# The Hurst Chronicles

## Reader Newsletter

Sign up for the Hurst Chronicles newsletter and be the first to hear about the next books in the series as well as reader offers and exclusive content, all for free.

Sign up now at Hurstchronicles.com

# Wildfire

Robin Crumby

Website: HurstChronicles.com
Twitter: @HurstChronicles
Facebook: Facebook.com/HurstChronicles

## Disclaimer

*Wildfire* is a work of fiction. Names, characters, businesses, places, events and incidents are either the products of the author's imagination or used in a fictitious manner. Any resemblance to actual persons, living or dead, or actual events is purely coincidental.

# Chapter One

*"He who is far off will die by the plague,*
*and he who is near will fall by the sword,*
*and he who remains and is besieged will die by the famine.*
*Thus will I spend my wrath on them."*

*Ezekiel 6:11–12*

The days had grown noticeably shorter. As autumn gave way to winter, darkness fell earlier. For those who clung to survival, the nights proved long, damp and cold. When the rains came, they seemed to last for several days at a time, washing the earth clean.

Word had spread far and wide. People came from all over the south of England, desperate to escape the Millennial Virus and the chaos of the mainland. They joined lines of refugees said to stretch for miles, waiting patiently for their turn to make the crossing.

The Isle of Wight had become a sanctuary. For those fortunate enough to clear quarantine, a land of plenty awaited, complete with fresh water, shelter and secure food supplies. The dull fluorescence visible at night from the mainland confirmed the rumours that they had got power back online. If they could do that, what else was possible?

1

The reality was a little starker. Camp Wight was an ambitious reconstruction project, a safe zone under military control. Naval patrols were tasked with preventing unauthorised access. Strict controls remained in force. Smugglers and people traffickers were routinely intercepted, their vessels sunk. Operating under impossible conditions, the allies were doing their best to take back control.

For all the hype, the island was at least free of the virus. Riley and the other survivors relocated from Hurst Castle could attest to that. That was not to say this was any kind of 'new paradise on Earth', as religious leaders had claimed. The island certainly hadn't flowed with milk and honey. In the political and moral vacuum that followed the breakdown, survivors grasped for new meaning. The Church and State were only too happy to oblige.

Those who feared for the future and yearned for the past found this approximation of freedom somehow disturbing. Like a funfair hall of mirrors, everything seemed distorted. Most had already come to terms with compromise. New arrivals traded their freedom for a fresh start. The allies promised security in return for blood, sweat and tears. In a wasteland of hope, Camp Wight offered renewal and purpose.

\*\*\*\*

Riley hobbled out of the rear doors of the Freshwater Bay Hotel, limping painfully towards the weathered bench seat which had become her favoured spot, overlooking the cliffs to the east towards the southerly point of the island. The bullet wound to her calf was taking an age to heal. She was at least mobile now, thanks to Sam. He had fashioned her a crutch from a broken broom handle recovered from the outbuildings at the hotel.

"I made it for you," Sam had said warmly, his hollow cheeks

a sign that he had not been himself lately as he waited anxiously for news of Jack.

"What would I do without you?" She ruffled his mop of blonde hair, pulling him in for a hug, noticing his sadness. "We all miss him, Sam."

"If anything's happened to Jack, I'll never forgive myself."

She noticed Sam repeatedly clenching his fists, staring at his shoes. She tried to reassure him. "Stay positive. I'm sure he's fine."

"It's not like him though. He would have sent a message by now. Someone somewhere must know where he is."

She had been worried about Sam for the last few days. He was bottling up all his anger, refusing to talk about how he was feeling, like a powder-keg waiting to explode.

Riley and the others had settled into their new life on the island with mixed emotions. They had their work cut out to restore the hotel at Freshwater Bay from a near derelict structure into something they could call home. The main building was sizeable but weather-beaten, stripped of furnishings by rival groups living nearby. Over the last few days, they had begun to scavenge beds and mattresses from the local area, doing their best to make the place habitable before winter set in.

They had much to be grateful for. This was a prime site in the west of the island. Set atop steep-sided chalk cliffs, the village of Freshwater was surrounded by farmland on one side and ocean on the other. She told everyone that she would never get tired of the views out across the English Channel, but privately, Riley acknowledged that the hotel was a poor substitute for the bleak beauty and high walls of Hurst Castle. They were all so vulnerable here.

"We should never have let Captain Armstrong take the castle," lamented Sam.

"We didn't have a choice. It was the only way of making the Solent safe. You know that," said Riley, stroking his arm. She would never admit it to Sam, but Jack had much to answer for.

No one liked the idea of giving up the castle. In the end, Captain Armstrong had left them little choice. Jack's hand had been forced. The allies needed Hurst to secure the western approaches to the Solent. Riley shook her head thinking back to the hardships they had endured to transform that place from a decrepit museum into a vibrant working community.

They had been happy at Hurst, living a simple, sustainable existence. Trading with other survivor groups, working the land, rebuilding lives, they had become a tight-knit group, pulling together. Now all that was gone, torn from their hands by Briggs and King.

Riley felt a lump in her throat, remembering what Briggs had done to Zed; torturing him until he told them what he knew. His inhuman screams had shaken her to the core.

"We've got to put the past behind us. Focus on the future. That's what Jack would have wanted us to do. We all need to look forward."

"You talk about him as if he's already dead."

"Sorry, I didn't mean that. Listen, all I'm saying is that Jack would have wanted us to keep busy. Winter's coming, and there's so much to do. We need to get on. We can't wait for Jack. We'll need food, water, and wood to burn."

She pointed at her leg and grimaced. "I just wish there was more I could do to help."

With Jack still absent, the other members of the Hurst council had rallied, but it still felt like their beating heart had been ripped out. As the days went by, her worst fears about Jack were playing out. No one knew for sure what had happened to him. They assumed he had been captured but, secretly, Riley feared he was already dead.

Riley had been one of Jack's fiercest critics, but now he was gone, she quietly missed his pragmatism. For all his faults, he had brought unity to the group. Without him, she worried their fragile harmony could fracture. A thirst for revenge would be irrepressible for Sam and those most loyal to Jack.

"Has there been any word from Zed?" asked Sam.

"Not yet. I'm sure he'll send news when he can."

Since Zed left for the new research station at St Mary's, Riley had grown increasingly frustrated, eager to follow him across the island to keep her promise. It still seemed improbable that Zed's daughter could have survived. The unexpected letter from Ryde Boarding School had confirmed that she had been evacuated from the mainland, along with all the other unaccompanied children separated from their families.

"I'll ask the soldiers in town if they've heard anything, okay?" said Riley.

Sam nodded and sloped off with his hands in his pockets. Riley shouted after him.

"If you find Tommy, you tell him that Liz has a whole list of jobs with his name on."

"He'll be fishing on the beach."

Riley watched Sam go before hobbling round to the front steps of the hotel to wait for her ride into town. Will emerged from one of the outbuildings, wheeling the largest of the communal bicycles. Even with the saddle up as high as it would go, it was still too small for his enormous frame. A narrow trailer cart was hitched behind.

Will held out his arm for Riley to steady herself as she removed her rucksack and lowered herself awkwardly into the trailer. He pushed off, standing up on the pedals, crashing through the gears until he picked up speed. With a bump, they bounced through the water-filled potholes that marked the short tarmac drive. It was an ungainly way to travel. At least she could get out and about to see what was going on.

On the main road into Freshwater, the military had set up a barricade, guarded day and night. The whole island remained under special measures. Freedom of movement was strictly limited to anyone with a military pass.

Each evening, like clockwork, a siren sounded to mark the beginning of the nightly curfew on the island. Anyone foolish enough to be caught wandering after dark was routinely rounded up. To many, the fences, barricades and curfews made it feel like an island prison camp, a distorted version of liberty.

Will supported Riley over to a wooden bench by the old Freshwater Lifeboat station. Sheltered from the wind, it was a pleasant spot to watch the world go by. She studied the notices and signs pinned to a community notice board. Locals and new arrivals searching for friends or loved ones. Scraps of paper carrying drawings and messages fluttered in the wind. The handwriting was hard to make out, its ink smudged and discoloured by the elements.

A commotion at the checkpoint drew their attention. The first of a convoy of red double-decker buses crested the hill and rolled to a halt before the barricade. Each of the buses was covered in colourful graffiti that Riley recognised from elsewhere in her travels. These stylised words and symbols were used by local groups to mark their territory.

One of the guards approached the convoy, his arm raised. Riley noticed his partner draw his sidearm, covering their approach. From a distance, Riley could still hear the diesel engines panting noisily. The engine housing at the back rattled, its rusting exhaust belching fumes into the morning air like some primitive machine.

The double doors hissed open and the driver emerged with a clipboard, followed by a soldier in uniform. The military men saluted each other. They seemed in no particular hurry to execute their duties, handing out cigarettes. Riley watched with interest, wondering whether she might recognise any of the new arrivals. After the news about Zed's daughter, they all secretly hoped friends or relatives might be next. So many people had been displaced in their attempts to make it here. The refugees were said to come from all over the south of England.

The driver finished his cigarette before climbing back onboard the bus. He revved his engine, thick smoke billowing into the air. The bus rolled forward through the raised barrier into Freshwater and, after a short delay, the rest of the convoy followed. Through the steamed-up top deck windows, Riley could make out dozens of expectant faces, eager to start their new lives on the island.

Each bus began disgorging passengers. The new arrivals stood squinting into the light, taking deep breaths of clean, sea air. One by one, the man with the clipboard called forward small groups and directed them in turn to designated accommodation. They set off up the road, staggering under the weight of all their worldly possessions. On their backs were rucksacks stuffed with spare clothes, sleeping bags and pots and pans, like ramblers setting off on some camping adventure.

Studying their grimy faces, some of them seemed almost shell-shocked, like returning veterans from the Western Front, struggling to readjust to civilian life. Perhaps the horrors were still fresh in their minds. The residual guilt of survival.

A shrill voice from the last bus interrupted the sombre procession. A woman in a headscarf and black overcoat was gesticulating at the soldiers. They seemed to straighten as she advanced towards them. Something about her gait and manner was familiar.

Riley blinked, widening her eyes. She hadn't worn her glasses for some time and had gotten used to being short-sighted. The woman seemed to recognise Riley and changed course towards her. It was only when she was a few steps away that Riley realised who it was.

# Chapter Two

"Riley! What on earth are you doing here?" exclaimed Sister Imelda, her cheeks flushed. She had noticed Riley's awkward stance and the crutch resting against the bench seat.

Riley's face remained expressionless, struggling to hide the conflict in her emotions. "I could ask you the same thing." She pointed up the hill towards the hotel. "We live just up there. I thought you knew." The memory of all the unpleasant things she had wanted to say the next time she saw Sister Imelda came flooding back. The sister seemed to read her mind.

"Look, I'm sorry for what happened back at the castle. Believe you me, I was as shocked as you were. We had no idea what Briggs would do." She swallowed. "How many of you made it across?"

"All but one."

"Jack?"

Riley's eyes narrowed, unsure how much the sister really knew. "I don't suppose you can tell us what happened to him after we left?"

"He was alive. I saw him with that other woman. She seemed to know you."

"You mean Terra? Yes, we know each other," Riley retorted with thinly disguised venom.

"I'm confused. I know Terra was captured in the attack on Osbourne House, but I got the distinct impression she was a willing participant. She didn't seem to be under any kind of duress."

Riley had last seen Terra at the forest camp near Porton Down. Back then, her behaviour made Riley suspicious. Always in the wrong place at the wrong time. Much as she disliked Terra, Riley didn't think she could ever be a willing party to torture and murder. What they had done to Zed was unforgivable. Terra would never allow Briggs to hurt Jack. Her Jack.

"Sister, I'm assuming this not a social call?"

"No. There are some rather troubling rumours about exploitation and brutality here on the island. Apparently, there have been multiple cases of people disappearing, human trafficking, slave labour, that sort of thing. Captain Armstrong asked me personally to oversee the transfer of refugees," she boasted.

"You're a curious choice to act as moral arbiter," challenged Will, overhearing their conversation.

Sister Imelda tried her best to ignore his barbed comment but knew he wasn't done.

"After the way you treated Joe at the Chewton Glen, the sisters' human rights record is hardly above reproach."

"Those men were willing volunteers."

"Is that why you keep them locked up? I'd love to know what Captain Armstrong makes of your breeding programme."

"Actually, he's one of our biggest advocates."

"I doubt that." Will laughed at the sister's hypocrisy.

Riley swallowed her anger, refusing to engage with the sister on this point. "What about Stella? Where's she now?" she asked, changing the subject.

"Not far from here, just along the coast. Over at the Royal Hotel, in Ventnor. There's a women's commune there. The sisters provide pastoral care and spiritual guidance to the new arrivals at Camp Four, just outside the town. That's where most of this lot have come from." She gestured towards the refugees. "They've all been assigned to the farms around here. All the skilled workers get sent to Newport, Yarmouth or Ryde. You should come and visit Stella and her little boy."

Riley hesitated. The sister knew full well how much Riley yearned to see Stella. After their brief time together at the Chewton Glen, she had come to think of her as an adopted sister. Riley knew the sister was twisting the knife again, playing with her emotions. Stella was so close, but with Riley's injury and no means of transport, she might as well be a hundred miles away.

"I'd like that very much." She sighed. "How is baby Adam?"

"He's gorgeous," Sister Imelda crooned. "Beautiful blue eyes and a good pair of lungs. There's a nursery set up now. Thirteen newborns already this year. We're expecting another fifteen by Christmas."

"So the programme is really taking shape then?"

"Captain Armstrong had set aside the whole of Ventnor," the sister said brightly. "We've set up hospitals, nurseries, you name it. In time, there will be a whole generation of children born there. Hundreds of young women are volunteering."

Something about the sister's enthusiasm for the programme irked Riley. She acknowledged the need for population renewal, but a breeding programme, for heaven's sake? Could no one else see where all this was heading? It all sounded so totalitarian.

The sister seemed distracted, looking over Riley's shoulder at the restless crowd, jostling among themselves to be next in line. Perhaps they worried they might miss out on the best accommodation.

"If you'll excuse me, I need to get these families settled. Perhaps I could pop up to the hotel afterwards? I'd like to say hello to Jean. Set things straight."

"I'll see what I can do." Riley nodded, watching the sister leave.

A group of four children were the last to emerge from the waiting bus. An exhausted man she assumed was their father followed behind, doing his best to chivvy them along. The youngest daughter looked half-asleep, emaciated, clothes hanging off her birdlike frame. Endless fatigue had robbed them of their childhood. The father seemed lost in melancholy, his parental responsibilities hanging heavy around his shoulders. The other two girls were holding hands, clutching each other for warmth, tears streaming down their cheeks. They followed their older brother who stood tall, grown old beyond his years.

Will wandered over and bummed a cigarette from one of the drivers. Riley hobbled after him, eager to listen in on their conversation.

"Where are they going to put all these people?" asked Will, drawing heavily on his cigarette.

"That, my friend, is someone else's problem. I just drive the bus. Let someone else do the worrying. Life's simpler that way."

"Ain't that the truth? So what's the latest from the mainland?"

"You hear that explosion last night? Rattled my windows, it did. You can see all the fires in Southampton from where we are. I tell you, this is the best place to be, as far away from the front line as possible."

"Assuming the fighting stays that side of the Solent."

"You lot won the lottery getting posted here. You should see what's happening out east. Looks like one enormous construction site. There's a whole patchwork of building projects, refugee camps, storage dumps. Row after row of armoured vehicles, jeeps, trucks and passenger coaches lined up ready for despatch."

Riley turned her back on the men. Hearing stories like this reminded her how lucky they really were. It sounded like the allies had their work cut out dealing with the rebels. Over the past few weeks, most of those relocated from Hurst had given voice to their fears. The consensus remained that things would get worse before they got better. It seemed that passive resentment was giving way to widespread anger, fuelled by exaggerated stories of brutality, conspiracy, injustice. She had no doubt that Briggs and King were somehow involved.

What had started as disconnected voices whispering their disapproval was growing steadily into a chorus of discontent. Riley had seen it with her own eyes. If left unchecked, in time, division could split family groups, even whole communities. If the rapid breakdown of trust between the local population and the allies continued, there would be a real danger of civil war. Sooner or later, Riley knew that they would need to defend this fragile island state. War seemed inevitable.

****

The arrival of the first spots of morning rain prompted a hurried departure from the seafront. Putting her hood up, Riley watched the last of the refugees scurry off towards shelter.

Beneath the graffiti covering one of the buses, she made out a faded movie poster, peeling in places. Some apocalyptic weather event featuring storms and earthquakes. Remembering the world's obsession with global warming and its consequences, she smiled at this outdated Hollywood vision of the future. Mother Nature had found an altogether more subtle method of bringing to a close this so-called 'Age of Mankind'. The factories, aeroplanes and air conditioning units had fallen silent as one. In the end, a microscopic virus had done more damage than all the hurricanes and earthquakes put together. What came next was anyone's guess. Riley found that thought somehow liberating.

Will laboured back up the hill towards the hotel, towing Riley in the cart, her legs swinging childishly over the back. He squeaked to a halt beside the front step, handing Riley her crutch.

Parked outside the dining hall was an unfamiliar black and chrome motorbike. A grey helmet was perched lopsidedly on its handlebars. She recognised the make immediately. It was a more modern version of the bike her father had kept in their garage when she was a teenager. The vintage Triumph had been his pride and joy, wheeled out each Sunday for a trip around the green. Riley and her sister took it in turns to ride pillion, wrapping their arms around his leather jacket, holding on tight, eyes closed. Her mother had never approved.

"Whose is the bike?" she asked Scottie.

He looked up from a blue-jacketed guidebook with a picture of the Needles rocks on the cover. "Some officer guy. I didn't catch his name," he replied dismissively.

"What did he look like?"

"Never seen him before. Black fella, asking for you."

She didn't remember any of Captain Armstrong's officers being black. From memory, they were all the product of Dartmouth Naval College, stiff-collared, upper middle class – not exactly a hotbed for diversity.

"What did he want?"

"You best ask him yourself. He's inside. Another administrator with a clipboard telling us what to do. Make him wait, I say."

Riley smiled at this last remark and hobbled over, waiting for Scottie to make room on the step. His attention had already returned to the book.

"What are you reading?"

"There's a shelf-full of guidebooks in the library. This whole island is fascinating. So much history. The Romans used to call this place 'Insula Vecta'? Means place of the division."

"Seems strangely fitting. I didn't know the Romans made it here."

"Four hundred years they were here. Must have been a bit warmer back then. Says it was famous for its wine." He chortled. "You know, people have fought over this island for millennia. Everyone's had a crack: the Vikings, the Danes, the French, even the Spanish Armada tried to land here."

"They won't be the last either."

"I don't know. All these soldiers? The whole island's locked down tight. You can't go anywhere. They tried to arrest me for bringing books back to the hotel. Accused me of stealing. Who's going to care about the odd missing book, I told them."

"Sister Imelda was in town. She's going to head up here when she's done."

"God help us. She's the last thing we need. Bloody do-gooders. Is she preaching her sanctimonious rubbish again? They think we need saving. Last time I saw her I said I was an atheist, just to shut her up. I told her this whole island was pagan up until the sixth century." Noticing Riley's puzzled expression, he explained, "You know, pagans? Stonehenge, druids, human sacrifice, that sort of thing?"

"I always thought there was something weird about this place, but I put that down to inbreeding." She giggled mischievously.

"Island-folk have always been a bit special. Mystical even."

"The morris dancers are a bit of a giveaway."

"They certainly have their own ways here. You know the New Forest used to be full of witches, probably still is. That's why they called this place the Isle of Wight. Wight used to mean spirit or ghost."

"Isn't that just what they used to tell the tourists? Ghosts and ghouls are the least of our concerns."

The front door creaked open, and Sam stuck his head out.

"Ah, Riley, there you are. There's an officer waiting for you in the drawing room. Arrived about half an hour ago. Said he was happy to wait."

Riley sighed. "Okay, Sam, I'll be right there. Just what I need, more census questions about skills and experience."

"No, this one is different. I think he's a priest or something. Don't forget to ask him about Jack."

"He may know something about Zed too," added Scottie, with a wink.

"Knowing Zed, he'll have forgotten all about us."

"I doubt that!" Scottie said, with a knowing smirk and a nudge to her ribs. "Anyway, I thought you'd be heading out that way soon?"

"Not until this leg heals. The doctor said the stitches can come out any day. Maybe the padre can give me a lift on that bike of his?"

"I doubt it." Scottie laughed. "Not without a pass, signed in triplicate."

"Come on, let's get this over and done with. You never know when we might need their help again. You want to tag along? Hear what he has to say?"

"Sure. I love winding up these clipboard guys. They're all so straight-laced and bloody English," he mocked in his best Glaswegian accent.

# Chapter Three

Outside the old manager's office, Riley knocked before entering, holding the door ajar for the others. The padre heaved himself upright and straightened his jacket over a sizeable frame, beret folded neatly under the arm.

There was something familiar about him, but she knew, from his army uniform, that he wasn't one of Armstrong's men. She thought she'd met most of the officers by now and would certainly have remembered the padre.

He looked about her age, and had dark hair, striking features and sharp brown eyes. By all accounts, he had spent much of his service behind a desk, overfed and under-exercised. That was one thing you noticed on the island: so many people seemed plump despite the food shortages. They hadn't suffered the same deprivation and rationing here.

"Sorry to keep you waiting," said Riley. "I was down in the village helping Sister Imelda with the new arrivals. Are you new here?"

"I got here a couple of weeks ago." The man smiled as he shook her hand. "Chaplain Bennett, First Battalion, Princess of Wales's Royal Regiment. Everyone calls me padre or Doug."

"Welcome. Everyone calls me Riley."

He looked surprised as if he'd just made a connection. "Sam tells me you are in charge of this place?" he said flatly, more a statement than a question. He noticed her limp for the first time as she leant back against the armchair.

Riley paused, not sure how to respond. In the absence of Jack, Zed and Terra, did that make her next in line? Scottie pulled a face as if to say "rather you than me".

"Well, at least until the others get back."

"Captain Armstrong asked me to do the rounds and make contact with all the different groups in this sector."

From his satchel, the padre unpacked an Ordnance Survey map of the Isle of Wight, spreading it out on the worktop. His nails were manicured, and Riley was struck by the contrast between the whites of his cuticles and the coffee colour of his skin.

He turned the map around the right way and pointed to some pencil markings highlighting an area that stretched most of the way north back to Yarmouth. An area of perhaps three or four square miles was lightly shaded in pencil, incorporating everything west of Freshwater, including the Needles Headland, Tennyson Down and up towards the village of Totland.

"This is your area. Sector Seven. You're going to be working closely with Corporal Carter and his platoon based up at the Old Battery." He pointed to the Needles rocks and the cluster of buildings on the headland above it.

"I'm going to need you to supervise these three farms here, here, and here. Your first priority is to secure food production. Our forecast models show the island population growing by two to three thousand people per month for as long as we can sustain that. By the end of the year, we estimate the island population nudging north of fifty thousand people again. In the short term,

ROBIN CRUMBY

we have enough food and water to last the winter. Beyond that, we need to move towards self-sufficiency. I understand your group has some experience with agriculture and farm animals?"

"That's right. We managed a similarly sized estate back at Keyhaven, near Hurst Castle."

"Good. Well, I'm told there's a herd of fifty-odd dairy cows at Warren Farm. That should keep you in milk and cheese. Over here, there are pigs, sheep, chickens and goats. Then over this side, there's a fruit farm."

"That all sounds manageable, but we'll need some extra hands if we're to increase production. Skilled workers would be a bonus to work any farm machinery, drive tractors, that sort of thing."

He made a note of her requests in a pocket notebook. "Anything else you need?"

"Well, we arrived here with next to nothing. For starters, we'll need basic medical supplies: bandages, antibiotics, painkillers, morphine and anything else you can find for us."

"Let me see what I can do. In the meantime, probably best to check what's left at the pharmacy in town."

"What's this zone marked here?" she said, pointing to an area marked with red chevrons.

"That's all off limits for now. Totland and School Green haven't been cleared. Leave that to the army. They're trained for that type of work."

Riley half-snorted at the suggestion they needed protecting. "We managed just fine before your lot showed up."

"Look, all I'm saying is that there's a minority of locals who don't take kindly to us being here. They resent the curfews, the forced relocations and the compulsory orders. And it's still possible there are pockets of infection."

"We were told they cleared this whole area weeks ago."

"Only in Freshwater. It's dangerous work, and it takes time. The clearance teams are due back here in a couple of weeks. Please just leave the house-to-house stuff to the soldiers. It's not worth the risk. Your priority right now is the hotel and the surrounding area. How much more is there to do?"

"Well, we've made a start fixing the roof, repairing the fences, getting the place ready for winter. We had a team clearing the wood over there for firewood. We'll put sheep and goats into that paddock behind the outbuildings here," she said, pointing to the field on the map.

"There's a pig shed we noticed a mile up the road we can use," added Scottie. "Maybe have some chickens in this sheltered area behind the car park. We'll need a few weeks, but I'd say we're getting there."

"Good. Next week we'll begin billeting more people to the hotel. I've got another forty labourers arriving in a few days. You can get them to do all the heavy lifting, the digging, the dirty work."

"Where are we going to put them all?" Riley wondered out loud, scratching her head.

"A building of this size? There should be more than enough beds for double that number," said the padre.

"I'm sure we'll manage."

"I suppose we can put mattresses in those rooms downstairs." Scottie suggested.

The padre reached into the breast pocket of his uniform and produced a list of names.

"The area commander asked me to confirm the names of those who've relocated from the castle. It says here there are seventy-three of you. Does that sound about right?"

"Yes, I think so," said Riley, noticing Scottie nodding, as he scanned the list.

"And I understand you have seventeen females aged between fourteen and thirty-five?"

"I'd have to check," said Riley, puzzled by the question. For some reason, it made her think of what Sister Imelda had said earlier.

"Good." He smiled, ticking off the information on his sheet. "I think that's everything for now. I'm going to need you to make it up to the Battery before nightfall. Corporal Carter will meet you there and show you around."

They all nodded, checking the distance on the map. Riley was thinking about her leg and what time it would get dark.

"Is that your bike outside?" asked Scottie, trying to reconcile the image of a vicar on a bike.

"The Triumph? She's a beauty, isn't she? One of the men at St Mary's found her for me. Needs a new carburettor."

"Padre, I don't suppose you could get me a lift later this week? With all the fuel rationing, it's next to impossible to get around."

"Where are you trying to get to?"

"There's a young girl, Adele, needs her check-up at St Mary's. She's part of the volunteer group. Then I'm trying to get to the boarding school at Ryde. The colonel said he would help, but I suspect he's forgotten all about it."

The padre blew out his cheeks. "Fuel's only half the problem. With all these checkpoints everywhere, you'd need an island-wide pass. Very hard to come by. I could get you as far as the hospital, but from there, you'd be on your own."

"I'm supposed to collect a friend's daughter from the school. Do you know Zed Samuels? He's working for the colonel. I made him a promise."

"Can't say I do. I know the colonel. Cold fish, hard to make out. Look, they're good people up at the school. She'll be in safe hands. They've had a lot of experience dealing with all these orphans and unaccompanied kids."

"I'd really appreciate it."

"No promises, but I'll see what I can do." He paused as if trying to decide whether to voice his thoughts. "I don't suppose you were based at Haileybury Court years ago, were you?"

"How did you know?" Riley blinked back at him, struggling to make the connection. "Yes, I was there for several years."

"You probably don't remember me, well, I don't suppose we ever met, but I remember you. You looked after my brother. He used to talk about you. You made a big impression on him."

"Good heavens. Very possibly. What was his name?" said Riley, wide-eyed.

"Reg. Private first class Reginald Bennett. Everyone called him Gooner."

Riley took a moment to reflect and clicked her fingers. "Of course, I remember your brother Reg very well indeed. Lovely smile, always made me laugh. He'd lost a leg, hadn't he? Came to us for weekly physiotherapy sessions."

"That's him. Roadside IED, just outside Basra. Blew off his right leg below the knee. He was never the same again, had severe head trauma, but your guys worked wonders, gave him back some dignity."

"Whatever happened to him? Is he still alive?"

The padre had been buoyed by reminiscences of his brother but now fell silent, staring over Riley's shoulder, a distant look in his eyes.

"He died some time ago. Took his own life."

"I'm so sorry. I had no idea."

"How could you? It was a huge shock to the family back home. He suffered from horrible bouts of depression, couldn't seem to get out of bed most days. Temper got the better of him once too often. Wife walked out on him, took the kids. He had nothing left to live for. After everything he'd been through, he came to believe that his service to this country counted for nothing. When his wife told him he couldn't see his own kids any more, it finished him, tipped him over the edge. Sorry," he said, regretting his momentary loss of control, "I can't abide people feeling sorry for themselves."

She reached out and touched his arm, but he shrank away from the contact. She persevered, gripping his sleeve.

"Your brother was an incredibly brave soldier. Everyone who knew him liked him." She paused, studying his reaction. "Look, I know what it's like. Having to be strong for everyone else. If ever you need someone to talk to, with someone who actually knew your brother, you know where to find me."

"I might take you up on that." He smiled weakly. "Still, it was probably for the best. Means he never got to see the outbreak and what followed. People with disabilities didn't really stand a chance, did they?" he said, shaking his head, blinking away tears.

Perhaps the padre was too proud to give in to emotion in front of strangers. Counselling veterans and their families, Riley had seen it a hundred times before. Those feelings never went away, but over time you got better at dealing with them.

"We've all had to adapt as best we can," he continued. "Survival is its own imperative. However profound our grief, life must go on. Ours is a stoicism borne from necessity." He looked at his watch, taking a breath. "Right, I'm sorry, I'm expected up in Yarmouth for 17:00. Don't forget about Corporal Carter at the Battery, will you? He'll be expecting you."

As he turned away, Riley sensed a veiled hostility. Her intuition told her it was more than merely residual grief for the loss of his brother. Something about his tone and body language made her think that, subconsciously, he blamed Haileybury Court for failing to prevent his brother's depression and slide towards suicide. She got the impression that somehow, deep down, he blamed her.

# Chapter Four

By the time Riley and the others had climbed to the top of the cliff path that ran along the headland out towards the Old Needles Battery, daylight was already beginning to fade. They had been told to make contact with the platoon before nightfall. Why the urgency? thought Riley. Nothing seemed to happen in a hurry around here any more.

Even with the crutch for support, the climb was physically demanding. She laboured up the slippery grassland, liberally embroidered with wildflowers. Her forehead beaded with perspiration despite the mild temperature.

As the others brushed past her, she took a moment to catch her breath, leaning heavily against the crutch. Will was the last to arrive and paused beside her.

"We'll rest at the memorial," he said, checking his watch and pointing to the top of the cliff.

Riley's leg was still throbbing from all the exertion. She gave Will's shoulder a grateful squeeze, her hand lingering there for a few seconds, wincing against her pain. Will was a bull of a man, with thick arms and a broad chest.

After what felt like a Herculean effort, they reached the stone cross that dominated the highest point of the headland. Will unhooked his rucksack and rummaged inside for a thermos flask, pouring out Rooibos tea into a single mug. He took a sip before offering it to the others.

Riley inspected the dressing on her ankle. She stood back with both hands on her hips, taking deep breaths, filling her lungs with sea air. The wind whistling through the low railings made her think of distant music, melodic and soothing.

Carved in large letters across the base of the weathered granite column she could make out the name Alfred Lord Tennyson. The upper-most section of the monument had been smashed off and lay broken on the ground. Spray-painted in red were the words: "Your God is Dead".

"Philistine," said Scottie with genuine bitterness.

"Who would do such a thing?" wondered Riley.

"Perhaps they hated poetry," joked Will.

"Tennyson used to live not far from here," added Scottie. "They say he walked up and down these slopes dressed in black with his broad-brimmed hat."

"You read that in your guidebook too?" Riley smiled.

"Half a league, half a league…into the valley of death rode the six hundred," started Scottie, trying to remember the lines from "The Charge of the Light Brigade".

Riley stood back and took in the view. As far as the eye could see, the English Channel stretched in all directions. Beyond the horizon, eighty miles to the south was the Cherbourg Peninsula and the coast of France. Directly west was Christchurch Bay and the Dorset coast. It wasn't hard to imagine why Tennyson found this place so inspiring.

On the way here, Riley couldn't stop thinking about Sam and Tommy. If the rumours were true that Jack had been killed by King, she worried what the pair of them might do. She made a mental note to talk to Scottie. He could always make Tommy see sense.

In the distance, she could just make out Studland Bay and Swanage. Jack always said it was one of his favourite places. There wasn't a single sail or ship in sight. An uninterrupted blue-green canvas of slow-moving undulations, topped by dirty-white crests. She watched as each new set of waves advanced rhythmically towards the base of the sheer chalk cliffs hundreds of feet below them. Nearing the end of their journey, they took it in turns to smash against the rocks. High above their bare heads, gulls soared effortlessly on a south-westerly breeze. Below her feet, perched precariously, hidden among crevices in the cliff face, she imagined nests filled with squawking chicks waiting for their mothers to return with food.

Will packed up the thermos and shouldered his bag before striding off on their final leg towards the Battery. "Come on, it's not far now," he said encouragingly.

In the gorse bushes to their right, a startled rabbit scampered towards the safety of its burrow, its white tail disappearing from view as fast as it had appeared. Starlings and other small birds were disturbed by the sudden movement. They had become unused to humans walking these once-familiar paths.

Further out, the lumbering shapes of cattle turned their heads, following the group's passing with disinterest. Riley made a mental note to send Tommy out in the morning to round up the cows and return them to their rightful field. Someone must have left the gate open again.

As they approached Needles Battery, the wind carried the hum of a generator from the old rocket-testing facility at High Down. From the mechanical sounds and shouting, it sounded like a work party carrying out maintenance. They got to within thirty metres of a furniture van before they were noticed.

The soldiers seemed startled by the sudden sight of the group. Two of the men jumped down from the van and reached for the rifles propped against the back wheel. The other men took the opportunity to take a break from their work, hands on hips.

"We're looking for Corporal Carter," said Riley, raising both palms defensively to show they meant no harm.

"This is off limits. Military personnel only." The older man said, scowling at them.

"We were sent up from Freshwater Bay by Chaplain Bennett. The name's Riley. This here's Will and that's Scottie over there."

The man scratched the back of his wiry hair, looking up at the overcast sky and dying light. It would be dark in an hour.

"Freshwater, you say? Bit late to be out walking the cliffs. You best come back in the morning. There'd be no finding you if you slipped and fell."

"We were told to come before nightfall." She shrugged nonchalantly as if she was just following orders. "Is Carter around?"

"He's over there." He gestured towards the bright light coming from the entrance to an underground bunker complex.

Riley had heard about this place. Back in the 1950s and 1960s, there were said to have been huge gantries above Scratchell's Bay used to test fire rockets for the British space programme. Seemed hard to imagine, but on a smaller scale this had been the British equivalent of NASA's Cape Canaveral. All that remained now were the concrete bases and underground bunkers.

They descended the stone steps into what looked like part of a museum whose exhibits had been cleared to make way for beds and living space for a dozen men. One of the work party broke off and strode towards them down the dimly lit hall, his hand outstretched, sleeves rolled up to the elbow.

"You must be the lot from Freshwater," he said, shaking their hands firmly in turn as he studied each of them carefully, sizing them up. "I heard you might be paying us a visit. How are you settling in? Got everything you need?"

Carter was a young man in his early twenties, blonde and good-looking. He had a scar across his right cheek that dragged at the corner of his eye. Riley noticed he favoured his left side as if self-conscious of his injury.

"We're getting there, thank you," replied Riley, avoiding staring at his scar. "There's still an awful lot to do. I understand we're going to be working together."

"Yes, the chaplain has some grand plans for this end of the island."

"How many of you are there?"

"Between High Down and Needles Battery, right now there are twenty of us, but we've been told to expect as many as seventy more over the coming weeks. We're just the advance guard."

"That many?"

"With the lighthouse keepers' cottages up there and the Old Battery, we should have more than enough beds. There's a canteen set up over there, a generator and fresh water. Food's the priority. That's where you lot come in. I gather you've had experience managing farmland and animals?"

"We did back at Hurst Castle. We had several acres of winter crops, plus some livestock. We had all sorts: sheep, cows, goats, chickens. It'll take time to recreate all that, but there are a couple of farms on the map that sound promising."

"Be careful how you go. There are a few dyed-in-the-wool locals living there." He raised his eyebrows. "Last time we went there, some crazy old woman fired a shotgun at the car. Friendly bunch. They don't like outsiders. They've taken full advantage to extend their boundaries."

"Wherever there's death, there's opportunity," added Scottie.

"I take it you're not from around here?" Riley asked the corporal.

"No, most of us transferred from Portsmouth a couple of weeks ago."

"Portsmouth? How was it?"

"A real hot mess. The whole place is one giant refugee camp. We're massively under-resourced. Too many refugees arriving every day, most of them sick or dying, too ill to make it across. Trouble is they have nowhere left to go."

"I suppose you're loving all the peace and quiet over here then?"

"Trust me, it won't last long."

"I hear there's been a fresh outbreak on the mainland?"

"So they say. I can't say I'm surprised. With so many refugees crammed into one place, it was always going to happen. Every Tom, Dick and Harry is trying to make it over here. Now there's cholera and dysentery to worry about."

"What about these rebel groups? The ones who ambushed our convoy coming through the forest?"

"I heard about that. Not much we can do though. We've got our hands full just securing the military bases. We've been attacked so many times, I suppose you just get used to it. Bit like back in Basra. What about Hurst Castle? Was it any better there?"

Riley lowered her head and bit her lip, choosing her words carefully. It wouldn't do well to blame the military right now. "Not really, but we were so remote, it felt safe."

"I heard about the attack," he continued. "It all sounded a bit chaotic. How many of your people made it across?"

"All but one. Our leader is still missing. No one's heard anything. We believe he was either killed or captured."

"I shouldn't give up hope. Miracles do happen."

"Maybe you're right."

"Before it gets too dark why don't I show you around the place? You're welcome to join us for dinner. We normally eat at seven. Then I can get someone to drop you back at the hotel afterwards. How does that sound?"

"Best offer we've had in days."

The sound of hurried footsteps drew their attention, and a uniformed man rounded the corner at speed, fighting to get his breath.

"Corporal, we just got a call from the *Chester*. They've picked up an intermittent radar signature approaching the Needles Channel from the west. They've asked the team at Hurst to be on high alert just in case they try and run the gauntlet."

"Sounds like another fishing boat trying to get through before it gets dark. Where are they now?"

"We spotted them staying close to shore, just rounding the Needles."

"Very well. Get a sharpshooter on the cliff top and get the GPMG prepped, can you?"

"Already done, sir. Someone's gone to find the Javelin."

"A missile, private? Do you have any idea how much those things cost?"

"Still, sir. Just in case they don't get the message, worth having handy," he replied straight-faced.

"Very well, but it'll be like using a sledgehammer to crack a nut. Carry on, private." He sighed, turning to Riley with a shrug.

"Want to tag along? We can show you what we're dealing with."

"Sure, why not?" said Riley, wide-eyed.

\*\*\*\*

By the time they reached the cliff top, looking back towards the mainland, it was almost too dark to see. Grey cloud threatened from the west, light rain falling beneath. On the mainland, she could see pinpricks of light from a dozen bonfires along the shoreline.

Riley shivered involuntarily, feeling the cold through her fleece. The view up here was stunning. Scanning to her right, she noticed Hurst Spit and the castle just across the water, no more than a couple of miles away. There was smoke rising from the canteen. Checking her watch, she realised it would be dinner time for the soldiers stationed there. She imagined the men assembling in the dining hall, tray in hand, waiting their turn for whatever slop was on the menu this evening. Fresh vegetable soup or a rabbit stew perhaps. Meat was so hard to come by these days.

Three soldiers were readying a tripod-mounted machine gun, removing the ties to a waterproof tarpaulin and bringing up ammunition boxes. Stepping close to the edge and looking over the low wall, she realised it was a long way down to the water, perhaps as much as three hundred feet. She could see nothing but grey water and stony shingle stretching round to the multicoloured chalk cliffs of Alum Bay. The smell of salt and seaweed carried to their elevated position. She could just make out the waves lapping at the shoreline.

"There she is, sir," said a man with binoculars, pointing to a skulking shape emerging between the Needles rocks, leaving behind a thin white trail. At first sight, it had the outline of a fishing trawler with a raised drum at the stern for its nets, several masts and lines strung above its wheelhouse. The hull seemed a brighter green colour, surging east at full throttle on the incoming tide.

"Looks like they're in a hurry to get somewhere," confirmed Carter, studying the trawler with his own expensive-looking Zeiss binoculars. "Maybe just a returning fishing boat. Any reason to be suspicious?"

"Yes, sir. Notice all the people on deck, just in front of the wheelhouse. I count at least ten. My guess would be they're people smugglers, trying to get back from Ventnor or Bembridge."

"Long way to go, isn't it?"

"Those are about the only places you could land a trawler like that on the south of the island."

"I see. Very well, let's give them a shot across their bows and see what they do about it."

"Private, you heard Corporal Carter. Two-second burst ten metres ahead of his bow. Fire when ready."

Riley took a step back and followed the corporal's lead, covering her ears. The sound of the machine gun firing was deafening. A ribbon of fire leapt out of the barrel and ripped up the water very close to the trawler. Considering it must have been at least a kilometre away, the gun was surprisingly accurate at range. She remembered Hurst Castle's own machine gun, just like this, set up on the Gun Tower.

Corporal Carter snatched the handheld walkie-talkie from his belt and raised it to his lips.

"Yarmouth command, this is Needles Battery. We have a small fishing trawler making towards the Needles Passage at ten knots. We've put a shot across their bows, and they're not taking the hint. What are your orders?"

"Needles Battery. We have him on radar. No authorised traffic at this time. You are cleared to engage."

Carter shook his head with some regret, raising his binoculars again and studying the trawler, perhaps hoping for some response. By Riley's reckoning, there was none.

"Try hailing them directly on channel sixteen," said Carter.

"Unknown fishing vessel, this is Needles Battery. You are entering a restricted area. Change course immediately, or you will be fired upon."

Riley watched enthralled, half-hoping that they would come about and avoid a confrontation. The man on the radio repeated his warning. The corporal shook his head.

"Private, you heard the man. You are cleared to engage. Short burst only. Target their bow, avoid the wheelhouse and passengers, if you can."

With a nod, the gunner depressed the trigger, and a line of bullets tore up the water, carving a line straight through the starboard bow, splintering its wooden deck. For a moment, Riley thought it had cut the whole boat in half, but through the spray and smoke, she saw them continue on their course. What was wrong with these people?

With a whoosh that could be heard from up high, flames engulfed the foredeck, and there were sounds of screaming from the passengers as they shrank away from the growing inferno. The boat's forward momentum seemed to slow as the bow sank lower into the water. The wheelhouse emptied in panic as one of the crew threw a life ring over the side and jumped after it. The passengers followed the crew's lead and abandoned ship, hoping to swim the hundred metres or so to shore through the infamous currents.

Suddenly, a massive explosion ripped through the engine

compartment and fuel tank, breaking the back of the hapless trawler. In a matter of seconds, she began to slip below the waves, before disappearing altogether. Left behind were two dozen fully clothed shapes in the water, fighting to stay afloat, surrounded by fishing gear and detritus. The fuel and oil on the surface caught, and panic turned to terror as the human shapes thrashed at the water trying to get away from the flames. Two or three people had the foresight to dive down and swim away, after which Riley lost sight of them.

"Why didn't they listen? Couldn't they see us up here? Didn't they know we're under orders?" said Carter.

"I'm afraid desperate people will do desperate things, sir."

"Private, get your men down to the beach and see if there are any survivors, can you?"

"Yes, sir."

"Oh well. We can't say we didn't warn them." Carter shrugged and turned to leave.

# Chapter Five

Zed stared at himself in the bathroom mirror. He barely recognised himself these days. If it wasn't the crow's feet around his eyes when he grimaced, it was the lines on his brow when he frowned. Admittedly, he'd been pushing himself hard. Maybe too hard.

He was still getting to grips with the prosthetic hand. It felt awkward and unnatural, strapped to his arm like a dead weight. The nurse said he would get used to it. In time, it would become as much a part of him as any other limb. Or so she said. Somehow he doubted that.

He gripped the side of the basin with his good hand, angling his head to catch the stark light from the overhead fluorescent strip. He studied the angles of his cheekbones. The last two years had eviscerated all traces of the man he once was. He struggled to remember suburban life. Wife, family, two kids, a steady job.

After what happened, hadn't he sworn to stay in the shadows? How had he allowed himself to become embroiled in politics again? Last time, it had cost him his family, his home, everything. He had shrunk from the limelight into a self-imposed exile and hidden from the world, teaching science in a secondary school near Croydon and working part-time on his PhD.

He had learned the hard way that the people he worked for would never leave him alone, and he only had himself to blame. His time at the Ministry of Defence was a chapter in his life he would sooner forget. In his experience, politics and science were uneasy bedfellows. If science was a search for the truth, then politicians had a nasty way of twisting that truth to their purpose. In the end, his whole family had paid the price for his obstinacy.

He tried hard to remember the last time he had showered, realising with some disgust that it was almost five days. Where had that time gone?

Peeling off the filthy threadbare T-shirt he had been wearing, he stripped to his underwear with some difficulty. Looking at himself in the mirror he realised he had gained weight these last few weeks, his ribs less pronounced. Tracing the scars on his arms and abdomen, he inspected the stump of his left arm. They had patched him up well. The infection was gone, the stitches removed.

He turned the tap and listened to the hot water gurgle its way through the Victorian-era pipework. Stepping into the shower, he closed his eyes, letting the water run down his face, filling his mouth. A single thought had been troubling him for days: what would he say to his daughter when he saw her again? After all this time, could she ever forgive him?

Since coming to St Mary's from Freshwater Bay Hotel, Zed had buried himself in his work, blocking out all extraneous thought. He spent as little time as possible in the small dorm room he shared with one of the lab workers. He could count on one hand the number of nights they had both slept in there at the same time, exchanging no more than a grunt and a nod before leaving again.

When Zed allowed himself the luxury of self-reflection, he

acknowledged a persistent weariness that sleep could never cure. Riley had been right. She was always right. He yearned for a return to a simpler life. A break from all this rushing around.

All those little things he had taken for granted. Being surrounded by people he could trust. What was it they said about absence making the heart grow fonder? Riley had pleaded with him to stay, and that had been playing on his mind. Her tenderness had rekindled something in him. Coupled with the trust the colonel had placed in him, he felt emboldened.

Knowing his daughter was still alive reminded him of his duty. Until he knew for sure what had happened, he owed it to his family to carry on. Right now, the colonel needed him, and that was all that mattered. A new purpose that overrode all other considerations.

Showered and shaved, he eased his prosthetic limb through the sleeve of a crisp white non-iron shirt and wriggled into a baggy hoody with Southampton University Squash Club written across the front. He wondered who these clothes might have belonged to. Some work-shy trustifarian, wasting away Daddy's fortune, or maybe a mature PhD student, like him, returning to education? He preferred to assume the latter. As he crouched down to lace up his shoes, the tight chinos cut into his thigh. Still, it felt good to be clean.

Stepping outside the accommodation block, he squinted into the daylight. It was less than a five-minute walk to the secure wing that housed the labs and offices set up for the Porton scientists. Considering the construction teams had converted several of the hospital buildings in less than six months, the facilities were impressive. They now had everything they needed to kick-start the search for a vaccine.

He stepped to the side of the road as another enormous

articulated truck rolled past him, laden with industrial machinery, stainless steel containers and other lab equipment. It was said that the allies had scoured the local area, requisitioning items from hospitals and pharmaceutical research centres. Doctor Hardy had been very specific in his requests.

The secure wing of the hospital was protected by armed guards and a newly installed keypad entry system. Zed and the men from Porton were treated like VIPs. He had only to ask, and whatever he needed was located and delivered the following day. As time went on, his requests had become ever bolder. Discretionary items and creature comforts. A new toothbrush, portable DVD player, electric razor. They even had cold beer. With a sigh, he remembered that the things he really longed for were intangible, impossible to scavenge.

He wasn't wearing a watch but guessed from the position of the sun and the scattered clouds hurrying across the island that it was probably mid-afternoon. From the moment he entered his office, time became an irrelevance. Meal times came and went. He ate when he was hungry and slept when he was tired, but neither of those things seemed to happen with any degree of regularity. He dismissed the daily routine of the facility as a distraction.

Walking through the compound, he nodded at two military types heading past. They saluted Zed, although he was not wearing a uniform. His status here as one of the colonel's trusted advisors was well known and respected.

All roads into the site were blocked by concrete barricades, overlooked by guard towers at fifty-metre intervals. For nearly three kilometres stretched a perimeter fence topped with razor wire, encircling St Mary's. Vehicle access to the compound was strictly prohibited to all but authorised military traffic.

Beyond the fence, he could see that many of the houses and buildings surrounding the site had been bulldozed. All that remained was rubble. Warning signs thrust deep into the muddy soil deterred the curious from approaching the fence. "Military personnel only - All trespassers will be shot". An explosion a few days ago had confirmed the widely held rumour that huge numbers of anti-personnel mines lurked unnoticed just below the topsoil.

Zed arrived at the front entrance to the newly built block where his office was located. Due to the sensitivity of the classified material he was reviewing, he had been granted a private room. Two soldiers broke off their conversation to check Zed's security ID and buzz him through the security door. He signed in at the front desk where a guard noted his time of arrival as 2.45pm.

"There you are."

One of the colonel's staff officers strode impatiently through the reception area, flanked by two orderlies. He wore standard issue camouflage fatigues, the multi-terrain variant, with highly polished black brogues and the name "Hannigan" above his breast pocket. Zed instantly disliked everything about the man. The moustache, the Brylcream, but most of all the condescension. Zed's school reports had always noted he had a "problem with authority".

"So what time do you call this?" challenged the officer, hands on hips. "The colonel was expecting you at the executive meeting this morning."

"Why didn't someone wake me up?" Zed said nonchalantly.

"Because we've got better things to do than babysit you civilians. Anyway, for some reason known only to the colonel, he gave orders that you were not to be disturbed, that you deserved a lie-in. Something to do with it being the weekend."

Zed blinked back unrepentantly, unaware that it was Saturday afternoon. The days tended to blur into one here.

"The colonel said you're something of a night owl. His words. He saw what time you left this morning in the register."

"I'm sorry. I don't have much use for a watch." Zed shrugged.

"Well, this isn't a bloody holiday camp, you know. Yours may be the colonel's private crusade right now, but you'll have me to answer to if you don't start towing the line around here."

"Look, if you have a problem with the way I work, I suggest you take it up with the colonel."

The staff officer glared at him, bristling with indignation. Zed softened his stance, remembering his advice to Riley about picking her battles.

"All I'm saying," he conceded, "is that we're all under pressure. Look, I get my best work done when no one else is around, that's all. Was there something in particular the colonel needed me at the meeting for?"

"That's hardly the point, is it?" the officer snarled. Backing down, he said, "The colonel had to leave urgently to meet with Captain Armstrong and Lieutenant Peterson. He wanted to see you before he left."

"Why the urgency?"

"There's been another attack on Portsmouth. We're just getting the report now. Apparently, several thousand refugees are massing just to the west of Chichester. The Royal Navy has set up a temporary humanitarian aid centre there. The numbers are unprecedented. We now have migrants arriving from all over Sussex, Surrey and Hampshire, trying to get to the island."

"The colonel always said this would happen. What about

Porton Down? Have there been any further updates?"

"You best ask the colonel when you see him. All I know is that the base has been reinforced by what remains of the 1st and 12th Armoured Infantry Brigades, from Bulford and Tidworth in Wiltshire."

"I thought we were evacuating Porton?"

"We were, but all that's on hold now. With everything we have going on here, we decided it was a good idea to keep Porton operational, just in case. Only the scientists are being evacuated for now."

"I could never understand how the colonel thought we could replicate Porton's facilities. They've been doing research into biological and chemical threats since the First World War. It's got everything we could possibly need."

"Except it's not here on the island. The decision to relocate was more about the security situation, but, with the help of the 1st and 12th Armoured, we should be able to safeguard things for a while longer."

"Good. When we're ready to start manufacturing a vaccine, Porton Down has all the laboratory facilities and production capabilities we'll ever need."

One of the orderlies coughed to get the attention of the staff officer. He was carrying a heavy-looking black metal storage box.

"Oh, I nearly forgot. Thank you, Smith. The colonel asked us to deliver this." He reached into his pocket and pulled out a key which he placed on top of the heavy box. He passed both to Zed.

This was the third such secure storage container he had been handed in as many days. It was a Herculean task to read and assimilate this amount of information, and the colonel seriously overestimated his abilities. Zed sighed at the prospect of another late night ahead.

If the last few days were anything to go by, there would likely be another consignment of documents in the morning once the tech person had decrypted more of the folders. They had barely made it through the first two data drives salvaged from Porton Down. The other two had been severely damaged in the bomb blast and resulting fire from the forest ambush, but they still hoped the data was recoverable.

Zed blinked away a yawn, apologising for his rudeness.

"Still having trouble sleeping?"

"If it's not my arm, then it's these weird dreams."

"I could find someone for you to talk to, if you like. About what happened..." The officer trailed off, noticing Zed's discomfort. Like most of the people who worked at St Mary's, Zed wasn't one for discussing the past.

Whenever he thought back to the interrogation, the torture, the things they had done to make him talk, his skin began to prickle. He had learned the hard way that Briggs would stop at nothing to get what he wanted. He didn't care who he hurt. Just the mention of Porton Down was usually enough to bring on waves of nausea.

"Keep yourself busy, that's what I tell my people. It helps to keep the demons away. Plus I highly recommend talking to a third party. I can have a word with the counsellor here. She's a very good listener."

"Thank you, but I'm not much of a talker." Zed grimaced.

"Let me know if you change your mind. The offer stands." He paused, inclining his head. "Now if you'll excuse me, I'll let the colonel know you're here."

Zed staggered up the stairs, labouring under the weight of the metal box, wondering what they had found for him this time.

He arrived outside a door with "4B" stencilled across it.

Inside was a cloister-like cubicle with desk, chair, computer, printer and piles of paperwork covering every surface. Zed flicked on the desk lamp and dumped the heavy box on the desk, sweeping the other folders and piles of paper to one side. He reached across the mess to grab a green folder stuffed with dozens of printed documents. The rapidly expanding ring-binder file was stencilled in black letters "Wildfire" with the MoD reference number underneath LRK/345762/CLS/923.

He retrieved the key from his trouser pocket, inserting it into the lock, and with a satisfying click the lid sprang open a few millimetres. Inside were two bound stacks of classified documents with an MoD cover sheet indicating who had already viewed these. There were only two names above his: Doctor Hardy and Colonel Abrahams. Underneath the reports, Zed found a snow globe with a Post-it note attached. He picked up the paperweight and shook it, watching large flakes of snow settling on the multicoloured spires and rooftops of Red Square, Moscow. He tore off the Post-it note and tried to decipher the colonel's handwriting.

*It's time we talked about Russia. You didn't think Iraq was acting alone, did you?*

Zed sat back in his seat and stared at the ceiling for a minute, trying to remember what the colonel had already told him. He knew only too well the rumours about Russian links with Saddam Hussein, but he had always dismissed them as unsubstantiated. The puzzle of the sophistication and scale of the Iraqi weapons programme had never been fully explained. Underneath the smokescreen and political wrangling, how on earth had Saddam built one of the world's largest weapons programmes, right under the noses of the United Nations?

He picked up the first stack of papers and turned to the title page marked "MoD submission to the United Nations Special Commission - Report on Iraq's Biological Weapons Programme". Some of the information sources, dates and locations had been heavily redacted, but flicking through the pages, Zed could see that much of the report remained intact. He remembered some of the research. After all, he had been one of the analysts who had worked on the original submission, though he had never seen what the MoD finally sent on to the UN.

He settled in to read the contents, noticing the colonel's notes in the margin. At the top of one of the inside pages written in capital letters were the words "Spanish flu?", underlined twice.

# Chapter Six

After what felt like a few minutes of reading, but was in reality nearly two hours, there was a knock at the door, and the colonel entered Zed's cramped office. Zed instinctively closed the folder.

"I got your message and came as quick as I could," said the colonel, shutting the door behind him. "You said you'd found something?"

"Well, I'm still working my way through the second folder, but I was curious about some of the items you'd underlined."

Puzzled, the colonel leaned forward, trying to see what Zed was referring to.

"Look, most of the documents you've passed me to date have been background material, MoD reports, low-level intelligence gathering, that sort of thing. Whereas this," said Zed, tapping the folder, "this is different class."

"If I remember correctly, those were some of the encrypted reports on the second data drive. The doctor was rather reluctant to allow us access until I threatened to send him back to Porton," said the colonel.

"It was your notes in the margin that were troubling me. You wrote 'Spanish flu', 'Biopreparat' and 'Alibekov' several times with a question mark. What did you mean?"

"Oh that. How much do you know about Biopreparat?"

"You mean the Russian biowarfare division? Not much. Just by reputation. I suppose we've all heard the stories."

"My long-held belief is that Iraq was not acting alone. The most likely partner was Russia. After the collapse of the Soviet Union, we know Iraq recruited dozens of their scientists. They went to the highest bidders. The US picked up a few high-profile names, people like Colonel Alibekov."

"Alibekov? Was he the one who defected?"

"That's right. He blew the whistle on the scale of the USSR's weapons programmes during the Cold War. He was the First Deputy Director of Biopreparat, worked there for many years. I got to sit in on one of his debriefing sessions. Incredible stuff. Happy to tell you over a pint sometime."

"I hear he's something of a legend in some circles," said Zed.

"We knew from Alibekov that some of his team went to Iraq. The two countries shared an obsession with developing biological agents, weaponised versions of the plague virus and smallpox, for example."

"Surely smallpox was eradicated in the 1980s?"

"Exactly, and that made the West vulnerable. All stocks of the vaccine had been run down. Smallpox had become a viable weapon again. The same was true of other pathogens. If their scientists could recreate something like the bubonic plague or Spanish flu, an outbreak could be devastating."

"What makes you so sure the Russians were helping Iraq?" asked Zed, leaning forward.

"Remember perestroika? Towards the end of the Cold War when Gorbachev came to power, it was no longer feasible for Biopreparat to maintain the scale of their research programmes. Things had started to change not long after the Convention on

Biological Weapons came into force in 1975. Reciprocal inspections between the Russians and Americans made it necessary to outsource some activities to overseas territories, beyond the reach of the inspectors. Iraq was definitely one of the partners they shortlisted."

"Why Iraq?"

"Because Saddam shared Biopreparat's ambition: to develop weapons of mass destruction and stockpile the vaccines needed to prevent such an attack happening on home soil."

"Interesting. We were always suspicious how Saddam was able to scale his programmes so quickly, to make breakthroughs that didn't seem possible from a standing start. It didn't seem to make sense. But colonel, if you don't mind me asking, how do you know all this?"

"I was stationed in Moscow for several years. Berlin before that. Last few years, I was at GCHQ."

"So you were a spy?"

"Not really. I prefer the term military intelligence." He smiled.

Zed studied the colonel more closely, not sure whether to believe him or not. He had never met a real spy before. The colonel seemed amused by his curiosity.

"Look, I'll tell you about it another time." He checked his watch. "Right now, I need you to concentrate on the body of evidence in front of you. I've called a meeting at 6pm. I want you to brief the others. Tell them what you've told me."

"Which bit?"

"About Project Wildfire and Iraq's weapon programmes. Keep it high level for now. By the way, I'd recommend you leave out the bits about Hitler, and Nazi wonder weapons."

Zed laughed, not entirely convinced that any of this was the right play. "I get the distinct impression they still think I'm some kind of conspiracy nut."

"No one is saying that any more. Things have changed. Confidentially, that US Navy Intelligence report Peterson showed us on the *Chester* proves that the Americans believed there was a credible threat against the West. Peterson's convinced there's more to Project Wildfire than meets the eye. I think Doctor Hardy and his team might be ready to listen to you. Remember, the Porton team are scientists. They're comfortable dealing with empirical facts, not theories. To them, the concept of a weaponised flu virus is implausible on a number of levels."

"Believe me, they're right to be sceptical. If I were in their shoes, I'd have a hard time believing all this. Until I can lay my hands on something in here that's tangible," said Zed, tapping the folder in front of him, "I'm never going to convince Doctor Hardy and the others. I'd rather keep my powder dry."

"Look, we're all on the same side. They're just impatient for answers. I've told Doctor Hardy to shut up and listen. He needs to give you a fair hearing, suspend his disbelief. Just tell them what you've been telling me. Who knows, it might spark something, nudge their thinking in new directions, but keep it factual. Keep the wild theories to yourself, for now. I'll see you in there at 6pm. That gives you about an hour."

"I'll see what I can do, colonel. What about Biopreparat?"

"That's just between the two of us for now." He winked.

As the colonel closed the door behind him, Zed blew out his cheeks, thinking through what he could possibly pull together in just over an hour. He slumped back in his chair, looking up at the cracks in the ceiling, shaking his head. Despite the colonel's encouragement, he had no doubt that Doctor Hardy would dismiss whatever he had to say. The scientists from Porton were so blinkered in their views, so wedded to their code. They suffered acutely from what he described as "not invented here" syndrome. He knew that he was asking them to take a leap of faith, to countenance another explanation for the worldwide pandemic. Yet, something about their intransigence made him suspicious.

Zed was the first to admit that there were dozens of unanswered questions, some of them fundamental. If the outbreak was deliberate, then who launched the attack? What was the target and why? He was no virologist, but he had learned a fair bit about biological weapons during his time at the MoD.

He had to assume that the Porton Down scientists knew more than he did about the virus. He knew they had electron microscopes and other state-of-the-art technology at their disposal. Chances were they already knew what they were dealing with. The CDC and WHO had been warning the West for years to prepare for the next pandemic. It just didn't seem possible that something so deadly could have caught the world by surprise.

Zed couldn't prove it, not yet at least, but he remained convinced that the Millennial Virus bore the hallmarks of a biological weapon. It had been engineered for a single purpose: to destroy human life.

He would love to get another look at the US Navy Intelligence report Lieutenant Peterson kept in that locked safe on board the *Chester*. From memory, it had referenced a Project Chuma, roughly translated as plague or pestilence. The report highlighted the activities of a rogue faction in the Russian military, suspected of providing technical assistance to Pyongyang. They had intercepted a communiqué suggesting they were working on a flu virus. Peterson confided that, at the time, no one had seriously believed there was a credible threat to national security, but in hindsight, it was hard to ignore.

Zed was still puzzling over the link between Russia and Iraq. Was it possible that the Russians had relocated their bioweapons R&D to Iraq to avoid the attentions of the US inspectors?

He leafed through a previous stack of documents until he found what he was looking for. It was a copy of a WHO report detailing an H1N1 outbreak in the seventies, which referred to an avian flu strain known as Russian flu. That particular strain had been dormant for nearly twenty years, frozen in time from the 1950s. It suggested an accidental breach or laboratory accident. It confirmed to Zed that the Russians had been running their own clandestine programme. Was it possible they had outsourced this particular Project Chuma to Iraq after all?

Buried within the thousands of documents contained within the Porton archive, there had to be something that could help explain what had happened. Working on his own, there was a limit to what he could achieve. He would need to push himself harder. Prioritise the most likely avenues of research. Back his hunches. He just needed more time.

His instinct was still telling him that what had happened in Iraq was vital. The colonel was playing his cards close to his chest. Perhaps he was trying to force Zed's hand. What choice did he have? Until he could be sure, his only option was to be economical with the truth.

What seemed like a short while later, the colonel's orderly arrived to escort Zed from his office. He grabbed a clutch of computer print-outs and stuffed them under his arm, suddenly flustered, feeling under-prepared.

He followed the stiffly uniformed orderly up the stairs and to the end of a brightly lit corridor. It led to the executive conference suite, where an armed soldier waited outside. By the looks of things, Zed was the last to arrive. The meeting had already started without him.

# Chapter Seven

"Ah, Mister Samuels, do come in. Have a seat. There's one near the back," said the colonel, gesturing towards the end of the long white table. "I hope you don't mind, but we started without you."

Zed squeezed along the wall behind a row of scientists and senior staff members, depositing himself in the only empty seat. It was a full house. He smiled weakly at Doctor Hardy who sat opposite. Hardy ignored him, staring blankly at the clock on the wall above him, watching the seconds tick by. From his body language, Zed could tell there was somewhere else Hardy would rather be.

For the first ten minutes, Zed listened disinterestedly to the base commander running through housekeeping items, enhanced security checks and new team members arriving from Southampton hospital. When the room suddenly fell silent, Zed realised everyone was looking at him.

"Mr Samuels? When you're ready. The floor is yours."

He got to his feet, nervously grasping the back of his chair, trying to remember what he had planned to say.

"Thank you. Well, as you know, I've spent the last week working through the Project Wildfire archive that was recovered from Porton Down."

"I'm sorry, Wildfire?" asked one of the senior staffers, removing his glasses. He was a grey-haired officer Zed had never met before.

"Yes, Project Wildfire was a DSTL research programme, born out of the second Iraq War, set up to determine whether it was feasible to weaponise a flu virus and the means by which this country could defend itself. We believed that Iraq was on the brink of some interesting breakthroughs in this field."

"The expert view was that the threat was negligible," cautioned the doctor. "Our own Common Cold Research Unit near Salisbury spent decades investigating strains of the influenza virus in the hope of developing a vaccine. Their counterparts at Porton assessed the future threat from a weaponised flu virus. It simply couldn't be done, by us or by anyone else for that matter."

"That was the opinion of the Minister of Defence at the time," agreed Zed. "For so many reasons, the UK and American teams dismissed these ideas as unworkable, and Project Wildfire was mothballed, its funding cancelled. In reality, the programme simply went underground and off the DSTL books."

Out of the corner of his eye, Zed could see the doctor shaking his head in disbelief, but he chose to ignore him.

"Believe you me, Iraq was not alone," continued Zed. "The intelligence reports I've seen suggest that other countries had their own parallel research programmes. The US, Russia, Syria, Iran, North Korea, Iraq and others. For several years, when I was a contractor working for the MoD and DSTL, some of that based at Porton Down—"

"Why are we wasting so much time on Iraq?" interrupted the doctor. "Russia or North Korea were far more likely candidates."

"Look, as we all know, throughout the eighties and nineties, Iraq developed one of the world's largest biological and chemical weapons programmes. Saddam was obsessed. He used his oil wealth to invest hundreds of millions of dollars, drafting in the best minds and the latest technology."

"And you really think it's credible that Iraq could have succeeded where so many others had failed?" asked one of the scientists, barely concealing his derision.

Zed held up a finger to acknowledge the question but refused to be thrown off his stream of thought.

"I spent the best part of a decade investigating Iraqi weapons programmes. The more I look, the more clues I'm finding. Are you familiar with the work of Rihab Rashid Taha al-Azawi?"

"You mean the legendary Doctor Germ?" sneered Doctor Hardy.

There was a stifled laugh from the far end of the table.

"Sorry, perhaps you can remind us all who this Doctor Germ was and why you think he is so important?" said the grey-haired officer.

"Certainly, but 'he' is actually a 'she'. Taha al-Azawi was an Iraqi-born microbiologist who did her PhD on plant toxins right here in this country at the University of East Anglia's School of Biological Studies. She was a brilliant scientist. Unmarried, no children, both of which were extremely unusual for a thirty-something Arab woman."

"Was she the same Doctor Germ who was name-checked in the infamous 'Dodgy Dossier' that justified the second Iraq War? The one that made the claim about Saddam's WMDs being ready to launch in forty-five minutes?"

"So, that's where I know her from," interjected the grey-haired officer.

"I believe she is key to all this. She had over fifty virologists and computer scientists running simulations at the bioweapons facility at al-Hakam. Our informant suggested they might have been modelling a large-scale pandemic."

"Wait, so you're saying that despite all the sanctions and UN resolutions and inspections, Iraq still managed to keep all this secret from the West?"

"It would appear so. The MoD team I was working with got drafted in to support the United Nations inspectors following the embarrassing revelation that the UK had been supplying Iraq with some of the equipment and technology used to produce biological weapons."

"Well, hold on a minute," interrupted the colonel. "The UK was certainly not the only one. France, Germany and the US were also implicated. We all unwittingly supplied critical technology to pharmaceutical production sites in Iraq. Everyone was hoodwinked into thinking it was for industrial use."

"How was the West that gullible? Why did no one put two and two together?" asked the grey-haired officer.

"It all comes down to so-called dual-use technology. With nuclear programmes where large plants are required to produce fissile materials, they're fairly easy to detect via satellite imagery. But as the team from Porton Down well know, bacteria and viruses are produced in the same way as everyday vaccines and antibiotics. That means that legitimate laboratories, breweries, dairies, even distilleries can be deployed to produce either. Hence dual-use," explained the colonel.

Zed took over. "Dual-use made the job of the international monitor extremely difficult. The Iraqi authorities were playing an elaborate game of 'hide the ball' with the UNSCOM team. UN resolution 687 mandated the destruction of all chemical and biological weapons. But how does one judge the purpose of a facility, whether it's being used for innocent, legal purposes or something more sinister?

"Back in the seventies and eighties, it used to be fairly straightforward to identify bioweapons plants from the large stainless steel or glass fermenters they used. Nowadays everything is about a hundred times smaller. Continuous-flow and computer controlled. The need to hold huge stockpiles is a thing of the past. Pathogens can be mass-produced relatively quickly now.

"Look, on paper, the UN team in Iraq had unlimited access to inspect whatever they chose. In practice, they were met with resistance, denial, and obstruction at every turn. Their teams were often delayed just long enough for facilities to be cleared of any incriminating evidence. In the end, the only way to be sure that Iraq was developing biological weapons was via covert surveillance. They had to find people on the inside who could help them get to the truth. Weapons programmes were too easy to conceal."

"So what makes you think this Doctor Germ is key to all this?"

"She ran the whole thing. Taha was secretly recruited by Saddam during her time at East Anglia University to become the Chief Production Officer at al-Hakam, the top-secret bioweapons facility just outside Baghdad. Saddam was obsessed with destroying his enemies. He tasked Taha al-Azawi with stockpiling a range of biological and chemical agents. Nothing was off limits. Anthrax, ricin, foot and mouth disease, smallpox. The UN estimated that more than 22,000 Irani prisoners were used for human experiments in the 1980s and 1990s. This scale of war crime was unprecedented since the atrocities of Auschwitz or Dachau."

Zed paused, his throat dry. He took a drink of water, his hand shaking with adrenaline.

"Years later, after the invasion of Iraq, Taha was captured and interrogated. Some of the audio files and transcripts of those conversations were found on the data drives from Porton Down. Hearing her voice was chilling. She stonewalled, denied everything. Only when she was confronted with incontrovertible evidence did she finally admit that they had multiple biowarfare divisions producing anthrax, ricin, plague virus, even smallpox."

"So you're really suggesting Taha's team might have created the Millennial Virus and launched an attack against the West?" interrupted Doctor Hardy, rubbing his tired eyes. "And I suppose you have at least some shred of evidence to back that up?"

"Look, what you have to realise is that by the time we got there the Iraqis had destroyed much of the evidence. What remained was at best fragmentary. It was like a giant jigsaw puzzle with most of the pieces missing. The inspection team weren't sure what they were looking for. At first, all they had were eyewitness reports that heightened their suspicions. They knew they weren't seeing the big picture. Admittedly, the physical evidence was at best flimsy."

"Flimsy? You could say that again!"

"But we should not be too quick to discount the possibility of an industrial accident or leak. None of us has forgotten what happened with the foot and mouth outbreak, doctor," Zed fired back, to the embarrassment of the scientists. "What was the official explanation? A missing vial from Porton Down? Or at least that's what I heard."

Again, there was a restlessness in the room. Zed suspected many of the Porton team knew far more than they were letting on.

"Another one of your wild theories, Mr Samuels. Please, can

we just stick to the matter at hand? I couldn't help noticing that your story about the interrogation of Taha made no mention of the flu virus."

"That's right. She swore blind that she was unaware of any such programme. If it had ever existed, then she assured us that programme had been shut down before her time."

"Then why are we wasting time talking about her?" said Doctor Hardy, removing his glasses and shaking his head in exasperation.

"Because we now know she was lying."

"How could you possibly know that?"

"Our informant referred to a Project Chimaera, or in Arabic, *Alkamir kayin khirrafi*. A research programme so secret that only a handful of the Iraqi leadership knew of its existence. Our assessment was that their research was cutting-edge and credible."

"Did you say chimaera? You mean like the mythical creature?"

"That's right. In Greek legend, the chimaera was a fire-breathing monster with a lion's head, a goat's body and a serpent's tail."

"Don't you think it's ironic that chimaera is also commonly used to refer to something illusory or imaginary that cannot be achieved? We might call that a red herring. Rather fitting, don't you think?" Doctor Hardy smiled.

"Except in this case where the Iraqi scientists appeared to have been close to a breakthrough. They had experimented on tens of thousands of Iranian prisoners of war, with dozens of separate strains of influenza virus. They were trying to engineer a virus that was easy to transmit and would ensure a high mortality rate."

"But that's impossible. It's been tried before," said Doctor Hardy dismissively. He leaned forward in his chair, casting his eyes around the room, looking at each person in turn, choosing his next words carefully.

"It's been a closely guarded secret that for over one hundred years, Porton Down has conducted research into every known pathogen. To stay one step ahead, it was imperative that our teams worked without limits, pushing the boundaries of what's possible to protect our nation from attack. Most of the world's most deadly chemical and biological agents were first developed at Porton."

"We're all well aware of Porton's record and achievements, thank you. Indeed, whether that work was undertaken for defensive or offensive purposes is an ethical debate for another time," confirmed the colonel.

"The Common Cold Unit spent decades looking at dozens of different strains of flu virus. They experimented on thousands of willing volunteers," said Doctor Hardy, growing red in the face. "In the last fifteen years, several laboratories attempted to create genetically modified flu strains. They wanted to see if it was possible to alter the rate of infection, splicing in genetic material from other viruses, such as Ebola or Marburg. The reality is that viruses are extremely unpredictable. They exchange genetic material with natural viruses all the time. An increase in the rate of infection is invariably countered by a decline in mortality. The Millennial Virus is a freak of nature. It simply could not have been man-made. It's too perfect."

"So you're saying that if you couldn't do it at Porton Down, it's just not credible that the Iraqis could have had any more success?" asked the colonel.

"Correct. The considered opinion of my team is that it's almost impossible that Iraq could have genetically engineered this virus."

"Well, hold on a minute," countered the colonel. "We believe Iraq was not acting alone. There were numerous links with the Russian biowarfare division, and they were almost certainly sharing data with Syria and North Korea. Iraq certainly had the knowledge, skills and the will to do this."

"Various witness reports confirmed the human experiments. We suspect that they were testing a new virus," suggested Zed.

"How do you know that?"

"One of the key witnesses was a truck driver who used to transport prisoners from Abu Ghraib prison to a military post in al-Haditha. He said that he saw canisters and drums marked with biohazard symbols. There were sealed airtight tanks just large enough for a single prisoner. The victims were said to have suffered from flu-like symptoms. Many of them died three to five days after exposure."

"But there are dozens of chemical or biological agents that could present as flu symptoms," argued the doctor. "It doesn't mean a thing."

"Well, we knew Saddam was stockpiling thousands of tonnes of chemical and biological weapons. The main concern was that he intended to fill the warheads of his Scud missiles with anthrax or some other biological agent. He planned to target his enemies in the region."

"But that claim was disproven, wasn't it? It was inconceivable that he could launch an attack in forty-five minutes. Anyway, warhead delivery mechanisms might be effective for some bacterial weapons like anthrax, but they are extremely unlikely to work for viruses. Air release is much too unreliable. Wind might blow the agent in the wrong direction. Extreme temperatures or even strong sunlight could reduce its effectiveness. The chances of success are tiny."

"The MoD certainly didn't take the threat of missile attack seriously. They were far more worried about human-to-human transmission."

Zed took over from the colonel. "The UN inspection team was highly sceptical until two disconnected pieces of information came to our attention. We discovered that the University of Baghdad had ordered frozen tissue samples from the Armed Forces Institute of Pathology in Washington. They were conducting research that required cell cultures from First World War victims of Spanish flu. Sixteen separate export orders were granted over the course of a four-year period in the nineties."

"And I suppose, at the time, no one thought that was suspicious?" asked the colonel.

"Well, it's not uncommon for pathogens and tissue samples to be exchanged between laboratories and universities," confirmed one of the scientists.

"We believe those tissue samples could have provided Iraq with sufficient quantities of the original Spanish flu 1918 pandemic strain to reproduce the virus," continued Zed, to the weary sighs of those around the table.

"Theoretically possible, but unlikely. Simply having those tissue samples is not proof that their team succeeded. Frankly, this chimaera nonsense is just another wild theory. Mr Samuels, the people round this table deal with facts. We're scientists, not fantasists. Find us some hard evidence, not this conspiracy nonsense about ridiculous miracle weapons. What did you call them before?" said the doctor, reviewing his notes from a previous meeting with some derision. "Nazi Wunderwaffen!"

Zed swallowed hard, feeling his cheeks redden. He was in danger of being laughed out of St Mary's. He decided to bite back, even if that meant revealing more than he had planned.

"Then what about the genetic markers you found, Doctor Hardy? You yourself said they were hard to explain. Wasn't that the real reason I was brought to St Mary's in the first place?"

Hardy leaned back in his chair, shaking his head. He let out a long sigh. "Yes, I admit that was our thinking at the time."

"Go on, doctor," instructed the colonel, with growing impatience.

"Look, when we first sequenced the virus, our preliminary analysis indicated the presence of third-party RNA strands."

"And what does that mean exactly?" asked the colonel.

"It suggested some level of human interference. Think of it as an artist's signature. Some labs use coded RNA sequences to tag viruses so that they can track their spread in laboratory tests. But we came to understand that there was a simpler explanation. Viruses exchange genetic material all the time. Even if there was evidence of third-party material, it didn't mean that the Millennial Virus was bioengineered. It's far more likely this was simply a natural mutation. Experts like Professor Nicholas have always said that they expected another flu pandemic, they just didn't know when."

"But they surely didn't expect the outbreak to bear such striking similarities with a long-dormant strain?"

"But why not? We know that the Russians sent teams to Siberia to retrieve dormant viruses trapped in layers of permafrost. It was something of an obsession. They believed that their enemies would have no defence against such rare pathogens. Like smallpox. No one keeps stocks of the vaccine any more. Smallpox no longer posed a threat."

"And you're suggesting that the same logic holds for a lethal strain of influenza?"

"Again, why not? Splice in some genetic material from

another virus and you have a pandemic the scale of which the world has never seen."

"Look, it's just not that easy. You people have no idea." The doctor laughed with open scorn.

"But just because your team failed, doctor, could it be done?" asked the colonel.

"I suppose it's theoretically possible. Just very unlikely."

The colonel's eyes narrowed, his palms resting flat on the table.

"Then, gentlemen, with all due respect, however unlikely, we have to assume that someone, somewhere, may have succeeded."

# Chapter Eight

Terra was one of the last to leave Carisbrooke Castle. The convoy of four vehicles crawled along country roads in complete darkness, heading for their new home. Staying well away from the main roads, they skirted allied checkpoints.

Terra rested her head against the window, staring at passing shapes and shadows, listening to the light rain. In the short time she had been at the castle, Terra had developed a strong attachment to the place. Lichen-covered stone walls reminded her just a little of Hurst. The austere accommodation was at best functional. She did not relish the prospect of spending the winter there. It remained a cold, unforgiving sort of place despite Briggs's best efforts to upgrade the living quarters. She consoled herself that if it was good enough for Princess Beatrice, Queen Victoria's daughter, then it was good enough for her.

The last few days, the whole castle had felt so empty without Briggs. His entourage had gone ahead to put the finishing touches to their new home, said to be a school on the mainland. At least his absence had allowed her some head space to make sense of the past few months as his so-called special guest. Her dreams remained haunted by that fateful night at Hurst. The castle had fallen because of her. She never should have trusted

Briggs to keep his promise. When he refused to stand up to King's demands for revenge, he said Jack had got what he deserved. What did anyone expect would happen after keeping King locked up at the castle all those months? The looping image of Jack's half-naked body twitching at the end of the rope made her nauseous once more. How could she have been so naive?

The convoy squeaked to a halt at a small landing area on the Medina River, opposite the Folly Inn. She stood shivering in the shelter of the tailgate. A rowing boat with a throaty Yamaha outboard took it in turns to shuttle groups of four out to a floating pontoon in the near darkness. Waterlogged shapes in disorderly rows suggested pleasure craft in various states of disrepair.

She blinked in the rain, struggling to catch sight of the passenger ferry that would transport them the rest of the way across the Solent.

"Shouldn't be much longer," whispered her companion, looking distractedly at the illuminated dial of his watch.

"How many hours do we have left?" she whispered anxiously.

"We're fine," reassured the minder, with an undertone of irritation, handing her the rucksack to carry. He had barely left her side these last few days. A rising star in Briggs's eclectic organisation. Most of them were former inmates from Parkhurst Prison or Albany, just up the road. Liberated during the outbreak, when the remaining guards could no longer care for them. The Governor's repeated requests for relief unanswered.

The younger man made no secret of his lack of enthusiasm for the task. He was only doing this as a personal favour. Briggs was a hard man to say no to.

Briggs hadn't trusted the allies to keep their word. He claimed the forty-eight-hour amnesty was a ruse to flush out those sympathetic to the rebels. Anyone attempting to leave the island would be rounded up rather than further swell the growing ranks of the disaffected. Briggs decided to slip away unnoticed in the night. With luck, they would catch the allies napping again. After all, it was a vast waterway to patrol with such limited resources.

Huddled in muted silence under a tarpaulin she listened to the rain falling all around them. The incoming tide tugged gently against the polystyrene floats. When the wind strengthened, the whole platform seemed to tilt at an alarming angle.

In the incessant downpour, water began pooling above their heads. The sagging material was stretched between four improvised poles. Terra was already soaked to the skin, holding a perfumed scarf to her mouth to mask the stench of mud and rotting fish rising from the riverbank.

From time to time, one of the others pushed against the sagging bulge in the tarpaulin to release a torrent of water into the flowing river.

On the far bank, a candle-lit lantern swung from a hook over the front entrance to the inn, casting shadows across the path. For a moment, she thought she saw a child's face at the window watching them, but the curtain fell back into place and the face was gone.

Their departure had been precipitated by Lieutenant Peterson's surprise visit to Carisbrooke by helicopter. The Americans blamed Briggs for his part in what had happened at Hurst. It would appear that their partnership of convenience had run its course. Briggs's presence at the castle was no longer tolerated. Did Peterson really believe that he could threaten Briggs? If there was one thing she had learned, to her cost, over the last few months, it was that Briggs could not be managed or controlled.

In the end, it had been Damian King's idea that they relocate to the new site on the mainland. He had made available to them what he described as a stately home, though Terra knew it was nothing of the sort. Walhampton was an independent boarding school, not a stone's throw from Lymington Hospital, well equipped for Briggs's growing entourage of nearly two hundred. King boasted that the three-hundred-year-old country house rivalled any National Trust site. It had even featured in the Domesday Book.

The hospital group had been using the school as overflow accommodation. Their numbers had swollen over successive months as more groups drifted south towards the island. The school was an obvious choice, surrounded by nearly one hundred acres, its grounds turned over to agriculture. Lush pastures dotted with grazing sheep, cows and almost forty pigs.

Victor said it was a tangible sign of the rebels' strengthening union that King had allowed Briggs to take over the school. She knew Victor had worked hard to bring the two groups closer together. Scattered along the coast back towards Southampton were several other newly formed communities sympathetic to the rebel cause. Together they had formed an alliance that might soon rival the allies.

Their heads turned in unison towards the sound of a low chugging noise coming from beyond the bend of the river. Terra glimpsed the powerful beam of the ferryboat's searchlight sweeping ahead for any obstacles. The man from the Folly Inn swung his lantern from side to side, guiding the approaching ferry towards them.

The bedraggled company got to their feet, herding closer together in expectation. Terra's minder cleared a path to the water's edge. They all knew who she was and what she represented. One by one they stepped aside to allow her through.

The small vessel put its engines into neutral and coasted towards them on the rising tide. When they were close enough to throw a line, with a nudge astern, the ferry bumped gently against the jetty. Hanging down to protect its painted wooden hull, the oil-stained fenders groaned in displeasure, compressed against the fibreglass of the pontoon.

The boat's skipper reached over to shake hands with the local man. The flashlight picked out his weathered yellow oilskin jacket and sodden flat cap. They exchanged a mumbled greeting before handing over a package wrapped in plastic. Terra assumed it must be payment of some kind, drugs most likely.

The remaining luggage from the castle was quickly stowed beneath a weatherproof canopy that stretched halfway back towards the stern. Once safely aboard they crowded together in the shelter of the wheelhouse.

The Folly man pushed the bow out into the tide, throwing their mooring lines to the waiting arms of the deckhand. They drifted silently along the length of the pontoon. Once clear of the line of moorings, the skipper threw the wheel over and powered the boat round to face back towards Cowes and the open sea beyond.

It was just after four in the morning. With any luck, they would make it to Buckler's Hard on the Beaulieu River before dawn.

"Did you have any trouble getting across?" asked Terra.

"Silent as the grave out there!" shouted the skipper over the steady rumble of the engine. "Most of the others left yesterday. We spotted one other fishing boat heading north out of Cowes. Trying to beat the deadline, I'd imagine."

"What happens when we get to the other side?"

"The boss said he's coming to collect you himself." He grinned lasciviously, several of his teeth missing.

Terra felt her cheeks flush. She pulled her jacket tighter, feeling the man's eyes wander down her like a piece of meat. She only had to say the word and she could have this man killed. She glanced across at her chaperone, who took the hint, glaring back at the skipper.

"Why don't you keep your eyes on the road, old man," he cautioned.

"I've known your Briggs since the beginning, you know. People around here would lay down their lives for him. He's like Robin Hood, stealing from the rich and giving to the poor."

"I'll be sure to tell him how well you served us. Your loyalty will be rewarded."

The skipper opened up their twin diesel engines as soon as they reached East Cowes, parallel with the burned-out shell of the old Royal Yacht Squadron. The bow rose higher as they powered into the black waves, sending spray flying either side. Looking behind, arms folded, she watched the island slowly fade into the pre-dawn darkness. The displaced water in their wake seemed to fizz with dull phosphorescence.

"We'll be back in no time. Briggs promised," reassured the minder, observing her body language.

She didn't doubt it. Victor had refused to divulge any of the details, but it was an open secret that the rebels were growing in confidence. They were nearly ready to execute their carefully prepared plans. Victor said it was safer that she knew little of what had been agreed. It must have something to do with the professor and why they wanted him.

She hated being kept in the dark like this. Victor had tried to placate her with repeated promises. Despite her misgivings, she swallowed her pride. Her conscience was screaming at her to get as far away from Briggs as possible, but where could she go? She was caught in a lie. Victor's veiled threats to expose her duplicity kept her within his power.

Fifteen minutes into their crossing, a sudden beam of light swept across the wheelhouse, as if alerted by their presence. The ferry was running dark, all navigational lights extinguished, relying on the experience of the pilot. As the searchlight swept back, it picked out the passengers. They turned as one to squint towards the light. The source was unlikely to be friendly; perhaps a navy patrol boat or large inflatable.

The skipper wasted no time in turning the wheel sharply to starboard, trying to break their lock. He nudged the throttle levers forward, reassuring himself that the twin diesel engines were at maximum power.

The water off their starboard bow seemed to erupt, spray cascading down on to the terrified passengers. The skipper jinked left, instinctively steering away from where the round had landed. He glanced anxiously over his shoulder, keeping track of where the other boat was. The light picked out his pursed lips and grimace.

Terra caught glimpses of the pursuing vessel as the searchlight fought hard to keep them in its beam. A larger patrol boat was quickly closing the gap, still perhaps a kilometre away to their right and certainly too far for small arms fire.

Ten seconds later there was a deafening explosion, much closer this time. The force of the water almost broached the ferryboat, showering the huddled figures in a fresh deluge of freezing cold seawater.

Little by little, they were finding their range. A third and fourth round fell close by, one in front and one behind. Terra could see the dark outline of the spit ahead of them, and the first of the channel markers flashed by.

The ferry turned sharply, lining up with the buoys ahead. Soon they would be within the narrow tidal passage that led to Buckler's Hard. Terra wondered whether the larger interceptor would attempt to follow them.

"Is it deep enough?"

"I don't know," said the skipper, looking over his shoulder. "Not at half tide."

Terra was relieved to see the searchlight power down as they broke off their pursuit, to a small cheer from all those on board.

"Sorry about that. Bit too close for comfort."

Easing back on the throttle, the ferryboat lost momentum as their bow sank back level so she could see ahead again. The ferry navigated the bends in the narrow river, sweeping past the ghostly outlines of yachts and power boats on river moorings. Either side of them were mudflats that looked perilously close.

"How much further?" she asked, checking her watch.

"Couple of miles yet. Don't you worry, Mrs Briggs. We'll have you there in no time."

Terra bridled at his condescension, but let it pass. She had grown used to the over-familiarity of these local men. She shivered against the bitter pre-dawn air, pulling her collar up. She followed her minder's lead and sank lower below the gunwale to shield her face from the wind funnelling between the trees. She fished out a pocket mirror and took a moment to straighten her wind-blown hair, apply some lip gloss and perfume in the dim light from the instrument panel. She wanted to look her best for the reunion with Briggs.

# Chapter Nine

Terra had heard so much about this place. The Beaulieu River was said to be beautiful, hence the name. She only wished she could see it in daylight.

It was hard to imagine, but Buckler's Hard was said to have been a major shipyard. Some of Nelson's ships that fought at the Battle of Trafalgar were built here with oak from the New Forest.

The skipper cut the power, and the ferryboat coasted towards the narrow jetty. He noticed her staring up the hill following the line of picture-postcard historic cottages.

"That's the old high street up there," he said, pointing up the hill. "Motor Museum and Lord Montagu's estate are further up. I could show you if you like, when you're next here."

"If I wanted a guided tour…" she started to say and then thought better of it.

"Sorry, I was only being friendly." He shrugged.

At the top of the hill, two school-liveried minibuses had their engines running, waiting to collect the last arrivals. Their headlights cast long shadows across the car park and roadway. She followed the man carrying her luggage, recognising the back of a pale-coloured Range Rover half-hidden behind a low hedge.

Two figures emerged, striding purposefully towards them.

With some excitement Terra recognised Briggs.

"I thought you weren't coming!" She smiled in feigned surprise. Briggs put his arms around her slender waist, lifting her gently off her feet. He squeezed her so hard she could barely breathe.

"I was worried. I heard there was some trouble."

"Nothing we couldn't handle. Were you worried about me?" She laughed coquettishly.

"Wait till you see this place. You're going to love it."

"I've heard it's beautiful."

He grabbed her again, pulling her in tight like a predator sniffing its kill, flaring his nostrils, inhaling her scent.

"They've got everything. Horses, tennis courts and a pool."

"Looks like someone missed me," she whispered into his ear. "I guess they're right. Absence really does make the heart grow fonder."

"Only the best for my princess."

"Darling, you're always thinking of my happiness." She beamed, hoping she wasn't overdoing it. Victor looked on amused, enjoying her performance.

"Come on, let's get you back. You hungry, gal? There'll be breakfast waiting."

****

The short drive from Beaulieu took longer than she expected, along narrow roads carpeted in wet leaves like some technicoloured tunnel through the woods. Several times they had to slow to a crawl as low-hanging branches brushed against the windshield.

After the cold night air, Terra was enjoying the heated seats. She leaned her head back against the window, closing her eyes.

"Here, take my coat," said Briggs from the front passenger seat. "If you're tired…"

"I'm too excited to be tired. I just didn't sleep much last night, that's all." She sighed, wondering if she was overdoing the whole "missing you" thing.

Round the next bend, Victor braked hard, almost ramming the stationary bus blocking the road. A crude barrier was guarded by two armed men. The guards approached the vehicle in their high-visibility jackets and asked to see their papers. One of them shone a torch into the cabin's interior and seemed to recognise Briggs. He stepped back and waved through the convoy.

Passing the East End Arms, they turned right at speed towards South Baddesley and Portmore. In places, the road surface was potholed and uneven, shaking Terra from her drowsy state.

The entrance to the school was barricaded. They slowed to navigate a chicane forcing them to stop in a heavily defended area. Terra noticed rusting sheet metal welded together to form narrow firing positions. Its surface appeared heavily marked with bullet indentations as if this site had been fought over many times. They passed a large pond to their left, reflecting scattered clouds and a brightening sky. It would be dawn in less than an hour.

Through the chicane and raised barrier, Victor tutted impatiently as the lead vehicle slowed for a speed bump. He steered round and accelerated the V8 Range Rover dangerously fast towards the tall pillars and iron gates framing the entrance.

Terra sat forward to get a better look at the three-storey period buildings silhouetted against the dawn skyline. Through the gates, Victor turned sharply left past a statue, tyres squealing, parking up outside the main entrance.

Briggs and Victor jumped out, slammed their doors and set off towards an ornate doorway, still lit by hurricane lamps either side. Terra recognised one of the guards from Carisbrooke who appeared to be wearing a radio mic. He touched his earpiece and mumbled something into his sleeve, holding the door open for them.

Briggs deposited the heavy suitcases in the hallway and with some theatricality threw open his arms to welcome Terra.

"So what do you think?"

"Very nice." She nodded, looking around with genuine surprise. Briggs clicked his fingers.

"Cyril, take these bags to the master suite, there's a good chap."

He turned to face Terra with a beaming smile.

"We're staying in the old headmaster's lodgings. It's not exactly five star, but it'll do. Do you want to change first or go straight into breakfast?"

"I'm starving. Food first and then I might have a lie-down." She winked at him.

"You'll find everything you need laid out in the hall."

"Are you not joining me?"

"I've got a couple of errands I need to attend to, and then I'll come and find you, okay?"

"No problem." She smiled. "Take your time."

Stepping into the dining hall, the sun was just breaking through the tree line, bathing the whole room in a soft yellow light. Row upon row of bench seats and long tables were set out, rubbish still strewn across the floor, as if there had been a welcome banquet the night before.

Right now, the place was virtually empty but for the silhouette of a lone figure reading a book.

The professor looked up from a well-thumbed textbook and waved her over.

"How lovely to see a friendly face." He greeted her with a warm smile. He removed his reading glasses and blinked up at her. "I trust you had a good crossing?"

"It was a bit hairy, actually. Luckily, the allies couldn't seem to get their range."

"So much for the amnesty then."

"More importantly, how have they been treating you?" she said, noticing some bruising underneath his left eye. He looked older than she remembered, dark shadows under intelligent eyes.

"I suppose I should be grateful that the punishment beatings have stopped. These days I even get to sleep in a bed."

"Progress indeed. What have you done to deserve all these privileges?" she enquired a little provocatively.

"I've been up at the hospital most days, working in the laboratory."

"I see. I hadn't realised you were helping them."

The professor seemed confused by the question. He glanced over her shoulder to make sure no one else was around.

"I wasn't exactly given a choice. Copper can be quite persuasive."

"Indeed he can. Sooner or later he always gets what he wants."

He studied her carefully, puzzling over something. She anticipated his concerns.

"Look, professor. If you're wondering whether you can trust me, I assure you we're in the same boat."

He didn't seem altogether convinced, refusing to look her directly in the eyes.

"Forgive me, but you don't strike me as someone being held against their will," he said.

"I've just had longer to adjust, that's all," she replied, tilting her head.

"Then what makes you stay?"

"We're all doing what we have to do to survive, professor. Surely as a scientist, you of all people should understand."

"Good heavens, it's not my place to judge." He smiled. "I don't blame you in the slightest if that's what you're thinking. I've always marvelled at the ingenuity of certain species to adapt when threatened. As ever, those best able to adapt have the greatest chance of survival. People like you and me, Terra."

Terra had forgotten how much she enjoyed their exchanges. Briggs was no great conversationalist, and she missed an opponent worthy of her intellect. She found deconstructing the professor's statements fascinating, for the same reason that she never tired of rereading her translated copy of Machiavelli's *The Prince* that she kept by her bed.

She was desperate to ask the scientist about his work but hesitated. She decided that the best approach would be to flatter his ego. After all, he struck her as the sort of gentleman who would never say no to a lady.

"Do you mind me asking what they have you working on at the hospital, or is it a secret?"

"Me? I'm helping them with their research."

"Research into what?"

"A vaccine, of course."

"But King doesn't strike me as being interested in saving lives."

"Don't underestimate him. He knows full well that whoever develops the vaccine first will have a huge advantage. There's still a long way to go. It may take years, decades even. For now, we're attempting to isolate the most potent strain of the virus, the one that has adapted most successfully."

"Why?"

"The more we can find out about the virus the more likely we are to find a vaccine. You see, if a virus kills its host too quickly, then the virus dies out. To be successful, a virus needs to walk a fine line between infecting the greatest number of people before killing its host. Viruses are always mutating, exchanging genetic material with other strains. Developing a vaccine is like trying to hit a moving target. Finding the most potent strain will allow us to focus our efforts."

"Professor, with all due respect, you don't know these people like I do. King is using you."

"I'm not a fool, Terra. I have no intention of being an accessory to genocide. I've answered their questions, that's all."

"The only thing they really care about is that island. They want it for themselves. Trust me, they have no interest in a cure. To King, that virus is a weapon."

"It did occur to me that they might be trying to start a fresh outbreak," whispered the professor, leaning forward.

"Could it work?"

"Unlikely. There are well-designed quarantine measures on both sides of the Solent."

"Then could they find a way to smuggle infected people on to the island?"

"Perhaps that's why they've been asking so many questions about incubation periods. No, it would still be tough. For a start, in the unlikely event that they were successful in starting an outbreak, the risk of it spreading back to the mainland would be too high. It would serve no purpose."

Terra leaned back in her chair, taking in everything the

professor was saying. An idea began to form in her head. She reached forward and grabbed the sleeves of the professor's jacket, looking deep into his eyes.

"We have to find out more about King's plan before it's too late."

He nodded weakly, looking over her shoulder as the dining hall began to fill with more of Briggs's men.

"Look, we can't talk here. Meet me outside in a few minutes. It's better if no one sees us leave together. Wait until I'm gone."

# Chapter Ten

As Terra finished her scrambled eggs on toast in the breakfast hall at Walhampton School, she pondered what she had learned from the professor.

She knew Briggs wanted the island for himself, but couldn't figure out how they planned to achieve that. Displacing the allies would be an impossible task, even with King's help. First, they would need to unleash the virus, deal with the Americans, wrestle back control, blockade the Solent, then starve out the survivors. That might take years. It was an impossibly ambitious plan, but knowing Victor was involved, she knew never to underestimate the man.

Shortly after seven o'clock, a bell summoned the remaining residents of Walhampton School to breakfast. The other tables around her filled quickly, and Terra checked her watch and took her cue to leave.

With a scrape of her chair, she approached the breakfast buffet, poured herself one last cup of coffee and made for the patio doors that led to the stone-paved terrace.

Outside, she found the professor standing next to the mirror-like surface of an ornamental pond. She blew on her mug and squinted into the dazzling morning sunshine.

The professor seemed oblivious to her presence at first, chewing his lip, mumbling something under his breath. She stretched and yawned, acutely aware of how tired she felt.

For a few moments, they stood side by side, enjoying the peace of the morning. There was a faint mist hanging over the landscaped gardens and fields that extended all the way down towards the shoreline. The sweeping views in the soft light were stunning.

He placed a hand on the small of her back and nodded towards the pathway. To their left, a high fence surrounded an old astroturf pitch, now serving as home to several temporary structures that protected farm equipment and vehicles from the elements. Where there had once been playing fields for rugby, football or cricket matches, there was now ploughed earth and row upon row of vegetables, enough even to feed a small army.

Following the line of trees, the path veered left towards a wooden bench covered with mildew. There was a dedication on the headrest that was hard to make out. In memory of Harvey someone. She couldn't read the rest.

Shaded by tall oaks, it was a beautiful spot overlooking a small lake. The water's surface was almost entirely covered in algae and water lilies, grown wild through the summer. Dragged up on the bank was a collection of kayaks and canoes, several small dinghies with their masts fixed in place. The tails of their tattered mainsails flapped gently in the breeze.

Terra sat heavily on the bench, letting out a weary sigh. She closed her eyes for a second, enjoying the earthy smell of woodland, wet leaves and lakeside flowers. Turning to face the professor, she snaked an arm along the back of the bench seat to rest a hand gently on his shoulder.

"If we going to get anywhere with this, I need you to trust me, professor."

He nodded, waiting for her to continue.

"How do you think Briggs and King intend to take the island back?"

He laughed. "Your guess is as good as mine. They're hardly likely to tell me. But if their team can perfect this strain of the virus, like you suggested, their best chance would be to smuggle infected people on to the island. You know at first hand that their defences are porous."

"But who would volunteer to be infected? It would be a death sentence."

"My dear, I don't suppose they would tell them, do you? They might say it was a prototype vaccine. The infected would never know they were carriers."

"I see," she said, trying to get her head around the idea. "Earlier you said the trick was not to kill the host too quickly. What did you mean?"

"Look, at any one time, there are dozens of virus strains in circulation. The most deadly strains tend to die out quickly, meaning the weaker ones prevail. Think about it. The longer a virus allows its host to live, the better chance it has of spreading further and faster. People with milder strains carry on their daily lives while infecting others, so natural selection tends to favour these milder strains."

"From what you've seen of King's operation, you really think they have the technical know-how to pull this off?"

"I'm not sure, but I certainly wouldn't underestimate them. There's evidence he's been experimenting on hundreds, maybe even thousands, of people. It's only a question of time before he zeroes in on the right strain. Mind you, there is one thing he's overlooked that might work in our favour."

"Which is?" she asked, hopeful.

"He's under the illusion that viruses can be controlled. In my experience, viruses are anything but predictable. That's what makes them so fascinating to dusty old academics like me."

"How so?"

"The behaviour of viruses has baffled brilliant scientists from Louis Pasteur onwards. That something so wonderfully small and simple can infiltrate much larger organisms and copy itself millions of time, spreading itself to other organisms. It's a thrilling game of cat and mouse as our immune systems devise a multitude of techniques to combat infection. But I don't believe King is trying to beat the virus; he's looking to redirect its energies against his enemies."

"And he really thinks he can pull this off?"

"He's smarter than you think. Take natural selection and what happened at the end of the First World War with Spanish flu. Those that got sick were taken out of the trenches and packed into overcrowded trains to be delivered to field hospitals already overrun with casualties. Those suffering from the milder strains stayed on the front line and died in their thousands advancing across No Man's Land against machine guns or in gas attacks. That reversal of natural selection worked to accelerate the spread of the flu. During the latest pandemic, hospitals and transport hubs were shut down as quickly as possible to try to slow the pandemic, exactly for that reason. Unfortunately, by the time the authorities realised what was happening, it was already too late. They were simply not fast enough to stop it."

"So, if viruses are so hard to control, there must be easier ways of disrupting the allies' operation. They're on an island, for goodness' sake."

"Well, for a start, there's a ring of steel round that island. Between the *USS Chester* and the Royal Navy, the allies patrol that waterway day and night."

"Officially, yes, but any number of smaller boats have made it through the blockade."

"True, but that's just the first line of defence. The allies were very specific in their choice of location. It's the second largest island in the United Kingdom with secure food supplies, water sources, power generation. That doesn't leave Briggs and King too many options, does it?"

"Could they poison the water?"

"They could, but it's actually much harder than it sounds. Most people on the island drink stored rainwater these days. The water that does come out of a tap has been through a purification process. Chlorine and other chemicals make it a hostile environment for any contaminant to survive. You'd need a trainload of bacteria to be reliable. It's simply not practical to mess around with their water."

"Then what about something nasty from the military base at Porton Down? Briggs is obsessed with that place."

"You mean like anthrax?" He sniggered. "No. It would leave the island uninhabitable for decades. If they want the island for themselves, then they just need a way to get rid of its unwanted guests. Anthrax would be like using a sledgehammer to crack a nut. But you're thinking along the right lines. They certainly can't match the allies for firepower. The beauty of biological weapons is that they leave all infrastructure intact and target the human population." He shook his head, chuckling to himself.

"What's so funny?"

"Oh, nothing, just reminds me of what happened during the bubonic plague. Are you familiar with the siege of Caffa? The Mongolian army used similar tactics. They catapulted plague victims over the castle walls to spread infection among the Italian defenders."

"Did it work?"

"Oh yes, the tactic was devastatingly effective. Any contact with the diseased corpses was normally fatal. Either that or infected rats breached the walls somehow. Anyway, my point is this: King is an educated man. He's fond of history. He'll have done his research. His questions confirmed that to me."

"So there have been other times when disease has been used as a weapon?"

"Certainly. Throughout history. The Japanese used the plague against China in the Second World War. Their bombers dropped porcelain jars containing rice and wheat mixed with plague-carrying fleas. Hitler tried it too. He infected livestock and feed with anthrax and glanders. The allies also have a chequered past."

"Really?"

"Of course. During the French and Indian Wars, English soldiers handed out blankets smeared with smallpox. During the American Civil War Confederate troops left animal corpses to rot in ponds along the path of Union forces."

"But surely never before with a virus?"

"Not that I'm aware of, no."

They both fell silent. In the branches above their heads, there was a flash of blue and green, and what sounded like a pair of parakeets calling to each other.

"There must be something we can do, professor. What makes this particular virus so deadly?"

"The Millennial Virus is actually not that different from seasonal flu. Headline symptoms are the same: high fever, runny nose, sore throat, aches and pains, coughing, feeling exhausted. In the vast majority of seasonal flu cases, those suffering get better after a week, whereas, with this virus, the outcome is quite different."

"How does it spread so quickly?"

"Simple. It's airborne. A single sneeze is enough to release thousands of tiny droplets into a public place, and just one of those droplets can cause infection. Fortunately, they don't stay airborne for long. Every winter, there are normally tens of millions of flu cases. Several hundred thousand die. This latest pandemic is simply a deadlier strain."

"If that's the case why can't they just make a vaccine?"

"Because vaccine formulation is not an exact science. Every year, drug companies used to supply hospitals with a new formulation targeting up to three of the most prevalent strains in each region, based on what they expected to spike. Look, we've been studying the 1918 Spanish flu pandemic for years. It killed more people than the war itself. There are still some things we simply don't understand."

"How is it that we can cure types of cancer, but not everyday flu?"

"Viruses are unpredictable, always changing. Even with the advances made from modern medicine and increased immunity, the same Spanish flu strain today would likely still kill tens of millions worldwide."

"So what's the point of antivirals and flu shots then?"

"Vaccines are the first line of defence. They generally work by fooling the immune system into thinking it's being attacked. Injecting a trace quantity of the virus allows the body to develop defensive capabilities. However, sometimes, when the human body encounters a virus for the first time, the immune system completely overreacts. In trying to destroy the virus, the body actually starts destroying itself. We call it a cytokine storm. It's caused when a defective feedback loop activates too many immune cells. Very dangerous. It can do untold damage to otherwise healthy organs and body tissue."

"So is that what you think happened this time?"

"Probably. We think that in both the Spanish flu and Millennial Virus pandemics, cytokine storms actually killed more people than the virus."

"Are the two viruses related?"

"Not directly, but in both pandemics, young adults seemed to be the most susceptible. We don't know why. The virus triggers an extreme immune response in otherwise healthy patients. It's almost as if the healthier the person, the more extreme the reaction. Multiple organ failure is not uncommon."

"You said Spanish flu killed more people than the war itself. Why is that not common knowledge?"

"It's hardly a secret. After the Great War people were convinced that the pandemic was somehow triggered by what happened on the battlefield. The poisoned gas attacks, the rotting corpses left decomposing in No Man's Land, coupled with rampant cholera. Last time I saw your friend Zed, he was convinced there was a connection, a conspiracy of sorts."

"Zed?" she half-snorted. "What would he know? He lied to all of us."

"Lied about what?"

"All that time he never once mentioned he'd worked for the government."

"What good would it have done? We all have secrets, things we'd rather stayed in the past."

Terra stared at him, wondering what he meant. She blushed and turned away, concealing her discomfort. Perhaps she was reading too much into it. After all, Terra found the professor so hard to read. She had been so careful, covering her tracks. Surely, no one could have discovered her real identity.

"Look," continued the professor, oblivious to the inner turmoil he had triggered, "if you study the history of pandemics as I have, you realise that large-scale outbreaks are actually fairly common. Roughly every thirty years. Think SARS, Bird flu, Asian flu. In most cases, they might infect hundreds of thousands only."

"But all the reports suggested hundreds of millions infected?"

"There's no way to be sure. For years, we scientists have been predicting a new pandemic. It was only a matter of time. I'm afraid we're all going through a very painful adjustment phase, like what happened after Spanish flu and the bubonic plague."

"Adjustment phase?"

"Yes, in cases like this, mass depopulation normally leads to permanent change in both economic and social structures. Right now, we're still at the beginning of that cycle."

"What does that mean?"

"That, in the short term, things are only going to get worse before they start getting better."

# Chapter Eleven

Riley stood outside Freshwater Bay Hotel waiting for the last few people to arrive. It was just before dawn, and they needed to be on the road at first light. She unfolded the map on the bonnet of a disused Mitsubishi Landcruiser that Will was fixing up in his spare time. The penlight in her mouth illuminated a crumpled Ordnance Survey map showing a detailed plan of the western half of the island, overlaid with a grid. Several grid squares were already shaded in a chaotic patchwork of grey pencil. Various sites of interest had been circled with a highlighter pen.

On the south-western edge of Totland, Riley committed to memory the location of a number of guest houses, farm buildings and private residences that they would need to investigate as part of today's search.

"Sorry I'm late," panted Joe, rounding the corner with Mila close behind. Riley checked her watch but thought better of reprimanding him. He was always late. Nothing she could say would change that.

"Now that we're all here, the plan is to head towards Warren Farm and check out these sites here," she said, pointing to the Old Coast Guard Station, a campsite and two B&B guest houses.

"What are we looking for?"

"All the usual stuff, tinned food, batteries, tools, but we're also keen to locate mattresses, bedding, gardening equipment, any sizeable wood stacks or coal stores, tables and chairs, and fuel for the generator."

"How are we meant to get all that back to the hotel?"

"Corporal Carter is lending us his furniture van. Anything we want bringing back here needs to be left at the side of the main road. The soldiers will pick them up later today."

"Depending on what we find we can always make a return trip tomorrow," said Scottie.

"Have the houses been cleared already? What about locals?" asked Tommy.

"Corporal Carter said they completed door-to-door checks when they first arrived. This whole area was evacuated weeks ago to make room for the new arrivals. Most of the houses should be abandoned, but they've had reports of illegal occupation. There's an old woman and her sons living up at Warren Farm. Apparently, she didn't take kindly to the soldiers being on her property, gave them both barrels when they tried to approach. With any luck, there shouldn't be too many others," reassured Riley.

"So what happens if we meet someone like her? The soldiers took all our weapons. What are we meant to use, harsh language?" said Tommy.

"First sign of any trouble, we call in the professionals. Carter gave me this," said Riley, fishing a walkie-talkie from her jacket pocket. "Hopefully it won't come to that. Listen, we need to make the most of the break in the weather. In a few weeks it's going to get colder, much, much colder."

"We're working as fast as we can," reassured Will. "Are you sure you wouldn't rather I stayed behind and finished the roof?

Some of the tiles have come loose; water was pouring through into one of the bedrooms last time it rained."

"We need you on this one, Will. There's going to be a lot of stuff to shift. You take Joe and Mila. Tommy and Scottie, you're with me."

She noticed Mila raise her eyebrows, annoyed at being stuck with Will again. The two of them rarely saw eye to eye on anything. Riley spun the map around, angling the penlight so they could all see.

Will nodded his approval and the six of them finished loading their equipment. They weren't completely defenceless. Riley had a long-handled machete strapped to the outside of the rucksack she carried. Will wore some army-surplus webbing with pouches stuffed with tools and supplies. He tucked what looked like a wooden short-handled rounders bat into his belt.

The two groups walked either side of the road, in single file, like Zed had taught them. As soon as they left the hotel grounds, their conversations stopped, relying on hand signals to communicate.

Riley still had the padre's warning bouncing around her head. "Leave it to the soldiers," he'd said. The truth was that they needed more supplies. The Hurst team prided themselves on their self-sufficiency. They couldn't afford to wait for hand-outs from the military. Anyway, it wasn't their style.

They reached the first cluster of two-up two-down cottages, observing them from a safe distance. The first one seemed deserted, curtains drawn, its owner's rusting estate car still parked in the drive. In all likelihood, their occupants never left. They had succumbed to the virus which meant there would be bodies to deal with. Seeing death at close quarters was something Riley still found distressing, though she got better at masking her emotions from the others.

Despite her best efforts to make as little sound as possible, her walking boots crunched up the drive. She signalled for Mila and Scottie to wait at the gate until she gave the all-clear. She scanned the upstairs windows, looking for any movement or sign of occupation. At the front porch, she checked under the doormat and behind the flower pot for spare keys. She waved the other two forward, pointing towards the Yale lock. Scottie removed a crowbar from deep within his rucksack. He forced the tip into the gap, levering it backwards and forwards, splintering the wood surround.

The door squeaked open on rusted hinges. The stench of decomposition made her flinch. She pulled a perfumed scarf over her mouth before entering the cottage. Letters addressed to Mr and Mrs Haverill lay on the doormat, along with colourful envelopes filled with holiday offers and credit card applications. It suggested to Riley that the occupants had died at the very beginning of the outbreak, at least before the postal service had ground to a halt, stranding millions of letters at postal depots.

She stuck her head through the doorway to the hall, listening for any sounds. It was deathly quiet. There was a dog bowl near the front door still half full with water. On reflection, it was unlikely a family pet could have survived its owners or stayed put for this long.

She waved Scottie and Tommy forward, indicating they search the kitchen while she took the living room.

Mr and Mrs Haverill must have been an elderly couple. The decor was tired and drab. There was an old record player with push buttons for medium wave and long wave radio, as if the modern era had passed them by. She rifled through the DVD collection and recognised a couple of newer titles. On the mantelpiece were silver photo frames with the smiling faces of grandchildren in school uniform, a group shot of a family gathering, birthday cards and a carriage clock that had stopped at a quarter to twelve.

The utility room proved more rewarding. There were boxes of matches, firelighters, cleaning products, coiled rope and a pair of sturdy walking boots, all of which went into Riley's rucksack. In the corner behind the door was a locked gun cabinet that might possibly contain a shotgun or rifle.

"Scottie?" she shouted. "Check the kitchen drawers. Any keys in there that might fit a gun cabinet?"

He didn't respond at first, but she could hear him rummaging through a kitchen drawer. He walked in and handed her several bunches of keys of various shapes and sizes to sort through. On the fourth attempt, the key turned, and the door swung open.

Inside were two antique shotguns with engravings on the stocks. She uncocked the first and checked the barrel. It was clean and well oiled. The firing mechanism seemed in good order, and there were more than a dozen boxes of cartridges. The other shotgun had a broken stock but she took it anyway in case it could be repaired. Before leaving, she loaded two cartridges, one in each barrel.

"Here, take this, it's loaded," she said, handing the weapon to Scottie. "Safety's on. Tommy, check upstairs."

"Let's not push our luck, eh?" cautioned Scottie. "We've got a good haul already."

He opened his rucksack wide so she could inspect their booty.

"Loads of tins, a can opener, cutlery, some sharp knives and some WD-40. Always comes in handy. Bedrooms are always a waste of time."

"We need bedding, remember?"

"I'm not going up if there are dead bodies to deal with."

"Good point. Leave it then. No one wants to sleep in a deadman's bed."

"What about the car in the drive?"

"Battery's almost certainly dead."

"Still, see if it'll start or not. I'll check the garage. Meet me outside in, say, five?"

She heaved open the garage door a few inches, wrestling with a rusted mechanism. It jammed a few feet up, but the gap was just large enough to crawl underneath. Riley clicked on her torch and looked around the darkened room. The retired couple must have been keen gardeners or DIY enthusiasts. There was an impressive collection of nearly new shears, spades, rakes, spanners, screwdrivers, saws and other tools neatly organised on the wall. A pristine lawnmower sat on airless tyres, covered in dust but otherwise immaculate. Holding the penlight between her teeth, she made a note of these items in her notebook.

From outside, she heard the Volvo's starter motor turn over several times, but the engine refused to fire. Then the battery died, replaced by the repeated click of the ignition. She heard a car door slam shut followed by animated voices from up the road. Will was shouting her name. She lowered herself to the ground again, slid back under the garage door on her stomach and reached back to grab the rucksack.

"Riley, you better come and see this."

"What is it?"

"A few houses up. I don't know what to make of it," he stammered. "It's messed up, that's what it is."

****

As soon as she walked into the dimly lit house, she knew something was wrong. The windows had been boarded over, and black plastic sheeting used to block out the daylight. There was evidence of recent occupation: half-burned candles in saucers placed around the room and a can of baby carrots, empty but still containing a fork inside. It smelled relatively fresh.

"There's no one here. We checked upstairs already, but you need to see the garage, Riley."

She assumed Will was exaggerating, but the look on his face said otherwise. He nodded towards the kitchen.

"I hope you've got a strong stomach this morning."

Riley took a deep breath and stepped over the threshold, holding the torch out in front of her with some trepidation.

It was an empty double garage with a dirty-looking wooden workbench at one end. She could make out a vice and a circular saw attached to the bench, and a chainsaw underneath. On the far brick wall, she noticed several metal fixing points with heavy chain hanging down, collected in a heap on the ground. Her hand was shaking as the torch beam edged right, pausing to identify what she assumed must be dried blood splattered up the wall. Underneath the fixings, more blood had pooled on the concrete floor.

Will's voice from behind startled her. "Some sadistic bastard has been using this as a torture chamber."

Riley swallowed, hardly daring to complete her search. She had seen rooms like this before. They all had. It was hard to imagine what drove a man – it was always men – to vent their fury, to punish, to inflict pain on others in this way. There would be no knock at the door, no consequences for their depravity, as if all morality and humanity had been wantonly cast aside like a change of clothes.

"Looks like they were still alive when they dragged them to that workbench then into the kitchen. You don't think—"

"Don't even say it. It's inhuman."

A whimper from the corner made Riley jump. She flashed the torch towards the source of the noise.

A woman's half-naked torso was hanging from two rings set high on the wall, almost reaching the flat roof. Her long matted hair masked her features, her head facing the floor in defeat. Her bare feet were secured by garden wire to a further ring just above floor level. The young woman was topless, her arms taut and filthy. Riley leaned forward and lifted her head up as gently as she dared. Her mouth was gagged, her eyes stared blankly back at her. She was likely drugged, barely conscious. Blinking into the light, her pupils were dilated. She tried to vocalise something but the words wouldn't come out, gurgling as she tried to wrestle free of the gag.

Riley untied the fabric and inspected the chains securing her hands.

"Will, there was a pair of bolt croppers in the garage of that last house. Would you mind? Scottie, Mila, keep an eye on the road, will you?"

She turned back to face the woman, leaning close to her right ear.

"Don't worry, we're getting you out of here."

"They'll be back soon," the young woman whispered, her throat hoarse.

"Which animals did this to you?"

"Two guys. I think they're brothers."

Will was gone a few minutes before reappearing with the bolt croppers. Riley shone the torch up to the rings so Will could cut through one of the links. The chain fell to the floor, clanking heavily in a heap. Riley braced herself as the full weight of the woman's body slumped forward into her arms. She lowered the woman gently down on to the floor. As sensation returned to her limbs, her whole body began convulsing, shivering from the cold. Riley took off her jacket and helped her sit upright, wrapping the coat around her half-naked torso.

Outside, they heard the distant sound of a car engine approaching the cottage, and Scottie shouting.

"Someone's coming," said Will. "What do we do, boss?"

She stared back at him, wondering whether they should stay and confront the men who did this, or run.

****

Between them, they carried the woman's barely conscious body out through patio doors towards a gate at the back of the garden that gave access to a narrow rat-run separating the back gardens. Through a bush, they could just see back into the patio area the way they had come. Scottie took aim at the doorway, covering their retreat.

"The rest of you follow this path up to the main road," she whispered. "Scottie and I will make sure whoever this is doesn't try to follow us."

From the house came the sound of someone kicking over a chair and shouting. A man's face appeared at the doorway. He had long, dark hair and a heavy beard. He was wearing combat trousers and an angler's jacket. He looked directly at where Scottie and Riley were hiding, and instinctively they both shrank down out of sight.

When she popped up again to take a look, Riley saw him striding towards them. There was a deafening boom close to her ear, and for a few seconds, she was disoriented, clasping her hand to her ringing ear. When she looked back, the man was writhing on the ground, and the door slammed shut behind him.

Scottie dragged her out, her hand still to her ear. Once they were further down the road, she got out the walkie-talkie and turned the power on.

"Corporal Carter, this is Riley!" she shouted. "You there?"

"Go ahead, Riley. What's up?"

"We need backup. We're searching the houses on Bedbury Lane on the way up to Warren Farm. Two hostiles, male, one in his early thirties, dark hair. One of them is wounded or dead, the other is likely following us."

"I told you to avoid Bedbury Lane."

"We didn't have much choice. It looks like someone's been torturing young women."

"That's terrible, but what do you want us to do about it?"

"I don't know. Arrest them? Shoot them, for all I care."

"If you're not in any immediate danger, I suggest you vacate the area as soon as possible." He paused.

Riley stared at the walkie-talkie in disbelief. "We only saw two of them, but there might be more. There could be other prisoners being held there. You need to do something," she implored.

"Look, I'll ask Private Dennis to swing by later when they pick up the beds and mattresses you need for the hotel. Tell him which house they're in, and we'll go and have a word with them."

Riley couldn't believe how desensitised he seemed, as if what she had just described was barely worthy of punishment. If the soldiers weren't prepared to deal with it, then she would. It was inconceivable that they would let murderers and torturers co-exist in the local area. Men like them had to be taught a lesson.

"Before I forget," continued Carter, "the padre said he'd swing by tomorrow and pick you up at 0530 hours. Said you'd know what he was talking about. Something about Ryde."

She turned off the power and put the radio back in her pocket. "Fat lot of good they are."

"What's the point of having soldiers here to protect us if they can't be bothered to lift a finger? At least give us some weapons, and we'll do it ourselves," suggested Will.

"Come on, let's get the girl back to the hotel. You lot finish your sweep of these houses. I'll come back and meet you at Warren Farm around eleven. I want to try and talk to that old woman, see if we can't come to an arrangement."

# Chapter Twelve

The padre had kept his promise. He collected them at five thirty sharp, hoping to make it back to his barracks near St Mary's by seven o'clock.

As the first light of dawn broke over the horizon, Riley was nudged awake on the back seat of an unmarked staff car. They had stopped at a checkpoint on the main road into Newport.

The chaplain had been kind enough to secure the relevant passes and paperwork. With any luck, she could drop off Adele for her hospital tests, pick up Heather from Ryde Boarding School and be back at Freshwater before the day was out.

Riley yawned and sat up straight. Her T-shirt had ridden up to expose her midriff. In the rear-view mirror, she noticed the driver staring at her. She met his gaze until he looked away.

The road sign to their right suggested they were not far from the outskirts of Newtown on the Bowcombe Road. In the dawn mist and gloom, she could just make out the silhouette of a castle high on the hill, dominating the skyline.

"Is that Carisbrooke Castle up there?" she asked no one in particular. The driver glanced out the window and nodded.

"Why are we stopped?"

"Checkpoint," he responded flatly, still red-faced at being

caught ogling her exposed flesh. Riley smiled at his embarrassment, quietly pleased that at least someone in this world still found her attractive.

"Would you mind finding out how much longer? We're on a tight schedule," she said, checking her watch.

The driver didn't move, recovering his sangfroid. Riley got the impression he was the type of young man who took issue with being told what to do by a stranger, let alone a woman.

"You heard the lady, private," barked the padre, eyes still closed. The front passenger seat was fully reclined, an overcoat clutched to his throat for warmth. He adjusted his position, struggling to get comfortable.

Reluctantly, the driver opened the door and stepped out into the chilly morning air. He set off up the road, hands thrust deep in his pockets, following the line of vehicles. The barrier remained down, the way closed to all traffic. It was just before seven. Curfew was still in effect.

She looked over at the curled-up shape beside her, straightening the blanket around Adele's shoulders. The little girl was fast asleep. Riley got out of the unmarked black saloon to stretch her legs. She massaged her frozen fingers, trying to get the circulation going again.

The vehicle in front was a split-screen vintage VW camper van. Inside the steamed-up windows, she could see a family arguing. The mother was wringing her hands while the father rummaged in their bags, shouting about something she couldn't catch. Perhaps they had mislaid their passes.

Further up the line, she could see their driver sharing a cigarette with the soldiers at the barrier. One of them was pointing towards Riley. The soldier seemed to straighten and shout something to the other guards.

The driver double-timed it back to her, gesturing for her to get back inside. He restarted the engine, breathing hard, and manoeuvred out of the line and up towards the barrier.

"Sorry to keep you, sir," said the guard with begrudging respect as they reached the barrier. The soldier leant on the driver-side window, chewing gum. The padre handed him the signed transportation order, which the guard angled towards the light to check the official military stamp. He looked at Adele in the back, sizing up the other occupants of the vehicle, before winking at Riley. When he was satisfied everything was in order, he nodded towards his partner who leant on the red and white striped counterweight to allow them through the barrier.

"Carry on, private," smiled the padre, touching his forehead in salute.

Something about their exchange pleased Riley. A mutual respect and military code still bound these men together, united by a common purpose to keep the island safe. Perhaps it was their professionalism or just an unshakeable faith in the chain of command.

The charade was plain to see if you chose to look. They were merely going through the motions. All of these people were locked in a repetitive cycle. Tied to their routines, enslaved by constructs designed in a different time. Riley chose to accept the display at face value. They were putting on a show for her benefit. A pretence of order and control.

She remembered a time when Britain had one of the finest professional armed forces in the world, before the chain of command became broken. Blind obedience was no longer enough. In a fractured organisation that had splintered into multiple factions, the operating parameters had changed overnight. An invisible enemy, civilian infrastructure that had collapsed, old rules that no longer applied, yet many still struggled to adapt, obeying orders that no longer made any sense.

The fatalist in her was whispering that these people were merely rearranging deck chairs on a sinking ship. If there was a fresh outbreak on the island, they would all be as helpless as each other. She remembered the professor saying that nature always found a way to disrupt mankind's best-laid plans. It was simply a matter of time.

As they drove slowly through the improvised security zone, Riley spotted a flurry of activity to their right. A battered old Ford Galaxy had its doors flung open. Three male occupants were hauled out and dumped unceremoniously on the grass verge by the side of the road, guns pointed at their heads. They looked no older than teenagers. The guard was shouting questions, his boot pressed firmly into the small of one boy's back. The guard leaned forward, pushing him into the dirt.

"Stay down!" he shouted. "I said keep your hands behind your heads."

The scene disappeared from sight as they continued on, but not before a single shot rang out, followed by a flurry of others.

Adele sat up violently, startled by the gunfire.

"Shhh," soothed Riley, stroking the back of Adele's head. "Just some kids trying to get through the checkpoint."

The driver flicked his eyes across at the padre who was craning his head to see what had just happened.

"Do you want me to go back?"

The chaplain shook his head, chewing his lip. "There's no point. If those lads were resisting arrest or trying to get through without a valid pass, then the soldiers have every right to use force. They're simply following orders."

"They were just teenagers," said Riley.

"We don't know the circumstances. It's not our place to interfere."

"Even so," started Riley before she was interrupted again.

"Look, I'll raise it with the area commander when I'm back in the office," he said, swivelling round to face her. "These are not normal times. These people have to learn that the control orders exist for their own protection. If one infected person makes it on to the island and we get another outbreak, we'll be right back to where we were two years ago."

"The soldiers are not above the law. You can't treat people like that and expect them to support you." Riley shrugged, crossing her arms. "And you wonder why the rebellion is gaining more and more support."

"You're right, but don't forget, we're all operating in challenging circumstances. Most of the island is under martial law. We don't have enough men or resources. Without civilian support, there's a limit to what we can achieve. Civilians can't just go wandering off without there being consequences."

"What about the people who still live here?"

"The same rules apply. Just because they were here first doesn't mean they qualify for special treatment. Even the kids," he said, looking over his shoulder at Adele.

Adele ignored him, well aware that his comments were intended for her. She continued staring out of the window. As if struck by a thought, she turned to face Riley.

"What's this new treatment they're going to try on me?" she asked.

Riley sighed. She had answered this same question half a dozen times but knew the little girl was terrified of going back there. It was the smell of the place, the men in white coats, not to mention the needles.

"I don't know. They're hoping your blood can still teach them more about the virus."

Riley noticed the padre's raised eyebrows.

"She has acute lymphoblastic leukaemia. They think it's affected her immune system in such a way that she has increased resistance, but they don't know why," she explained. Turning back to Adele, she continued, "They'll give you some more of those pills you don't like. Remember what that nice American doctor told you?"

"You're 'special'," she mocked, mimicking the American doctor's voice. "Can't be that special if I'm still going to die."

"We don't know that. Anyway, the pills should start making you feel better, sweetie."

"What about that machine he said would kill the cancer cells?"

"You mean the radiation therapy? He said there was a machine at St Mary's, but I doubt it's still working. Don't get your hopes up until we know."

"It doesn't matter. I just want to help them find a cure if I can," she said with an air of resignation.

The doctors were all sanguine about her chances. Without a bone marrow transplant, their best hope was to reduce her symptoms and alleviate her pain when the time came. In the meantime, they were accelerating their tests, hoping to learn more about why she was one of the few to catch the virus and get better. They seemed to think that Adele's defective immune system was the cause of her increased resistance.

"You're a brave girl, Adele," added the chaplain from the front seat, trying hard to put a positive spin on this macabre exchange. "Who knows, maybe they'll name the vaccine after you."

Riley shook her head, discouraging him from continuing. Adele had been so stoic about her illness.

"I didn't tell you. I had another nosebleed yesterday. Took ages to stop. It's getting worse, isn't it?"

Riley pulled Adele in tight and whispered in her ear, "Listen, we'll get through this. We all have to hope for the best."

Adele nodded weakly, staring off into the distance. The car fell silent, bar the low rumble of the road.

With every mile they were another step closer to St Mary's. She had wanted to send a message to Zed, hoping she could see him. She hadn't heard a peep from him since he left. She was beginning to wonder whether he was even still at the hospital, or had moved to another location. Come to think of it, this was the longest time they had ever been apart.

She had been replaying their last conversation over and over. Unburdening herself, telling him how she felt, was liberating and a huge weight off her mind, but in hindsight, she worried that she'd gone too far. It might taint their friendship somehow.

The more she learned about Zed's former life, the more things fell into place for her. He had always been so reticent, so unwilling to open up. To a trained counsellor like herself, it remained a puzzle. She knew about the family break-up, the separation from his wife and kids, but imagined there must be more. The revelations about Iraq, Project Wildfire, and the political fall-out had provided more pieces of the jigsaw. She knew now that Zed had been demonised, driven out, made a scapegoat for so-called flawed intelligence that had led Britain to war. She was sure she still only knew a fraction of what had really happened.

She had counselled enough combat veterans to recognise depression in all its forms. In her experience, the mental scars of war ran much deeper than the physical. Coming to terms with disability was one thing. She knew that prosthetic limbs and plastic surgery had transformed the lives of those in her care, even returned to some of them a semblance of normality and self-respect. The memories of the horrors of war were far harder to erase.

If you had never served in the military, it was impossible to imagine the pain of watching helplessly as a squad member and buddy died in your arms, or seeing non-combatants, innocent women and children, suffer terrible injuries. The second-hand stories of atrocities, genocide and mass graves were hard enough to hear, let alone see first-hand.

It had been Riley's job to support the individuals who came to her weekly sessions, to put those horrific events in context, to help them to compartmentalise and move on. But in truth, she assumed some of that burden on their behalf. It was impossible not to be affected by their stories. The nightmares, the anxieties, the sense of helplessness. It was stupid really, but in some way their pain and sadness were somehow contagious.

She knew that Zed's role had been office-based, not frontline, but the mental scars could run just as deep. Despite her probing, he still refused to talk about his departure from the MoD. Reading between the lines, there had been suggestions of impropriety, errors of judgement, guilt by association. Those rumours had followed him to his next job.

She knew the man she had grown close to had a good heart. She found it impossible to believe he could have willingly done anything illegal or immoral. Her only hope was that he would get some form of closure from re-engaging with his old life. Reopening the Project Wildfire files and trying to get the answers he so badly craved might explain what really happened. Not knowing was perhaps the hardest thing.

\*\*\*\*

As they progressed through the outskirts of town, they arrived at another checkpoint that controlled access to what the padre said was the island's most significant military compound which encircled the hospital and several other large buildings in the vicinity. The whole base was ringed with high fences, imposing brick buildings beyond. She could see a group of three bulldozers clearing a residential area to make way for new buildings.

Newport seemed much changed since her last visit. The island's capital was in truth no bigger than a small town, the size of Chichester or Farnham, near where she had grown up. Its population had swelled dramatically in the last few weeks, back towards its pre-outbreak peak. There was a buzz about the place, which surprised her. Most of the houses and apartment blocks looked occupied again. People going about their daily lives. On the roads, there were a number of military convoys shuttling troops and equipment back and forth.

Beyond the checkpoint, they drove alongside high walls topped with razor wire that could only belong to a prison. The driver pulled up parallel with a row of perhaps a dozen identical vehicles with white numbers stencilled on the doors. The padre jumped out and set off towards a low-rise building.

"I'll be as quick as I can."

A few minutes later he emerged with the requisite passes and handed them to Riley.

"There you go. Look after them. These should get you to Ryde and then all three of you back to Freshwater. They're good for seventy-two hours. Whatever you do, don't overstay your welcome. You saw what happened to those lads."

"Thanks. These should give us plenty of time. We're not planning on staying."

Riley looked out the window at the imposing facade of the main building. "Is this the old prison?" she asked.

"That one there is Albany Prison, and the other is HMP Parkhurst."

Riley shivered. "Isn't that where they put all the mass murderers and gangland criminals?"

"So they say. The Kray twins, the Moors murderers, the Yorkshire Ripper, they were all there."

"Until some genius let them out. Men like Briggs." She sighed. "So how do your men like being locked up in prison?"

"If it means a warm bed and some privacy, then it's better than what they're used to. They were the only places around here we could find with accommodation for several hundred men. Besides, we don't lock their doors or anything; they're free to come and go. Right, I'm afraid that this is where I leave you. The driver will take you to the hospital just over there," he said, pointing to the far side of the compound. "Then he'll take you on to Ryde and back here afterwards."

Riley leaned out of the window and took the chaplain's hand.

"Thank you again. You know, your brother would be proud of you. I can't tell you how grateful we are for the lift and your kindness."

The chaplain's right eye twitched at the mention of his brother. "It was the least I could do, after everything you did for him. I hope you find what you're looking for. God be with you."

He banged his hand on the top of the car, and the driver pulled away.

# Chapter Thirteen

Zed had worked through the night, trying to get through the latest batch of classified documents. He reached for the coffee mug on his cluttered desk and took a sip before realising it was stone cold. He spat it back into the cup. He stood up too quickly and almost stumbled. His right leg had gone to sleep from the hours of inactivity.

Down the hall was a small kitchenette with a portable gas stove. He filled a saucer of water from the tap, lit the gas and warmed his hands against the flame. On the window ledge beyond the glass was a jug of cold milk.

At this hour of the morning, he still had the place to himself. Most of the team didn't seem to troop in until after breakfast. Waiting for the water to boil, he massaged his shoulders, stiff from hunching over the desk all night. In the cupboard were some digestive biscuits and a half-eaten bar of rum and raisin chocolate. It wasn't much of a breakfast but better than nothing. He stuffed a couple of the biscuits into his trouser pocket for later.

He heard footsteps coming along the hall and the sound of his office door opening.

"Check the kitchen. His light's still on."

He recognised the colonel's voice. A man in uniform stuck his head around the door of the kitchenette and seemed relieved to find him.

"He's in here."

"Do you want a cup of something, colonel?" Zed shouted down the hall.

"No, got one, thanks. I'll be in your office when you're ready."

Back in the tiny room, Zed cleared some desk space, moving several stacks of reports to the side. Top of the pile, the cover sheet was stamped with the United Nations seal. It remained Zed's job to hunt for the proverbial needle in the haystack. Any clue that could reveal the origin of the virus.

"Did you find anything of interest in those UN briefing documents?"

"Nothing we didn't already know. Useful to have independent verification, I suppose. How's Doctor Hardy's team getting on?"

"He's as elusive as ever. Still refusing to answer questions. By all accounts, they're struggling to explain the presence of certain proteins and gene sequences, but they still reject any suggestion of human interference. I was very clear in my instructions. They need to investigate all possibilities, however unlikely."

Zed rifled through the pile and handed the colonel a number of sheets stapled together in one corner.

"This one piqued my interest."

"What is it?" said the colonel, quickly scanning the cover sheet.

"A leaked extract from an Iraqi autopsy report. The Iranian soldier had died in captivity. He had suffered horrible asphyxiation, his lungs were filled with liquid choking his airways. Frankly, it reads like something from the First World

War, yet this was nearly seventy years later. The symptoms are consistent with Spanish flu."

"Or more than a dozen other chemical or biological agents. It proves nothing."

"Well, it proves that Saddam Hussein was conducting human tests on prisoners of war, and that's just the tip of the iceberg. It's all documented in here. Between 1983 and 1988 more than twenty thousand Iranian soldiers were killed by gas attacks, or in chemical and biological weapons tests, not to mention the thousands of civilians who were killed by canister bombs. The first-hand accounts of experiments at Abu Ghraib make for grim reading."

"I thought all the patient records were destroyed before the invasion?"

"Most of the written records were, but we still have sworn statements from the guards obtained under interrogation by our inspectors. They admitted the widespread use of biological agents against prisoners of war."

The colonel shrugged as if unimpressed by these revelations.

"Any proof of Russian involvement?"

"Not yet, but I did find countless examples of Western nations supporting the Iraqis' programmes, whether knowingly or unknowingly."

"Such as?"

"Blueprints for the construction of a factory designed by Neuman Corporation in the US, CBW hazmat suits from a DuPont factory in the UK, industrial plant equipment and chemicals sourced from Germany, Holland and France."

"Yes, we know all that. Dual-use was their get-out-of-jail-free card. What else?"

"How about this?" said Zed, reaching for another sheet on

top of a different pile. "Papers signed by Saddam himself, personally authorising the production of nerve gases such as tabun, sarin and VX. And here, reports from UN observers independently verifying the terrible consequences. My point is these documents confirm that this was a regime without scruples, prepared to flaunt international regulations and kill civilians without hesitation."

"But what does it tell us about his biological weapons programmes? We already know Saddam was using nerve gas and twentieth-century chemical weapons against the Kurds and other civilian targets."

"I'm coming to that. Chemical weapons were like gateway drugs to Saddam. He was so delighted with their performance that he gave orders to accelerate research into biological weapons that could target enemies in other regions. In 1988, he began test-firing rockets and bombs filled with anthrax, ricin and botulinum toxins. At al-Hakam, in the western desert, the Iraqis produced over half a million litres of biological agents. In December 1990, special forces seized evidence that he was attempting to convert his Scud missiles to carry a biological warhead."

"And yet, when the inspectors reached al-Hakam, they found no trace of those warheads or biological weapons?"

"Colonel, we both know that there was a massive cover-up. Unofficially, the UN destroyed over thirty-eight thousand munitions loaded with, or capable of being loaded with, CBWs. The Scud threat was real. According to the Pentagon, even if one of those Scuds loaded with anthrax had been launched, it could have contaminated an area of three thousand seven hundred square kilometres for several decades. That's a hundred times more lethal than the Hiroshima bomb."

"Hold on, that's stretching the truth a little, don't you think? I remember that report. It stated that munitions were, quote, 'capable' of being loaded with CBWs. Those biological weapons were never found, were they?"

"Officially, that's correct. But unofficially, the UN inspectors knew the stockpiles existed, but they proved impossible to locate. Their efforts were consistently frustrated by a lack of cooperation from the Iraqis. In all likelihood, they were simply buried in the sand somewhere."

"After the war, what happened to the UNSCOM team you worked with?"

"As far as I understand, the team was wound up and disbanded. Many of them left under a cloud. Rumours about US interference and CIA espionage. It became a political football. The lack of cooperation from the Iraqis certainly didn't help matters."

"And what about you? I understand you left the MoD payroll not long afterwards."

"Me? Oh, I stayed on for a bit, hoping the inspection programme might force some meaningful change. After all that hard work, I suppose I became disillusioned. The sanctions that followed only made things worse. The civilian population was hit hardest. Rates of malnutrition and infant mortality soared. It was a terrible price to pay for our collective failure."

"I wouldn't be too hard on yourself. There's only so much you can do in that situation. And this business about your own departure? I've read what little there is in your personnel file. What really happened?"

"The September Dossier happened."

"You mean the 'Dodgy Dossier'?"

"I remember it like it was yesterday. September 2002. The

lead-up to the second Iraq War. I was one of those so-called experts they wheeled out before various intelligence committees. We briefed ministers, advised the Defence Department, but in the end, they used us. They twisted the truth to make the case for war. When public opinion turned, they made us the scapegoats. The '45 minute' claim was preposterous. It sullied our reputations, made us laughing stocks. Kelly was the real victim. I never believed he committed suicide. One way or another they killed him, plain and simple. It was the final straw for me. I quit, went into hiding. Then they had the temerity to come after me?"

"Why?"

"They turned my life upside down, launched a half-hearted investigation. Made allegations that I'd been passing documents to the Americans. It was complete nonsense, but that kind of stink tends to stick. Someone higher up the food chain was pulling all the strings."

"Yet none of that was in your file."

"It's because it was all made up. In the end, I moved abroad, worked for a biotech start-up, but the MoD wouldn't let it go. They threatened to have me extradited to face unspecified charges. I ended up coming home voluntarily after six months. Being away from my family was terrible. The Official Secrets Act meant that I couldn't talk about it, and no one could ever understand what I was going through. Most of what I knew was classified. Not being able to see my kids tore me apart. They were still only little back then."

"It sounds like there was a bigger political agenda. You were just a pawn. Expendable. In my experience, politics and science rarely work well together," admitted the colonel.

"What's really frustrating is that most of these documents are heavily redacted. At best, they're incomplete. I suspect the originals would tell a different story. If I could get access to the original archive at Porton where they keep copies of everything…"

"I can get you up there, if you like. Doctor Hardy's team needs to retrieve more vaccine samples. I can get you on that helicopter?"

Zed sat upright, suddenly energised. "The Porton library should have thousands of documents, going all the way back to the First World War. Some that apparently never got digitised."

"I could introduce you to a couple of people there. One is the archivist, the other is someone I used to work with back in my Moscow days. He's something of a Biopreparat specialist. He could tell you a lot more than I can about what Russia was up to with biological weapons."

"If it can short-cut my investigation, absolutely."

"Doctor Hardy boasted that the Porton archive chronicles the entire history of chemical and biological weapon development in Britain. If it's not there, then it probably never happened. They call the librarian Ephesus."

"Ephesus?"

"Come, come. I took you for an educated man. Surely you've heard of the great ancient libraries of Alexandria in Egypt and Ephesus in Turkey? They were said to have stored the largest collections of handwritten books of antiquity. What's in Ephesus's head is so sensitive, they say he'll never be allowed to leave Porton."

"That sounds more like a prison sentence than a job."

"He's lived there most of his life. His work is everything to him. Wife died years ago, no other living family."

"With someone like Ephesus to work alongside, I could really accelerate my investigation."

"I'll make the necessary arrangements. You might want to pack an overnight bag. See you back here at 1500 hours."

"Thank you, colonel."

# Chapter Fourteen

Zed scanned the skies, listening for any sign of the helicopter. It was already ten minutes late.

The colonel had been the last to arrive. He nodded at Zed and the Porton scientists waiting in the shelter of the hospital building nearest the helipad. There was a steady drizzle that limited visibility. A fine mist settled on everyone and everything, soaking into clothing and equipment. Zed was keeping his distance from Doctor Hardy; he still hadn't forgiven the doctor for his outburst in yesterday's meeting.

A grey helicopter with Royal Navy markings roared into view, sweeping low over the hospital before banking hard and coming into a hover, one hundred feet off the ground. Zed could make out the pilot looking down at them, skilfully guiding the aircraft into land.

The arrival of the Royal Navy Merlin confirmed the rumour that had been doing the rounds. The story went that Captain Armstrong had sent an expeditionary party in search of any serviceable aircraft they could salvage from Bournemouth or Southampton Airports. In the end, they made it all the way to the naval base at Culdrose on the Lizard Peninsula in Cornwall and returned with two Merlins loaded with equipment. It meant the allies were no longer dependent on the *Chester*'s Seahawk for urgent transportation of men and equipment. Zed had overheard one of the staff officers boasting about their new assets.

As soon as the Merlin touched down, the hydraulic ramp at the back lowered to allow the group onboard. Sat either side of the spacious cabin was a squad of Royal Marines wearing helmets and combat gear. As soon as the ramp whirred shut, they lifted off.

Once they were airborne, Zed moved seats so he could see out the window. Gaining altitude, they swept over Cowes and out towards the Solent. Visibility seemed much better the higher they got, and he could make out the American warship at anchor off to his right. In the distance, several smaller vessels were shuttling in and out of Portsmouth Harbour. As the helicopter crossed the five miles of open water, they followed the estuary north towards Southampton docks.

Zed was surprised how empty the container port seemed. Thousands of red and blue rectangles processed one by one, their contents searched and catalogued. As far as the eye could see, acre upon acre of shipping containers were lined up in orderly rows. With no new ships arriving for as long as anyone could remember, and the *Maersk Charlotte* unloaded of the bulk of its containers, the port looked more like a graveyard than a commercial hub.

Most of the cargo was redundant in a world without power. He noticed what looked like stacks of white kitchen appliances, fridge freezers, ovens, washing machines and tumble driers dumped in irregular pyramids. The reminder of domesticity made him smile.

Among the millions of tonnes of goods, it was also said that they had discovered building materials, tools, equipment, farm machinery, steel, humanitarian aid supplies, and trucks which collectively would accelerate the allies' reconstruction efforts. Captain Armstrong said they now had everything they needed to realise their plans for Camp Wight.

Leaving behind the suburbs of Totton and Calmore, they banked north-west towards Salisbury and Porton Down, crossing open countryside. The grey strip of the M27 motorway briefly interrupted a lush carpet of green. A bulldozer had cleared a path, pushing the abandoned vehicles to the side of the road, to make way for a convoy of oil tankers, flanked by armed escorts, ferrying fuel from Fawley Refinery.

When there was nothing left to see but field after field, Zed turned back to face his fellow companions. The faces of the scientists were lit up by the grey light from their laptop screens. The soldiers were resting their eyes or playing cards. The colonel sat next to Doctor Hardy, shouting at each other, trying to make themselves heard over the din of the engines. Zed closed his eyes and tried to get some sleep.

He sincerely hoped Ephesus and the Biopreparat expert were even half as good as the colonel had implied. Either one of them could provide the clues he needed.

The pitch of the engines changed, and the Merlin started to lose altitude. Zed peered out of the window, hoping to catch his first sight of Porton Down. The military base looked tiny from a distance, but in reality was a sprawling complex containing a large number of office buildings, labs and warehouses surrounded by farms and villages. As they swept lower over a wooded area, he noticed half a dozen people emerging from the tree line, pointing up into the sky. Several of them broke into a run following their path.

The pilot skimmed low over the newly repaired perimeter

fence with the addition of timber supports and rolls of razor wire. The Merlin pirouetted neatly round into a cleared area beyond the staff car park, where a cluster of uniformed men was standing ready, shielding their faces from the down draught. He recognised the base commander, Major Donnelly, among the welcome party sheltering behind three waiting transports.

Once the helicopter touched down, Zed grabbed his rucksack from beneath the seat and stood waiting with the others for the ramp to be lowered. The Royal Marines exited first, making straight for the truck where one of the base personnel was beckoning them over.

"Welcome back, colonel," said the major, saluting his superior officer.

"You can dispense with the pleasantries, major. Did you get my message?"

"I did. We were under the impression that Doctor Hardy already had everything he needed."

"So did I. It seems that, for the time being at least, your facility is not entirely redundant."

As the helicopter powered down, Zed became aware of the unmistakable sounds of a large crowd approaching the fence behind them. He turned in surprise to see almost a hundred men and women surging towards the landing area, running from every direction, shouting and gesticulating. The Porton guards unholstered their side arms and shepherded the new arrivals towards the safety of the vehicles.

"That bloody helicopter never fails to draw a crowd."

"Is the compound secure, major?"

"It is now, yes. We had to repair several sections of fencing after the last attack. The team of engineers from 12th Armoured laid razor wire this week and built those guard towers you see over there. There's no way in, but let's not stick around to test that theory."

The major's second in command added: "Sir, they wouldn't dare attack in daylight hours after what happened last time. They sustained heavy losses."

"How many men did the 12th Armoured send you?"

"Three platoons. I suggest we talk once we're inside. The crowd have a habit of throwing stones if we linger too long," said the major, gesturing towards the lead vehicle. The driver was already holding open the rear doors for the passengers.

"Mr Samuels, why don't you tag along with us?" suggested the colonel to the apparent displeasure of Major Donnelly.

****

The five-minute journey from one side of the compound to the other revealed a base in much better shape than the last time they had been here.

"How are your food supplies holding up? I'd imagine the addition of the men from Bulford and Tidworth isn't helping?"

"We're managing. The 12th Armoured brought two lorry-loads of dry stores. Three thousand ration packs. It won't last forever, but it at least buys us some time."

"What about vehicles?"

"Just what they arrived here with. A couple of trucks, two armoured personnel carriers, oh, and a Scimitar."

"What's that?" asked Zed.

"It's an armoured reconnaissance vehicle equipped with a thirty-millimetre cannon."

"That should give the locals something to think about." Zed smiled to himself. A tank? Now that he would like to see.

"They don't scare easily. They're a persistent bunch. There's normally someone nosing around, keeping an eye on us. Particularly when anyone arrives or leaves. They know we have food and weapons here."

"Well, if they're anything like the survivor groups near us, they won't give up. Desperate people will resort to desperate measures, especially if they see lorry-loads of food and supplies arriving here."

Major Donnelly turned to face the colonel. "Sir, now that we're in private, may I ask why Mr Samuels is back here again? Am I to assume that his investigation is ongoing?"

"You may."

"I thought we had given him everything he asked for."

"You did but, unfortunately, some of the drives were damaged in the ambush. Mr Samuels is going to need full access to the archive."

Major Donnelly hesitated, unsure how to respond. "May I remind you, sir," as if deference required a special effort, "that access to the archive is restricted to military personnel with 'Top Secret' clearance only."

"I'm aware of that, major."

"I am only authorised to grant access with the written approval of the Minister of Defence himself."

"Well, in his absence, I'm giving Mr Samuels authorisation," replied the colonel, somewhat tersely.

"As the commanding officer responsible for this facility…"

"Do I really need to spell it out to you again?" he spat, before relenting slightly. "With all due respect, major, if you're concerned about Mr Samuels putting his snout in where it's not wanted, I suggest you assign a chaperone. Make sure he doesn't go wandering around helping himself to state secrets. I'm not sure what you're afraid of. It's not as if you have the Loch Ness Monster in here."

"Sir, the archive contains a complete record of every chemical and biological warfare experiment since the First World War."

"That's why we're here."

"If you can let me know the focus of your investigation, perhaps I can—"

Zed was about to launch into an answer when the colonel cut him short.

"Mr Samuels reports directly to me. I'll brief you as soon as circumstances permit. In the meantime, your team will afford him every assistance, extend every courtesy. I expect Ephesus himself to be made available."

Major Donnelly inclined his head reluctantly. Their vehicle slowed to a halt outside the entrance to the main building leading to the subterranean levels. Two armed guards stirred from their seats and held the door open for the new arrivals. The major turned to address one of his staff.

"Can you let Ephesus know that we have visitors from St Mary's? I expect you'll find him in the library."

The orderly hurried off towards the stairwell. The Porton scientists followed Doctor Hardy towards a maze of passageways that led to the underground laboratories where it was said they undertook all the more hazardous research into deadly pathogens.

Zed tuned out of the conversation between the major and the colonel, suddenly anxious about meeting this so-called "Sage of Porton Down". Could it be possible that all his questions might finally be answered? Besides Doctor Hardy, Ephesus might be the only person in the country who knew the truth. The sound of footsteps on the metal stairwell jolted him back to the present.

"Ephesus will see you now. Gentlemen, will you follow me?"

# Chapter Fifteen

Terra left Briggs snoring late into the morning in their new bed. She washed quickly in a handbasin filled with cold water and finished her hair and make-up in front of an antique Venetian-style mirror that must have belonged to the headmaster's wife.

Their living quarters at Walhampton School were modest but comfortable, supplemented by antique furniture salvaged from nearby houses and shops. It wasn't what she would have chosen for herself, but it was passable.

She ran her fingers along a rail of more than three dozen designer dresses and haute-couture outfits liberated to order from Southampton's finest fashion outlets. Tilting her head and posing in front of the floor-length mirror she chose a knee-length Vivienne Westwood dress matched with a pure cashmere sweater. The alterations she had requested were amateurish, the stitching crude in places. This was the dress Briggs said "turned heads".

She spent the next hour exploring all the different former classrooms, dormitories and sports facilities. People stopped what they were doing when she entered, taking off their hats, or awkwardly curtseying like she was some lady of the manor.

There was a smell about the school that was so evocative. It took a moment for her to place it. Somehow it reminded Terra of her mother. Dusty books, disinfectant, spilt milk and burned toast. Her mother had always been so disapproving. Nothing had ever been good enough. That same bile and bad humour had eventually driven her father away. Terra had never forgiven her for that.

On the top floor, she discovered stunning views across the fields back towards the sea. Below were two additional levels of dormitories crammed with single iron-framed beds in neat rows, set out for the many workers who called this place their home. They were split up by function with kitchen staff occupying one, housekeeping, security and administration in the rooms next door.

Surveying the magnificent grounds and generous accommodation, she now understood why Victor had chosen the school for their displaced group. It was far more practical than a medieval castle.

Out of the second-floor window, she followed the progress of a small convoy of vehicles approaching the school along the drive from the main road. Bouncing over the speed bumps was a convoy of school-liveried minibuses followed by an Audi estate.

As the minibus slowed to navigate through the car park, the dirty faces of several men pressed excitedly against the windows as they pointed up towards the grand building. The convoy continued straight past without stopping, towards the sports hall and theatre beyond.

Before it disappeared out of sight, one of the forlorn occupants seemed to rush to the back window, banging his fists against the glass. The image was frozen in her mind. It was hard to tell from this distance but she half-recognised his face. Dark hair, handsome, deep-set eyes, olive skin, and a heavy beard in urgent need of a trim.

She took the stairs two at a time. On the landing, she barged into the back of Victor, almost knocking him over.

"Where are you going in such a hurry?"

"Sorry," she said breathlessly. "I was trying to catch the minibus. Do you know where they're taking them?"

"Who? The last group from Carisbrooke?"

"I thought *we* were the last group?"

"The men from the *Santana* came separately."

Suddenly it all made sense. The *Santana*. She had first seen the crew from the tanker when they were marched across the castle courtyard, hands secured tightly behind their backs, imprisoned in the old dungeon beneath Carisbrooke. She remembered the truck that brought them to the castle. The tanker was found by the allies with its engines disabled, drifting helplessly off the Needles in the storm.

"Why bring them here?"

"Peterson wanted them dead. Briggs is convinced they know something."

Terra remembered Briggs's laugh at the mafia phrase the American had used. Something about "concrete boots".

"Have they been interrogated yet?"

"We've tried, but they only speak Spanish. We're waiting for the translator to arrive."

"I could have a go?" offered Terra. "I'm a bit rusty, but…"

"I didn't know you spoke Spanish. Anyway, they've already found someone. King knew a teacher from Lymington. He'll be here later."

"Mind if I tag along?"

"It might be useful to have you there. We don't know if this translator can be trusted. I won't tell him you speak the language."

\*\*\*\*

Near the old stables, a solitary figure stood guard outside the locked storeroom where the *Santana* crew was being held. As Victor and the rest of the group approached, the guard removed a bunch of keys from his coat pocket and made to unlock the door. On the third attempt, he wrestled the padlock open, levering the door wide enough to reveal a darkened room.

Terra followed closely behind Victor and the translator. Inside, the stench was overpowering. She was suddenly self-conscious in her designer clothes.

The group hesitated near the door, waiting for the guard to find his torch. The beam of light arced around the room, picking out the recumbent shapes of the *Santana* men stirring back to life. The man closest to them looked barely able to stand. The others stared back at the rectangle of light that framed Terra.

"*Eres un ángel?*" she heard one of the men say.

"What did he say?" asked Victor.

"He thinks she's an angel," scoffed the translator.

Terra smiled, covering her mouth with the perfumed scarf she wore, trying to mask the stench of sweat and piss. The guard's torch flicked from one face to the next until he found the person he was looking for. He kicked at the man's legs until he got unsteadily to his feet.

"This is the guy I was telling you about."

"Mateo, find out what this man knows," said Victor, gesturing to the translator.

"What do you want me to say?" Mateo replied in lightly accented English.

"Start by asking him why the Americans wanted them all dead."

The tanker skipper looked terrified, his face smeared with dried blood. The translator spoke quickly, using words that were half-familiar to Terra, reassuring him that he would not be harmed if he cooperated. The skipper raised his hand to protect his face, cowering as if he expected to be struck at any moment.

"He says his name is Jorge Sanchez. He's the First Officer, from Puerto Cabello in Venezuela. The rest of the crew are from Chile or Argentina. Those two in the corner are Filipino."

"Ask him why they were in the English Channel," continued Victor, waiting impatiently for the translator to relay the question.

"He says the *Santana* was carrying refined petroleum from Kuwait City to the Rozenburg Refinery near Rotterdam in Holland. When they heard how fast the *enfermedad* was spreading in Europe, they decided to anchor off La Coruña and wait for further instructions."

As the Puerto Capello man finished each sentence, his words were translated into passable English.

"They tried to reach the company for several days. They left messages but got nothing back. In the end, they decided to continue on their journey to Rotterdam."

"So what happened? Why are they here?"

"He says they were chased by pirates off the French coast, near Roscoff. The *Santana* couldn't outrun them, so he did what they were trained to do. He cut his engines and disabled all power. They hid in the compartment behind the engines, but the pirates found them and locked them up. When they couldn't get the engines restarted, they must have abandoned them. He says they drifted for days until a fisherman called Jack set them free."

"Did he say Jack?" interrupted Terra, hardly believing her

ears. "Jack saved these men?" she repeated in astonishment, watching the skipper's face.

"That's what he said. Jack and some soldiers from a *castillo*."

"So why did the Americans have them in custody?" pressed Victor.

The translator relayed the question, and the skipper seemed on edge, shaking his head, repeating that he didn't know. Victor loomed over him, his fists clenched. The threat of further violence seemed to loosen the skipper's tongue.

"He's worried we're working with the Americans, says they intercepted his ship weeks before in the Bay of Biscay, just west of La Rochelle. They boarded the *Santana* at gunpoint, seized some of their food and syphoned off most of the marine diesel. They interrogated each of them for hours, trying to find out what they knew about the *enfermedad*."

"The virus? What about it?"

"The same questions over and over again. About other groups, other countries, where there were survivors. They seemed particularly interested in islands. Majorca, Minorca, Greek Islands, the Channel Islands, Sardinia, Corsica."

"Why islands?"

"He doesn't know. He thinks they were looking for a place to land."

"What about the rest of Europe?"

"They had intermittent radio contact with different groups all along the coast. North-western Spain, around Bordeaux and Brittany. He says there was a large group of British survivors in Cornwall."

"Ask him about the virus."

There was a brief exchange as the translator clarified the phrase he had used.

"He calls it the 'English Flu'. He says very few have survived."

"He means the Millennial Virus?"

"No, he said where he comes from, everyone calls it 'English Flu'. Apparently, the UK is under some special quarantine order. No ships are allowed to land for fear of infection. That's why they were so worried about coming here."

"But that makes no sense. We all saw the same news reports. The virus was everywhere, not just here. The Americans confirmed that. Why would they start calling it 'English Flu'?"

"He doesn't know. It's just what he's heard everyone else calls it."

"No wonder no other ships have come here. What if the United Nations has established an exclusion zone around the whole of the UK, and only the Americans have dared to ignore the mandate? It would all make sense," said Terra, thinking out loud.

"Then why did Peterson want these men killed?"

"Maybe it's because they know something about the outside world. Or perhaps this scare story about the UK was invented to keep others away. Who knows who started that rumour?"

"There's something else. He says that their radio stopped working when they entered the Channel. They couldn't raise anyone any more. They lost contact with the French groups in Brittany."

"You think someone could be jamming the signal?" asked Terra.

"Well, it's not us."

"What about the Americans?"

"But why?"

"I don't know. To keep everyone in the dark? Right now, the Americans control the flow of information. That's to their advantage. These men might be the only ones who know the truth. Maybe that's why Peterson wanted them dead."

"Briggs guessed there was more to this. That's why he wanted them kept alive. He thinks they might be able to provide leverage when the time comes to negotiate with the allies," said Victor.

The interrogation complete, Victor, Terra and the translator were ushered towards the open doorway. They were all keen to get some fresh air. Terra lingered by the door, struck by a thought.

"But how on earth would you go about jamming radio signals?"

"Beats me." Victor shrugged. "Perhaps the military has the equipment."

"Or the police."

"Ask Copper. He might know."

"I couldn't help overhearing, but there's a teacher who worked here that knows a lot about radios," said the guard. "I think his name is Gerry. Lives in one of the houses just over there. He taught design and technology, or something."

"Perhaps you can find this Gerry. Before I take this to Briggs, I want to know if what he says is even possible."

The guard set off towards the cluster of staff houses on the far side of the school grounds, leaving the visitors with the *Santana* men. Looking into the darkened room, nobody had moved an inch. Victor closed the door and clicked the padlock shut.

"I wouldn't put it past Peterson. I don't trust that guy," admitted Victor.

"I never understood why the Americans were here in the first place. Who chooses the Isle of Wight when you could be sunning yourself in Majorca, Malta, Gibraltar or Corsica?

"Then that's the question we need an answer to."

\*\*\*\*

A few minutes later, the guard returned, pushing a reluctant Gerry, who didn't seem to understand why he had been brought there. Victor looked him up and down and put his arm around his shoulders.

"So, Gerry, I hear you know something about radios?"

"Bits and pieces. I taught design and technology at the school."

"Excellent," said Victor, squeezing his shoulder. "Now, say, for the sake of argument, you wanted to disrupt all communication between the UK and mainland Europe, how would you go about that?"

Gerry blinked and smiled, pushing his glasses up his nose where they had slid down. He seemed amused by the simplicity of the question. Terra wasn't sure what he had expected; perhaps Victor's reputation had preceded him.

"Well, it's fairly straightforward to block communication at a local level, but to do so at a regional level requires a bit more grunt."

"Go on."

"Basically, there are two ways. You could raise the noise floor or try spoofing."

"Meaning?"

"Okay. Raising the floor is a way of drowning out the signal by transmitting 'white noise'. Basically, you broadcast static. It makes it harder, though not impossible, to separate out any radio signals from the background noise. It's a bit like trying to talk over machinery or engine noise. It requires a bit of specialist equipment and a lot of power to drown out the other signals, but in theory, you could jam anything. It's very difficult to overcome this."

"And the other way?"

"Spoofing is similar. The idea is not so much to drown out the signal but to send out another signal that's very similar. That makes it very hard to isolate one from the other. Bit like trying to make yourself heard in a crowd when lots of people are talking at the same time. Or when you drive between two broadcast areas, you sometimes get that with radio stations overlapping each other."

"Let's go with door number one. How would you broadcast this 'white noise'?"

"First you'd actually need to get your signal into the antenna. Direct connection would be best."

"So where would you go to do that?"

"Not far from here actually. There's the Rowridge Transmitter right there," he said, pointing south-east.

"You mean that massive tower on the island?"

"Yes, you can't miss it. It's the main transmitter for the whole of the south of England. If you took control of the site and installed your own equipment, you could drown out all other signals. Well, theoretically anyway."

"And all wavebands would be affected?"

"Not exclusively. There's a chance that very local point-to-point line of sight transmissions would still work. Below the radar, if you like. Also, ELF might still work."

"What's ELF?"

"It's what US submarines use to communicate over very long distances. They have dedicated transmitters based in the middle of nowhere, with incredibly low ground connectivity. I think the US system is called Seafarer. They have a base station somewhere in Wisconsin with very long cables up to fifty kilometres long that can send out coded transmissions. They can be received virtually anywhere on the planet. Britain tried to build an ELF system up in Scotland, but they couldn't get it to work, or someone withdrew the funding."

"So you're saying that it's possible that the Americans are the only ones who have this ELF way to communicate over long distances. Interesting. Thank you, Gerry. You've been very helpful. You can go now," said Victor, patting him on the back. He motioned for Terra to walk with him so they would not be overheard.

"So whether it's Peterson or someone else, we know someone may be trying to block communication in this region." Terra sighed. "The next question we need to answer is why? What are they up to?"

"Why would anyone want a news blackout in southern England?

"How much do we really know about Lieutenant Peterson?" asked Terra.

"Why? What are you thinking?"

"What if the other senior officers on board the *Chester* didn't die of the virus? What if Peterson got rid of them somehow?"

"No, Terra. It would require a grand conspiracy to keep something like that secret from the rest of the crew."

"But it's not hard to imagine, is it? Once an alarm is sounded that infection had been detected onboard, the crew would be confined to quarters. Peterson could have found a way to control things. Told the crew what they wanted to hear. Kept them in the dark. Pretended that the commanding officer and XO died of the virus."

"But why, Terra? Why would Peterson do that? He's a career naval officer. What does he gain?"

"Men like Peterson crave power and control. Who's to say that they didn't choose this island? It has natural advantages. Big enough to sustain a large group indefinitely. The presence of that antenna is a clincher, don't you think? Anyway, where else would you go in Europe?"

"But what about the rest of the Americans? Someone would have stood up to him. You're not suggesting they're all in league with Peterson?"

"It would only take a few of the senior officers to make this work. Who knows? If you ask me, Peterson went rogue a long time ago. He saw an opportunity, and he took it. He's smart and ambitious. Who's to say he didn't plan this whole thing? In the absence of outside influence, he controls the message. Their version of events is absolute. Who are we to know better?"

Victor didn't seem entirely convinced, but he had to admit that it was an intriguing explanation.

"We need to talk to Briggs, right now."

# Chapter Sixteen

Riley felt terrible leaving Adele at St Mary's hospital on the island. When it was time to leave, the little girl clung to Riley's arm, fighting back the tears. One of the nurses standing nearby broke off her conversation with a colleague to come over.

Bending down on one knee, she took Adele's hand and whispered gently, "Are you one of our brave volunteers?"

Adele wiped the tears from her eyes and nodded back at the nurse. Underneath her uniform, the nurse wore thick woollen tights but still shivered against the bitter wind. She noticed Riley staring at her legs.

"I know, they're hideous, aren't they? But there's no heating here, and it gets so cold."

Riley smiled back at her and pulled Adele in tight, squeezing the breath from her lungs. She was the closest thing Riley had to a daughter.

"I'll be back before you know it," she promised, stroking Adele's hair.

"Don't worry. We'll look after her," reassured the nurse. "Anyway, with all the soldiers around here, this is probably the safest place in the country right now." She winked playfully, pointing towards the prison.

The child seemed comforted by the nurse's words and released her grip on Riley's arm. The admissions nurse handed Riley a clipboard with some paperwork to complete.

"Are you her mum?" she whispered.

"Actually, she's not my daughter."

"Just put 'guardian' then. I don't suppose it really matters; no one checks any more. The director still insists we do things properly. The NHS wouldn't let a little thing like the end of the world get in the way of paperwork, would it? What would the world come to, I don't know."

"With any luck, I'll be back before dark."

"Well, if you get stuck, I'm sure we can find somewhere for her to stay for the night."

Riley continued filling out the form, pausing at one of the questions, as the nurse leaned forward to help.

"I've put Zed Samuels as next of kin. He's actually based here at St Mary's."

"Oh, right, very local then. Is he a soldier or a doctor?"

"Actually, neither. He's working with the colonel and the team of scientists that arrived from Porton Down."

"Oh, I know. That lot keep themselves to themselves. They don't mix with the rest of us."

"Any idea where I might find them?"

"They work in that new building on the far side of the compound. I think you've probably missed him though. A big grey helicopter arrived this morning. Made quite a racket."

Riley looked crestfallen.

"I can check if you like. See if one of the others knows anything?"

"Don't worry. I can try again when I come back for Adele after her tests. He might be back by then."

Riley said her goodbyes, and the nurse led Adele into the main building. Riley watched the pair of them leave, secretly hoping Adele might turn and look back, but she disappeared down the corridor and out of sight. It broke her heart to leave her here, but she had a promise to keep.

****

The journey to Ryde was further than she expected. The driver said it would take them another couple of hours from St Mary's. His body language betrayed the fact that today's assignment was anything other than a burden. He slumped against the headrest, absent-mindedly playing with the radio dial, searching through static for a signal. When he did it for the third time, Riley asked him to stop.

"Sorry, more habit than anything else. I suppose I keep hoping there's someone out there, or just some music."

Riley had run through every scenario in her mind, wondering how Zed's daughter would react to the knowledge that her father was still alive. How could she explain why Zed was unable to come himself without making it seem that he had more important priorities?

She knew that Zed and his wife were separated and that the kids had been living with their mother before the outbreak. It didn't sound like the family was particularly close. Something reminded her of his muted reaction to the letter from Ryde Boarding School informing him that his daughter was still alive. It was almost as if he was numb to the news. His behaviour had puzzled her at the time.

He had confessed that his weekends with the kids had slipped to monthly visits, whether through travel or work commitments, but they were so understanding. He always made it up to them, spoiling them with gifts, meals out or pizza nights in. Riley wasn't sure, but it sounded like the type of excuses you told yourself to ease the guilt.

She cursed her luck that she had not had the opportunity to speak with him. Since telling him how she felt on the clifftop at Freshwater, she felt unburdened. Gone was that sense of emptiness that had gnawed at her soul. The regrets and recriminations after losing everyone she cared about during the pandemic. For the first time in as long as she could remember, she looked forward with anticipation, rather than dread.

The car swerved around a sharp bend and onto the main road at high speed, without slowing to check for oncoming traffic. They seemed to be the only vehicle on these back roads. Suddenly, she realised that she hadn't been paying attention for the last few minutes. This wasn't the road to Ryde.

"Where are we going?" she asked, leaning forward in her seat, looking around for a landmark or something she recognised. "I don't know your name."

"It's Terry," the driver said, stretching out his right hand for her to shake over his shoulder. "The main road from Newport to Ryde is reserved for military convoys during the week. Trust me, this way is much quicker."

Looking out the window, there was only field after field of open countryside. Now and again they passed entrances to construction projects where plant and machinery were digging holes or erecting structures needed to cope with the vast influx of personnel.

"So, Terry. How long have you been here?"

"Me? I've been on the island most of my life. My parents lived on the south coast, near Sandown."

A strange structure caught her eye to the right. From a

distance, it looked like a cross between an obelisk and the giant sculptures of Easter Island, remembering the conversation with Scottie about druids and pagans.

"What's that weird pyramid thing?"

Without taking his eyes off the road, the driver replied, "Oh, that old thing. Ashey Seamark. In the old days, it guided ships into Spithead Harbour. Apparently, you can see it way out to sea."

"I imagine the island's changed quite a bit since the allies arrived."

"You could say that again." He laughed dismissively as if it were the biggest understatement of the year. "We were lucky in the outbreak. We didn't get it nearly as bad as you lot on the mainland."

"So I hear."

"But when the ferries stopped running, we were cut off. It didn't take long for all the supermarkets to run out of food. We had to make do with what we had. When the military showed up, things started changing quickly. They claimed all the best stuff for themselves, took over the big houses, commandeered the remaining stores. To us locals, it felt like an occupation."

"Wait, I thought you'd be grateful. Didn't they bring security, get the electricity working again, make it safe from the virus? They must get some credit for that?"

"Not really. If you ask me, I wish they'd leave us in peace."

"I appreciate things look different on the island. You have a different perspective living here."

"Always have, always will."

They both fell silent again until Riley pointed off to their right at a grass-covered military installation on top of the hill. Something about it reminded her of Hurst Castle.

"That's Bembridge Fort," he said. "Been there for hundreds of years. There's a bunch of soldiers living up there now."

"There must be lots of forts like that all over the island. I hear they were built to defend the south coast against invasion by the French or Spanish."

"If you say so. I never did have much time for history."

"I only know that because one of our group is fanatical about local history. He's always collecting things. Memorabilia, paintings, sculptures, art. All sorts of things that no one else seems to care about these days. He thinks that if we don't keep history and culture alive, then our children's children won't know what life was like."

"He's got a point."

"All that knowledge will be forgotten, forever."

"You're not from that place in Ventnor then?"

"Which place?"

"The one where they invite young men to sign up for the breeding programme."

"I heard about that. Run by a bunch of nuns. They used to be based at the Chewton Glen Hotel before they relocated to the island. I've had a few run-ins with them. They're not very nice people."

"Still, I hear the waiting list is about a hundred names long right now. Lucky buggers." He winked in the rear-view mirror. "Still, you can't blame them, I suppose. There aren't that many of us good-looking folk left."

"Don't get your hopes up. They're only taking blue-eyed blondes with A-levels," she teased.

"I don't suppose…" His voice trailed off, staring at Riley in the rear-view mirror, running his eyes down her sweater.

"Do I look that desperate?" Riley frowned, remembering the

way she had caught him staring at her this morning. "Actually, don't answer that."

"No harm in asking is there? You won't tell the chaplain, will you?"

"How old are you anyway? Eighteen?"

"Nineteen."

"Well, I'm nearly twice your age. I could be your mother for goodness' sake! Cheeky sod." Riley shook her head and did her best to ignore him for the next five minutes, secretly flattered that a nineteen-year-old could still find her attractive.

The centre of Ryde had the look and feel of an occupied town during wartime. The first things she noticed were the dark green military vehicles on every street corner. She had seen the same thing in Yarmouth. The soldiers were maintaining a visible deterrent. They wanted to manage the experience of new arrivals. A show of order and control. The reality, she now knew, was somewhat different.

Ryde seemed relatively unscathed by the lawlessness that had laid waste to more populated areas. Market stalls and shops were open for business. Mothers dragged reluctant children along crowded pavements, pushing shopping trolleys loaded with items.

"It all looks so normal here."

"It was very different before the soldiers showed up. Don't be fooled by appearances. There were raids from the mainland, and widespread looting."

"But the shops and people. I wasn't expecting that. What do they use for money?"

"Everything's bartered these days."

"Makes sense. That's what we did back at Hurst. We traded with all these other groups. We grew our own vegetables, made our own cheese and beer. We were mostly self-sufficient, but for everything else, I suppose, well, we found a place in the new economy."

"Bet the fishing was good at the Needles?"

"Like you wouldn't believe. Crab, lobsters, prawns, shrimps, cod, haddock, skate, plaice, you name it."

"That's what I miss most, fish and chips on a Friday, and a few pints of local ale."

"Tell me about it. It's the little things you miss most. There's something so satisfying about being self-sufficient."

"On the island, we've been doing it for years. I never liked having bottled water and food flown halfway around the world. It was such a waste."

"You're right. Being dependent on the land and the sea again has brought us all back closer to Nature. Eating what's in season, following her cycles. We got so used to eating bananas from St Lucia, avocados and strawberries from Israel all year round. Makes the winters hard though, eating potatoes, carrots and turnips all the time."

On their left, they passed a large cemetery, overgrown with weeds. Smoke drifted across their path from a large burial pit. Before she could close the small crack in her window, the whole car filled with an intolerable stench Riley was all too familiar with. The mental image of their own plague pit at Hurst was hard to forget. Bodies piled on top of others, charred and blackened beyond recognition. It was the only sure way to kill the infection and safely dispose of the bodies.

They passed All Saints' Church, its rafters and brickwork exposed to the elements where the roof had caved in. Ahead of them, she glimpsed the Solent, stretching back towards the mainland. They turned left and pulled over on the right in front of the school gates. Terry flung his door open and jumped out to help with the rucksack.

"I won't be long. You coming in?" asked Riley.

"I'll wait here if that's all right."

Riley hobbled inside to the sparsely furnished reception area where an officious-looking woman behind the wooden counter had her head buried in a large ledger. She was scanning pages full of names and details. Without looking up, she barked, "Can I help you?"

"I've come to pick up one of your students – Heather Samuels," said Riley brightly.

"I know who she is. And you are?" growled the receptionist in a supercilious manner that Riley took an instant dislike to.

"Riley Stephens."

"Relative or guardian?"

"Neither. I'm a friend of her father's. I have a letter from your principal," said Riley, handing the woman the envelope. The receptionist removed the letter and scanned the handwritten sheet through glasses perched on the end of her nose.

"You'll need to talk to the principal. Mrs Shirley is not here this morning. She's been called away. You can try again later or come back another day, it's up to you."

Riley felt her hackles rising at the woman's intransigence.

"We've come all the way from Freshwater. I've got a car waiting outside."

"I see. I'm afraid without Mrs Shirley's permission, there's nothing I can do."

"Can I speak to Heather?"

"She's not here either," she said, checking her ledger.

"Sorry? Where is she then?"

"I'm not allowed to discuss student whereabouts without—"

Riley slammed her hands down on the counter, rocking back on her heels, infuriated by this woman's attitude. She leaned forward and grabbed hold of the woman's lapels, ruffling the mauve jacket and dislodging the floral pin that clattered on the counter.

"Now you look here, you crusty old bat, you either tell me what I want to know or I'll get my friend outside to put a ferret up your dress."

The woman looked genuinely terrified at the prospect of wild creatures in her underclothes and started whimpering, struggling to free herself. At her cries for help, there came the scrape of a chair from the next door room. A hunched man in his early seventies hobbled in, his expression thunderous. He had an unlit cigarette hanging from his lips. From the look of him, Riley thought he must be the school janitor.

"What on earth is going on here?" he yelled, his eyes narrowing to slits. "How dare you come in here like this? You leave Mrs Thompson alone, or you'll have me to answer to."

"No, not until someone tells me what happened to Heather Samuels," said Riley, releasing the receptionist who fell back into her chair, cowering in fear.

"There's no need to be uncivilised," he reprimanded with a wagging finger. "Heather was picked up yesterday. Mrs Thompson wouldn't know; she wasn't here."

"Picked up by whom? Her father?"

"No, it was a woman. One of the sisters from Ventnor."

"Sister Imelda?"

"I think that was her name," he said, running his finger down the register. "She wrote her address here in the ledger. Here we are. The Royal Hotel in Ventnor."

Riley felt her eye twitch involuntarily. What possible reason could the sisters have had to remove Zed's daughter? They had interfered once too often. She promised herself that this would be the last time.

# Chapter Seventeen

With a curt knock on the door, Zed and the others entered a vast library with thousands of books and reports lining all available wall space. At the head of an old oak table was a stooped man of advancing years with bright blue eyes. He looked like an academic, slightly eccentric with white hair, combed to the side, a green tie and sports blazer. He remained seated, studying the colonel and Zed, clearly sizing them up.

"These are the visitors I was telling you about, Ephesus," said the orderly in a raised voice.

The old man seemed to angle his head as if struggling to hear. "Yes, yes, do sit down. I hear you've come a long way. What exactly can I do for you?"

"Ephesus, my name is Colonel Abrahams, formerly of GCHQ. We're hoping you can help us. Mr Samuels here would like to ask you a few questions. He's conducting an independent investigation," said the colonel in a loud voice.

"I'm afraid you'll have to speak up. My hearing is not what it used to be."

"I said Mr Samuels here is exploring various alternative theories about the source of the outbreak, such as a terrorist attack or accidental leak. He needs your help to learn about any state-sponsored research into flu viruses you may know about."

"I've been through all this before with one of Doctor Hardy's team."

"Then perhaps you would be so kind as to show Mr Samuels here what you showed them."

"Assuming the major will allow that. He's quite protective of who he lets me talk to these days."

"Major Donnelly has authorised you to answer Mr Samuels' questions."

"Only the questions relevant to his investigation," added the major.

The old man laughed to himself, tickled by something. "Very well. I'll do my best. Where would you like to start?"

Zed reached into his briefcase for the notepad containing his many questions. "We're looking for any pre- or post-war documents that track attempts to use viruses as biological weapons."

"I see," said Ephesus, raising his eyebrows.

"If you indulge me, I'd like to go all the way back to the Second World War," said Zed, leaning forward in his chair and unbundling the folders he had brought with him. He noticed the doctor shaking his head.

"The colonel was kind enough to provide me with a number of documents from the Porton archive that reference the earliest known attempts to develop biological weapons. From what I understand, both sides developed a range of chemical and biological weapons in the Second World War, but they were never used. Is that correct?"

"I may look that old, but I'm afraid that's a little before my time. Professor Durant was in my role back then. He started this whole archive. He convinced the Minister that the government should have a permanent record of its various research programmes. He realised how important it was that we compile everything into one central archive for posterity. Of course, back then, Porton Down was just a few humble sheds and warehouses filled with amateurs."

He sighed, a nostalgic glint in his eyes as he surveyed the packed shelves and dusty box folders, reports and books.

"This is where it all started, you know. We documented every chapter of chemical and biological warfare. If you ask me, this remains the finest institution of its kind anywhere in the world. But then, I'm sure the Americans or Russians would have something to say about that now."

"Mr Samuels is going to be talking to our Russian expert later."

"Anton? Yes, he's always good company. Full of stories."

"One of the earliest intelligence reports I found claimed that the Nazis explored the potential use of influenza as a weapon of war."

"Yes, that's right. I suppose they were inspired by the success of 'Nivum 11'. It was one of the Nazis' so-called Wunderwaffen they hoped might turn the tide of the war."

"Was this in 1943?"

"Probably, but that's debated by various experts. The Allies certainly had earlier suspicions, but nothing was confirmed until 1943."

"It was a coup for British Intelligence, as I remember," boasted the colonel.

"That's correct. They captured a top-ranking German scientist in Tunisia. His name doesn't appear in the official war records, but we know he was a biologist based at the main research laboratory at Spandau. Under interrogation, he confessed that they were working on an experimental agent he said mimicked the effects of Spanish flu. It stimulated the victim's immune system to attack itself, similar to the effects of Blitzkatarrh, or lightning flu. The codename the Germans used was 'Nivum 11'."

Zed was scribbling everything down as fast as he could, underlining 'Nivum 11'.

The old man continued in a faltering voice, "It caused quite a stir in Whitehall, I can tell you." He chuckled. "Developing new Allied biological weapons was considered of vital importance to the war effort."

He was wracked by a coughing fit as he took a slug of water from a glass.

"Churchill was convinced that 'Nivum 11' marked a new era in modern warfare. He authorised a massive increase in funding and resources for the team at Porton Down to accelerate research into our own biological weapons, in the hope that they could come up with a defence against this new class of threat. So began the research programmes into better understanding different viruses and their potential as weapons. But without a sample of 'Nivum 11', there was a limit to how much we could do to prepare the country against such an attack."

"Surely," deflected Major Donnelly, "biological weapons were in their infancy? The Allies were much more worried about nerve gas and other chemical weapons."

"Yes, but Churchill was equally worried about the scale of Hitler's ambitions with biological weapons. He secretly ordered half a million anthrax bombs from the US. You see, most of the large-scale weapon production at the time was outsourced to Fort Derrick, in Maryland."

"Was there any evidence these new biological weapons were ever used?"

"Had the war not ended when it did, there's no doubt that anthrax would have been used for the first time in Europe."

"What makes you so sure?"

"They were desperate times. America had just dropped the first atomic bomb on Hiroshima. The Allies were using firebombs to destroy civilian population zones. The scale of destruction was unimaginable. The prevailing wisdom was that the Allies would stop at nothing to bring an end to the war."

"But if Hitler had those weapons, why did he choose not to use them?"

"Indeed. His V2 rockets were already terrorising British cities. What was stopping him from using the rockets as a delivery mechanism for an anthrax payload? The result could have been devastating."

"Surely he was facing certain defeat. Using anthrax would have turned the tide of the war."

"True, but it would also have opened a Pandora's Box. An anthrax attack on London would have rendered most of the south-east of England uninhabitable for decades. If the Allies had retaliated in kind, the same would have been true of large swathes of Germany. It would have been a terrible price to pay, greater even than atomic weapons."

"And what about this 'Nivum 11'? Is there evidence that it was ever used?"

"Good Lord, no. It was still experimental. It would have taken many more years to perfect as a weapon. No one at Porton seriously considered a virus could pose a credible threat."

"The technology of the time was much too primitive to turn a virus into a viable weapon," added Major Donnelly. "Nerve gas was the real threat."

"Our team's energies here were going into defence. Mass-producing innovative ways to protect our soldiers from chemical or biological attack. Clothing, respirators, detectors, that sort of thing. The major is right. Attack by nerve gas was considered most likely. Just the threat of attack was enough to render most of our forces completely useless."

"The challenge they faced was that once a soldier is wearing a respirator, he can barely fire a weapon."

"And that, my dear chap, is half the battle won. Cast your mind back to the first chemical weapons. In 1916, soldiers were dying in their hundreds of thousands on the battlefields of Ypres and the Somme. The generals were desperate to gain any advantage to break the stalemate. Their first breakthrough was to release clouds of chlorine gas and then mustard gas to drift over the enemy trenches. The generals had the temerity to argue that these new chemical weapons offered a more humane way to kill than throwing the flower of youth at enemy machine guns. They described this new warfare as a higher form of killing."

"The holy grail of modern warfare is to find a way of incapacitating one's enemy without destroying their infrastructure and buildings. Atomic bombs, by contrast, are such clumsy weapons."

"In 1942, Henry Stimson wrote, and I quote, 'any method which appears to offer advantages to a nation at war will be vigorously explored.'"

"My point precisely. What if the Millennial Virus was a state-sponsored attack on the West with a view to eliminating the human threat while retaining all of their towns and cities intact?"

Ephesus seemed tickled by the naivety of the question. "If I were you, I would start by looking at which nation or group stood to gain the most from such an attack, if that's what you really believe this was."

Zed stood up suddenly, electrified by a single thought. "So perhaps the question we should be asking ourselves is not why did this outbreak happen, but why did this happen now?"

"What are you thinking?" asked the colonel.

"Well, if my hunch is right, there must have been a catalyst. Did something happen to precipitate this attack? A provocation, a scientific breakthrough? I believe the virus was an act of war."

"Like the 9/11 attack or the assassination of Archduke Ferdinand in Sarajevo?"

"Exactly. Ephesus, perhaps you could be so kind as to show me where to find these documents? I've made a list."

Zed handed him some lined notepaper, folded many times. He had been carrying it around with him for days, adding to the growing list of questions and information requests. The old man put on his wire-framed glasses and scanned the handwritten page, scratching his head and frowning.

"Right then, we'd better get started. Tom, can you make some tea and I'll dig out these project folders. Wildfire, eh? I haven't heard that name in years."

"We'll leave you to it, Zed. I'll be downstairs in the command centre if you need me," said the colonel, rising to leave with Major Donnelly.

# Chapter Eighteen

After more than three hours of discussion, Zed and the Porton Down archivist took a much-needed break.

The old man seemed exhausted by the relentless barrage of questions exploring the different research programmes, both domestic and foreign that related to viruses. Zed was satisfied that there was full disclosure of material. There appeared to be little subterfuge. A couple of times, Ephesus hesitated, but he blamed his faltering memory. For a man his age, he seemed distinctly together.

Zed's wrist was aching from the dozen or so pages of notes he had been scribbling. Porton rules forbade the direct copying of classified documents, though in the circumstances that was hardly the issue. There was no mains power in this part of the building.

Zed was escorted back to the main canteen just in time for lunch. The sounds and smells of hot food were unmistakable. More than a hundred workers were collected around dozens of small tables. Half the personnel were military; the rest seemed to either wear lab coats or civilian clothing that gave no clue as to their role at the facility. In the far corner, he spotted the colonel seated with several other men he didn't recognise. In front of them each sat a humble bowl of rice and chilli.

"How did you get on?" asked the colonel, when he'd finished his mouthful.

"Very informative. It was like drinking from a firehose." Zed sighed.

"In a good way?"

"Oh yes. Ephesus knows more about the history of scientific research in this area than anyone I've ever met. It would take a week to read through all the reports he suggested. There's a lot to assimilate."

"We don't have a week. The helicopter is coming back for us tomorrow. We need to be back at the hospital before dark. Did you get the impression he was holding anything back?"

"Hard to say for sure. He knew most about post-war and Cold War-era programmes, but when it came to the last ten years, his knowledge became a bit sketchy.

"Hardly surprising. Since everything was scanned and computerised, he's more a curiosity these days. A relic from another era."

"He admitted as much himself. Said there's been little need for his skills of late. He did mention that some of the most highly classified documents were never digitised, for obvious reasons."

"Hardly surprising. They wouldn't want them in the official records."

"Nevertheless, they kept paper copies just in case. He might just be the only person who knows of their existence."

"What about Iraq and Wildfire? Was he any help?"

"Not really. Perhaps I had unrealistic expectations. I just hoped someone could shed more light on what happened after the project was terminated."

"If the archivist doesn't know, then Doctor Hardy and Major Donnelly are probably your last hope, if we can get them to talk.

As for Wildfire, I suspect there are very few people left alive who know more than you do."

The man next to the colonel stirred at the mention of Project Wildfire. He nudged the colonel to get his attention, waiting for an introduction.

"Oh, my apologies. Zed Samuels, may I introduce Anton Peters? Anton is the Russia specialist I was telling you about."

Anton stood and inclined his head. "It is a pleasure to finally meet you. The colonel has told me much about your investigation."

He spoke in an educated voice, with a slight affectation that suggested English was not his first language.

"I hear you've been asking questions about Russian links to Saddam?"

"That's right," Zed replied, lowering his voice so that the neighbouring tables would not overhear their conversation. "We know Iraq was getting outside help. My working hypothesis is that Russia had outsourced some of its research and development to Iraq. The colonel suggested you might be able to shed more light?"

Anton smiled knowingly, giving nothing away. "Why don't we take a walk outside?" He slid his chair under the table and gave a small bow to his fellow diners.

On their way out towards the main hall, Zed felt he was being watched. Out of the corner of his eye to his right, he noticed a well-dressed woman sitting alone. He was pretty sure she was following their departure. He gave into temptation and glanced towards her, but she instantly looked away. There was something about her that seemed so familiar. She was attractive with shoulder-length mousey-brown hair, and wore a dark trouser suit and cream blouse. He estimated she was roughly his age.

Zed and Anton left the main building, past the security guards stationed near the swing doors. Outside, the temperature was already dropping as the sun sank lower behind the tree line.

There were very few people out here, other than soldiers at their posts. Further down the road a team was unloading boxes and stores from a waiting truck. In the watchtower at the far end of the compound, he could see two soldiers pointing at something in the distance, beyond the fence.

"So, Mr Samuels, you have my full attention. What is it I can help you with?"

"The colonel told me you had first-hand knowledge of Russian weapons research, is that correct?"

"Of course. My real name is Anton Vasily Petrovich. The colonel helped me relocate here shortly after the fall of the USSR."

In the cold autumnal air, his breath was just visible when he spoke. Anton kept checking around him, keeping his voice low.

"So you actually worked for Biopreparat?"

"Yes, I was based at the Vector Institute for many years. Do you know it?"

"I've heard of it."

"It's in Koltsovo, south-western Siberia, not far from the border with Kazakhstan. It's the Russian equivalent of the American CDC or the US army's Chemical and Biological Defence Command. When I was there, Vector was the centre of Biopreparat's research operations in the eighties and nineties."

"So Vector was not dissimilar to Porton Down?"

"I suppose so. We undertook research into many different pathogens, such as smallpox, Marburg, bubonic plague."

"What was the purpose of the research? To evaluate known threats or to develop weapons based on them?"

"In my view, they are one and the same. Doing one without the other is hard. When I was there, Biopreparat already had more than sixty thousand employees and was still growing."

Zed struggled to hide his surprise at that statement. It suggested that the USSR had covertly maintained its weapons programmes. "Surely by the early nineties the USA and USSR were rolling back their size and scale? Hadn't both countries signed up to the Biological Weapons Convention?"

Anton stopped and studied Zed, perhaps unsure whether the naivety of the question was feigned or genuine.

"They were paying lip service to international pressure. You have to remember that during the Cold War, there was minimal trust. The Kremlin believed that America would stop at nothing to destroy us. After the atomic bombs dropped on Hiroshima and Nagasaki, we knew the Americans were prepared to use weapons of mass destruction against their enemies. Our only chance was to maintain a viable deterrent. To build a lead in the arms race. Nuclear weapons were no longer politically acceptable, which meant biological weapons development took centre stage."

"How did Biopreparat manage to conceal its scale and purpose for that long?"

"With difficulty. There were regular inspections. It became a full-time logistical operation to stay one step ahead of the inspectors. We got very good at moving around any incriminating equipment." He laughed unapologetically.

"They did the same thing in Iraq with the UN inspectors. They mounted a whole campaign of deception and disinformation."

"The Kremlin was deluded. They believed that, far from dismantling their programmes, the Americans were accelerating their research. Biopreparat had to keep pace, to stockpile ever increasing quantities of anthrax, plague virus, smallpox, tularaemia and other viable agents."

As they turned a corner, their stroll through the compound took them past a high-security unit with biohazard symbols on the outside door and a sign which read: "Hazardous waste: strictly no admittance". There was a three-person maintenance team preparing to go inside, wrapping duck-tape around their wrists to seal their suits. One of them nodded at the two men as they passed.

"That's odd," said Anton once they were out of earshot. "The power must be out in this section."

Looking back, Zed saw what Anton was referring to. The door's three-bar brushed steel locking mechanism was disengaged and its keypad entry system deactivated. Unlike the other buildings they had seen, the security light above the door was not illuminated.

"Remind me to ask the front desk to send someone to check it out. They're always cycling through the grid trying to turn off power to the buildings they're not using."

"Going back to what you were saying, surely the Americans must have known what the Kremlin was up to?"

"I suppose so. Concealing ever-growing stockpiles of chemical weapons became impractical. We needed a way of continuing our research beyond the interference of the American inspectors. It was imperative that Biopreparat developed new biological weapons and pathogens that America would have no defence against."

"And those biological programmes were based at the Vector Institute?"

"Vector was chosen because it was state of the art, heavily protected, almost impossible to penetrate. A whole Red Army regiment was based there. Security countermeasures like you would never believe. The Americans made many unsuccessful attempts to recruit Vector scientists, to infiltrate the facility."

"So what happened?"

"Eventually they found a way in. The colonel tells me that MI6 had a deep cover agent, working in one of the labs, feeding them information. They were particularly interested in a former student of mine, Doctor Sergei Netyosov. Back then, he was already a rising star, a brilliant young scientist. MI6 were convinced that Sergei was on the brink of some dramatic breakthrough that might give the Soviets an unassailable lead."

"Do you know what he was working on?"

"He was a pioneer in genetic engineering. He was attempting to splice together different strains of a virus. He called it a 'chimaera virus'. A hybrid."

Zed thought back to the UNSCOM files documenting the various Iraqi programmes led by Taha al-Azawi. "The Iraqis had a parallel research project," he said.

"I assure you, that's no coincidence."

"And yet Doctor Hardy was so dismissive of this research. He said that the creation of such a hybrid virus was pure science fiction."

"He would say that." He laughed. "The British were sceptical that another team could have pioneered this gene-splicing technology before them. They were blinded by their own arrogance. I assure you, the real experts were based at Moscow's Ivanovsky Institute of Virology. To my mind, they were the ones who first created a hybrid virus. They were said to be able to control how it behaved, in some respects."

"Such as?"

"I don't know. Make it more resistant, extend its incubation period, insert a kill switch?"

"Do you think it feasible that they could have programmed the virus to target certain geographies or demographics? Specifically the West?"

"Theoretically, yes. Sorry, I forget, you're not a virologist, are you? This has actually been proven before. The Russians were not the first to design a biological agent to target certain ethnicities. Have you come across Project Coast in your research?

"Not that I remember."

"During the apartheid regime, the South African government launched a notorious inoculation programme designed to lower fertility rates in the indigenous black population. It was hidden within a vaccine for Yellow Fever. That was just the start. Wouter Basson headed up Project Coast. He was authorised by President PW Botha himself to use all means necessary for so-called social engineering. They researched the potential deployment of other biological agents such as anthrax, cholera, thallium, Ebola and Marburg for use in smaller-scale activities such as assassination attempts of human rights activists and prominent ANC leaders."

"I'm familiar with the apartheid regime but I've never heard about the rest. How did they get away with it? Surely there was international outrage?"

"It only came to light much later on. My point is that it wasn't just the South Africans and Russians who were looking at bioweapons. Saddam Hussein was an early adopter, particularly against ethnic minorities in Iraq and Iran. There was no question. Collaboration between South Africa and Iraq was later proven. Apartheid regime scientists visited Baghdad on several occasions, inspecting factories and production facilities. I also know that some of my former Vector team ended up working in Iraq and Libya."

"So this gene-splicing technology you mentioned, do you

happen to know which viruses they were experimenting with? I'm specifically interested in Spanish flu."

"It was a closely guarded secret. Sergei Netyosov's research was classified. I heard rumours that he had perfected a strain of the plague virus, resistant to all antibiotics. If true, it could easily have been deployed to wipe out large numbers in targeted population areas."

"With so many defectors, were they not able to confirm any of these rumours?"

"If anyone would have known, Vladimir Pasechnik would have. He defected before me in 1989. He swore he had no knowledge of Sergei's programmes."

"But you still think it's credible that they could have outsourced Sergei's work to the Iraqis? I keep hearing rumours that there was a team at al-Hakam working on something like this, off the books."

"Why not? I'm saying it's possible, yes. Biopreparat had prioritised research into viruses."

"Such as?"

"I'm sure the colonel has told you about our early work with smallpox."

"Remind me."

"For several years we fell in love with smallpox. The Americans had run down their vaccine stocks. Smallpox was no longer considered a threat."

"Then why the change of heart?"

"The problem was that smallpox does not occur naturally. Humans are the virus's only known host capable of spreading the infection. So any outbreak could be quickly contained with quarantine measures. Even if the virus had been genetically re-engineered, an outbreak would be, at best, limited."

"I see. Whereas with influenza, humans are not the only hosts."

"That's right. Birds and pigs can also incubate and contract the virus."

They had walked as far as they could in the compound, reaching a new area of fence prematurely sealing off several disused buildings that had fallen into disrepair, cannibalised for building materials.

To the right, new foundations had been laid. Tools and wheelbarrows abandoned where they had been left at the end of a shift. The exposed steel skeleton of an unfinished building whistled in a gust of wind.

Something beyond the fence caught Zed's eye. Two half-hidden figures watching them through binoculars. He cradled his left arm and wrist instinctively, remembering what had happened last time he came here. The ambush, the explosion, the vehicle rolling on its side. Pulled from the smoking wreckage by Briggs's men. The interrogations and torture that ended in his rescue. Suddenly he felt vulnerable so far from the main building. He turned on his heels and gestured Anton to start back.

"Look, I don't claim to be an expert on influenza," continued Anton. "Doctor Hardy is the real expert. He knows a lot more than he's letting on."

"So if he is the key to all this, how do I get him to talk? He's clearly not going to help me voluntarily."

"He's protected by Major Donnelly. Not even the colonel can get him to talk. "

"There must be a way. Everyone has a weakness."

"I once saw the KGB file we kept on him. His vices were listed as 'none'."

"He must have a weakness, a pressure point."

"If there is, no one has ever found it. Don't waste your time. He's unbreakable."

Anton checked his watch and realised they were late for Doctor Hardy's briefing in the lecture hall. "Perhaps we should be getting back."

"They won't start without us. Come on, I'll show you a short cut."

# Chapter Nineteen

"I need to talk to Briggs right now," demanded Terra, resting her hands on the darkly stained wooden counter at the school's reception.

"Well, he's not here," replied the bespectacled janitor, without looking up.

"Hey!" shouted Victor, getting his full attention. "It's important. Where is he?"

"He's up at the hospital." He blushed. "Been there all morning."

"Come on. I'll drive us up there." Victor huffed, grabbing the keys to a top-of-the-line Jaguar saloon from a hook by reception. Climbing in, the interior still smelled of new leather. It was practically in show-room condition. The engine roared into life, and they pulled away.

At the main road, he turned right, tyres squealing on the tarmac, as they headed away from Lymington. Victor seemed to notice Terra's confusion.

"I never go through town. Too many soldiers. Too many questions. This way is longer but much less hassle."

It was only a couple of miles as the crow flies, but it took them nearly half an hour to wind their way through narrow country lanes before rejoining the main road through the Forest that led to Lymington.

From the mini-roundabout on the outskirts of town onwards, Damian King had converted the entire industrial estate into a fortified compound ringed by a high-security fence. The estate contained more than a dozen warehouses and storage units that served as an Aladdin's cave of items recovered from the local area.

Terra was amazed that the allies had allowed this group leave to remain. After all, the site was a mere stone's throw from their command post in Lymington and just the other side of the river from the ferry terminal. It was undoubtedly only a matter of time before the site was cleared and King evicted by force like they had threatened to do at Carisbrooke Castle. Unless there was some other agreement in place that gave them protected status. In return for what, thought Terra.

At the barrier to the compound, one of King's men gestured for Victor to slow down. He seemed to recognise the car and immediately waved them through the open gateway. Parking directly in front of the main entrance, they hurried inside to find Briggs.

The hospital buildings were more modern than she remembered, certainly built within the last decade or so. Inside the front entrance was a large atrium with high ceilings and multicoloured walls. At the bottom of the glass and steel staircase, they found a group of more than a dozen men conversing animatedly. One nudged the other until they all fell silent, staring back coldly at the newcomers.

"We're looking for Briggs," said Victor breathlessly.

A familiar voice from above greeted them.

"He's up here somewhere," shouted King, leaning over the railing, mumbling something unintelligible over his shoulder.

"Something I can help you with?" He smiled, head tilted.

"It's private." Terra smiled back.

Briggs joined King at the railing, their elbows touching. He looked different somehow. The two men were relaxed in each other's company. There was a growing momentum behind their partnership that gave grounds for self-satisfaction as more and more local groups rallied to their cause. Terra was burning to know what they were planning.

"Private, eh?" Briggs laughed, observing their impatience. "We've nothing to hide from our friends."

Terra hesitated, readjusting what she had planned to say. "Are you familiar with the radio mast at Rowridge?" she asked, skipping the preliminaries.

"The one on the island? It's hard to miss."

"We've figured out why none of the radios work around here."

"Go on."

"Someone's broadcasting static."

King glanced suspiciously at Briggs, but he shrugged as if to say "nothing to do with me".

"Why would anyone do that?"

"To enforce a news blackout."

King blew out his cheeks, half-mocking Terra. "Or a simpler explanation is that the power may just be out?" He exchanged another glance with Briggs, who leant further over the railing, peering down at her, ruminating on this new theory.

"I suppose it could explain why only short-range radio seems to be working. Copper, remember that police jammer you found for us?" said Briggs.

Terra couldn't see Copper from where she was standing but heard a grunt of agreement from above.

"And you figured this out all on your own?" sneered King.

"She had some help," added Victor, feeling left out.

"If it were an act of sabotage, then surely the military would have figured this out by now. They're not stupid."

"Unless they're the ones who did this in the first place?" suggested Terra.

"The military? What would they have to gain from knocking out the transmitter? They need to coordinate their activities more than anyone."

"Not if they had their own communication systems that weren't affected."

"I suppose it's possible. Just seems like a lot of effort."

"The person we spoke to said someone could be broadcasting static to mask all other signals. So if other regions or countries have been trying to get in contact and getting no response, then…"

"They'd assume everyone was dead."

"Exactly. That might explain why no one has come here. For fear of infection."

"Hold on. What about the Americans? Why did they come here?"

"We don't know yet."

"We weren't the only country affected. Radio blackout or not, someone would have organised a relief effort by now."

"Not if the whole of the UK remained subject to an international quarantine order."

"Why would they do that?"

"The *Santana* crew called it 'English Flu'. We think that no one has dared to land here because it's still considered too dangerous. There might be a whole exclusion zone around the UK. No one comes, no one leaves."

"And you really think no one would have chanced it? The whole country is wide open. It's a looter's paradise."

"Correct. That quarantine order would attract every petty criminal with a rowing boat."

"If the UN is really involved, by now they would have sent clean-up crews, inspection teams, that sort of thing. They wouldn't just leave us to rot like this. It's been two years."

"Or no one's been here because the rest of the world is in just as much of a mess as we are. That's the only logical explanation. If the Americans thought the UK was riddled with infection, then why would they bother? There are probably hundreds of places less affected."

"The more rational explanation is that the transmitter stopped working because there's no power, that's all," cautioned King. "I'm telling you, if they get the transmitter back online, they'll restore comms."

"Terra, this isn't just another of your wild theories, is it? I suppose you have some actual evidence?" challenged Briggs.

Terra looked flustered as if someone had taken the wind out of her sails. "You have to admit, it makes a lot of sense…" She blushed, realising everyone was staring at her. "But no, I wanted to bring this to you as soon as we found out."

Briggs glanced at King, who shook his head.

"And you did the right thing," Briggs replied with a hint of sarcasm. "Look we're in the middle of something, yeah? Why don't we talk about this later, back at the school?"

Terra thought about pushing the point, but Victor cautioned against it with a glance.

"Perhaps if you need me here," said Victor, "I can get someone else to take Terra back?"

Briggs smiled mischievously at King. "No, I think we have

everything under control. I'll see you both back at the school."

Victor looked bruised by the dismissal. Since joining forces with King, he too had felt his power over Briggs had waned somewhat.

As they turned to leave, Terra noticed chalk markings on the floor and realised what they had been looking at from above. It was an outline of the Isle of Wight, with major towns marked out and various areas shaded in different colours.

"Dividing up the spoils already?" asked Terra.

"Something like that." King shrugged.

"Aren't you getting a little ahead of yourselves? How exactly do you plan to get everyone off the island?" she asked bluntly.

"Ask nicely?" One of the men laughed.

"Well, they're not going to leave willingly. You're not thinking of starting a new outbreak, are you?" Her eyes flicked from Briggs to King and back again, gauging their blank reactions for any clues.

"What an active imagination you have."

"How else do you plan to get everyone to leave?"

King strode to the top of the stairs, taking them two at a time, clearly irritated by Terra's refusal to leave. She instinctively retreated towards Victor.

"You're a little nosy parker, aren't you?" he snarled, grabbing her by the throat and almost lifting her off the ground. Terra glanced at Briggs as she struggled to breathe, imploring him to intervene.

"I'm sorry, I didn't mean—" was all she managed to get out.

"That's enough," commanded Briggs. "Let her go."

King released his grip, and Terra clutched at her throat, gasping in pain. Far from rushing to her defence, Briggs seemed almost amused by King's response.

"Go on, Terra. Say your piece."

"I know these people." She coughed. "I know how they think. Armstrong, Peterson and all the others. Remember, I was on the other side. I know their plans for Camp White, their quarantine measures. Don't you think I might be able to help?"

"Why do you think we kept you around till now," said King.

"I told you already," added Briggs. "It's safer this way. The fewer people that know what's planned, the better."

"But surely…" she started and then thought better of it. She knew from experience that once Briggs had set his mind to something, there was no changing it. It would be like trying to prise a mussel from a rock with your bare hands.

"Go and find the professor, will you." demanded King. "I'd like a word."

The momentary look of alarm on Terra's face betrayed her complicity. A few minutes later the guard returned, pushing forward the professor. He was still in his lab coat, frowning in annoyance.

"Perhaps you'd like to explain why Terra here is asking so many questions about our plans?"

"I don't know what you're talking about. We barely know each other," batted back the professor dismissively, avoiding eye contact with Terra. There was a fresh welt under his left eye.

"Didn't I warn you what would happen if you betrayed me?"

"I've told no one," he insisted wearily.

"So it's done?"

"I did everything you asked. It's too late to stop them."

"Stop who?" challenged Terra.

"You still here? I thought I told you to head back to the school," barked Briggs, taking her by the arm and leading her towards the front entrance. She wrestled her arm free and pulled up.

"Stop keeping me in the dark, Briggs. I'm not stupid. I know what you're up to. I just need to hear it from your own lips."

He motioned for her to head outside. "What more do you want me to say? That you're right?"

"Right about the virus? That you intend to start a new outbreak?"

"The volunteers were chosen at random," he admitted. "I don't even know their names."

"Volunteers?"

"Yes. To receive the experimental serum. We told them it was a prototype vaccine, and packed them off on the last ferry to the island."

"But they'll never make it through quarantine."

"I wouldn't be so sure. We found a strain with a longer incubation period," said Briggs, checking his watch. "With any luck, they'll clear quarantine long before the symptoms present themselves. No one will ever know."

"My God. How many of them are there?"

"It only takes one to make it through."

"So what are you going to do now?" She blinked, feeling suddenly faint.

"Sit back and wait for nature to take its course."

"No, I meant how are you going to stop the virus spreading back to the mainland?"

"You let me worry about that."

Terra's knees almost buckled, and she sank down on a nearby bench. She looked up at Briggs, searching out any sign of compassion. "But you'll kill everyone. It will be genocide."

"Not everyone," conceded Briggs "But in a few months, those that don't die of the virus will be dead of starvation or some other disease. Then we can start the clean-up process."

Terra was momentarily speechless. As the impact of Briggs's words hit her, she mumbled, "Men, women and children."

"They should never have gone there in the first place."

"They were promised sanctuary. A fresh start."

"Yeah, on my island," added Briggs. "Look, one day you'll understand. It's better this way, believe me."

"I'll never understand—"

"You'll see, eventually. There's a war coming. We can't match the allies in a fair fight. When we're finished, the island will be free again. They'll be no one left to challenge us. You'll have everything I promised you, Terra. Everything."

"But, Briggs, you're going to a place I can't follow you," she cautioned, fighting back the tears, trying to hide her despair. She broke free of his grasp and backed away, shaking her head.

She was dumbstruck, realising the implications of what King and Briggs had set in motion. She stumbled towards the car, tears streaming down her face. She was desperate to get as far away from these people as possible, back to the school, anywhere but here.

Looking back through the semi-opaque glass doors as she waited for Victor, she watched them all laughing, pointing in her direction. Their features were distorted by the glass. The door was still ajar, and King's voice sounded almost demonic, racked by coughing. In a moment of clarity, she saw them for what they really were. The horror of what they planned was now plain to see.

Something made her think of Jack and Hurst. For all his faults, she missed Jack's pragmatism, his ability to determine right from wrong. Terra's moral compass had been a spinning dial since his murder. She could no longer deny that she was in league with criminals, men so depraved they had consciously cast aside all remaining vestiges of compassion. What remained was barely recognisable as human.

She now knew that they calmly planned to plunge the whole region into a Biblical hell. Like the four horsemen of the apocalypse, pestilence and famine, death and destruction would be unleashed on the allies.

She could no longer stand by and do nothing. Her only chance was to somehow get word to the allies. She just wondered whether Peterson and Armstrong were any more trustworthy than the rebels who plotted against them.

# Chapter Twenty

After what seemed like an eternity, the unmarked staff car carrying Riley finally reached the outskirts of Ventnor, in the south of the island.

With time running out before the evening curfew, her driver threw caution to the wind, taking the most direct route through the picturesque seaside towns of Sandown and Shanklin, roads he seemed to know well.

There was little traffic to speak of this far south from the militarised zone, but successive checkpoints had resulted in unforeseen delays. Their final destination was the Royal Hotel in Ventnor where they were hoping to find Zed's daughter, Heather.

Riley was still seething with anger at Sister Imelda for interfering. She was wracking her brains, trying to remember whether she had mentioned her planned trip to Ryde when they last met in Freshwater. What possible reason could the sister have had for removing Heather from the school?

The roads narrowed as they entered Ventnor. The sweeping sea views were replaced by stone-built houses and trees overhanging steep-sided slopes as their route snaked back and forth, heading down towards the waterfront. Riley pressed her face against the glass, trying to catch sight of the Victorian-era hotel.

Another sharp corner and Riley's stomach lurched. She opened the window a crack to get some fresh air. The smell of the sea reminded her of Hurst. Other than the apple she had brought with her, they had skipped lunch to save time.

The driver veered off the main road and screeched to a halt outside the hotel porch. Riley flung the door wide, striding up the drive with her rucksack slung over her shoulder. There was a gaggle of women chatting near the front entrance, whispering into their sleeves. One of the women seemed to recognise Riley and ran off to find one of the sisters. The crowd parted, clearing a path towards reception.

"Riley," exclaimed Sister Imelda with genuine surprise, "I didn't expect you so soon. Stella will be thrilled."

"This isn't a social visit."

"Sorry?"

"I've come to collect Heather Samuels. Zed's daughter? You collected her from Ryde Boarding School yesterday."

"Heather? Well, yes, I vaguely remember a girl by that name. I had no idea she was Zed's daughter."

"But, sister, I told you last week that I was coming to collect her. There's no point denying it. This poor man has been driving me around all day trying to find her. I came all the way from Freshwater this morning."

"How silly of me. Yes, of course." Sister Imelda seemed confused for a moment. "I'm sorry, I don't know how I could possibly have forgotten. Perhaps I got my wires crossed, somehow. It's so easy to lose track of names. We've taken in so many girls over the last few weeks. You see, the school needed to make room for the new arrivals."

"But Heather's thirteen. She's far too young to join your programme."

"My dear Riley. Whatever you've been told, we're a charity for homeless young women. We've taken girls far younger than Heather. They have to be at least thirteen years old to join the programme."

"So it's true then. You really are press-ganging all these vulnerable women into joining?"

"Hardly. We don't force them. Barely half decide to join," the sister whispered, imploring Riley to lower her voice. "Why don't we take a walk in the gardens and I can explain properly."

"I really don't have time for all this. I'm meant to be back at the hospital by 5pm." Riley looked at her watch. There were only three hours until the soldiers closed the roads again for curfew.

"At least allow me the opportunity to explain. I'm sure you'd like to see Stella and Adam before you leave."

Riley relented. She knew she was being manipulated. The sister's calm authority seemed to relax her. As she often found when dealing with these people, it was impossible to refuse without appearing ungrateful. It was one of the many reasons she found the sisters both beguiling and frustrating.

Sister Imelda linked arms with Riley and led her down the lane towards Ventnor Park. The wrought-iron gate was hanging from its hinges and the entrance overgrown, but within, the sheltered beauty of the park was inviting.

"This is one of my most favourite places on the island. The locals say there's a microclimate here."

"It's beautiful," Riley said, distractedly.

"You should see the Royal Botanical Gardens. When the sun comes out, it's a small slice of heaven. Palm trees, trumpet flowers, fuchsia, magnolia, the colours are stunning." The sister sighed, leaning her head to study the trees.

"Another time, I'd like to see that," said Riley impatiently. "But right now, I need to find Heather and get going. I so wish you hadn't meddled."

"Is that the thanks I get for rescuing Zed's daughter from that school? Who knows what happens to young children there?"

"I appreciate you have the best of intentions, but let's not pretend that this was pure altruism."

"If you're suggesting an ulterior motive, I assure you, you're mistaken. Our only concern here is protecting the vulnerable, giving young people a fresh start. Most of the young women who come here have suffered terrible hardship or been abused. Can't you see? This is a sanctuary from that world. We can give these young people back a future, teach them new skills, finish their education, restore their hope. We're doing God's work."

"You may fool everyone else, but not me. Your judgement is just as subjective and questionable as any other survivor group. You're doing what you believe is necessary to survive. At the end of the day, we're all in competition for resources."

"How can you say that about the Sisterhood?"

"You fail to appreciate how your behaviour could be perceived by others. I suppose it's a matter of perspective. Heather is only thirteen, for goodness' sake."

"Regardless of what you think you've heard, no one is forcing these young women to do anything against their will. I assure you, all the girls who choose to join the regeneration programme are volunteers. Motherhood is Nature's greatest gift."

"But they're still children. They're much too young for that responsibility. I understand full well what you're trying to do, but really?"

"As soon as girls reach puberty they are eligible for

consideration. Sister Theodora is the final arbiter. We insist on a level of emotional and physical maturity. You do realise that it's a modern invention that women should put their careers ahead of their biological function. Back in Victorian times, the average age of first-time mothers was much younger. Circumstances demand that we adapt."

Riley felt her eye twitching again. "And what happens to these newborn children? Is it true they're sent to St Mary's for testing?"

"Good heavens, no. We're not monsters."

"Sister, I've just come from St Mary's. I've seen it with my own eyes. Do you have any idea how many children are there?"

"They're crying out for volunteers. I'm fully aware of the vaccine trials they are undertaking. We do whatever we can to help. Stella's son, for example, is a regular visitor there."

"Why Adam?"

"Because he's one of the first of the newborns to exhibit increased resistance. I'm told he has natural antibodies that help counteract infection."

"This place is acquiring quite a reputation, you know. Every man on the island is talking about your regeneration programme. They're queuing up to enrol."

"So I've heard. It's a testament to the levels of support we enjoy, but we don't just take anyone. First, the men have to undergo various tests to make sure they qualify. We need to be sure they are fit and healthy."

Riley was shaking her head in disbelief. The sister's naivety was blinding. "Don't you see? We're all just meat for the grinder. They're using you. They're using all of us. This whole vaccine trial rides rough-shod over people's human rights. They're all so focused on finding the cure, they don't care about individuals."

"I don't blame them. Finding a cure is paramount."

"Even if it means only the genetically pure get put forward? Medical screening for those with family histories of illnesses? Racial profiling? Screw the rest of us."

"These are just stories, Riley. You're seriously accusing a hospital of prejudice and bias?"

"Absolutely. And to think I've just left Adele in their care. What was I thinking?"

"Look, these last few weeks, we've all been under a huge amount of stress. You of all people know how that affects us," she said, stroking her arm tenderly. Riley softened at the contact.

"Look, set aside your misgivings for a moment. You must see that we're building something that matters. We already have almost two hundred volunteers in the programme, and there are probably a hundred more waiting to enrol. You should see it, Riley. Accommodation spread over large houses and B&Bs throughout Ventnor. We have our own maternity unit, full to bursting with expectant mothers. It's the most wonderful sight. We'd love to have you stay with us. Join us?"

Hearing it from the sister's point of view, made Riley question whether this regeneration programme was really all that bad. She didn't like their methods, but in the face of an uncertain future, she found it hard to argue against this biological imperative. If they didn't compromise, then what hope was there for the survivors? If science could find a way to alter the odds in their favour, then surely it was worth the cost? Right now, survival was no better than a lottery.

"What happens to the children?"

"Other than monthly check-ups, they get to stay right here with their mothers. They will go to nursery and the local school. I assure you, it's all perfectly normal."

Coming towards them along the footpath were half a dozen mothers with pushchairs. They were each dressed in a royal blue uniform that reminded Riley of Wrens, the female volunteers in the Royal Navy during wartime. The group was in high spirits, laughing and talking loudly above the wail of several over-tired infants. Riley spotted Stella from a distance. She shouted her name and ran towards her. Stella's laugh froze on her lips, eyes wide in disbelief.

"Riley!" she shouted, embracing her tightly, "My God. I've been praying for you."

"And who's this?" Riley cooed, peering into the folds of blankets to get a look at the angelic face of a child who must have been nearly six months old.

"Please don't wake him. I just got him off to sleep."

Stella turned to address the other mothers who were watching them. "Why don't you ladies go on? I'll catch you up."

Riley noticed a couple of girls were probably no more than fifteen or sixteen. She turned her attention to baby Adam. Now that the buggy was no longer moving, he was beginning to stir.

"He's gorgeous. You must be so happy."

"I can't begin to tell you. It's been amazing. Say hello to your godson."

"Me, a godmother? Really, I'm touched. Thank you."

"The sisters have been great, but being a single parent is hard work. Now that Adam's going into the crèche, I'm volunteering to be a mother again."

"Again? So soon?"

"They need all the help they can get. Why don't you stay? You might like it. It's different here now. "

"No, I'd go crazy. I get why you like it, but really, it's not for me. My place is with the others back in Freshwater. Adele needs me."

"Of course. How's she doing?"

"Actually not great. She was diagnosed with leukaemia a while back. Without a bone marrow transplant, there's not much they can do, but she's putting on a brave face. She has some pills to relieve the symptoms. She's volunteered to help with these vaccine trials."

"Adam too. He's been back and forth to St Mary's most weeks. The doctors seem to think he's special."

"Do they know why?"

"They say that because I was immune, he will be too. All I know is that they keep taking more and more of his blood. That's why they're so insistent that I volunteer again. Apparently, there's a male volunteer, like me, with very high levels of resistance."

"I'm told they're trying to genetically engineer immunity in the next generation."

"When there's a chance you can make a difference, it's hard to say no. Who knows? Maybe Adam's little brother or sister might help them figure out the answer."

Riley reached out and placed her hand on Stella's arm. "I'm sure you're right. I just don't like the idea of them taking advantage of you like this."

"They're really not. I wouldn't do this if I didn't believe in it."

Riley checked her watch and realised they were running short of time if she was going to make it back to the hospital with Heather before curfew.

"Listen, I promise you I'll come back another time, but I really have to get back. My driver won't wait forever."

"Why don't you stay the night?"

"I can't. Adele will be waiting for me."

They set off back towards the hotel, linking arms again.

"So how come Zed couldn't be bothered to pick up his own daughter?" said Stella.

"It's a long story. He's been working up at St Mary's. Some investigation for the colonel. Wildfire, I think he called it?"

Recognition flickered briefly in Stella's eyes, before she shrugged and made light of it. When they got back to the car park, the car and driver were nowhere to be seen.

"Maybe he parked around the back," said Riley, looking in all directions.

At that moment, Sister Theodora emerged from the hotel entrance, her long robes dragging across the dirt. "If you're looking for the man who was here, he said he couldn't wait any longer. He's gone back to the hospital."

"Without me? How am I meant to get back?"

"I told him we would make arrangements to get you back in the morning."

"You told him not to wait?"

"Child, curfew begins in two hours. He wouldn't have made it back otherwise. It's not worth the risk of being caught out in the open."

"That wasn't your decision to make. You realise a little girl's waiting for me. She'll be worried if I don't return."

"Your driver will inform the hospital of the change in your plans. It will give us a chance to talk."

"Come on, Riley," said Stella cheerily. "Stay and have dinner with us. There's so much to discuss."

"I will ask Sister Imelda to take you both back to the hospital in the morning. I trust you can ride?" asked Sister Theodora.

"You mean horseback?"

"Stella, perhaps you can find Riley a bed for the night and tell the kitchen we have a guest for dinner." To Riley, she said, "We eat at seven."

# Chapter Twenty-one

Zed followed the Russia specialist through a maze of underground service tunnels that snaked beneath the Porton Down buildings. There was a low rumble of machinery down here. The air smelled musty and damp.

At the end of a long dark passageway, they reached a heavy steel door protected by a CCTV camera. A tiny pin-prick of red light on the camera housing suggested the power was active here. Anton knocked three times, and with a scrape of metal, the top and bottom security bolts were released.

Inside, a uniformed guard waved them through into a modern interior. Beyond a pressure-sealed door, a further security checkpoint granted access to sub-level two. By the time they took their seats in the theatre-style auditorium Doctor Hardy and his team were ready to begin their presentation.

In the pit of the generous subterranean lecture theatre, Hardy introduced a series of awkward-looking eccentrics who mumbled through their prepared statements, barely looking up. Zed tried to follow but found the endless acronyms and technical language impenetrable. As far as he could tell, they were conducting more than a dozen parallel vaccine trials, two of which were showing promise, and worthy of further study. The rest had already been abandoned.

Zed was absent-mindedly looking around the room when he noticed the striking woman from the canteen sitting at the far end of the row in front of his. She was twiddling a strand of light brown hair, listening distractedly as she scribbled notes. She leaned back in her chair. Her navy-blue trouser suit, patent leather shoes and cashmere cardigan marked her out as civilian.

From where he was sitting, Zed could safely study her profile from a distance. There was something so familiar about her, yet he struggled to place her. A colleague of his wife? Another parent from school? Someone he had known when he was younger?

She wore silver hoop earrings, her shoulder-length hair pulled back into a ponytail. There was a healthy glow about her, considering how little daylight the team enjoyed down here. She had soft eyes, high cheekbones and naturally olive skin. Her cheeks seemed to redden, perhaps aware of his attention.

The meeting broke up, and the assembled crowd began to disperse, returning to their offices and laboratories. The object of his gaze seemed to linger, taking her time to put her papers back into a small leather briefcase. Zed took his chance and wandered over.

He pretended to look at a community noticeboard covered with faded sheets advertising book groups and football tournaments, lift shares and social clubs. Out of the corner of his eye, he waited for her to notice him. She abruptly stopped what she was doing and looked up at him.

"You don't remember me, do you?" she challenged.

At first, he wasn't sure if she was addressing him, but when she spoke again, there was no question.

"You're Zed Samuels, right?" She squinted, waiting for the penny to drop. "I'm Gillian Forrester. Carol's friend?"

As soon as she said the name Carol, he instantly made the

connection. She studied him carefully as he shook her hand, holding on a little longer than was strictly necessary, noticing the prosthetic.

"Of course, I'm so sorry. It's been how many years now?" He shook his head, still trying to recall whether she was Carol's disapproving flatmate.

"Nearly fifteen." She smiled. "You're forgiven."

"Remind me, you and Carol shared a place when she lived in Salisbury?"

"You see, you do remember. We did until I got my own place."

"What was that pub around the corner called?"

"The Cloisters?"

"That's right, off Friary Lane. That brings back memories."

"I used to love that place. You really didn't recognise me? I haven't changed that much, have I? You certainly haven't."

"I assure you, your powers of recognition are much better than mine."

"Did you keep in touch with Carol then after Salisbury?"

"Not really. We were always on and off. I could never work her out. I think she met someone else." He sighed, remembering how keen he had been on Carol Farman. "I suppose we drifted apart. Our careers took us in different directions… How long have you been working here? I didn't know you were a scientist."

"I'll take that as a compliment. Actually, I'm an epidemiologist."

"So what exactly does an epidemiologist do?"

"Basically we're data geeks. You should meet my team. Wall-to-wall nerds. We're the ones who come up with all the models and simulations to show the impact of different variables in an outbreak. Containment strategies, deployment of vaccination, quarantine procedures, that sort of thing."

"Interesting."

"If I'm honest, it's pretty dull." She laughed, noticing his raised eyebrows. "But since the outbreak, we're like rockstars round here."

"I would have thought Doctor Hardy's team got top billing?"

"We don't all work in a lab, you know. There are all sorts working here: geneticists, mathematicians, computer scientists, physicists, pathologists and programmers."

"So you must work with Doctor Hardy?"

"Not directly, but I know some of his team."

"What's he like?"

"Other than a charisma bypass, I hear he's all right once you get to know him. So how about you? What brings you to Porton?"

"Long story," he said, tapping the side of his nose. "I'm conducting an investigation."

"Does that mean you're sworn to secrecy?"

He leaned forward and half-whispered, "Not really, but then again, you might be able to help. I'm working for Colonel Abrahams. He's got me looking into the causes of the outbreak."

"But pandemics aren't your field, are they? I thought you were the Iraq specialist. What's the connection?"

"That's the sixty-four thousand dollar question. I need to rule out the possibility that this was an accidental leak or terrorist attack." He paused, suddenly struck by a thought. "I don't suppose you've ever heard of Project Wildfire?"

"Should I have?"

"No, I suppose not. It was an MoD research programme, set up after the second Iraq War. They were trying to determine whether a modified flu virus had potential as a bioweapon."

She sighed and raised her eyebrows. "You're not seriously

suggesting that the Millennial Virus was a bioweapon, are you? Don't you think we've looked at that already?"

"And?"

"We dismissed it, of course. There was no evidence whatsoever. It's a conspiracy theory, nothing more." She shrugged, checking her watch. "Look, I have somewhere I need to be right now, but why don't we meet in the bar? Buy me a drink, say 8pm, and I'll tell you what little I do know."

"There's a bar here?"

"Of course there's a bar here. What else would we do cooped up underground? It's one of the few advantages of being stuck with microbiologists and lab technicians. They make a mean homebrew."

"Okay, 8pm it is."

"I'll treat you to some good old-fashioned Porton hospitality." She winked.

"Best offer I've had in weeks. See you there, Gillian," he said, enunciating the syllables of her name, now he remembered it. She snorted in mock offence.

"Only my mum called me Gillian. Call me Gill."

Zed watched her leave with a boyish grin. Gill Forrester. He could remember her so clearly now. They had all been much younger back then. Their whole lives ahead of them. The few times he had stayed over at their shared flat, she was always so disapproving. Carol always said Gill was jealous, but she didn't seem in the slightest bit interested in him. She was so private. She never once brought anyone back.

Zed noticed a small commotion at the back of the lecture theatre as one of the junior assistants struggled to help Ephesus up from his seat back into the wheelchair. Seeing the old man again, Zed was struck by how old and frail he seemed. In any other circumstances, he would have been retired to a local care home for ex-service personnel. Unfortunately, right now, Porton needed Ephesus more than ever. No one knew more about chemical and biological weapons than he did. He had already proven those credentials, many times over, in that first series of meetings. Zed walked over to offer his assistance.

"Perhaps I can take you back to the library?" said Zed, interrupting the old man's tussle with his assistant.

"As long as you promise to go easy on him. He's worn out after your last conversation," said the young man protectively.

"Stop trying to mother me, Charles. Yes, Zed, that would be very kind. Thank you."

Zed smiled and steered him through the departing crowd towards a service elevator that would take them back above ground level. Once the metal gates were firmly closed, Zed pushed the oversize button, and with a lurch, they started their slow ascent. Ephesus turned to face him.

"I saw you talking to Gill Forrester. She's somewhat of a rising star around here. The major is not a fan. She's far too irreverent and subversive for his liking."

"I knew her from when I was based here, in the nineties."

"Is that so? Still, I wouldn't tell her too much. They're all as bad as each other. Covering their own backs."

"What makes you say that?"

"Nothing personal but you're an outsider. There's too much at stake. It's all right for me, I've got nothing left to lose. But the others? They have too much invested here."

"Well, they can't duck my investigation forever. The colonel won't allow it. Doctor Hardy's not untouchable."

"You shouldn't blame him. He's always had the best intentions."

"Didn't they say the same about Gerhard Schrader and the Nazis?"

"Doctor Hardy is no Schrader. He is a scientist first and foremost. Politics come a distant second. Before I became the archivist here, did you know I worked in the labs as a chemist? I've experienced at first hand the challenges Hardy faces. Too much political interference, too much scrutiny. The public would never understand what we do here."

"You mean research 'without limits'?"

"Nothing so dramatic. I mean that defending the nation against all known threats requires understanding one's adversary. Thinking as they do. Studying their weapons and tactics. Learning everything one can."

"That line between defensive and offensive research is all rather murky, don't you think? A bit chicken and egg. The end result is always a new arms race, just like the last."

"You're underestimating the purpose of a deterrent, the fear of retaliation. Think about how effective the possession of nuclear weapons has proven over the years. The same logic holds true of chemical and biological weapons. If we bury our heads in the sand and refuse to investigate the potential of bioweapons, it hands an unassailable advantage to our enemies. Why do you think Hitler didn't arm his V2 rockets with anthrax during the Blitz on London?"

"Because an escalation would have quickly led to Armageddon on European soil."

"Exactly. Because deterrents work."

"Am I to assume that Porton still holds illegal stockpiles of chemical weapons then?"

"I'll let you draw your own conclusions."

"What if there was a leak? Surely the very presence of those weapons on home soil poses an unacceptable threat to national security?"

"Not if precautions are taken. The risks are minuscule," he said, waving away Zed's concerns.

The service lift shuddered to a halt, and Zed slid open the heavy gates, bumping the wheelchair over onto the smooth linoleum walkway.

"Richard Nixon was right. Mankind already carries in its hands too many of the seeds of its own destruction. The world looked down on biological weapons as the poor man's nuclear weapon, but they were wrong," said Ephesus.

"Nixon always struck me as an unlikely flag carrier for peace."

"He is often misunderstood. It was Nixon who formally ended all offensive aspects of the US bioweapons programmes. He deserves our praise."

"Are you familiar with the Latin expression *Armis bella non venenis geri?*"

"No."

"It means war should be waged with weapons, not with poison."

"If you truly believe that, then you really are a fish out of water here."

"If you had seen at first hand the human cost of these despicable weapons, you'd understand. What Saddam did to those Iranian prisoners of war, in the name of science, was barbaric."

"You're lecturing a third-generation Polish Jew. My grandmother and grandfather were gassed at Auschwitz."

"Then how can you defend weapons research at Porton Down?"

"Were it not for human experimentation, we would only know half of what we now know. As ever, the interests of the many must outweigh the interests of the few."

"Hitler said something similar to justify the experiments that killed your grandparents."

"Hardly. That's totally different. Hitler believed that those of inferior racial or social classes had no rights. He called people like my grandparents the *Untermenschen*. Their lives were expendable. They had no intrinsic value as humans. They were fit only for scientific experimentation to support the war effort."

"And yet, here we are all these years later repeating those same mistakes. What about all those so-called volunteers they have locked up downstairs, forced into taking part in Doctor Hardy's experiments?"

"Rumours and scare stories spread by the locals. Those brave people are volunteers."

"Open your eyes, Ephesus. The major has snatch squads roaming beyond the fence, hunting for your so-called volunteers. Every week they bring back fresh meat for the grinder."

"Believe what you like. I choose to believe that the survival of the human race is what matters. This country is at war with itself. National security interests must come before medical ethics. In times of crisis, it has always been necessary to suspend the humanitarian rights that act as an impediment to progress. This is no time to worry about ethics."

"Ethics? Human rights? You bandy these terms around like bargaining chips in a casino."

"When you have lived as long as I have and seen what I have seen, can you really blame me for dispensing with political correctness?"

Zed took a deep breath, feeling like he had reached his limit. In the absence of outside scrutiny, he was beginning to think that Porton Down had cast aside all concerns of morality and ethics.

They had come to believe that their version of reality was absolute, whatever the cost to others.

"If you'll excuse me, I'm afraid I need some time to process all this," said Zed, shaking his head. "Is there somewhere I can work without being disturbed?"

"You can use my assistant's office. Third door on the right. It's not locked."

As Zed was gathering up the stack of papers he had made earlier, he relented. "Look, Ephesus. I'm grateful for your help. I really am. I'm sorry if my investigation is inconvenient for you."

"Don't take this so personally. We all want the truth. You shouldn't blame Doctor Hardy. He's just doing his job."

Something about that last sentence sounded confessional to Zed. The phrase "just doing his job" had haunted him for days. It reminded him of the Nuremberg trials after the Second World War. "*Befehl ist Befehl*" was the line used by so many to defend their actions when implicated in the extermination of six million Jews. They were just following orders.

It was as hollow a defence now as it was back then. Everyone had a choice, a moral responsibility, a conscience. The staff at Porton Down still had so many questions to answer.

# Chapter Twenty-two

At seven o'clock sharp, Sister Imelda collected Riley for dinner from a small attic bedroom on the top floor of Ventnor's Royal Hotel. She was led downstairs to a private room in the back corner of the old restaurant where assembled guests of Sister Theodora sat in silence, waiting for the last members of their party to arrive.

The sister said grace with her head bowed, pausing at the end of each sentence to lend resonance to her words. When she finished, quiet conversations resumed, and the woman next to Riley passed around a bowl of steamed rice served with a vegetable curry sauce and garden vegetables.

Riley became aware of Sister Theodora staring at her from the other side of the table. The sister cleared her throat and interrupted someone mid-sentence.

"I'm so glad you were able to join us, Riley. It gives me a proper chance to clear the air."

Riley paused mid-mouthful, wondering how the sister could possibly justify her complicity in the attack on Hurst that had cost Jack his life.

"I wanted to express my sincere regret for what happened. Sergeant Daniels placed me in an impossible situation."

"By Sergeant Daniels, I assume you mean Copper? I assure you, he's not the man you think he is."

"I should never have trusted him. He lied about their intentions. His concern for the welfare of those people was a smokescreen, I can see that now. It was all a ruse to gain entry to the castle. I suspect Sergeant Daniels is as much a victim in this as we all were. It's obvious he was being manipulated too."

"Copper is the worst of the lot."

"I had my suspicions, of course. We'd all heard the rumours. Back when I knew him, the sergeant was a pillar of society. His wife was in my church group. I can't understand what could happen to make a man change like that."

"Is it so hard to imagine? The breakdown, the collapse of institutions, the failure of the police and government to get a handle on the crisis. It was a bonfire of vanities. That newfound freedom corrupted too many in positions of power. It offered them all a licence of impunity."

"Good people are not so easily corrupted."

"It's all a game to Damian King. He delights in leading people astray. We all have pressure points, and he knows exactly which buttons to press."

"I knew the sergeant's wife." The sister sighed. "They had their marital issues, the same as every other couple. She always hinted at a darker side to his character, but I would never have imagined in a hundred years he was capable of this. He always seemed so resolute, so committed."

"We all have our demons."

"We have all sinned. I take comfort in the knowledge that sinners such as the sergeant will be made to feel the heavy hand of God's vengeance. This is a time of repentance for all of us. A chance for those who have sins to redeem themselves through changes in behaviour. As Jesus said: 'He that is without sin among you, let him first cast a stone'."

"Sister, good people died that night. Your faith in Copper, Sergeant Daniels, was totally misguided. You're as much to blame as anyone."

The sister put down her cutlery and leaned forward with renewed intensity. An unmistakable indignation burned brightly in her eyes. "I trust you're not suggesting I should be held responsible for what happened. My priority was towards the hundreds of starving refugees who came to that castle seeking shelter. I had no way of knowing what Briggs and King intended. What they did was unconscionable."

"It was cold-blooded murder. No one has seen Jack since that night."

"Why ever not? I remember Briggs's men saved him from drowning. After that, the soldiers were in control. I can't believe Corporal Flynn would have allowed anything to happen to Jack."

"Briggs was the reason Jack was in the water in the first place!" exclaimed Riley in disbelief.

Stella interjected, "So Jack was the man they pulled from the water?"

"Yes, Stella. Do you know what happened to him?"

"He was trying to get away. Briggs didn't rescue Jack; they captured him, dragged him back half-naked." She swallowed hard, closing her eyes, trying to picture the scene. "He was terrified, blue with cold. Someone told me that, after we left, they hanged him."

"That's just a rumour, child," said Sister Theodora, dismissing the idea. "The soldiers would never have allowed such a thing."

"You didn't see the murderous look in that man's eyes. They did, sister. One of them strung Jack up by the front entrance."

"Which man?"

"They called him King. He was the prisoner at Hurst."

"Why didn't Flynn stop him?" shouted Riley, banging the flat of her hands down on the table, silencing the conversations around the table.

"The only person who did anything was a woman. Terra."

"Terra was there?"

"Yes. She gave him her coat. He was freezing cold. I didn't know who she was. She was crying. I'm telling you, the soldiers did nothing."

"I had no idea," said Sister Theodora, shaking her head, "I must have been so preoccupied with the welfare of the refugees I didn't pay enough attention to what was happening. But if this is true, then killing Jack in cold blood is murder."

"This was revenge, pure and simple."

Sister Theodora fell silent for a few minutes, staring at her plate. Riley watched her with a mixture of pity and regret, wrong-footed by her inability to countenance a generalised propensity towards evil. Riley had seen the same flaw in Jack. He had assumed in others a predisposition towards charity, kindness and generosity. He believed that, given the right conditions, nurture would triumph over nature. They were all learning the hard way that the rules had been changed to suit people like Briggs and King. In an increasingly toxic moral vacuum, everyone else was still struggling to adapt.

Sister Theodora spoke quietly. "Rest assured, God is all-seeing. Their punishment will be terrible. In the end, justice will be done."

"I really hope you're right."

"My child, this whole pandemic was divine retribution."

"Sister," interrupted an eager woman at the far end of the table, "do you believe that those among us who have sinned will be similarly punished?"

Riley struggled to contain a smile.

"Those guilty of loose morality, certainly."

"It is said that an avenging angel stalks among us, spreading disease," added Sister Imelda.

"During the Spanish flu pandemic, they called the avenging angel 'The Spanish Lady'," said Sister Theodora. "She was a physical embodiment of death, dressed in a black flamenco dress. A skeletal woman whose face was hidden by a veil, holding a fan in one hand, impossible to resist." Her hand grasped the air as if reaching out to touch this ghost.

"In Greek mythology, they had something similar," added another. "They were called the Furies. An instrument of destiny."

"And you believe man's attempts to find a cure are futile?" asked Riley, amused by their religious fervour.

"God alone can spare our lives."

"Scientists have mocked our long-held beliefs and belittled Church leaders for too long."

"Is it really so wrong to try to save lives?"

"They're wrong to meddle," cautioned Sister Theodora. "God alone is the author of the evil brought upon us. He is the supreme judge and jury of our punishment. Those who ignored his Gospel deserve to be punished. Believe you me, St Mary's and Porton Down are stains upon this land. Places of such wickedness and immorality that God will unleash a great punishment on them. Like Sodom and Gomorrah, they will be reduced to ashes and columns of smoke."

"I understood from Chaplain Bennett that the Sisterhood was helping St Mary's and their search for a vaccine."

"The padre and I don't always see eye to eye, but we want the same thing. The final Day of Reckoning is nearly upon us when we will all be counted," Sister Theodora answered, rising from her seat. "The wrath of God does not distinguish between good and evil. We will all be buried in the same grave and suffer the same fate on this Earth. The difference will come in the Afterlife."

"The Afterlife?" said Riley, struggling to keep a straight face. She decided it was best not to mention that her father had raised her to be sceptical of all religious beliefs.

"Yes, when the sinners will be brought forward, one by one, to stand trembling before God and he will look upon them as they cry in horror, begging for mercy until he takes his vengeance upon them." Her voice rose to a crescendo. "The good will be welcomed into the Kingdom of Heaven, and the evil sentenced to the flames of an eternal fire in the darkness of Hell."

As she finished her "fire and brimstone" sermon, Riley realised that the room had fallen silent as everyone listened earnestly to the sister.

"What about all those who fall somewhere in between?" countered Riley. "Is it really so binary?"

"Ask yourself whether you are guilty of aping piety, maintaining the outward appearance of devotion without actually embracing God in your heart. Such hypocrisy and flattery reveal a rottenness in our very souls. By even entertaining thoughts of adultery, theft, or murder, we all deserve to be punished."

The others nodded, accepting this pronouncement. Riley pushed her half-finished plate away. She had lost her appetite.

\*\*\*\*

After dinner, Sister Imelda led Riley through to a well-furnished sitting room where a group of girls were playing cards on a Persian rug. An older woman sitting in a high-backed leather armchair was explaining the rules.

One of the girls looked up as the sister and Riley entered. The resemblance to Zed was unmistakable. In profile, she had handsome features, long eyelashes, and brown hair. She looked older than her thirteen years, already a woman. There was an earthy vitality and natural curiosity that Riley recognised from her father.

"Heather? Can we borrow you for a few minutes? I have someone I would like you to meet."

Rather reluctantly, the girl placed her cards on the rug and sidled over. A lock of hair tumbled across her face, half-concealing unmistakable defiance as she met Riley's gaze, waiting for someone to explain.

"Why don't we sit over here," said the sister, gesturing towards a quieter corner.

"If this is about what happened yesterday…" Heather began to say.

"Heather, this is Riley, a friend of your father's."

"My father?" She blinked back with no hint of emotion.

"Yes, your father sent me to collect you, to bring you to him," Riley said.

"My father is alive?" she repeated. "I don't understand. Why didn't he come himself?"

"It's a long story."

"No offence, lady, but you could be anyone. How do I know you're a friend of my dad's? The school warned us about people like you. You could be trying to abduct me."

"What?"

"Human traffickers forcing kids into slavery. It happens all the time."

"I can vouch for this woman," said the sister.

Heather continued to stare at Riley, sizing her up. "Okay. Let's say you are who you say you are. What's my dad doing that could possibly be more important than collecting his daughter?" She snorted in disbelief.

"He's working for the colonel. Ask him yourself when you see him tomorrow."

"Typical. He was always putting his work before his kids. If you expect me to trust you, prove to me that you know my dad."

"What do you want to know? He's tall, dark hair, beard, bit grumpy, prefers his own company. Mole on his left, no, right cheek, piercing blue eyes, bit like yours. He has a slight scar on his nose where he broke it playing rugby."

"Go on."

"Your mum is Tracy, and you have a younger brother called Connor. Satisfied?"

As Riley ran through the details, Heather's eyes seem to widen as she came to terms with the fact her father really was alive. Her expression was a mixture of emotions, oscillating between wonder and anger.

"You said my dad works for a colonel? But he's a teacher."

"Before he became a teacher, he worked for the Ministry of Defence. You would have been just a baby."

"You sure?"

"I've seen his service record. He was an Iraq specialist. Back in the nineties, he was assigned to the United Nations team investigating illegal weapons programmes. I'm not making this up," added Riley, noticing Heather's incredulous expression.

"It doesn't matter." Heather shook her head. "I couldn't care less if he's alive or dead. You don't know him like I do. He left us, moved out. Went to live somewhere else. He's a pig. We only got to see him once a month. What kind of father deserts his family when they need him most?"

"I'm sure you have every right to be angry. Not knowing what happened to you tore him apart. Your father is a good man."

"Mum promised he would find us. We waited so long for him. He was probably too busy saving himself."

"I know it's hard to believe but a lot of people owe your dad their lives, myself included. If it wasn't for him, I don't know what would have happened. Your father saved us. We would have been killed or driven away."

"You make out like he's some big hero. Well, he's not. He never had any time for us. He couldn't have cared less."

"When you're older, you'll understand."

"Don't patronise me. You weren't there. You don't know what happened. You only know his side of the story."

"Look, I'm sure I can't begin to imagine what you and your family went through. Whatever you may think, I'm sure your father had his reasons."

"What happened to your mother and brother, Heather?" asked Sister Imelda, trying to defuse the exchange.

"Mum died not long after the outbreak. Connor didn't make it through quarantine. For all I know, he's dead too." She closed her eyes in torment. "They said he had the virus, but if he had it, then I had it too."

"Not necessarily," corrected the sister. "It doesn't work like that. Do you know where they took him?"

"They put him with all the sick people. They said that if he got better he would be sent to the school. I waited and waited, but he never came."

Listening to Heather, it was impossible not to be moved. Underneath the overwhelming sense of sadness, Riley became aware of something she had not felt in some time. As mercenary as it sounded, if Zed's wife had passed away, it meant Zed was a free man, and Heather was her responsibility now.

# Chapter Twenty-three

After a troubled night's sleep disturbed by dark dreams of avenging angels and demons, Riley was woken early by the muffled noises of a large hotel stirring into life. Outside, it was still dark, but they needed to make an early start if they were going to make it to the hospital in good time.

After a meagre breakfast of porridge and fresh fruit, Riley found her way to a small stable where a young girl about Heather's age was fastening bridles to three horses.

"Can you ride?" asked the stablehand.

"Not since I was about your age," said Riley.

Heather appeared, struggling under the weight of a heavy leather saddle which she handed to the other girl.

"There's nothing to it. You'll be fine."

Did nothing phase this girl, thought Riley.

"Bess here is as gentle as they come. She'll not cause you any trouble, will you, Bess?" said the stablehand.

The large white mare whinnied, snorting at the attention. Riley was helped up into the saddle as the party of three was led out into the courtyard.

"How far is St Mary's from here?" she asked Sister Imelda.

"Around fifteen miles. With any luck, we should arrive by lunchtime."

Bess was as well behaved as Riley could have hoped for, trotting obediently behind the other horses. Beyond the outskirts of Ventnor, the gentle slope made for a tiring climb. Once they got beyond the narrow tree-covered lanes flanked by high bushes on either side, the landscape opened up, and they enjoyed views across wide open fields and farmland.

Alongside the road were numerous caravan parks and tented areas where the allies had created temporary accommodation for several hundred new arrivals. Even at this early hour, there were teams toiling in the fields, digging irrigation ditches and turning the soil. The dirt-smeared faces of diligent workers stared up at the passing group with mild amusement, hands on hips. Riley had to admit, the three women on horseback made a curious spectacle.

Sister Imelda insisted they stayed off the main roads, keeping to bridleways and farm tracks where there were fewer vehicles. They stopped at a footbridge over a small stream to refill their water bottles and stretch. The sister had brought with her some oat biscuits, and a hard cheese wrapped in greaseproof paper. She cut the cheese into slices with a pocket knife and handed them around.

Riley had been keeping her eye on Heather. The girl seemed taciturn and withdrawn.

"You're not still sulking about seeing your father, are you?"

"It's my choice," she argued.

"Heather, you're still a minor," Sister Imelda pointed out. "You belong with your father."

"None of the other girls are being forced to leave."

"That's because most of them are orphans. They'd give anything to see their families again. You do realise that, don't you? If I were you, I'd be a bit more grateful to all the people taking time out to reunite you with your father."

"I don't know why you're bothering. He couldn't care less about his family."

"You're wrong. No father ever loved his children more." In truth, Riley too was puzzled about Zed's relationship with his daughter. The amateur psychologist in her was whispering that these behaviours were most likely inherited. Zed's own father was probably to blame. A poor role model who never showed his son any real affection. Zed would have grown up emotionally stunted in some way. Perhaps the Sisterhood had encouraged these same feelings in Heather. Riley knew they were no great fans of Zed.

Sister Imelda listened to their exchange, finishing her snack before packing everything into the rucksack. She checked the map and traced their route with her finger. Without looking up, she addressed a question to no one in particular.

"Have you ever asked yourselves why the virus struck the mainland so hard but the island was mostly spared?"

"Geography, I suppose," suggested Riley.

"So you think the Solent acted as a natural barrier to infection?"

"That is unless you're going to tell us it was actually God's will and that we brought this on ourselves?" mocked Riley, rolling her eyes. "I suppose the islanders were all saints."

"Don't listen to her, Heather. You should not make fun of what we believe."

"The sister believes God hears everything. That we should 'seal our lips with silence'."

"Enough of your cheek, young lady."

"Sorry, sister, my father was an atheist. He taught me to be sceptical of all religion."

"You must believe in something."

"Personal responsibility, shared accountability, and reciprocity."

"Then it is not too late to change your ways. All our lives have been spared so that we may give thanks for God's mercy. I choose to believe that this was no natural disaster. The sins on the mainland were simply too great to go unpunished. Sister Theodora tells us that the island was spared so that we may begin again. A new promised land: a new Jerusalem."

"Amen." Heather sighed.

"Your vile generation deserves as much blame as any," continued Sister Imelda.

"What did we ever do?"

"Did you never wonder why this pestilence is called the Millennial Virus?"

"I don't know, because it was discovered around the millennium?"

"No, because it was sent to cleanse young people of their sins."

"Why us?"

"Your generation was singled out for the greatest punishment. Social media was the catalyst for your transgressions."

"We deserved to die for a little screen time?"

"You all displayed such wanton gluttony, greed, and pride with your phones and devices, your Facechats and your Snapbooks."

"Not all of us. I had one of those cheap push-button phones. The only vice I had was some snake game."

"Then perhaps that is why you were spared."

Heather and Riley exchanged a glance, and they continued on in silence for a while, lost in their thoughts.

On the farm track just ahead of them, three youths stepped

out from behind a small shed. One brandished an iron bar hanging loosely from one hand. He gestured for the three riders to stop. Riley glanced behind them and noticed three more teenagers sealing off the way they had come.

Heather's horse whinnied and reared up a little, frightened by the youth closest to her. He reached out to try and grab the bridle, but the horse shook its head, baring its teeth.

"Easy now," soothed the sister, patting her restless horse. "What do you want?" Her voice trembled slightly.

"Perhaps you ladies missed the sign back there." The youth grinned, two teeth missing from his lower jaw, and pointed behind them. "This here is a private road. If you want to get through, then you have to pay, like everyone else."

"Who are you then? Dick Turpin?" Riley mocked, while her fingers groped for the small blade she kept hidden in her belt buckle. "How old are you lot, anyway?"

"Old enough," said the tallest of them, who looked about fifteen. "Why don't you start by giving me that watch?"

"This old thing? It's practically worthless."

"I'll be the judge of that. Anything that works without batteries is worth something."

"Now look here," demanded the sister unconvincingly. "You wouldn't want us to tell the soldiers at the next checkpoint about a bunch of junior highwaymen trying to hold people to ransom, would you?"

"Soldiers? You mean Dad's Army? We're not frightened of that lot." He laughed. "Briggs runs things around here."

"Briggs?"

"That's right. If you ain't got nothing to offer..." His voice trailed off. "Well, then, I'm sure we could work something out. Why don't you get off those horses and we can discuss this in my office?" he sneered, gesturing towards the farm building nearest them.

Riley glanced nervously at Heather, whose horse was the more unsettled, pacing around. The sound of the huge mare's hooves on the driveway made the young men keep their distance. Heather did not seem in the least bit frightened. She was sizing up the three lads in front, while keeping an eye on the more timid ones behind. Riley was worried Heather might do something stupid to precipitate matters.

Without warning, Heather clipped her heels and drove the mare forward, shouting him on, making straight for the boy in front. As she galloped past, the teenager dived out of the way. Heather beckoned to Riley and the sister to follow.

One of the boys made a grab for Riley's bridle, but he was too slow, and the horse barged him out of the way, knocking him flat on his back. The iron rod in his hand was sent clanking down onto the concrete. The sister didn't hold back and set off after them.

When they caught up with each other, Riley could hear Heather roaring with laughter, like this was all one big joke to her. Over her shoulder, she was relieved to see the youths had not tried to follow.

"That was reckless and stupid, Heather. What if they had grabbed one of us?"

"They were just kids. Bullies like them are everywhere. Relax."

The sister was flush with all the excitement. There was a hint of a smile on her lips. "Well done, Heather. For a moment, I thought we were in trouble. I don't know what we'd have done without you."

Riley shook her head disapprovingly. "You could have got us all killed, that's what."

****

Riley and the others reached St Mary's just after lunch. She wished she could have photographed the look on the soldiers' faces as the women approached on horseback. By the time they reached the gate, a crowd had gathered.

"Where can we leave our horses, officer?"

The silver-haired guard at the checkpoint was dumbstruck, scratching at the back of his neck. "Can't say I know, really. I suppose you could put them behind the mortuary. Just follow the road down to the pond. There's a small park with some grass. You can't miss it."

They thanked the guards and entered the heavily fortified compound that surrounded the hospital buildings. Inside the perimeter fence, there was a bustle about the place. Smoke rose from the large chimney that dominated the main building where Riley had left Adele the day before. Everyone would be wondering where she had got to. Riley had never expected to leave the girl there overnight.

They dismounted and tied the horses to a railing that fenced off one side of the small park, leaving the mares to nibble at the grass.

At the reception desk, an officious-looking woman rifled through a sheaf of paper that contained lists of visitor names. "Adele Crabtree, yes, she's in the Louis Pasteur ward, second floor. First stairwell you come to on your right-hand side," she said, pointing down the corridor.

Riley recognised the same nurse from the previous day waiting outside. There was a serious look on her face that worried her.

"Thank God you're here. We had no way to reach you."

"What is it?"

"There have been some unexpected complications. I'm afraid that Adele had an adverse reaction to her treatment. Let me get the doctor, and he can explain properly."

# Chapter Twenty-four

After several wrong turns and dead ends, Zed finally found the staff bar situated on level three of the underground bunker complex at Porton Down. The lighting in here was so low it took him a moment to locate the person he was meeting.

"I was beginning to think you weren't coming," said Gill, seeing Zed squinting at the doorway.

"Sorry, I'm late, I got completely lost. This nightclub lighting doesn't help either."

"Don't worry. This is probably the only bar on the planet where a female can sit in peace without being harassed by some idiot."

Zed looked around the bar and saw what she meant. Everyone was working or reading, minding their own business. The couple in the corner were engaged in quiet conversation, interrupted by the occasional laugh.

The Porton staff had tried their best to make the place look like a traditional English pub, with stools at the bar, dart board, pool table, soft furnishings, and a large TV screen in the corner. Multicoloured chalk on the blackboard announced that they would be screening a recording of the 1981 FA Cup final between Tottenham and Manchester City with "that wonder goal by Ricky Villa". Set around the walls were several seating areas with large black PVC sofas, several of them occupied.

The barman made eye contact as Zed approached, rubbing his hands together at the prospect of a new customer.

"What'll it be?"

"I'll have two more of whatever the lady over there is drinking." He pointed to Gill back at her table as she raised her half-empty glass of dark brown stout.

"Two pints of Porton Dark then." When he'd finished pouring the drinks, the barman held out his hand for payment. "That'll be two tokens, please."

Zed tapped his pockets and looked around despairingly at Gillian. She held aloft two red casino-style chips which he collected and handed to the barman. Placing the pints on the table without spilling them, he sank into the leather-backed chair with a weary sigh. He took a sip and winced at the bitter taste.

"I know what you're thinking. It takes a bit of getting used to."

"You could say that."

She leaned forward in her chair. "So, listen, about Wildfire, I asked my team already, discretely, of course. A few of the senior guys have been here much longer than me. Even they only knew bits and pieces. Happy to share, if that might help you out."

"Absolutely. I'm still getting the run-around. I'll take anything. Right now, it's like a giant jigsaw puzzle with most of the pieces missing."

"I'm not surprised. First thing they teach us around here is not to ask questions. Everything is compartmentalised. Fraternisation between different teams is discouraged. From the sound of things, this project was off the books. "

"I get that impression. Don't tell me, the only people with

oversight of different programmes would be Doctor Hardy and Major Donnelly?"

"Correct. But since the outbreak, there's been a steady collapse of those Chinese walls, at least unofficially. It turns out they had competing teams working in parallel, completely unaware that anyone else was involved."

"I'm sure this place still has a lot of secrets to give up. One hundred years of military experiments must leave a few scars."

"If you only knew the half of it."

"Why did no one blow the whistle?"

"Look, we're watched all the time. You just get used to it," she said, noticing his scepticism. "See that guy over there by the dartboard, the one reading his book?"

Zed scanned the room and found the ball-headed man she was referring to. His body was angled towards them so that he could surreptitiously observe them, but he was too far away to overhear their conversation.

"He looks harmless enough. How do you know he's watching us?"

"Trust me, he followed me down here. Since you arrived, I've noticed some new faces hanging around the department, spying on us. I don't care. What are they going to do? Lock me up for having a drink with an old friend?"

Zed was encouraged by her defiance. If more people spoke up, maybe they would never have got into this mess in the first place, he thought to himself.

"What you need to understand is that here at Porton, we maintain a deliberate separation from the norms of society. First and foremost, we are scientists, we're taught to be objective. I can see you judging us, but you're wrong to do so."

"Look, I appreciate your reality is somewhat different to

mine, by necessity. I'm just trying to get to the truth, that's all."
He shrugged, taking another sip from his glass. The stout was
less bitter second time around, but still had a spice kick to it.

"Look, as soon as my teammate started talking about
Wildfire, we all agreed that there must have been a link with the
Common Cold Research Unit. They spent decades researching
the flu virus. It's an open secret. Maybe their work was merged
with Project Wildfire. My friend mentioned something about an
Iraqi translator who was relocated here. Does that mean anything
to you?"

Zed sat forward in his chair. "Does he remember a name or
what they looked like? Male, female?"

"He was a bit hazy on the details, but I can ask."

"The colonel passed me various reports from the CCRU. It
closed down in 1989."

"Weirdly, the CCRU is what first brought me to Porton."

"You were a volunteer?"

"I was desperate for money. Carol said they were looking for
young, healthy professional people to take part in a medical trial
for a prototype vaccine. It was easy money. I stayed here for a
week."

"How much did they pay you?"

"Not much, but there were a few of us who did it together. It
was a laugh, a cheap holiday. They told us the vaccine was
completely harmless. They injected us and then watched as we
did all these mental and physical challenges. It was like a
recruitment programme. They'd roll out the red carpet, make us
feel welcome, encourage us to come back for the next round of
trials. What can I say? I must have dazzled them with my charm
and intellect. They ended up offering me an internship."

"I always wondered who volunteered for those things. They

make it sound so safe, and then you hear horror stories about toxic shock and adverse reactions. If you ask me, putting your life in someone else's hands like that is terribly irresponsible," said Zed bluntly.

"Not really. Clinical trials are the best way to learn about infections and how to stop them. Sure, they're not without risk. A few years ago, we did a lot of work around Gulf War Syndrome. There was pending litigation claiming MoD negligence."

"I remember. Did they ever figure out why so many veterans returned from the Gulf with life-changing conditions?"

"The symptoms were very broad. Headaches, asthma, dermatitis, chest pain, chronic fatigue, poor concentration. There were a number of theories."

"Didn't some people claim it was exposure to Saddam's chemical weapons?"

"That's right. Others blamed the Uranium-tipped munitions the allies used, but a silent majority believed that the inoculations themselves were to blame."

"What do you mean?"

"The MoD was paranoid that one of the vaccine shots was contaminated. They worried it might have been rushed out and not properly tested. Or used in combination with other shots in a short period. The interaction of those different vaccines can prove unpredictable. It's likely that in the rush to vaccinate the troops, they didn't spend sufficient time checking whether they were safe or not."

"So you think Gulf War Syndrome could have been self-inflicted?"

"I'm just saying it's possible."

"If that's true, it would be the worst own goal since Lee

Dixon's back pass for Arsenal against Coventry in 1991."

She seemed confused by the reference.

"Forget it. It doesn't matter. So, reading between the lines, are you saying there could be a parallel between Gulf War Syndrome and the Millennial Virus?"

"How do you mean?"

"That the flu shot could have had unexpected side effects."

"No, I wasn't suggesting that. I'm just saying that a lot of the work we do here is actually preventative. Vaccines rather than weapons. Don't go twisting my words to your purpose."

"How much do you know much about the Spanish flu pandemic?"

"I wouldn't be very good at my job if I didn't know much. Spanish flu, H1N1, bubonic plague. They're all core case studies. We use them to model future pandemics. Why do you ask?"

"Based on your models, is it reasonable to expect that the outbreak could die out abruptly, like the Spanish flu?"

"Sometimes one strain dies out, and a milder one takes its place. Mutation is non-linear. It can happen very suddenly. But frustratingly, it remains somewhat of a mystery."

"There's another question that's always puzzled me…"

"Go on."

"Why did they call it the Millennial Virus?"

"Good question. It's actually a common misconception. When the outbreak first started, we identified anomalies in the data that suggested those most prone to fatality were young adults. At the time, the worse affected were born around the time of the millennium, hence the name."

"Oh, I see. So it's just coincidence. There's no connection with the millennium itself?"

"It was the same with Spanish flu. It had a disproportionate impact on young adults. Around the end of the First World War, it was assumed that the higher mortality was related to wartime service in the trenches, or at least their exposure to others infected with the virus. Years later, they actually discovered that young adults were simply more susceptible, though they're still not clear why this is the case. In the modern age, some experts blame lower rates of inoculation, but I'm not convinced."

"Did they ever figure out the causes of the Spanish flu outbreak?"

"Not definitively. Some European experts suggested that infected poultry and pigs imported from Fort Riley in Kansas resulted in the flu virus jumping directly from birds and pigs to humans. Understandably, the Americans disagreed."

"I suppose they're hardly going to admit to causing a global pandemic."

"A few years ago, I was corresponding with a US team trying to discover the origin of Spanish flu and why it proved so deadly. They managed to recreate the original 1918 strain from tissue samples they found frozen in Alaska. They were able to prove conclusively that most of the victims died from an overreaction of their immune system rather than the virus itself."

"I've read about this. Is that what they call a cytokine storm?"

"I'm impressed," she mocked, inclining her head. "If true, it would in part explain why the flu had such a dramatic effect on young adults. It stands to reason that their immune systems would have never experienced a virus similar to this. Their bodies simply reacted more strongly to rid the body of infection, and the consequences of that would have been terminal for the victim."

"So an overreaction of the immune system can actually be more deadly than the virus it's attempting to counter?"

"Precisely. A team at the University of Ghent in Belgium were trialling a new universal flu vaccine. They were able to fully sequence the influenza genome for the first time. That allowed them to substitute new antigens into a pre-existing vaccine strain and reprogramme the immune system to attack the flu virus. Unfortunately, their prototype was still in development when the outbreak occurred."

"So, let's assume that Porton has been tracking the Millennial Virus for nearly two decades. Why then has it proved so difficult to manufacture an effective flu vaccine?"

"It's much more complicated than it sounds. I'm no expert, but from a modelling point of view, the continual mutation of the virus means it's simply not possible to develop a vaccine until an outbreak actually occurs. They often don't know what they're dealing with until the first cases present themselves. Different strains of the virus compete with one another all the time, sometimes exchanging genetic material with other viruses."

"So if your job is to model these outbreaks and predict the next mutations, it sounds like there's a lot of guesswork involved?"

"You'd be surprised. We're not just throwing darts at a board, blindfolded," she said, pointing to the bar. "We make heavy use of tech. AI and phylogenetic analysis."

"If you're trying to impress me…"

"It's sort of like building a family tree, to help determine the biological ancestry of a virus and map how it might spread geographically."

"And that helps you understand why one strain is more lethal than another?"

"It provides clues as to how the virus might further mutate. It's not a perfect science, but it allows us to zero in on the correct vaccine formulation and potential treatments for those already infected."

"Between the two of us, how far away do you think we are from developing an effective vaccine, realistically?"

She shrugged her shoulders, taking another swig from her half-empty glass. "Hard to say."

"Doctor Hardy mentioned in his speech that they have two promising clinical trials."

"Don't believe the hype. Even if they have had a breakthrough, the trials will be very small scale. They'll have no way of knowing how effective it will be on larger groups. It could take months, if not years."

"The stakes are sky-high. Every week that goes by, tens of thousands more people will die in this country alone."

"I'm aware of that, but expectations are unrealistic."

"So what does this testing process involve?"

"Typically, they would expose the test subject to a weakened strain of the virus to encourage the body to develop antibodies. This acquired immunity creates what we call immunological memory so that the next time they are exposed, the body knows how to combat infection."

"So once they've landed on something that is effective, they can presumably mass-produce the vaccine quickly?"

"It depends. They have some state-of-the-art tech here. They use bioreactors to accelerate the manufacture of cell cultures so that, in theory, they should be able to produce a sufficient quantity of the vaccine to be able to deal with a large-scale outbreak."

"What about the trials that are not successful? What happens to the test subjects?"

She looked over her shoulder to make sure they weren't being overheard. "In extreme cases, injecting test subjects with even a trace element of the virus can be terminal. In others, those cytokine storms we touched on can ravage the body, produce swelling, rashes, fatigue, nausea, or worse, even organ failure."

"Do people know the risks when they volunteer for those trials?"

"What do you want me to say? I'm not going to lie to you."

"But, Gill, those people still have rights. Just because they're volunteers doesn't mean they're expendable."

"They gave their consent. They all signed a waiver."

"I doubt that constituted informed consent in the eyes of the law."

"Look, we're well aware of our duty of care. We fulfil our obligations."

Just then an orange flashing strobe blinked on and off in the corner, followed swiftly by the deafening wail of an alarm. For a moment, everyone in the bar seemed to stare at the strobe and each other in disbelief, until a recorded announcement began looping.

"Warning: containment breach. Please remain calm and await further instructions."

"Is this real world or just a drill?" asked Zed.

"I don't know. It wouldn't be a drill at this time." She pointed at the double doors to the corridor which had a red light flashing above them as the air seals activated around the doorway and the room began pressurising.

"What's happening?"

"Any kind of leak detected in the facility and each room seals automatically."

"So we're stuck here?"

"Until the all-clear is given, yes. Trust me, there are worse places to be stuck."

Zed seemed reassured by her sangfroid. "If we're not going anywhere, got any more of those drinks tokens?"

"We don't have time for that," she said, jumping to her feet. "We need to find out what's going on. There's a phone over here."

# Chapter Twenty-five

"There's no answer," said Gill, as she dialled the next number on the phone list attached to the wall. "Where is everyone?"

"Try Major Donnelly's office. The colonel said he would be there."

She hung up and dialled a different extension number. Someone answered on the first ring.

"Hello? Yes, it's Gill Forrester." She paused, listening to the request for identification. "Of course, it's Delta-Sierra-Zulu seven-three-one. I was looking for Major Donnelly or Colonel Abrahams. Well, if you can let them know that I'm here in the staff bar with Zed Samuels. Yes, of course, let me just do a head count. There are seventeen of us here. Can you tell me what's going on?"

She listened for a few seconds, nodding and exchanging concerned looks with Zed.

"Okay. Perhaps you can let us know as soon as they know more. We're on extension 4378." She replaced the receiver. "He said they've had sensor alarms sounding in multiple sectors."

"What does that mean?"

"That there's been some sort of breach event. Look up there," she said, pointing to a grey electrical box near the door. "There are sensors in every underground section that go off if they detect any kind of airborne toxin. It's only happened once before in all the time I've been here."

"False alarm?"

"It's possible. The laboratories are two floors below us. As soon as they detect a leak, all sections automatically seal to limit the spread of whatever set off the alarm. It didn't sound like they knew where it originated from."

"So it could be serious?"

"I doubt it. It's unlikely to be coming from one of the P4 containment laboratories. Those are the ones that handle dangerous pathogens."

"How can you be so sure?"

"All the P4 labs are completely secure. Each unit has negative pressure, meaning if there was ever a leak, air leaks in, not out. All the technicians work in pairs in positive pressure suits with their own filtered air supply. The units dealing with airborne pathogens have their own separate air supply. There's no way it could have contaminated other areas."

"So if it didn't originate from the labs, where did it come from?"

"It's too early to say. There's a computer terminal in the office over there we can try. Let's see what we can find out."

Zed followed Gill through behind the bar to a room where three disused workstations sat, gathering dust. She powered up the nearest one and, after a short delay, keyed in her security details. She pulled up the system diagnostics and navigated through several submenus before she found what she was looking for. She sat down, and her fingers flew over the keyboard, entering command codes.

"As soon as the sensors detect a toxin, the computer starts

analysing the sample to see if it can find a match against a pre-built database of biohazards. It's fairly rudimentary, but it should give us a fast-cycle answer to what we're dealing with so we can adjust our response. Doesn't look like it's finished its analysis yet."

The vent above their head had fallen eerily silent. It was already noticeably warmer now the air conditioning system had stopped working.

"The backup ventilation system should have kicked in by now."

"It's going to get really hot down here without it."

"Even if the main supply is cut off, the backup system should keep recycling and filtering the air in this section." She pulled up the screen showing the ventilation system and noticed several amber warnings. "That's odd. Those backup systems seem to be down as well. I can try rebooting from here." She tried a couple of entry commands but shook her head. "I don't have access. It needs a system administrator to activate."

She opened a dialogue window and drafted a message to the maintenance team to look into it. The phone on the wall beside the bar started ringing, and they heard one of the others answer.

"Gill Forrester? Hold on."

Gill leapt up and ran through between the tables to snatch the receiver from the barman.

"Thanks. Gill Forrester speaking. Yes, sir." There was a long pause as she listened carefully. "Do we know when this happened? Okay. How many did you say? I don't see how that's possible, do you? Yes, I'm on workstation D487 if you need to reach me again. Can you tell the maintenance team they need to get the air back on in here as soon as they can? It's beginning to get really stuffy."

She put the handset back in its cradle on top of the base station and addressed the sixteen others stuck in this section. "The whole base is on lockdown. Looks like we're going to be here for a while."

"Did they say how many casualties?" asked Zed.

She ran her hand through her hair, retying her ponytail. "They're still waiting to hear back from some of the other sections. So far they have five people seriously injured and another fifteen with milder symptoms."

"Any idea yet what it could be?"

"Well, that's the odd thing," she whispered, leaning in. "From his description, it sounded more like exposure to a chemical agent to me. No biological agent I know works that fast. He said the victims were struggling to breathe, chest pains, unexplained rash on exposed skin, loss of motor skills. Let's see if the computer has completed its analysis."

She rekeyed her ID and password and progressed through to the sensor analysis area of the intranet. The status was showing as "Red: Organophosphate Detected". She clicked on the item to display further information, and it showed a paragraph of standard text offering a list of potential hazards and their symptoms.

"Organophosphate? You mean like a garden fertiliser?"

"Except a thousand times more deadly. Organophosphates include gases like VX, Sarin, Tabun. Really nasty stuff."

"Do you mean to tell me you still keep stockpiles of those gases here?"

"I have no idea."

"How do we know if we're safe in here? Shouldn't we evacuate to the surface?"

"And risk further contamination? This is the safest place.

We're sealed off from the rest of the facility."

"What about oxygen levels?"

"It's a big room, and there are only seventeen of us. If we stay inactive, then we should be fine until they rescue us."

"We better make ourselves comfortable then."

"You can. I've got work to do. Just because we're stuck here doesn't mean we're completely useless. Why don't you come and join me in the office? We can carry on talking. You haven't asked me what I found out about Doctor Hardy yet."

****

Zed watched Gill work from the comfort of a threadbare two-seater sofa. He had tried lying down with a cushion under his head, but the furniture was just too small, his legs hanging over the armrest. Whichever position he tried, he just couldn't relax.

"Will you stop fidgeting! You're worse than my old dog."

"Sorry," he said, sitting up. "Give me something to do then."

"I'm waiting for a couple of database queries to come back, and they're eating up all my processing power. This machine is ancient," she replied, gesturing at the grey monitor and PC tower under the desk. "No wonder no one uses it any more. Ask me more questions, if you like. I can multi-task."

"Tell me again what you're looking for."

"Clues. I'm trying to figure out how an organophosphate could have gotten into the ventilation system."

"Sabotage?"

"It would have to be an inside job."

"Why would anyone do that?"

"To disrupt Doctor Hardy's team, for starters."

At the bottom of her screen, an incoming message icon started blinking, and she clicked on it.

"It's Freddie. He's one of my team. He says: 'Sorry to hear you're stuck in the bar. Count yourself lucky! The rest of us are chained to our desks in the office, watching the temperature climb, with no food or water. We've just been told they're evacuating the building room by room, so hopefully, it shouldn't be much longer. Have a drink for us, won't you?' Cheeky sod."

She typed something back and turned to face Zed. "They're clearing the floor above, so with any luck, it shouldn't be too much longer."

Just then there was a massive rumble, and everything in the room began to shake, tipping books from the shelf on to the floor and disrupting the power. The lights flickered off, and her monitor went dead, plunging the room into darkness. After a couple of seconds, the dim emergency lighting in the other room cut in.

"That sounded like an explosion to me," said Gill. She picked up the phone and began pushing buttons to dial out. There was no ringtone. "It's dead. Phone lines are down. That's never happened before. Grab that torch, will you, just in case the emergency lighting fails. Let's go and find the others. They'll be worried."

\*\*\*\*

In the main bar area, dust was drifting down from the ceiling, settling on every surface. Several of the group were still hiding under tables, fearing the worst. The barman was already sweeping up the broken bottles and smashed glasses.

Over by the sealed metal doors, a woman had her face pressed to the small square of glass, trying to see what was going on in the corridor.

"Can you see anything?"

"Nothing. Power must be out on the whole floor," she lamented, rattling the handle again.

Gill reached out and put a hand on her shoulder. "Why don't you come and sit down over here?"

She led the frightened woman over to one of the tables where two people were getting back to their feet. They made room for her on the leather sofa.

"Why hasn't the air come back on? It's getting hot in here," someone asked.

"It shouldn't be much longer now. I just spoke to my team on level two. They're being evacuated. We all need to sit down and conserve as much air as possible. Everyone stay hydrated."

She led Zed away back to the office, eager to see if they could get the computer back online.

"How long do you think we've got?" whispered Zed.

"A few hours max. After that, it's going to be unbearable in here."

\*\*\*\*

Gill removed her jacket, and they both sat down on the small two-seater sofa, its tired springs groaning in displeasure under their combined weight. Zed wiggled into the corner against the cushioned armrest, his forearm prickling with perspiration. He could feel the warmth of Gill's skin through the trouser suit. She noticed his discomfort and patted his leg with a little too much familiarity for Zed's liking.

"Nothing like a crisis to bring people together."

"I'm glad we got to spend some time together. I'm just sorry it has to be under these circumstances."

Her breathing was heavy, as if the heat and accumulation of carbon dioxide in the room were beginning to have an impact on them both. The people around them were languishing on the floor or slumped on chairs, staying as still as possible, trying to conserve energy.

"So you never got married then? Any kids?" he asked, wiping sweat from his brow.

"No. I was never one for settling down. Married to my work, I suppose. Maybe I never found the right person." She sighed unconvincingly. "I wouldn't have minded kids. I just didn't want the relationship bit that went with that. Does that make me sound like a monster?"

"Not at all. After my separation, that's kind of where I landed. It wasn't ideal. I got used to seeing my kids on my own terms without all the emotional baggage that goes with it."

Out of the corner of his eye, he noticed Gill staring at him with a knowing smile.

"Still wearing that ring though?" she teased.

"Old habits die hard, I suppose. What about you?"

"Me? Oh, don't pretend you didn't know already. I'm sure Carol told you."

"Told me what?"

"I always had a massive crush on you. It's why Carol and I argued so much."

"Really?" he said, turning to face her, unsure whether she was joking on not. "I always thought you…" He hesitated. "Played for the other team…"

"Is that what Carol told you? She's such a conniving cow. She only said that because she knew I liked you. She probably felt threatened, thought I was going to steal you away from her. I can't believe she said that."

He rolled his head back against the wall, staring up at the ceiling. "Wow. I should be flattered. Women fighting over me. That's never happened before."

"A heartbreaker like you? Don't be so coy."

"Me?" Zed laughed, amused by her attention.

"Yes, you. You're just too thick-skinned to notice."

"Well, it's news to me."

"Carol always said you had the emotional intelligence of a rhino."

"She always did have a way with words."

"And something tells me that ring on your finger is more a deterrent than a treasured memento."

"This old thing?" he said, twiddling his wedding band. "It simply means that until I know what happened to my wife, I'm still married."

"So there is someone else. Come on. Spill the beans. Who is she?"

"It's nothing. We're good mates, that's all."

"Pull the other one. Name?"

"Look, it's a long story. She's called Riley. We've been through a lot together. She saved my life, twice."

"I knew it. You're such a romantic, holding a secret torch for her."

"It's not like that. Anyway, what about you? There must be someone special here at Porton? A good-looking single woman like you?"

"Here? Are you joking? We're not exactly spoiled for choice in the scientific community, unless you're into goatees and bad teeth." Her breathing seemed laboured. "Anyway, Major Donnelly doesn't approve of personal relationships. It compromises security. This whole place is like one giant fishbowl. Mind you, it doesn't exactly stop people." She winked, her eyes struggling to focus.

Zed was also finding it harder to talk and breathe, clutching at his chest. It had grown very quiet in the bar area as everyone fell silent. Perhaps they were sleeping. He was beginning to feel so tired, his thoughts slurred. He yawned, overcome with fatigue. Her hand fumbled for his wrist, holding on tightly.

"Zed, I'm frightened."

\*\*\*\*

When he opened his eyes again, he was aware of the repeated dull thud of someone knocking on the door and voices coming from outside the room. It took him a moment to get his bearings. Gill was asleep beside him. She refused to stir when he nudged her in the ribs.

The knocking continued, and with a superhuman effort he levered himself upright, collapsing onto the linoleum floor, dry retching on all fours. He winced at the pain from his forearm that had taken the force of the impact. He crawled across the floor between the tables towards the doors, stopping every few moments to catch his breath.

The banging at the door intensified. He was nearly there. He could see masked faces in the glass panel staring down at him, muffled voices shouting for him to do something. Their instructions were indistinct. It was like they were spoken in a foreign language. His vision was blurred, and the shapes danced in front of his eyes.

A woman's voice he recognised sounded so close. Crying out in desperation.

The glass panel in the sealed door buckled and then smashed inwards, releasing a delicious breath of cooler air from the corridor outside. The sound of a heavy axe set to work on the door, splintering the wood around the glass and handle, just large enough for a hand to reach through, groping for the release mechanism. Zed could see it now, just a few inches from their fingertips. His breaths were still short, but with one massive effort he braced himself against the wall and pushed the large green door release button before he slumped to the floor.

Four figures dressed in biohazard suits surged towards him, checking his pulse and looping the strap for an oxygen mask around the back of his head, before attending to the inert body of what he assumed to be Gill a few feet away. Within seconds, his head began to clear as he greedily gulped down the oxygen, tuning into the conversations around him.

"Non-responsive. Quickly get her into the corridor and start CPR."

It was a relief she was still alive. He could only assume that the oxygen levels had fallen faster than expected in the bar area and that slowly but surely they had been slipping towards asphyxia. Another half an hour and they would all have succumbed to oxygen starvation.

"Zed, can you hear me? It's Colonel Abrahams. How are you feeling?" he asked, helping Zed upright. "We came as quickly as we could, but we had our own problems to deal with."

Zed rubbed the back of his head, feeling for injury, checking his arms and legs for bruising or fractures. He seemed fine, but, in his experience, it paid to be careful. His senses were clearing, and when he spoke, his voice sounded hoarse and unfamiliar.

"I'm fine, colonel. What happened? Gill said it was an organophosphate."

"We're not sure what happened, but the whole base is on lockdown."

"Was it a leak from one of the labs?"

"We don't believe so."

"Then where the hell did it come from?"

"We think it was a deliberate act of sabotage."

"But why?"

"We don't know yet, but it sounds like someone fed nerve gas into the lab's ventilation system."

"My God."

Zed had a hundred questions but was too tired to articulate them. He shook his head and coughed for a full ten seconds, his throat dry. The colonel handed him a bottle of water.

"Let's get you out of here and back to the upper levels."

"What about Gill?"

"Someone will bring her up separately. She's safe now."

# Chapter Twenty-six

In the near darkness of the headmaster's house, Terra waited all evening for Briggs to come back from the hospital. Her face was pressed against the glass of the first-floor window, keeping watch over the drive. She was still clutching a cold mug of tea to her chest.

Finally, after several frustrating hours, headlights on high beam announced Briggs's return. She rushed down to reception just as the doors were flung open and his entourage surged in. He spotted her and shook his head.

"Not now, Terra."

"Please, babe. I need to talk to you."

He paused for a second, gesturing for the others to continue without him. "You were an embarrassment back there."

"Me? An embarrassment? I'm trying to stop you from making the biggest mistake of your life."

"Look, I'm not in the mood. I told you, you're too late."

"You said we were in this together. Stop shutting me out."

"I'm not going to let you mess this up."

"This whole plan is half-baked."

"Stop sticking your nose in where it's not wanted. You're a liability."

"That's King talking," she said, shaking her head. "You're better than them. You really want to be remembered as a mass murderer?"

He pushed her away again. "It's out of my hands."

"It's never too late. Please, I refuse to believe that. Think about the kids, all those innocent kids. There must be some other way for us to get what we want? This can't be a zero-sum-game."

"Trust me, there isn't."

"King's manipulating you—"

He slapped her hard across the cheek, his eye twitching. She clutched at her stinging face, but the pain subsided quickly. This was nothing compared to the previous times he had hurt her.

"If you try and get in the way again…" he said, leaving the threat hanging. "King is not as forgiving as I am."

"I don't care about King. I care about you." She reached out to touch his face, but he pushed her hand away.

"Don't try my patience."

"I'm begging you, please. I can't stand by and watch you destroy everything we've worked so hard for. Those deaths will be on your conscience forever."

Briggs studied her carefully, and his stance seemed to soften. He let out a deep breath and looked deep into her eyes, tenderly stroking her face. She smiled in the hope that he wasn't altogether lost to her. She still had some influence. He was yet completely immune to her power.

For a moment, she imagined an inner conflict of indecision and uncertainty caught between two opposing poles. He pulled her towards him, squeezing the breath from her lungs in a bear-like embrace.

For a few delicious seconds, she felt totally vulnerable, all pretence gone. She had faked it for so long, sometimes she couldn't tell what was real any more. She tried to remember the point when she had stopped pretending.

His eyes narrowed and the moment was gone. He disentangled himself and pushed her away. "Like you said, I'm going to a place you can't follow."

"I didn't mean it like that."

"This is for the best. Trust me, you don't have the stomach for this," he decided, twisting her arm painfully to the side.

"Wait, what are you doing?"

She was shaking her head, terrified what he might do. She knew all too well what he was capable of. Those who ceased to please Briggs didn't tend to last long.

"I can't have you messing up again. Nasser?" he shouted to the guard standing at the door. "Put her in the professor's room. She'll be out of harm's way there."

"Briggs, please," she pleaded as he strode away without looking back.

Her cries turned to sobs as she was led towards the professor's cell; a spartan cloister with an iron-framed single bed, a writing table and a wooden chair. The guard pushed her into the cell, slammed the door and turned the key, leaving her to cry herself to sleep in the darkness.

****

Terra tried to get some rest but found it impossible to relax. She rolled over, trying to get comfortable on the bare mattress and pillow, her mind churning on their earlier exchanges.

There was still no sign of the professor, and it was getting late. A noise from outside made her sit up. She heard a key in the lock, and the heavy oak door swung open.

It took her a moment to recognise the figure standing in the doorway.

"Well, well, well. Behold, the Whore of Babylon." King laughed, holding up his hands. "The false Queen who conspires against us."

"If you've come to taunt me, you're wasting your time."

"Come, come. Don't give up so easily. Briggs may not be able to see what you're up to, but I can."

Terra was confused and struggled to maintain her composure. Had Victor sold her out? Had he betrayed her confidence in some desperate attempt to win back favour?

"I don't know what you think you know—" she started.

"There's no point pretending. You're not as good as you think you are. Don't flatter yourself. I can read you like a book." He waved his hand like a magician casting a spell. "Don't worry, your secret is safe with me."

"What the hell are you talking about?"

"You, Terra. You've got more faces than Big Ben, but you got sloppy, didn't you? You thought you were cleverer than everyone else. Victor's told me everything."

"Victor knows nothing. He's lying."

"Well, I've known Victor for a long time, longer than you, that's for sure. I know what he's capable of. He's ambitious, I'll give him that, but he doesn't have your guile. He told me the truth about your little pact."

"The truth? That he's working his own angle, like everyone else around here."

"Don't get me wrong, if I had my way, you'd be strung up like Jack, but Victor convinced me that we still need you. Forget your lovers' tiff; Briggs is still very much attached to you. Mind you, what do you think Briggs would say if I told him the truth?"

"He'll believe me, of course. He trusts me."

"You really think he'll listen to you after the stunt you pulled earlier," mocked King. "Not any more."

"Look, your blackmail won't work with me. You think you can manipulate everyone, don't you?"

"You of all people should know that everyone has their weak spot. You just need to know where to exert pressure."

"Did you tell Jack that, before you killed him?"

"You know what Jack's problem was? He refused to face up to reality. He seriously thought he could save the world, one person at a time."

"Jack was a good man."

"You wouldn't say that if you knew how many hours I had to listen to him babbling on about there being 'good in everyone' and how you just had to 'find it and channel it'. He was an idiot. I'm not surprised you managed to twist him around your little finger."

"People like you never built anything; you only know how to destroy. Jack and I made that Hurst community what it was. We were partners. Before you came along and ruined everything."

"In your own special way, I suppose you cared for him, didn't you? Like a virus needs its host. How did Jack never figure you out? You're so gauche, so obvious. For someone who claimed to be a 'good judge of character', he was blind as a bat."

"Don't underestimate me, King," she snorted.

"Oh, I don't. I take my hat off to you, Terra. After what you've done with Briggs? I'm your biggest fan. But then you've had a life-time of practice, haven't you? I thought Victor was manipulative, but he's a schoolboy compared to you."

"You've got me all wrong. I don't suffer from delusions of grandeur. I'm just doing what I can to survive."

"We're all susceptible, even you. You've been fooling other people so long, you fool yourself. You think you're in control, but you're not."

"I never claimed I was in control. I leave that to you geniuses."

"Have you ever heard of Stockholm Syndrome? They should use you as a case study. Long-term captives developing imaginary feelings for their captor. They think they're in love with the person who's been inflicting pain and suffering. It sounds messed up, but it's scientifically proven."

Terra was silently digging her fingernails into her wrist, trying to keep her composure, but finding it more and more difficult. Perhaps he was right. She had been doing this for so long, she had forgotten what real feelings were like. She felt exposed and defenceless, fighting back tears of anger, tears of shame at what she'd done.

"Just admit it. You're using Briggs to get what you want, just like you used Jack."

She shook her head, refusing to confess. She knew that denial and silence were her best defence.

"So what's Victor promised you then? I suppose you're going to shack up with him next, once you've got rid of Briggs. Or is that your moment to break free of the shackles and reincarnate yourself as something new? Start calling yourself Debbie again?"

Terra stared back at him dumbstruck. She had told no one, not even Victor. She decided to ignore the question, hoping he would let it go.

"I wouldn't trust Victor if he was the last man on earth."

"Maybe it will come to that."

"You just called me Debbie…" She couldn't resist temptation.

"Debbie Sanderson. That's your real name, isn't it? One of the officers we captured at Osbourne House said he knew you, but he couldn't figure out why you blanked him at the reception. You pretended not to know him, didn't you? It took him a while to figure out why."

"Whatever he told you, it's not true."

"At first, he couldn't remember the specifics, just the rumours of some ugly little fraud. What did you do? Con someone out of their life savings? He remembers you disappearing, leaving the country all of a sudden. You just walked out on your life, left everyone and everything behind. He said you had a kid. You abandoned her when you thought you'd been rumbled."

"It wasn't like that. Izzy lived with her father. It was all a big misunderstanding."

"What was it? Drug habit? Gambling?"

"Look, I was stupid, that's all. I borrowed from the wrong people, ran up some debts."

"Shit happens. It's not like you killed anyone. The guilt's the same. Must be hard to live with though, walking out on a kid like that?"

"Yeah, it hurts," she conceded. "Not knowing what happened to her. She'd be nearly six now."

"We've all done worse. Look, this virus did us all a favour. It wiped our slates clean, gave us a fresh start without all that..." He searched for the right word. "Baggage."

"I did what I had to do. That's all."

He was staring at her, trying to figure her out, enjoying her discomfort. She decided to return fire with fire.

"Don't tell me, you're the only honest person around here? A man like you, you must have deserted people you cared about? How did you learn to live with yourself?"

"Let's just say, unlike the rest of you, I prefer to keep my past where it belongs: in the past."

"Man of mystery, eh? From the accent I'm guessing you grew up near Manchester," she gambled, wiping away the tears. "Somewhere posh though, like Altrincham."

"Close. Go on." He nodded, folding his arms.

"But I reckon you lived abroad." Her eyes narrowed. "Judging from the sun-damaged skin and the clipped vowels, you spent time in South Africa?"

"You have a good ear. I'll give you that."

"You're not the only one who can read people."

"Touché. I've clearly met my match."

"Sometimes it's subtle. A word here, an intonation there."

"No, you spent far too long with that South African Neanderthal back at Hurst."

"You mean Will? How did you—"

"He used to visit me in the dungeon each week to remind me what we did to him at the hospital. He was very expressive with his fists."

"Well, he's no friend of mine."

His eyebrows furrowed, unsure whether she was telling the truth. "I always wondered what Briggs saw in you. He could have had anyone, but he chose you. I could never figure that out, before now. Maybe now I see."

"Look, King. Help me get out of here, and I'll do whatever you want me to."

"Victor was right about you. You'd turn on anyone in a moment to save yourself. Morals of an alley cat."

"Just give me a second chance. I'm begging you."

"Why would I help you, Terra? You're right where I want you." He sniffed loudly and turned to leave. "It's a shame really. You falling out of favour with Briggs, just when things are about to get interesting."

He slammed the door behind him as he left, and she heard the key turn in the lock. His footsteps grew fainter down the corridor.

# Chapter Twenty-seven

Riley, Heather and Sister Imelda were shown into a small waiting room at St Mary's hospital while the nurse went to find the doctor who had been treating Adele.

The sister put her hand on Riley's shoulder. "She's in good hands. They know what they're doing here."

"I hope you're right."

"Baby Adam has been here several times for tests."

Riley closed her eyes, clutching her hands together in supplication. She spotted the doctor and nurse conferring at the end of the corridor.

A stooped Asian man in a white coat shuffled towards them, his rubber-soled shoes squeaking on the linoleum floor tiles. There was a sheen about him that suggested things had not gone their way in the operating theatre. Beads of sweat on his top lip caught the light.

"Adele's a fighter. It was touch and go for a while, but she's stable now. She's had quite a night while we fought the infection," he said, shaking his head. "You can go straight in. She's sitting up and talking. She'll be relieved to see you. I warn you, she's on some strong medication so she might be a little confused."

"Do you know what happened?"

"We've not seen a reaction like this before, and we've been running these trials for days now."

"What are you testing?"

"We call it 197C. It's a phase two trial. There are twelve of them in Adele's volunteer group. We administer the vaccine to each of them and then monitor how their immune systems respond."

"So what should have happened?"

"We inject a trace amount of the virus itself. Trying out different variations until we find the one that works best. Inevitably there's a degree of unpredictability. There's a lot of trial and error. Hundreds of different combinations."

"Doctor, Adele knew the risks when she signed up. She wanted to help."

"She's a courageous girl. We're very grateful."

"Was the reaction something to do with her leukaemia?"

"We're not sure why but the leukaemia seems to be causing her body to produce very high levels of antigens. Antigens fight the infection. At 5.30pm yesterday, she was injected with 197C. Almost immediately she experienced respiratory problems. Something similar to anaphylactic shock."

"That sounds serious."

"In rare cases, the body's immune system overreacts to an infection and literally starts attacking itself."

"Why?"

"Well, vaccines generally work by fooling the immune system into thinking it's being attacked. Injecting a trace quantity of the virus allows the body to develop defensive capabilities, but sometimes, when the human body encounters a virus for the first time, in trying to destroy the virus, the body actually starts destroying itself. It's caused by a defective feedback loop where too many immune cells are activated. It can be very dangerous if not treated immediately."

"Then you know what to do?"

"Luckily, we caught it early. We've been using a dialysis machine to filter out the cytokines and other toxins. Generally speaking, anti-inflammatory and immunosuppressive drugs have limited impact. She's still got a high fever, but she's stable."

"Well enough for visitors?"

"Yes, go ahead," said the nurse, glancing at the doctor for his approval. "She was asking after you when she came round."

Inside the small wardroom were six beds, each of them occupied. Adele was at the far end, hidden behind a curtain to afford some privacy from the other adult patients. Surrounding her bed were several machines connecting wires and sensors to her wrist and forehead.

Adele stirred as she saw Riley, but was too weak to move her head. There was a rash across her exposed neck and chest. Riley gripped the little girl's hand and felt Adele faintly squeeze back. The effort seemed all too much for her. Her swollen fingers resembled fat little sausages, tender to the touch. Riley lifted the hand a few inches and gestured to the nurse.

"It's fairly common. Nothing to worry about. The infection is dying down now. You should have seen them earlier."

Adele seemed to stir at the sound of voices, her lips parting, but no sound came out.

"How are you feeling, sweetie?"

"Bit better."

"You're going to be fine now," said Riley, stroking her hair and resting her hand on her burning cheek. It felt clammy to the touch. The beep of the monitor next to the bed struck a regular rhythm, watching the pulse chart bounce up and down.

Adele closed her eyes, leaning her head against Riley's hand, enjoying the cool touch.

"She'll be exhausted," added the nurse. "She's been up and down all morning. Why don't I get you all a chair?"

"Actually, I really should be getting back," said the sister, readying herself to leave. "I don't want to leave it too late, travelling on my own, especially with the likes of those boys we met roaming the countryside, taking the law into their own hands. I'll stick to the main road this time."

Riley stepped back from the bed and hugged the sister. "I appreciate you bringing us here. Promise me you'll look after Stella and Adam?"

"I will." She smiled, turning to face Heather. "Good luck. I hope you find your father. He's a good man."

Heather nodded but showed no sign of emotion. When the sister had gone, they settled in to watch Adele sleep, listening to the conversations around them. In the bed next door to her sleeping figure was an elderly man watching the pair of them.

"She's lucky to get visitors."

"Are you one of the volunteers too?" asked Heather, studying the man. He had silver hair, but Riley suspected he was younger than he appeared. There was something off about him, something that didn't seem right.

"I know what you're thinking. Why do we do it? I can't pretend it hasn't taken its toll. I'm fifty-three, you know. People say I look much older."

Riley tried her best to hide her surprise. From his wrinkled hands and age spots, she might have said he was in his late seventies. She imagined the cumulative effects of all these tests had accelerated the ageing process.

The man rolled up his sleeve and revealed a series of scars and what looked like burns on his skin. "That's nothing. You should see the rest of me."

As he began to unbutton his shirt and expose his chest and left shoulder, Riley glimpsed the true extent of his sacrifice. Heather recoiled and turned her head away to the amusement of the recumbent man. He was horribly disfigured by successive exposure to whatever it was they had tested on him.

"I've been volunteering for medical trials for years. Ever heard of the CCRU?"

"Cybernetics?"

"No, the Common Cold Research Unit based up near Porton Down. Closed years ago. They used to call me the Duracell Bunny. You remember the TV ad. Always coming back for more? They said I was longer lasting." He smirked playfully.

"Must have been before my time." Heather shrugged.

"When they were doing their PR campaigns in all the national newspapers in the 1980s, I got interviewed in the *Daily Telegraph* and *The Guardian*. They even did a piece in *Vogue* magazine, if you can believe that."

Riley angled her body back towards Adele, but the man continued undeterred. He seemed determined to make the most of the opportunity to talk.

"Back in the day, they used to advertise a week's stay at the CCRU as the best package holiday anywhere. All sorts were going there. Students, small groups, married couples, all getting away from it, earning a bit of spare cash, staying in nice accommodation. We all thought we were doing our bit, helping science develop a cure for the common cold. Little did we know it would all end up like this."

"What do you mean?"

He leaned across and lowered his voice. "No one really believed they were trying to find a cure for the cold. They were testing all these different strains, trying to find out more about the virus."

"I don't understand. Why did you volunteer if you suspected they had ulterior motives?"

"I've never really thought about it." He shrugged. "But I'd do it again in an instant. That's why we volunteer, isn't it? If a few years less of my life might mean I can help save others, then it's a small sacrifice, don't you think?" He rolled his head back against the pillow and struggled to catch his breath as if the effort of the conversation was all too much for him.

Riley was startled by a loud noise outside their building and the distant wail of a siren. Looking outside, she couldn't see anything unusual and returned to her seat. She had always wondered what made people like him put themselves forward for human trials. The naivety of the volunteer surprised her. She remembered Zed's barely believable stories about clandestine weapons testing up at Porton Down. By all accounts, after the war, the search for a cure for the common cold had been a cover story for countless chemical and biological weapons programmes. Zed had suggested there were dozens of conspiracy theories swirling around at that time.

She thought back to the waiver she had signed for Adele to take part in the trial. Riley wondered whether the volunteers were ever truly made aware of the risks they were exposing themselves to. Without that knowledge, could volunteers ever be said to have given their informed consent? She doubted it.

It made her deeply suspicious of what was really going on at Porton Down and St Mary's. Hearing the sister liken them to Sodom and Gomorrah had struck a chord. Volunteers like Adele were expendable. Their suffering or death was an acceptable price to pay in the search for a vaccine.

The siren outside continued unabated and Riley went to ask the nurse what was going on.

"It's probably just another drill. They do them all the time here."

Through bitter experience, Riley knew better than to ignore a warning. She grabbed Heather by the hand and hurried down the stairs to the main entrance. There was a small group of soldiers barking orders at the receptionist as they approached, pointing towards the main gate.

"What's going on, corporal?" she asked the man standing nearby, who looked a little flustered.

"We're getting reports of a security situation on the island. The base is on lockdown until we know more."

Heather and Riley backed away slowly towards the stairs.

"You said we'd be safe here with all the soldiers around."

"I know, Heather. Like he said, I'm sure it's just a precaution."

# Chapter Twenty-eight

Riley and Heather stood outside the main building at St Mary's watching a flurry of activity. Soldiers were hurrying from one end of the complex to the other, laden with weapons and equipment. The pair felt like spare wheels, wondering what they could do to help.

"I thought you'd be long gone by now," said Riley, noticing Sister Imelda striding back towards them.

"So did I. They've told me I can't leave. No one's allowed in or out," she said, bustling towards the staircase. "I'm going to take it up with the captain. They can't hold me against my will, it's outrageous."

"Did they give a reason?"

"I don't think they know themselves," she said, making a beeline for the reception desk. "They're just following orders."

They followed the sister back inside as she fought her way to the front of the line, nudging military personnel out of the way.

"I need to speak to the captain," she demanded of the receptionist.

"He's in the main office." She pointed down the road. "Third building on your right-hand side."

All three of them bustled up the road, passing a long line of vehicles moving slowly towards the front gate. Above the distant wail of the siren, the unmistakable sound of a belligerent mob could be heard.

At the entrance to the command centre, a single guard watched their approach with some suspicion.

"IDs, please?" he insisted.

Riley went through the motions of checking her pockets and made as if she had forgotten hers.

"No pass, no entry. You know the rules, ladies."

Turning her back on the guard, Riley whispered, "Come on. Let's try round the back."

Next to a fire door, propped open with a brick, they found a group of uniformed men and women smoking. Riley nodded casually at one of them and went through.

"Excuse me," shouted one of the men, but it was too late. They were already inside.

The emergency exit led through to a darkened service area that would normally have been filled with the hum of machinery. The air conditioning unit stood idle, salvaged for parts, dismantled and broken. Beyond the swing door, along a narrow corridor were various blue hospital signs, that had been repurposed with handwritten notices directing visitors to all the various different departments. The captain's office was on the third floor.

An armed guard on the stairwell seemed distracted, cupping his ear as if trying to listen to an exchange on his walkie-talkie. Riley strode towards him, bold as brass. He held his hand out to ask her to wait, but she ignored him.

"We're here to see the captain."

He acknowledged an instruction over the radio and turned back to give Riley and the others his full attention. "He's upstairs with the commander and some Americans. And you are?" he said, reaching for his clipboard.

"Just tell him Riley and Sister Imelda are here. He knows us."

He relayed the message and stepped aside, directing them up the stairs. The padre was waiting for them on the next floor, hands on hips.

"So this must be Heather." He nodded in her direction. "Glad to see you found each other. Look, sister, I'm sorry, but if this is a social visit, your timing is pretty terrible."

"I've just been told I'm not allowed to leave. Am I to understand we're prisoners here?"

"It's a precautionary measure. The whole base is on lockdown."

"Then what the hell's going on?"

"You're welcome to wait, and I can explain afterwards. We're just in the middle of briefing the Americans."

The sister was not in a forgiving mood, so he gestured for them to follow. Weaving behind a maze of desks and workstations bustling with military types, he led them into a small office with the name Bennett stencilled on the door, and a wooden cross underneath.

"We're getting initial reports of a fresh outbreak."

"Where?" interrupted Riley, worried about the rest of her team in Freshwater.

"Camp Three. It's just south of here. They're reporting nearly a dozen infections in one day."

"How? Haven't most people on the island had their booster shots?"

"We don't yet know. We only found out this morning."

"Could someone have got through?"

"I doubt it. All the beaches and landing points are patrolled.

We have checkpoints on every road. The island is watched day and night."

"Then the virus must have found a way."

"They're doing everything they can to contain the outbreak. We just have to hope that we can nip this in the bud."

"And if that doesn't work?"

"It has to work."

"Well, then," said the sister in resignation, "if we're all stuck here, what can we do to help? Perhaps I could lead some prayers."

"I was going to suggest that. There's a chapel at the far end of the compound. There will be a lot of worried people here who would appreciate your spiritual guidance. I'll let everyone know you'll be there for them."

"What about all the people outside the fence?" said Riley, pointing out the window towards the main gate where she could see several hundred locals clamouring to be allowed in.

"There's not much we can do for them. They can't stay there. They'll be told to disperse."

There was a knock at the door. One of the orderlies stuck his head round, tapping his watch.

"Now, if you'll excuse me, Lieutenant Peterson is waiting."

Riley joined Heather on the red leather bench seat where she had left her. She slumped back against the wall and blew out her cheeks.

"Those poor bastards," she whispered under her breath. "I knew this place was too good to be true."

"They told us it would be safe."

"I know, Heather. It's no one's fault. Somehow, I guess nature finds a way. If it's anything like the last outbreak, then our best bet is to get as far away from towns and cities as possible.

The south and the west of the island are probably best."

"Nowhere's safe," cautioned the sister. "This is what Sister Theodora said would happen: that the first outbreak was just the beginning."

"We should never have left Hurst," conceded Riley. "I've never felt truly safe on this island."

**** 

After nearly half an hour's wait, the conference room door opened and the meeting participants filtered out. Riley could see Lieutenant Peterson and his team members still in the room, poring over a map of the Isle of Wight.

She spotted Sergeant Jones waiting patiently by the door. He looked up and smiled, making his excuses to leave.

"Riley, how are you?" he said, looking her up and down, before enveloping her in his arms. "And who's this?"

"This is Zed's daughter, Heather."

"Of course, you have your old man's eyes." He grinned, studying her carefully.

"How do you know my father?"

"We've been in a few scrapes together." He shrugged. "For a pencil-pusher, he's got real guts. How's his arm healing up?"

"His arm?"

"My bad. I take it you haven't seen your father yet?"

"Sorry, Heather," said Riley, shaking her head. "It must have slipped my mind. He lost his arm in an incident."

"Look, I didn't even know he was alive until yesterday."

"We think he's up at Porton Down with the colonel."

"That's what I heard too. Hey, listen, I guess we're all sticking around here for a while. If the boss doesn't need me, you want to grab a coffee?"

"Go ahead, I'll keep the sister company," said Heather. "We'll be at the chapel."

\*\*\*\*

Riley was reluctant to leave Heather alone for too long, so they collected a styrofoam cup of black coffee each and took a quick stroll around the compound. They talked and talked, about life at Freshwater, what they had both seen and heard, their hopes and fears, and the family and friends they had both lost. Pete had been married with two kids; a boy and a girl.

"I was never the settling down type," admitted Riley. "Do you think you'll ever make it back home, find out what happened to them?"

"Sometimes I think it's better not knowing. Then I can just pretend this is just an extended tour of duty. That I'll be home in time for Thanksgiving or my daughter's birthday."

"I suppose we all hoped that the US would have been better prepared, better funded. The UK's so overpopulated. Didn't geography help slow the outbreak in North America?"

"I don't think distance made much of a difference. Turns out we were all vulnerable. Everything was so interconnected back then with people travelling far and wide. Life's different now."

His shoulders seemed to slump talking about home. It was the same reason people avoided talking about the way things were before the outbreak. It was just too painful.

"When was the last time you got a proper break?" she asked, touching his arm.

He blew out his cheeks. "It's been a while. I had a couple of days back in September. Just took off on a bicycle along the south coast and back up."

"Must have been nice to tour the island, see what's changed."

"It's slowly getting better. I've been overseeing the new recruits. They're doing more of the heavy lifting work now. Seven units so far, three more coming online by the end of the year."

"So you think things are on the up?"

"Until this new outbreak, I'd say we had everything under control."

"What about the rebels?"

"I wouldn't worry about them. We're keeping an eye on them."

"Do you know what happened to Terra and the professor?"

"We tracked Briggs back to Carisbrooke Castle, but then they disappeared a few days ago. We think they may have gone back to the mainland. Maybe joined up with Damian King's group."

"If you know where King and Briggs are holed up, why don't you just take them out, once and for all?"

Jones found that amusing for some unknown reason. "Unfortunately it's not that simple."

"I don't see why not. You've done it before. Remember? You rescued us."

"That was different. Do you have any idea how much trouble I got into last time I listened to you and Zed? I disobeyed a direct order, nearly lost my command. They threatened me with court martial if I turn vigilante again."

"Seriously?"

"Seriously. So don't go fluttering those eyelashes and ask me to do you any more favours."

"You know they hanged Jack. Strung him up outside the castle gates like some common criminal."

"I'm sorry, okay? There was nothing we could have done. I didn't like it any more than you did. It was a miracle we got the rest of you out."

"Are you worried about the professor?"

"If we find out he's been helping them with their research, then we'll be forced to take steps."

"You mean silence him?"

"If we can't get him out, then yes, that's exactly what I mean."

# Chapter Twenty-nine

The colonel half-supported, half-dragged Zed back up the underground passages beneath Porton Down, making for the stairwell to the upper levels.

In Zed's semi-delirious state, the hazmat suits made the colonel's men seem like astronauts exploring an unknown world. Their movements were exaggerated, their features distorted and monstrous. Through the perspex panel of the bright yellow hazmat suit, he could see the colonel inside, perspiring heavily from the effort.

Zed started to laugh, prompting concerned looks from those around him. Every time he tried to remove his oxygen mask, the colonel would stop and insist he place it back over his mouth and nose.

Their small group reached a sealed airtight door giving access to the next zone. It was marked "Authorised Personnel Only". They pushed the button to release the outer airlock. It was just large enough to accommodate five men at a time. Once the outer door was sealed, they were exposed to a high-pressure jet of air from above. They turned around and let the air stream wash over their suits and clothing.

When the decontamination cycle was complete, the

colonel rattled the handle, waiting for the locking mechanism to disengage. For some reason, it remained closed. From a speaker embedded in the ceiling came a woman's voice, polite but firm.

"I'm holding you here, gentlemen. Major Donnelly's orders."

"Perhaps you can let him know that Colonel Matthew Abrahams is outside." He smiled towards the camera, head tilted.

There was a short delay before Major Donnelly's voice came over the intercom. "Welcome back, colonel. We've had to seal this section until we know what we're dealing with. We can't risk further contamination. Is Corporal Chappell with you?"

The corporal pressed himself against the airlock door and manoeuvred the colonel to the side before taking his place in front of the camera.

"Sir, we found no signs of contamination or toxins on the lower levels. Casualties seemed to be suffering from dehydration and exhaustion only. All the sensors down there were green."

"How's Mr Samuels doing? Any signs of exposure?"

"Nothing at all. Other than oxygen deprivation, he seems fine."

The speaker fell silent again. Zed braced himself against the wall. He felt a little giddy, but other than that, as far as he could tell, he was unharmed.

"Very well. Proceed to the medical centre. They'll check him over. The rest of you get scrubbed down. As soon as we've finished our sweep and got a full situation report, I'll come and find you."

The colonel nodded, waiting for his turn to exit the airlock. The medical centre was on sub-level one, back the way they had come.

"Really, I'm fine," said Zed, "I'd rather get back to work."

"For once in your life, just follow orders, will you?" barked the colonel.

**** 

With a hiss of air, the inner door to the medical centre cracked open, and they were helped through by one of the nurses. She wore a face mask and gloves but no other protection. She led them through to a shower area where they were asked to remove their clothing.

"Is this really necessary?" asked the colonel irritably, stripping to his underwear. His thighs were white and podgy under the bright strip lights.

"Sorry, colonel. We have our orders. It will only take a minute."

They were handed some antibacterial soap that smelled like hospital disinfectant. The nurse scrubbed them down with a long-handled brush. Their groans and protestations at the jet of cold water brought a smile to the nurse's face. She made no secret of her amusement at their discomfort and embarrassment.

When their ignominious treatment was over, she handed them each a grey-green towelling dressing robe and escorted them through to a changing room where army-issue clothing was neatly folded in various sizes.

They were ushered barefoot through another sealed doorway into a long corridor that was abuzz with activity. The communal space had been recommissioned as a clearing centre for others like them who had been disinfected and were now waiting to return to their own sections. A guard showed their group through to a meeting room where they were told to wait for the major.

A few minutes later, there was a rap at the door, and the major and his entourage surged inside. He slapped a pile of papers on the meeting room table.

"The lab just got back to us. They confirmed the agent is VX."

"How is that even possible?"

"We don't know yet."

"How many casualties?"

"So far, we have three confirmed dead and more than a dozen injured, but we're expecting many more. Lab Four seems to be the worst affected."

"Could this have been a spill?"

"This was no accident. There's been no research involving organophosphates for decades here."

"Then where the hell did it come from?"

The major unrolled a large map showing the Porton Down site and the various buildings within the perimeter fence.

"Over here, there's a secure biohazard storage bunker deep underground that contains trace quantities of various pathogens and agents. We keep them for training purposes. I suppose it's possible that there could have been a break-in."

"Has anyone at ground level confirmed that?" challenged the colonel.

"We're still trying to get confirmation, but unfortunately, our communication systems are out temporarily."

"Since when?"

"A few hours ago."

The colonel's face turned puce with rage.

"Until we know for sure, we have to assume that the whole base is under attack," conceded the major. "We don't even know whether the perimeter is still secure."

"We're trying to restore contact with the surface."

Zed noticed the colour slowly drain from the colonel's face as if he were facing up to his worst fears for the first time.

"We know there was an explosion inside the perimeter fence around 2110 hours. We think it came from here," he said, pointing to an area shaded grey on the map. "In the maintenance area. We lost power to some of the lower levels around the same time. For some reason, the backup systems never kicked in. I have an electrical team working on rerouting power. Most of the surface camera systems are offline. Right now we're blind."

"What's your best guess, major?"

"To target the underground labs would have required someone on the inside."

"A disgruntled employee? Someone with a grudge against Porton?"

"There must be one or two of those around," muttered Zed under his breath.

"But why attack the labs?"

"Lab Four is where the vaccine trials were taking place. It'll be out of action until we can get a clean-up crew in there. Several of the clinical trials team were injured. Worse-case scenario: we're potentially looking at a delay of several weeks."

"It gets worse," continued the major. "We've lost power to the refrigeration units where we keep stocks of vaccine. We've rigged a couple of portable generators down there, but it's not a long-term fix."

"So this was a deliberate attempt to disrupt our operations, pure and simple," confirmed the major.

"And the agent? What exactly are we dealing with?"

"VX is extremely toxic. Invisible, no taste, takes the victim entirely unawares. Nasty stuff. By the time you realise it's there, it's already too late."

"Presumably banned under various conventions?"

"Yes, but several countries still maintained large stockpiles, which is why we train our forces in how to defend themselves against VX."

"Nerve gas is a dirty, indiscriminate weapon," said the colonel.

"We knew Pyongyang was testing an intercontinental ballistic missile capable of delivering a chemical or biological payload. VX was still listed as a current threat to national security."

"Saddam was a big fan of organophosphates," confirmed Zed. "Back in 1988, the UN inspection teams found hundreds of men, women and children suffering from exposure to a nerve agent. Their injuries were horrific. Even mild exposure led to rapid convulsions, paralysis and death."

"It's a horrible way to die. A lingering, painful death. Paralysis then suffocation." The major shook his head.

"How does it work?" asked the colonel.

"Nerve gases disrupt a key enzyme in our nervous system, meaning muscles stop working properly," continued the major. "With paralysis in the chest, lungs quickly fill with liquid, your heart doubles in size, blurred vision, degradation in mental and physical capabilities, disorientation, depression, and despair. It moves unseen, killing without sound. I won't bore you with all the details."

"VX was a British breakthrough," acknowledged Zed.

"Trust me, be grateful it was just VX. VX is primitive compared to some of the other biological agents they could have used."

"Why did most of the safety systems fail?"

"Someone must have planned this meticulously. They knew our weaknesses," suggested the major. "We've had to shut down power to all non-essential areas. We're still running on backup. We're moving staff to the upper levels, for their own safety."

"How long can we last on the backup ventilation system?"

"Twelve hours, possibly longer if we close off the sub-levels."

"Then we can't stay down here indefinitely."

"We've got enough food and water to last weeks. This whole bunker complex was designed to withstand a nuclear attack."

"Not without air though. The planners never considered a ground assault. Disabling the ventilation systems and backup power was a masterstroke."

Zed listened to the exchange with growing alarm. The colonel had always maintained that this was the most secure site in the country. Right now, Porton Down seemed as vulnerable as anywhere else.

"We've checked the computer log files," said the major. "There's no trace of a hack or unauthorised access, which suggests that it's something mechanical. It's going to take longer to find. Whoever did this knew how to cover their tracks."

"Right now, the safest thing we can do is to stay put. This whole place is designed to withstand a direct hit by ground-penetrating ordinance. The blast doors at the main entrance are three feet thick. There's no way in."

"That's hardly the point. We think they may have been barricaded from the outside."

"If the blast doors are blocked, there must be another way out of here?"

"Once the base goes into lockdown, there's only one means of access, and that's sealed."

"Can we cut our way through?"

"We have a team at the main door now with an acetylene torch. It's going to take time."

"Keep trying to reach the base commander on the surface. We've got a chance of coordinating a breakout."

"Whatever we're going to do, we need to hurry," said the colonel. "The air down here is going to become unbreathable in a few hours."

"Colonel, I think you're overestimating their chances of success. We've got some of the smartest people in the country," challenged Major Donnelly. "If they can't figure it out, then God help us."

"There is one option we should consider, sir," suggested the major. "Doctor Hardy's team can produce any number of toxic substances. All we need are those samples from the storage bunker. We could fight fire with fire."

"And risk contaminating the whole base and killing more of our own people?"

"We are at war, gentlemen. At this stage, we cannot afford to rule out any options, however unpalatable."

"But surely not this," cautioned Zed.

"If they take any more of our core systems offline, things could quickly deteriorate."

# Chapter Thirty

Riley and Heather took their places in one of the empty pews at the back of the chapel within the secure military compound at St Mary's hospital. Heather was reluctant to go anywhere near the front in case the sister picked on her generation again.

In a raised voice from the pulpit, the sister was giving a combative response to a question from the congregation. She looked up and nodded at Riley as they took their places.

"But hasn't he punished us enough?" shouted a voice from the back.

"Did you really believe that things could just go back to the way they were? We've still learned nothing. The pandemic was the beginning of God's punishment, not the end. His anger still burns bright."

"So what does he expect us to do?"

"Repent before it's too late. God has spoken to us through the virus."

"Haven't we lost enough?"

"We still have so much more to lose. He tried to warn us, and we ignored him. People chose not to see or hear. Did you not notice the great storms and floods? The forest fires, tsunamis and earthquakes increasing in ferocity each year? Politicians and scientists have argued for years about climate change and pollution, but no one saw these events for what they really were. These were his warnings."

"Don't we deserve a second chance?" asked an adolescent near the front. "Is it not too late to seek forgiveness?"

"The chance for redemption has passed. The doors of mercy have been closed in our faces. I believe God is now irreconcilably angry."

"What did we do that was so wrong?"

"How many of you can claim to be without sin?" she said, surveying the room, waiting for anyone brave or foolish enough to raise their hand. "How many of us are guilty in thought as much as deed?"

She pointed to the same adolescent who had asked the earlier question, now shrinking in her seat, hoping the ground would swallow her up.

"Your generation was the most worthy of blame. The vanity and conceit of social media, heads buried in your phones. The rest of you are just as guilty of hypocrisy and pride. You should all be grateful your lives were spared."

The double doors at the back of the chapel creaked open, and a gust of cold wind swept down the aisle, causing Riley to wrap her coat tighter. The door slammed shut again. Everyone turned to see the chaplain striding towards the lectern, carrying a cumbersome cardboard box.

"Don't let me interrupt you. I just came to hand these round." His voice echoed around the half-empty pews and arches. He pulled out a large stack of white surgical face masks, counting out the requisite number and passing them to the person nearest the aisle in each of the pews.

"Father, I was just explaining to these good people why God is so angry."

"That's right. We are like souls on a sinking ship in the middle of a great storm," added the padre. "Our vessel is perilously close to the rocks, but the passengers are oblivious to the danger. Unbeknown to them all, the ship is already holed below the water line. If we don't wake ourselves from this comfortable slumber, we will all drown."

"The choices we make now," continued Sister Imelda, "will determine whether we steer a course away from those rocks or disappear into the darkest depths, never to be seen again."

"I choose to believe that we are not helpless, and nor should we act so," encouraged the Padre.

"Our fate and the fate of mankind are in God's hands."

"We can all start by wearing the masks I'm handing out. The base commander requires that we wear them in public places, starting immediately."

Seeing alarm in the faces around him, he added quickly, "I'm sure it's just a precaution."

"Padre, the sister told us that this pandemic was only the beginning. Do you believe that too?"

"Absolutely. Do you not remember the story in the Bible about the plagues of Egypt?" He paused, looking around the congregation, seeing a few heads nodding. "That's right. God punished the Egyptians and its Pharaoh for refusing to set the Hebrews free. If we still refuse to repent, then we should expect not just more pestilence, but civil war, famine, and deprivation until all remaining evil is purged from the Earth."

"I'm starving. Can we get out of here?" whispered Heather, struggling to conceal a yawn. Riley nudged her in the ribs to behave herself.

"There can't be too much more of this," said Riley, secretly quite enjoying it.

"I've heard it all a hundred times before. At the school, they were forever telling us it was our fault. I'm fed up with this brainwashing nonsense. Please?"

As they stood up to leave, the sister looked up from the book of Isaiah and glared in their direction.

"'According to what they have done, so will He repay wrath to his enemies and retribution to his foes; He will repay the islands their due.'"

"Does Isiah mean this island, sister? Or all islands?"

"Not literally, child, but his coming will be 'as brilliant as the sunrise'," she continued with a flourish. "Pestilence will 'march before him', and plague will 'follow close behind'. It says there will be a terrible harvest, and souls will fall from the tree of life like leaves in the autumn."

"Then how should we prepare?"

"Know thyself so that you may repent before your sins are exposed. The Day of Judgement is upon us," proclaimed the sister. "For those of you who have lived a penitent life, your suffering will be at an end. For those you who have sinned, you can expect an eternity of pain and suffering."

"Come on," whispered Riley. "I think we've heard enough."

Outside the chapel, they found Sergeant Jones waiting for them. Light rain was just beginning to fall, and they sheltered inside the chapel porch.

"I've been looking everywhere for you. We just got our orders. I wanted to say goodbye."

"I see. When will you be back?"

"I don't know. Maybe tomorrow. Depends when we complete our mission."

He seemed more guarded than usual with Heather standing there. His body language seemed off, awkward somehow. She couldn't decide whether his feelings for her were getting in the way or whether there was something else.

"Well, you look after yourself." She smiled. "Make sure you come back in one piece."

He said her name and then stopped. It was suddenly apparent that there was something he needed to get off his chest.

"Heather, can you give us a minute?"

The girl shrugged and set off towards the main building. Sergeant Jones closed the gap between them and put his huge hands on her shoulders.

"What is it?"

"Look, there's no other way to say this. You need to get as far away from here as possible."

"Why?"

"No one here is safe. They're already losing control. Things are getting crazy. If the outbreak reaches St Mary's, they won't be able to stop it. Lieutenant Peterson is ordering all non-essential US personnel back to the *Chester*, effective immediately."

"You're all just going to leave?"

"We have too. Here," he said, reaching into his backpack and pulling out an army-issue surgical mask. "Wear this at all times."

"It's going to take more than that."

"I know, but it's better than nothing."

"What do you expect us to do? I'd go back to Freshwater, but this place is on lockdown."

"Then find another way out. Remember the outdoor education centre I told you about at Medina Valley? It's north-east of here. Find a boat and leave. It's your best chance. Don't wait too long." He pulled Riley in tight and hugged her. "I'll see you soon, okay? Stay safe."

"I will," she said, her eyes closed as she squeezed him back.

**\*\*\*\***

Riley hurried after Heather who was nearly back at the main hospital building.

"Is he your boyfriend?" sneered Heather.

"No, we're just friends. Anyway, he's not my type."

"Didn't seem that way to me. I saw you two."

"It's not like that. He's leaving, going back to his ship. He just wanted to say goodbye." She stopped and waited for Heather to walk back to her. "Look, as soon as Adele is well enough, we've got to find a way out of here."

"Why the sudden urgency?"

"Because if this new outbreak gets worse, we want to be as far away from the crowds as we can. Hospitals, military bases, refugee camps are going to get hit the hardest. We need to get back to Freshwater."

As they approached the main complex, Riley became increasingly aware of the crowd gathered outside the front entrance.

Turning the corner, they saw hundreds of people with placards. They were chanting something she couldn't make out at first. It sounded like "Let us in."

Strewn around the grass verges was the detritus from several canvas tents destroyed by the soldiers in their latest attempt to clear the area overnight when the crowds had thinned. Faces were pressed against the wire mesh. Soldiers dressed in hazmat suits looked on passively, keeping watch on the crowd.

Heather lingered, puzzled by the scene. They were shouting at her, trying to get her to approach the fence until Riley pulled her away.

"Come on, let's go and find Adele."

In the hospital ward, they were surprised to find Adele sitting up in her bed, alert and close to her usual self. She was still a little pale, and there was a drip attached to her arm.

"Look at you. Who's made a speedy recovery?"

"I've been waiting ages. They say I'm well enough to leave tomorrow."

"That's fantastic news."

The nurse spotted them and wandered over. "She's responded well to the treatment so providing there's no relapse this afternoon, she's all yours."

# Chapter Thirty-one

Major Donnelly slammed the door behind him, hands on hips. He looked flustered, his usual mask of calm and control temporarily absent. Zed set aside the document on quarantine controls that Gill had passed him.

"We've completed our search of the lower levels. We're evacuating all remaining injured to the medical centre," announced the major.

"How many more?" asked the colonel.

"Three more seriously injured," he said, shaking his head. "That makes seven dead and eighteen wounded."

"Worse than we hoped, but less than we feared."

"Much worse. None of this should have happened."

"There's nothing we can do about that now. Have you got hold of the base commander yet, major?"

"Just now. They came under sustained attack by a large force. First incursion was reported at 2045. It was a slaughter, but they just kept coming. Apparently, they used kids as human shields. They knew we wouldn't risk killing children. Sniper teams picked off a couple of their leaders, but by the time reinforcements arrived, at least a hundred had made it through the fence. Our guard towers were flanked and overrun."

"Have we heard anything from 12th Armoured?"

"They fell back towards the vehicle compound. An hour ago they reported intermittent contact. The rebels seem content to contain our men for now."

"Show me on the map. Where are they?"

"They've regrouped here," he said, pointing to Building Four on the western edge of the complex. "There's a small armoury in that building. Lieutenant Thorogood says they're rearming and will be ready to move within the hour."

"How far away from their position is the biohazard storage unit you mentioned?"

"Less than four hundred metres. We've already briefed them. They'll retrieve the items Doctor Hardy requested. We're making securing that storage unit our top priority."

"Do they intend to evacuate us?"

"Colonel, this bunker is one of the most secure places in the country. We just need to take back control and get our systems back online."

"At some point, we'll need to get the team and the vaccine samples back to St Mary's."

"I'll pass that on."

"You're not still thinking of using chemical weapons?" asked Zed in disbelief.

"We're not at that stage yet, but I've asked the doctor to give us a range of options, should we choose to deploy those assets. I suspect he'll go with something like chlorine or mustard gas."

"But those are primitive First World War weapons."

"Exactly. Simple to produce and very effective in confined spaces."

"You can't seriously be considering authorising their use, colonel?"

"I understand your concerns, but right now all options are on the table. We hold a technological advantage. We should use it."

"They knew the risks in attacking a military facility," agreed the major. "They deserve to face the consequences. Our men are equipped with hazmat suits. I suspect theirs are not."

"I simply cannot support the use of chlorine gas against women and children," Zed objected vehemently.

Major Donnelly's eyes narrowed as he stared back at Zed. "Mr Samuels, all methods of killing are distasteful."

"But there must be another way," Zed appealed to the colonel.

"Look, we've encountered these groups before. They'll stop at nothing to get what they want. They think we have a vaccine. This is our opportunity to deal with the threat once and for all."

"Why not get word to the *Chester*? We're in range of their weapon systems."

"And risk collateral damage to this facility and its personnel? Look, if it comes down to a choice between losing more of our people in a firefight and eliminating a rebel threat without a shot being fired, then chemical weapons are an option we must consider."

"Let us hope then that it does not come to that. Major, let me know as soon as the 12th Armoured are ready to begin their assault."

"Yes, sir."

\*\*\*\*

After the meeting broke up, Zed took a much-needed break to clear his head. He was still haunted by what he had seen years ago. Photographic evidence of chemical attacks from the Bloody Friday artillery and air bombardment of Halabja. Hundreds of images of children's bodies contorted into agony. Thousands dead and wounded. He would never support the deployment of those same tactics here.

He went to look in on Gill at the infirmary and found her in the waiting room where a nurse was checking her pulse.

"What's with the bandage?" Zed asked, pointing to her forehead.

"Oh, that. I must have whacked my head when I passed out. Next time you take someone out for a first date, you might want to warn them they'll wake up in a strange bed stinking of disinfectant."

"You can talk! Ever since I drank that Porton Dark stuff, I've had a splitting headache."

"You'll get used to it."

"I normally save the disinfectant for the second date." He sniffed.

"Who said there'd be a second date, you charmer?"

"Look, I'm just glad you're okay."

"It could have been worse. Sealing the room did its job, maybe saved our lives."

"You were right, you know. They've just confirmed that it was VX."

"I knew straight away it wasn't a leak. It had to have been sabotage."

"I still can't believe you keep VX on-site."

"Why not? This is where it was invented. If you knew half of what else they keep down there, it would do your head in."

"So why did no one ever speak up? The tabloids would have died for that story."

"We've all signed the Official Secrets Act. Everything we do here is classified."

"And this wall of silence is getting us nowhere, Gill. If Porton Down is concealing the truth, then it's your duty—"

"You don't know these people. They'd never let anyone speak out."

"The colonel can protect you, give you immunity, move you someplace safe. Please, Gill."

"You don't understand. This place is my life. I've spent my whole career here. You can't ask me to risk everything I've worked so hard for, to betray these people. We're part of one family."

"Just talk to the colonel, please. See what he has to say."

"I'll think about it, okay?"

Zed nodded and got up to leave.

****

Half an hour later, there was a light knock on the door. Zed found Gill waiting outside, with a wan smile.

"Thank you for coming," he whispered, grasping her hands in his. "Colonel, there's someone I'd like you to meet. Gill Forrester is the epidemiologist I mentioned earlier."

"Yes, of course. Ms Forrester. I've heard a lot about you. How are you feeling?"

"Much better, thank you."

"I'm familiar with your work. We followed your team's advice on quarantine procedures on the island."

"At least someone reads those reports."

"I was telling the colonel what you told me earlier," said Zed. "About vaccines and unintended consequences."

"You mean Gulf War Syndrome? I'm sure the colonel has heard this all before."

"I'm familiar with the official version but suspect someone

with your access knows the real story."

"With genetic engineering, it's all very new and mostly trial and error. With some of these experimental vaccines, there's always a small risk that things can backfire."

"How exactly?"

"Basically, whenever you roll out a large-scale immunisation programme, occasionally you get side effects. With so many combat vets suffering unexplained symptoms, it suggests there's a problem either with the vaccine itself or an incompatibility between the different shots. Occasionally you see some sort of reaction in the subject. In extreme cases, a vaccine can actually make people more susceptible to a virus."

"Doesn't that defeat the whole object of a vaccine?"

"Not entirely. It's still effective for the vast majority, but for a small number, when they do become infected, they can actually have a more severe infection."

"Could there have been similar issues with batches of flu vaccine?"

"Unlikely, but I can't rule it out. Influenza vaccines are big business. Hundreds of millions of shots administered annually. Before they move to production, numerous approvals need to be sought. They're normally very thorough. Normally. Maybe there was a rogue batch, I don't know."

"Has that ever happened before?"

"There was a case a few years ago with Dengvaxia, a vaccine for dengue fever. It was a public relations disaster for Sanofi, the French drugmaker. For some reason, they ignored the early warnings about side effects and went ahead and vaccinated more than a million children in the Philippines. They tried to hush it up, but word got out. It prompted a crisis in confidence for other vaccine programmes. We're all still suffering blow-back from that mistake."

"Earlier you said that these emerging gene therapies require a degree of trial and error. What did you mean by that?"

"Look, gene therapy has been a medical dream for years. The ability to repair faulty genes or enhance their function to perform better. They already had limited success against inherited diseases such as haemophilia or cystic fibrosis. A few years ago, there was some pioneering work going on in the fight against flu. They were trialling new approaches."

"I remember. Squirting antibodies up people's noses or something?"

"That's right. After the last avian flu pandemic, our teams got very excited about a universal treatment against the multitude of influenza strains, but a breakthrough always eluded us."

"Didn't they do something similar with malaria?"

"The intended outcome was similar. They were looking to genetically modify mosquitoes to be incapable of transmitting malaria to humans. It was hoped that successive generations of mosquitoes would inherit this trait and in time malaria could be eradicated altogether. Before genetic engineering, they tried to eliminate whole populations of indigenous mosquitoes using pesticides like DEET in the Vietnam War, but it was a disaster. There were numerous side effects to human health."

"Playing God usually has unintended consequences."

"True, but the health benefits of wiping out malarial infection were too great a prize to ignore. Forty per cent of the world's population lived in areas prone to malaria. Five hundred million cases annually."

"And that same prevent strategy presumably held for influenza? By vaccinating the world's entire population, you could theoretically wipe out influenza?"

"There was a lot of money at stake. It was worth billions of dollars annually to whichever pharmaceutical giant came up with a universal flu vaccine, not to mention the health benefits, productivity gains, and cost savings for the NHS alone meant it paid for itself. Gene therapy had the potential to change medicine forever. The promise of herd immunity."

"Except in the wrong hands that same technology could just as easily be deployed to weaponise any number of viruses or bacteria."

"In the scientific community, we call that 'gain of function' research. It's still a very specialist field of science. Very closely regulated, a bit like nuclear technology. Much of the science of pathogens is still very poorly understood. There are probably less than two hundred people in the world capable of undertaking that type of research on viruses. Even fewer now. Most of those would have been in the US or Russia."

"So, say a team was assembled with the requisite skills, what would they actually need to create an effective virus? I don't suppose they have a Haynes manual for that yet?"

"Look, I'm a data geek, not a virologist, but I'm told you can find any number of genetic sequences for viruses published on the Internet. As far back as 2001, a British team published the genetic code for the bubonic plague. A few years later, another team did the same with smallpox and cholera. It's a bit like the Human Genome Project, except no one stopped to think of the risks."

"My point exactly, but surely a student with a Petri dish could hardly recreate the bubonic plague from a recipe they found on the Internet?"

"That's the thing with viruses. Once you have a live sample, you don't need much in the way of special equipment at all. A single chicken egg could be used to provide enough virus to kill every human being on the planet."

"If that's the case, then why were terrorist attacks using biological agents not more common?"

"For starters, you can't just walk into a supermarket and buy these pathogens. They're stored in secure facilities, like this one. Anyway, even if terrorists did get hold of a virus sample, it's still unlikely that they could start a pandemic. Viruses are extremely vulnerable outside a host. They don't react well to sunlight, wind, or temperature change."

"Is there any way of tracing where a genetically engineered virus sample came from?"

"It doesn't come with a barcode, if that's what you mean. As soon as a virus is released from a laboratory environment, it quickly becomes unrecognisable, exchanging genetic material with natural strains."

"Doctor Hardy told me once that gene therapists are like artists. They have their own quirks and traits, patterns in their work. I was rather hoping that, like Van Gogh or Rembrandt, they might have recognisable brushstrokes."

"I suspect he was pulling your leg. It's messier than you think. I suppose they all use short cuts, the same as anyone else. If they always spliced in the same sequences from other viruses, then it might just give you enough to act like a signature. You'd have to ask Doctor Hardy. Come to think of it, another theory you might want to ask him about is whether someone resurrected a paleo-virus."

"A what?"

"A paleo-virus. You know, like pre-historic viruses. A few years ago, one of the earliest known examples of a virus was discovered frozen in the Siberian permafrost."

"Like a dinosaur virus?"

"Yes. At the time it was said that modern-day humans, even homo sapiens, might never have been exposed before."

"So we might have little or no immunity?"

"Correct. In fact, we simply have no idea how the human body would react at all."

The colonel had been taking copious notes during their conversation. He underlined the final sentence and put his pen down.

"Miss Forrester, how do you feel about going on record? I'd very much like you to act as an expert witness in the enquiry I'm organising."

She glanced at Zed who smiled his encouragement.

"You don't know these people. They'll close ranks."

"We could protect you. Relocate you to the island if necessary," added Zed.

"Without documentary evidence, there's very little we can do. Rumour and hearsay are not going to be enough. If I'm right, this goes right to the top. Beyond even Major Donnelly," said the colonel.

"Everything here is compartmentalised. It would be impossible for me to gain access. I suppose I could try and use my boss's login."

"We'd need copies of project folders, internal memos or correspondence. Whatever you can find."

"I've already looked," added Zed. "None of those are in the main archive. I believe they may have been systematically deleted."

"There might be a departmental backup. With all the power outages, we kept local copies of files on our team server. I can see what I can find and report back."

"We will still need you to testify against Doctor Hardy."

"You know he'll deny everything."

"Leave that to me," reassured the colonel. "I'll find a way to make him talk. You have nothing to fear."

# Chapter Thirty-two

Terra sat up in bed, jolted awake by raised voices outside her room. The key rattled in the door, and two heavy-set figures stood framed by the dim light from a lantern.

Without ceremony, they strong-armed Terra to a waiting car and drove her to Lymington Hospital in silence. There was a palpable tension between them that suggested something had happened. A setback, their plans disrupted, perhaps a counter-strike by the allies. They were refusing to answer her questions.

In the empty staffroom, sat two hooded figures with their hands tied behind their backs. The denim jacket of the male on the right was darkly stained with dried blood. At the sound of footsteps, the captured prisoners looked up anxiously.

"Why am I here?" asked Terra, gesturing towards the pair. She didn't recognise their clothing but instantly feared the worst.

Hearing her voice, one of the hooded figures sat up straighter, suddenly alert.

There was a knock at the door, and one of the guards let Copper in. There was a sheen about him, his chest heaving as if he'd jogged here. His black shirtsleeves were rolled up, exposing richly tattooed forearms. The snarl on his lips suggested he was far from happy about something.

"Where's Briggs?" she demanded.

"He's with King."

"Then what am I doing here, Copper?"

"We found these two creeping around the place. They had this." He picked up what looked like a hunting rifle with a wooden stock and matt black telescopic sight.

"Who are they?" she said, almost dreading the answer.

The hooded figures seemed very animated as they listened to the exchange, wrestling against their bonds, their mouths gagged.

"I was rather hoping you could tell me," he mocked.

Copper strode over and removed the first man's hood. Terra stared wild-eyed at the frightened figure, barely believing her eyes. It was Tommy. There was a large swelling above his right eye and a cut on his cheek which had bled profusely, soaking into his jacket and collar.

She swallowed hard, realising that the other person had to be Sam. Her Sam.

With some theatre, Copper removed the last person's hood, enjoying Terra's reaction.

"You know them, don't you?"

Terra considered whether there was any point denying it, as she struggled to come to terms with the state of Sam's swollen face.

"You know I know them from Hurst. They're just kids," she said, shaking her head.

"Well, these kids just tried to kill Briggs."

Terra clasped her hand to her mouth, not sure what to believe. Copper's face was a mask, giving nothing away, watching her reaction.

"Is Briggs all right?" she asked, her eyes flicking between them. "Tell me, please."

"He's fine, but King and the professor weren't so lucky."

She didn't know what to say or think. Her thoughts were a jumble. She was struggling to take it all in. "Not dead?"

"King's in the operating theatre now. He's still in a bad way, lost a lot of blood. The professor was hit in the leg."

"When did this happen?"

"Last night. Victor set up a parley with a group from Southampton. He's been trying for weeks. They said they wanted to join us, but then these two here started taking potshots." He was enjoying her confusion as she tried to make sense of what she was hearing. She didn't for one moment believe Sam and Tommy were capable of killing anyone in cold blood, let alone with that toy rifle.

"They've already admitted it. Said it was revenge, for what happened to Jack. Isn't that right?"

Tommy and Sam shook their heads, still fighting against their bonds, pleading with Terra to make this stop. She knew full well what Copper would do to them. She had seen it so many times before.

With Copper's permission, she approached the pair to get a closer look. She lifted up Sam's chin. There was a sad, disappointed expression in his eyes that cut her to the quick. She wasn't about to admit it to Copper, but Sam was the closest thing she had to an adopted son.

She remembered when he first came to Hurst as a scrawny teenager. She'd taken him under her wing, nurtured him, became the mother he so dearly missed. It gave her a purpose, a distraction from the inner turmoil and self-loathing she had experienced in the beginning. The last time she had seen Sam was on the *Nipper* before Briggs's attack on Osborne House. The night she was kidnapped.

She took a deep breath and knelt before him, unsettled by the darkening bruise and swelling across his forehead. His nose was bloody, possibly broken. She wondered how long they had beaten these two. Knowing Copper, he would not have stopped until they'd told him what he wanted to know.

Sam's breaths seemed to come in short gasps as if he was finding it hard to breathe. She leant forward and ran a hand over his abdomen and chest, feeling for the source of his pain. A sharp intake of breath suggested a broken rib or a punctured lung.

"He needs a doctor."

"Not until he answers my questions." As if to hammer home the point, Copper kicked out hard towards Sam's midriff, eliciting a renewed groan.

"That's enough!" She turned on Copper with a mother's fury. "I know these two, they wouldn't hurt a fly. They're just boys."

"Then how do you explain them being here with this rifle?"

That was the thing. She couldn't explain it, but she knew in her heart that something was wrong. Copper was on edge, and that made her suspicious.

Tommy fought against his ties, moving his head from side to side to dislodge the gag. He was trying to say something.

"Why don't we let them speak for themselves?"

"No, they've as good as confessed. Said there were more of them. That South African was here too, ran away when we chased them."

"If they've already confessed, then why am I here?"

"Because King reckons you were in on this too."

"Me? He said that?" she challenged. "What about Briggs? What does he believe?"

"Like I said, he's busy."

"Well, let me tell you, Copper," she said, rising up and

puffing out her chest in a display of defiance. "Briggs doesn't tolerate failure. Where were you when all this was happening? Weren't you responsible for their protection?"

Copper laughed but seemed to bridle at the suggestion that he was somehow to blame. He stiffened, an ironic smile forming on his lips. "Victor warned me about you."

"How did you figure I was involved? I can see why you made detective," she sneered. "I've been locked up at the school. Remember, these two Neanderthals came and woke me up."

The two armed men standing at the back of the room flinched at the slur, glancing at Copper, who nodded back as if to say "Relax, I've got this."

Turning to Terra, he said, "You never did know when to put a lid on it, did you? No one's saying you pulled the trigger, but you've been acting suspiciously since you got here. Creeping around, talking to the professor, then this happens. It doesn't look good for you."

Terra reached out and grabbed the rifle propped against the wall. The two guards reached for their weapons, but Copper motioned for them to be lowered.

"I used to have a rifle like this when I was twelve," she said, handling the weapon with unmistakable expertise, pulling back the bolt, sniffing the chamber, checking the sights and taking aim at one of the guards who swallowed uncomfortably.

"For a start, it's single shot. You said there were two shots."

"Three, actually. We know this was not the only weapon, if that's where you're going. You really think I need a ballistic report?"

"Look, I know how it looks, but I'm telling you, these are not the guys who did this."

"Don't tell me how to do my job," Copper snarled, leaning

in close. "They were caught red-handed. They had a weapon, a motive. It's about as open and shut as they come." He turned and gestured to the men at the back. "Take these two back to their cells. We'll see if a few more hours in solitary confinement can't loosen their tongues a little."

"What about the woman?" asked the guard.

"I'm not done with her yet," smiled Copper.

Once Tommy and Sam had been hauled to their feet and dragged out, Terra softened her tone.

"Look, let me talk to them. I'm sure I can get to the bottom of what really happened."

"I don't think that's a very good idea, do you?"

"Then at least let me talk to Briggs?"

"Get it into that pretty little head of yours, he doesn't want anything more to do with you."

As Terra was led out, she wrestled her arm free and reared up in Copper's face. "I know you're lying. Just wait till Briggs finds out about this."

There was a momentary flash of alarm that made her think she was on to something. "I've always wondered what made a decorated police officer go bad. It was King, wasn't it? I bet he didn't have to try very hard. Or perhaps you've always been on the take," she mocked.

He stared back at her impassively.

"That's it, isn't it? This wasn't your idea at all. People like you are only good at doing what they're told, following orders. That's what you are. You're a follower, Copper."

He slapped her hard across the cheek, confused by her reaction as if he had just played into her hands in resorting to violence. She smiled back at him, fighting back the stinging pain.

"You've wanted to do that for some time, haven't you?"

"Don't tempt me," he snarled, clenching his fists. "There's no one left to protect you."

"You think I need protecting? I fight my own battles. Once King and the professor are out the way, who do you think Briggs is going to listen to?"

"I should have dealt with you weeks ago, you stupid cow."

"You lay one more finger on me, and I swear it will be the end of you."

Copper seemed to hesitate, wrong-footed by her confidence. "Take her away," he commanded with a knowing grin, leaving a relieved Terra to her small victory.

# Chapter Thirty-three

Zed and the colonel found Major Donnelly in the Porton Down command centre, huddled around a black-and-white CCTV monitor showing a live feed from the surface.

"What's going on?" whispered Zed to one of the orderlies, who turned to look him up and down.

"They've just reached the main bunker entrance."

The orderly turned back to the monitor as a blurry shape appeared close to the camera in the semi-darkness. The soldier wore full combat gear, his face obscured by a gas mask. He looked anxiously over his shoulder as muzzle flashes lit up the covered area behind them. The figure ducked lower and was joined by two other soldiers, pointing back towards the way they had come.

"Say again, commander," shouted the major, his voice clipped, leaning forward, gripping the microphone. The soldier on screen lifted his walkie-talkie to speak.

"The rebels are falling back. They've sustained heavy casualties. We're establishing a perimeter. The engineers are starting work on repairing the blast doors."

"What's their initial assessment?"

"It's a mess. Someone used shape charges to disable the release mechanism. The hydraulic pistons are damaged. It's going to take time to replace them."

"Can we drill through?"

"Sir, the blast door is three feet thick. Reinforced steel and concrete. They're bringing up the welding gear. The quartermaster says there's a diamond-tipped drill on-site we could use."

"How long will that take?"

"We don't know yet. Several hours, at least. In the meantime, we've got another team at the substation working to get the remaining systems back online."

"Do we have surface readings on the VX?"

"Negative. We found two bodies by the ventilation stacks. Whoever did this died in the process. I don't think they'll try that stunt again."

There was a loud explosion on screen that made the CCTV feed flicker and disappear. When the picture came back online, there was smoke billowing from the entrance area.

"Commander? Commander?"

"We're okay. Close call. Looks like an RPG. The 12th Armoured units should be approaching our position any moment. I'll report in as soon as I know more. Out."

The major turned, drained and deflated, to face the others. "Let me know as soon as they report in, will you?"

"Yes, sir."

"Major, can I have a word?" asked the colonel, leading him to one side. "Mr Samuels' investigation has reached a critical juncture. I'd like to convene a formal inquest to put Doctor Hardy on the stand. So far he's refused all our meeting requests."

"With all due respect, I hardly think this is the right time. Half of my team is in the infirmary, and the rest are trying to figure out a way out of here."

"Until they can get that blast door open, no one's going anywhere. I can't think of a better opportunity, can you?"

"You're wasting your time, colonel. Doctor Hardy is never going to volunteer anything useful to your investigation."

"I wouldn't be so sure. I'm relying on you to make him talk."

"I can try, but his team has always worked in the greatest secrecy. He's under no obligation to reveal the nature of his work, even to me."

"Either he cooperates, or I'll have him arrested and this place shut down," he said, inclining his head.

Major Hardy considered his options, glaring at Zed and the colonel. "Very well. I suggest we meet back here at midnight. That should give me some time to prepare the ground and explain your position to the doctor."

****

By the time Zed led Gill back into the hearing, there were already nearly a dozen senior personnel gathered. A U-shaped table left a seat for Doctor Hardy at the front of the room. The colonel and the major took their places at the head of the table, shuffling their stack of printed documents.

The doctor was the last to arrive. He looked surprised by the number of attendees but soon regained his composure and took his seat. He glared at Gill, perhaps wondering why she was at the meeting.

"Thank you for joining us, doctor. Major Donnelly has informed me that you intend to cooperate with our investigation."

"Absolutely. I have nothing to hide," he replied with unconvincing sincerity.

The colonel tapped the folder on the desk in front of him.

"New information has come to our attention which outlines a number of DSTL programmes active here in the lead-up to the outbreak of MV-27."

Doctor Hardy's face drained of all its colour. He threw a confused look towards the major, who avoided his gaze, staring blankly at the wall. The doctor sighed in frustration, realising that the trap was closing. Like a cornered animal, he looked determined to fight his way out.

"I'd like to start by asking you about so-called 'gain of function' research."

"Yes, of course." He cleared his throat, blinking at the innocuous opening question. "Gain of function is a fairly well-established methodology used in microbiology and genetics to investigate, for example, respiratory pathogens with pandemic potential, so SARS, MERS, or influenza."

"And this is a field of science that's still fiercely debated?"

"Correct. Until a few years ago there was a complete moratorium on this type of research. All projects required approval from an independent scientific panel."

"Because of the high risk of triggering an outbreak?"

"That's right. This was never about bioweapons. The objective was to develop an effective vaccine. It was always scoped as preventative. In the three years immediately after the moratorium was lifted, the National Institutes of Health gave the go-ahead to ten separate projects in the US, five of which concerned flu strains."

"So, for the record, you're saying there were other teams worldwide working on these types of projects. And to your knowledge, were these predominantly military programmes or was there oversight from civilian agencies?"

"Generally, these were run by the military. We learned the

hard way that these types of projects were best kept secret. I'm sure we all remember *The Guardian* headlines about H5N1 research."

"Go on."

"*The Guardian* broke the story about labs in Wisconsin, and the Netherlands' pioneering work with bird flu. Scientists there were attempting to speed up transmission between hosts. There were experiments on ferrets, but the perceived danger to humans was still very high."

"Doctor, let me cut to the chase. Did you, or did you not, undertake similar projects here at Porton?"

"I'm unable to answer that question without the personal approval of the Minister of Defence." He smiled.

The colonel took a deep breath, the colour rising in his cheeks. "Very well. Then speaking theoretically, when working with live pathogens like this, what sort of safeguards would this independent scientific panel insist on?"

"Typically, they would be very specific about safety protocols and security. Experiments would have to be conducted in level four containment laboratories within secure military facilities."

"You mean like this one."

"Yes. Porton Down is one of the only facilities in the world that qualified."

"But accidents do happen, don't they, doctor?" countered Zed.

"Of course, but they're very scarce."

"To your knowledge, did Porton ever ship samples of live viruses to other laboratories?"

"Not to my knowledge."

"So you deny that laboratories like this one regularly shipped samples through commercial carriers?" asked Zed.

"No doubt these are more urban myths peddled by the media."

"Then let me enlighten you," Zed shot back, reaching for his notes. "A few years ago, the CDC in Atlanta mistakenly FedExed a sample of H5N1. They blamed an administrative error. There was a public enquiry."

"That could never happen here." The doctor shrugged. "We would never ship live samples to or from other laboratories using commercial carriers."

"And yet, previously, you said that collaboration with the Americans was common. Which international body provided oversight to this combined operation?"

"Each country and region has their own system of approval. For reasons of national security, most of these programmes would be kept off the books. Precedents for this type of research were established in the Cold War during the race to develop atomic weapons. Physicists learned to distinguish between what can be made publicly available and what should be classified. We simply wouldn't want our scientific breakthroughs made public."

Zed leaned back in his chair, admiring the doctor's performance.

"Why don't we change tack," suggested the colonel. "You've expressed your opinion previously that the Millennial Virus, and I quote, 'could not have been a bioweapon'. For the record, can you remind us what those reasons were?"

"Mr Samuels has repeatedly suggested that Iraq, and by extension, I understand, Russia, were implicitly responsible for the pandemic. He maintains that Iraq was experimenting with genetically modified viruses. From my perspective, that's simply not plausible."

"How can you be so sure?"

"Because, back in the late 1980s, my team flew to Iraq to inspect their facilities and assess the maturity of Iraq's chemical and biological weapons programmes. Our view was that the technology they were using was decades behind the West."

"To be clear, that was before Russia began outsourcing its R&D to Baghdad. From the 1990s onwards, we know that Saddam was ploughing a lot of money into germ warfare. We also know they ran a series of tests in the 1980s and 1990s, using rockets to deliver a bacterial payload."

"If that's true, all they were really doing was copying pre-existing twentieth-century technology. Mass-producing anthrax is one thing; genetically engineering a virus is completely different. It's so far beyond their capabilities as to be absurd. It's only in the last ten years that breakthroughs in this area were made. Iraq's bioweapons programme was simply not credible."

"Even with the help of the Russians?"

"Not to my mind. Like I've said before, to bio-engineer something as exquisite as the Millennial Virus would require an unprecedented level of sophistication. Maybe in ten, twenty years, but not with current technology. The virus is simply too perfect."

"Is it more plausible that the outbreak could be linked to so-called paleo-viruses?"

The doctor seemed to hesitate, reluctant at first to answer. "I'm not sure where you're going with this."

"Let me refresh your memory. A few years ago, a French team from CNRF retrieved a sample of a virus frozen in the Siberian permafrost. *Pithovirus sibericum*, I believe it was called," said the colonel, referring to his papers. "To everyone's surprise, even after something like thirty thousand years in suspended animation, the virus was still viable. It was said to be totally unknown to science."

"Correct, but *Pithovirus sibericum* is harmless to humans."

"In its current form, yes."

"And its genetic structure is significantly more complex than, say, the influenza virus. Hundreds of genes. Very different."

The colonel glanced across at Anton Petrovich, who seemed to be enjoying their exchanges.

"Anton, perhaps you'd like to explain why the Russians were so excited by this discovery?"

"Of course. We hoped that *Pithovirus sibericum* could teach us about the evolution of viruses. The CNRF find was right on our doorstep," admitted Anton, sitting forward in his chair. "We began scouring Siberia for other viruses that might have become trapped in the permafrost during the last Ice Age."

The colonel had been staring at the doctor, watching his reaction.

"Doctor, you implied that this virus was 'harmless to humans'," said Zed, leaning back in his chair, "but how can you be sure? No human has come into contact with these primitive viruses for at least thirty thousand years."

"I suppose it's possible that they could become harmful eventually, but only if they were released outside the laboratory and allowed to mutate and exchange genetic material with other viruses."

"Can you confirm whether samples of these primitive viruses were ever brought here for study?" asked Zed.

The doctor declined to respond and simply shook his head. The colonel ran his finger down the list in front of him.

"There's no mention of such a programme on the official record, but that doesn't mean it didn't exist."

The doctor glanced at Major Hardy. "Look, no one could afford to ignore a scientific discovery that challenged our fundamental understanding of viruses. Our job is to investigate all known biological and chemical threats."

"Surely there are considerable risks in resurrecting a long-dead virus?"

"No more so than working with any other virus. Providing teams follow normal protocols, there would have been minimal risks."

"How can you be sure?"

"Because we've been doing this for years, colonel. Science doesn't stand still. It was only a matter of time before that layer of permafrost melted. Global warming was accelerating that process."

"The doctor's right," admitted Anton. "The virus samples were discovered in an area rich in minerals and oil. Sooner or later drilling equipment or vehicles would have disturbed them. Finding those samples still frozen allowed the world a unique opportunity to study a still dormant virus."

"So it's purely coincidence that only a few years after resurrecting these viruses, we witness a pandemic the like of which the world has never seen?"

"Pandemics have occurred throughout history. There's little evidence to suggest that this one was any different."

"In the interests of time, I'd like to move on. What can you tell me about Operation Pandora?"

"Pandora?" he said, his eyes widening in surprise. "That's going back a while, isn't it? You'd have to ask Major Donnelly. Pandora was outside the remit of my department."

"Then major, perhaps you can explain?"

"Certainly. Pandora was set up after the end of the Second World War to determine whether the civilian population might be vulnerable to a large-scale biological terrorist attack. It was put on ice in the 1970s and 1980s due to budget cuts, but after what happened on the Tokyo Subway with Sarin gas, they reactivated the programme."

"For the record, my understanding is that Operation Pandora conducted a series of live release tests on the British mainland."

"Back in the 1960s, scientists from Porton were involved in a number of simulated attacks on the London Underground. They set out to deliberately infect millions of civilians with what were said to be harmless bacteria. One of these tests chose Colliers Wood underground station for the release of a sample of *Bacillus globigii* on a packed commuter station during rush hour. The experiment exceeded all their expectations. Twelve days later, traces of *Bacillus globigii* were found in Camden station over ten miles away."

"But the proxy wasn't harmless at all, was it? They subsequently discovered that the sample was responsible for long-term health problems."

"The risks were greatly exaggerated. *Bacillus globigii* affected a tiny minority with prior health conditions only. Pregnant women, for example, had a slightly elevated chance of miscarriage or birth defects. That sort of thing."

"Colliers Wood wasn't the only public test. Porton scientists have been running similar experiments for years," claimed Zed. "I believe your tests may have claimed the lives of hundreds of civilians through secondary complications. Heart failures, tumours and cancers."

"Colonel, are we really expected to endure these endless conspiracy theories?"

The colonel rifled through his stack of papers until he found a memo relating to Zed's claim.

"Setting aside the public health implications, there's no point denying it. We have evidence that suggests similar experiments were carried out in major population centres including Southampton and Bournemouth. Porton scientists also ran tests at Sandown Bay on the Isle of Wight."

"I'm not sure where you're getting your facts from, but we would flatly deny such allegations."

"Good Lord, major. These experiments were conducted not just here but all over the world. As far back as the 1950s, the Americans staged simulated attacks on the cities of San Francisco, Minneapolis, Panama City and St Louis. On Porton's recommendation, the Americans used the same supposedly harmless agents. The bacteria were released in clouds offshore and allowed to disperse over the city. During six or so experiments, it was said that they successfully infected every single person within one hundred and twenty square miles of the downtown San Francisco area."

"Every single person in one hundred and twenty square miles?" repeated the colonel.

Anton seemed to find that amusing, rocking back in his chair with a broad smile.

"What could possibly be funny about that, Anton?"

"It was something of a standing joke at Biopreparat." He shrugged. "The Americans were so paranoid that their coastal cities could fall victim to a Russian biological attack by submarine."

"Over the next twenty years, I understand that America staged two hundred and thirty-nine separate open-air tests."

"And no one made the link between those tests and spikes in cancer or birth defects in later years?" asked Zed.

"I don't believe so, but what scientists quickly realised was that not only was a large-scale biological attack possible, it was actually frighteningly easy."

"At Vector, we always had our suspicions about Porton Down's ambitions." Anton smiled.

"Concerning?"

"Industrial accidents are surprisingly common. During the Cold War, we had a Communist sympathiser here who leaked details about Porton programmes. For example, in the 1980s, we were obsessed by the pioneering work with neurodegenerative diseases. Mad cow's disease, I think you called it. Then soon after, you had the unfortunate accident with BSE. In my line of work, I don't believe in coincidences."

"You're seriously suggesting that BSE was an industrial accident?" interrupted the doctor, rising from his seat. "That's preposterous."

"Sit down, doctor," cautioned the colonel. "Let him continue."

"Sure, why not?" continued Anton. "Leaks are inevitable, despite all of the precautions we take. The USSR also had its problems. You've probably heard what happened at Sverdlovsk in 1979?"

"Go on," said the colonel.

"Some mix-up with a clogged filter removed for repair. An accidental release of anthrax spores. When the shift changed over, no one remembered to tell the new guys. They switched an evaporator back on that released spores over the whole city. By the time they realised their mistake, hundreds of people downwind of the plant were already dying. Had it not been at night, when the civilian population was indoors, the accident would have been far worse."

"How did they manage to keep that out of the news?"

"There was a cover-up, of course. Brezhnev was a master of deception. TASS, the Soviet news agency reported that contaminated meat killed hundreds of people. Just like your cover-up with BSE."

"Colonel, are you really going to allow any more of these wild conspiracies? My participation in this enquiry was on the understanding we would be discussing serious scientific questions."

The colonel sat back in his chair and rubbed his tired eyes. "Very well. I suggest we all take a half-hour break and resume at 1am."

# Chapter Thirty-four

Zed grabbed a plastic cup from the dispenser in the hall and waited impatiently for the slow trickle of drinking water. He was still replaying what he had just learned. If Anton was right, what else had Porton Down been responsible for?

An industrial accident was one thing, but the intentional release of biological agents, not just once but dozens of times in heavily populated areas? The scale of the cover-up exceeded even his wildest imagination.

Down the corridor he could see shapes posturing in the shadows, one figure towering over the other, a finger jabbed in someone's face. Among the lively exchange, he thought he heard Gill's voice. Draining the cup, he set off to investigate. The figure noticed Zed's approach and stepped back.

"Everything okay?"

"Stay out of this, Samuels," said the doctor, moving into the light. He seemed irritated by the interruption, red in the face about something.

"I wasn't asking you," Zed cautioned, inserting himself between them. "Gill?"

"I'm fine," she said, wiping spittle from her face. "The doctor was just reminding me of my obligations, that's all. He wrongly assumed that I was the source of the leak."

"You still haven't denied it," spat the doctor.

"Seems a bit late to be developing a conscience," challenged Zed.

"You people have no idea what we do here, do you?"

"Just admit it. Your team was operating off limits, given far too much freedom. When you started playing God, you crossed the line."

Doctor Hardy laughed at Zed's high-handedness. "I hadn't figured you for a flat-earth proponent. Genetic engineering is mankind's greatest gift. The ability to improve human health."

"And it's also its greatest curse."

"People like you blame science for everything bad that's ever happened. Geneticists are the custodians of our future. In a few more years, people like me will help eliminate a whole host of common diseases, maybe even find a cure for cancer. So what if we make a few mistakes along the way?"

"That arrogance contributed to the deaths of hundreds of millions of people."

"You're certifiable if you believe that."

"People like you sowed the seeds of our own destruction. Scientists had a moral duty to evaluate the risks, not just the opportunities."

"There you go again, mixing science with politics. Independence of thought is the true hallmark of a scientist. It shouldn't be up to us to impose constraints on progress."

"That's a little too convenient, don't you think? Why did no one stop to think through the consequences, reject the areas of research likely to be hazardous to human health?"

"Political correctness and moral flimflam have impeded progress for far too long. The potential benefits of our research are unlimited."

"And so were the risks."

"Would you say the same about nuclear research? One of the greatest energy revolutions this planet has ever seen. And you're saying it should have been shelved because someone, somewhere, might misuse the technology at some point in the future?"

"You're missing the point."

"No, Mr Samuels, with all due respect, you are. Science has never been morally neutral. That so-called 'moral barrier' was breached decades ago. Once it's broken, it can never be remade."

"Scientists must draw their own lines in the sand and never allow the military to dictate terms."

"You and I, Samuels, we are links in the same chain."

"Then I blame a systemic failure to hold science to account," snarled Zed, breathing hard, their noses almost touching.

"Gentlemen, gentlemen, please," said Gill, pushing them apart. "This is getting us nowhere. A viable vaccine is what matters. We all want the same thing."

"No, Gill, you're wrong. This was never about the vaccine, it was always about power. I want the doctor to start taking responsibility for what he's done."

"What exactly are you accusing me of?"

"Genocide."

"You've got this all backwards. My team is this country's best chance of salvation."

"I think you've been drinking your own Kool-Aid for too long. You know what your problem is? You're drunk on power."

"I couldn't care less about power. We have a real chance of making a breakthrough here."

"I saw the same God-complex in Iraq. The architects of Saddam's weapons programmes suffered from a dangerous form of narcissism, of infallibility. Don't you realise that the technologies you've worked so hard on, once created, can never be unmade? They risk falling into the hands of rogue states and terrorist groups."

"Like Iraq, you mean?" he mocked.

"That's right. We gave them the skills and knowledge to exploit these technologies, helped train their scientists. Well-meaning universities and pharmaceutical manufacturers were much too naive."

That seemed to chime with Gill, who had remained on the fence until now.

"Zed's right. There should have been much tighter controls on exports. We've all been living in a fool's paradise."

"The government thought biological war was unthinkable." Zed shrugged, shaking his head.

"They were wrong," added Gill.

"Can't you see?" ventured the doctor. "The whole war on terror was a grand deception. We've all been manipulated. A sinister ploy to secure massive increases in defence funding."

"That benefitted scientific institutions much like this one?"

"The threat of attack was always inflated. The government propaganda machine walked a fine line between maintaining public awareness and creating blind panic. Fake news designed to create fear. Fear that could be channelled into votes and political support. The pretence for war, the invasion of Iraq, Afghanistan, of missile strikes against Syria and Iran, it was always fabricated."

Zed shrugged off the deliberate attempt at provocation.

"What's your point, doctor?"

"All I'm saying is, if I were you, I wouldn't ignore the vested interests. Stop pointing the finger at people like me trying to help, and ask yourself who really stood to gain from all this."

"Who could possibly benefit from the death of billions

worldwide?" Zed indulged the doctor, playing along, thinking out loud, keeping his guard up. He already had a working hypothesis, but he wasn't prepared to share it publicly just yet.

"A biological attack doesn't fit the profile of Islamic Fundamentalists. Jihadis preferred the spectacular. Crashing planes into buildings, blowing up public transport, not some microscopic, unseen virus. An attack of this sophistication had to have been state-sponsored. North Korea would be top of my list," stated the doctor.

"What makes you so sure?"

"Because North Korea is unique. A repressive regime, fanatical support of its people, hard borders, minimal transport links with the outside world. Let's just say Pyongyang decided to vaccinate its entire population against a virus they engineered themselves…"

"Then their chances of survival would be considerable." Zed nodded, trying to conceal his scepticism. "And I thought I had a monopoly on far-fetched theories."

"Granted, there are still a lot of ifs and buts," admitted the doctor.

"Could a virus be programmed to target the West?"

"I don't see why not. It's been done before. Theoretically, you could target specific demographics or ethnicities with higher concentrations of certain blood types. The likelihood of it backfiring would still be considerable."

"You know that's actually not as far-fetched as it sounds," agreed Gill. "A few years ago, we recommended to the MoD that they vaccinate all our high-readiness units against a variety of biological threats, including anthrax. In the end, only 3 Commando, Air Assault Brigade and some Royal Marine units were vaccinated. Trouble was, a good number of personnel opted out. Word got around that the side effects were simply too bad. People said they'd rather get sick than go through the vaccination programme again."

A loud buzzing noise from further down the corridor sounded as a light above the meeting room changed to green. Several others made for the door, waiting to be allowed back into the hearing.

"They're calling us back in."

"I'll catch you up," said Zed, hanging back.

Something about what the doctor had volunteered was troubling him. He didn't trust him in the slightest. Was he just throwing a dog a bone, trying to keep the investigation focused anywhere but on Porton itself? His instinct was still shouting that Russia was to blame. If Russia had been offshoring research and testing to Iraq, then it might also be possible they were outsourcing weapons development to North Korea. Was it possible that Peterson had already shared the US intelligence assessment directly linking Pyongyang with research into viral weapons? Or was that just what the doctor wanted him to think?

\*\*\*\*

Once everyone had settled back into their seats, the colonel brought the meeting to order.

"At the request of Major Donnelly, I'd like us to turn our attention to the UK's response to the outbreak and how our vaccine resources were deployed. Miss Forrester? As our resident epidemiologist, perhaps you can explain more about the Sentinel Programme?"

"Certainly," began Gill, almost as if she had expected the question all along. "Porton Down was a member of Sentinel, the World Health Organisation's early warning system, linking more than one hundred research centres in over eighty countries. The WHO threw a lot of money and resource at the problem. State-of-the-art systems for tracking and analysing over five thousand different strains of influenza via antigenic maps."

"What was the extent of Porton's involvement?"

"My team would input our research data into the Sentinel system, and their AI would analyse all the variables and extrapolate the best response."

"If it was that sophisticated then why did it fail?"

"Sentinel did the job it was designed to do. Their forecast models correctly predicted Singapore or Hong Kong as the epicentre of the next outbreak."

"We didn't need a billion-dollar computer to tell us that," sniped the doctor. "It's the same reason DSTL had a mobile unit permanently based in Singapore."

"Why?" asked the colonel.

"Because villagers in rural Asian communities live in very close proximity with all manner of wildlife: chickens, ducks and geese," added Gill. "These rural areas are so often the hosts for influenza viruses like H5N1 bird flu."

"It was the same in the First World War," confirmed the major. "Some of the big army training camps such as Étaples in France or Fort Riley in the USA were ideal breeding grounds for influenza outbreaks. Troops from different regions and countries thrust together, some with no previous exposure to strains of viruses."

"The more densely people are packed together, in close contact with chickens and pigs, the harder it is to control the spread of infection."

"So Sentinel got the location right but simply bet on the wrong virus?" asked the colonel.

"Yes and no. The Sentinel system was far from perfect. It was a huge leap forward but, in the end, surveillance was only half the battle. To be effective, Sentinel relied on a network of government agencies and civilian contractors to react in real-time to any identified threat."

"So, if I've understood you correctly, you're saying that the system collapsed because those third-party agencies were simply too slow to respond?" clarified the colonel.

"Precisely. You see, compared to other viruses, the Millennial Virus has such a short incubation period," explained Gill. "Most of our preventative measures proved insufficient. For example, we took the precaution of administering booster shots to all health workers, but that resulted in no more than a thirty per cent improvement in their resistance. It still left critical personnel vulnerable to many strains."

"We know now that withholding most of our stockpiles of Tamiflu and Relenza was a critical error," admitted the major.

"Hindsight is a wonderful thing. I suspect they simply underestimated the scale of the outbreak until it was too late."

"Do you believe an earlier release of those stockpiles could have made a difference?"

"Without question."

Zed was riveted by the exchange. It was the first time he'd seen Gill go toe to toe with the doctor and openly contradict his earlier statements. He had always defended the actions taken by the MoD. With every successive answer, the scowl on the doctor's face became more pronounced.

"Were there parts of the country which you believe would have been less affected in the outbreak?" asked the colonel.

"In our simulations, rural areas, far from major transports hubs and cities, normally fared best. We could expect some areas to avoid infection altogether. For example, the Highlands, the Dales, Lake District, parts of Wales, even the Isle of Wight."

"It's entirely logical. Lower population density equals lower levels of infection. And what, may I ask, were the simulations based on?"

"We use sophisticated stochastic prediction methods, analysing thousands of variables and complex probabilities to forecast the likely spread of disease. It allows us to make the best use of our limited resources. The models were built off the back of previous pandemics such as the Black Death in 1348 the Great Plague of 1665-1666 and the Spanish flu in 1918. Even though the country is a lot more connected, the spread of infection is fairly consistent."

"Low levels of vaccination didn't help."

"I'm sorry, you've lost me."

"He's referring to so-called anti-vaxxers," whispered Zed to the colonel. "Flu jabs were supposed to be mandatory for key workers, but they chose not to have them."

"That's right. After the whole Andrew Wakefield scandal, there was admittedly a great deal of mistrust when it came to vaccination."

"Andrew Wakefield?"

"You remember, the British GP who claimed there was a link between MMR shots and autism. People became so sceptical. Rumours and lies magnified by the echo chamber of social media. It was all part of a wider trend towards fake news."

"Anti-vaxxing was a global movement. In the US, France and other countries, people came to believe that immunisation was unsafe. It led to a huge rise in preventable diseases. Cases of whooping cough, mumps and measles were all on the increase."

"I suppose we all lost faith in the big institutions to act in the collective interest," conceded the colonel.

"People thought they knew better. They distrusted science. It was open season. Climate change, vaccination, even the moon landings. Science was seen to be no longer trustworthy."

"That was doubly true of Big Pharma. People thought mandatory inoculations were just a money-spinner."

"Religious leaders didn't help, claiming only God could grant immunity, encouraging parents to opt out on behalf of their children."

"Some even claimed that the vaccine actually caused the outbreak itself."

"Can we please return to the facts? This is getting us nowhere," sighed the colonel. "The whole country went to hell in a handcart when people stopped trusting media outlets, qualified scientists and health experts, and started listening instead to the rantings of noisy individuals on a soapbox."

"I agree. Evidence and scientific fact became overrated. There's always some group who thinks they know better than science," sneered the doctor, staring directly at Zed. "Too many people believed that the state was trying to control their every waking thought, to manipulate them. Everyone's suddenly an expert."

"The truth becomes a choice, rather than a matter of opinion," admitted the colonel.

There was a rapid knock on the door, and one of the orderlies entered the room.

"Major, sorry to interrupt, but they've just broken through the blast door. The base commander is looking for you."

"Colonel, with your permission, I propose we call a halt to proceedings and resume once we know what's happening up top."

"Very well," he conceded.

# Chapter Thirty-five

The base commander and Lieutenant Thorogood from 12th Armoured were waiting for them in the command centre, deep within the bunker complex at Porton Down.

The two officers were taking it in turns to gulp greedily from a two-litre water bottle. With her hood and mask removed, Zed could see the base commander's face was streaked with dirt and sweat from the fight, her long brown hair pulled back in a ponytail. Zed imagined doing anything physical in those protective suits must be intolerable. He stood at the back with Gill, stretching on tiptoes to see above the sea of heads.

The major shook hands with the two officers, relieved to see them and eager to hear their report.

"We've set up a perimeter around the entrance, but we won't have long. They'll be regrouping and rearming."

"How many are there?"

"Hard to say. Maybe a couple of hundred."

"More than last time?"

"Yes, sir, and they're well-armed. Semi-automatic weapons, tactical shotguns, mortars, RPGs. They have at least one tripod-mounted machine gun."

"Where the hell did they get that lot?"

"Any one of the army bases near here." She shrugged. "Most of them are abandoned. There would have been plenty of equipment left behind when our units pulled out."

"Did you bring the items the doctor asked for?"

"Yes, sir. They were delivered to the labs a few minutes ago."

"And the storage bunker?"

"We left a team there to secure the rest. They'll radio in if they have any further trouble."

"Very good, commander. Was there something else?" asked Major Donnelly, noticing her hesitation.

"While your comms have been out, we picked up a number of high-priority messages from St Mary's."

The commander handed the major a folded scrap of lined paper which he scanned and passed to the colonel. The expression on his face spoke volumes.

"This message is nearly seven hours old! Why are we only just getting this now?"

"By all accounts, they've been trying to reach us all day. The rebels must have taken out the main antenna. We only got this by chance. It was relayed by an allied unit operating north of Southampton."

"By the sounds of things," sighed the colonel, "St Mary's is in just as much of a mess as we are. The sooner we get back there the better. Commander, it's imperative we get word back to St Mary's as soon as possible."

"I'll see to it right away."

The colonel made a beeline for Zed and Gill, and took them to one side. He looked rattled for the first time Zed could remember.

"There's been a fresh outbreak on the island."

The pair stared back at him, lost for words.

"Has it been contained?" asked Gill.

"I believe so."

"How?"

"They've all trained for this. The whole island goes into lockdown. Face masks and protective equipment are mandatory for all personnel. No one comes in, no one goes out. Reserves of vaccine stocks are released."

"Is that going to be enough?"

"It has to be. We can't afford to lose the island…"

The major interrupted Zed mid-sentence.

"Colonel, the helicopter is coming for your team as soon as it completes its current mission. You'll need to be ready to leave at thirty minutes' notice."

As the colonel rose to speak privately with the major in the corridor, Zed reached across the table and took Gill's hands in his. She still seemed to be weighing up her options.

"Come with us," he implored.

"This is my home."

"Just wait till you see what the island is like. You won't need to live underground any more. St Mary's has got all the same facilities now."

"I know. I want to. It's just…" Her voice trailed off. "Let me think about it, okay? I need to talk to my team."

"Maybe they could come with you. We could relocate the whole lot of you."

She slid around on the bench seat until she was sitting next to him, snaking an arm behind his back, resting her head against his shoulder.

"I want to. I really do. Perhaps this is our chance at happiness."

She nuzzled up against him, her eyes closed. He kissed the top of her head, enjoying their quiet moment of intimacy, allowing himself to forget. It had been a long time since he had felt this relaxed in someone else's company. Even Riley. Was this what happiness felt like? It was intoxicating. Yet something didn't feel right. He took a deep breath and pushed her upright.

"What's the matter?" she said, looking up into his blue eyes.

"I don't know. This is all happening too fast." He shook his head, unsure what to say. "I can't stop thinking about my daughter. What was I thinking coming here? What kind of father hears his daughter has survived against all the odds and can't be bothered to go and see her?"

"You were doing your job," she replied tersely, sitting up straighter. "You said yourself, you hadn't seen her in years."

"I know. It doesn't make any sense."

"Look, if I come to the island, then I'm going there because of you. You need to be honest with me if you're having doubts. What am I to you exactly?"

He looked away, marshalling his thoughts. It was a good question. He felt like a kid on a merry-go-round, holding tight, trying not to fall off. His head was spinning. Feelings he barely remembered came flooding back.

"If it's Riley, just tell me."

"No," he replied unconvincingly.

He was beginning to doubt his instincts more and more. Perhaps Doctor Hardy was right. Who did he think he was? Out of his depth, grappling for answers. A fish out of water. His conscience was screaming at him. Surely, his place was with his family, not here on this wild goose chase.

In a moment of clarity, he remembered what was really troubling him. Everyone he truly cared about was in danger on the island, while he was stuck here. After what happened last time he promised himself he would never leave others to face their fate.

All those soldiers and quarantine procedures had not prevented this. His duty was to his family. Maybe, just maybe, it was not too late to make a difference. He needed to get back to his daughter, to Riley and the others.

He stood up, determined to get out of there, whatever the cost. Suddenly he felt claustrophobic. The hairs on the back of his neck began prickling in a cold sweat. Gill shook her head disappointedly.

"Is that really all you have to say to me?"

"I wish things were different, I'm sorry. I just need time to think. Right now all I can think about is getting back to the island."

"Look, I get it. Carol once said you never could commit," she said with a note of bitterness she instantly regretted. "Perhaps it's better I do stay here." She stroked his arm one last time, managing a weak smile. "Go on. Do what you have to do. I'm not going anywhere. I'll be right here when you figure out what you want."

\*\*\*\*

Zed found the colonel making final preparations for their extraction. He was hunched over a map of Porton Down, with the major and some of his team.

"There's nowhere for the helicopter to land anywhere near the main building. As soon as they're on final approach, we'll need to relocate to this site here."

"We'll send an advance party to secure the landing area. Once they've given the all-clear, we'll ferry you there in the APC. You'll be flanked by three other armoured vehicles, including the Scimitar."

"What about those RPGs and the heavy machine gun?"

"The Scimitar will deal with them and clear a path for the

transport. The APC is impregnable to small arms fire."

"So how long do we have?"

"From St Mary's the flight time is around thirty minutes. As soon as they're inbound, they'll radio ahead."

"How many can they take?"

"Depends what they send. If it's one of the Merlins we can all fit in, but if they're sending the Seahawk, say crew of three, four marines, plus five or six passengers."

The colonel looked across at Zed studying the map, listening to their exchange. Zed looked up. The colonel didn't need to say anything; the question was obvious.

"She's staying put." Zed shrugged.

"Then it's the doctor's team and the two of us. The rest will have to wait for the next trip. Gear up, gentlemen. We meet back here in fifteen minutes."

****

Zed packed up his notebook and paperwork into the day bag he had borrowed. He couldn't get Gill out of his head, regretting the way they had parted. He couldn't leave without saying a proper goodbye. He owed her, after what she had done for them all.

She had already shown him her office on sub-level two, but he still had to ask a couple of times along the way, zigzagging through various subterranean spaces and passageways.

Eventually, he found the door to her department, marked anonymously as room D725. He knocked lightly, not waiting for an answer. Inside, he found six workstations, four of them occupied. From a spartan corner office, Gill looked up. Her shoulders seemed to sag on seeing him.

He closed the glass office door behind him, noticing her colleagues watching him closely.

"I couldn't leave without saying sorry."

"No, it's me who should be apologising. It wasn't fair to put you on the spot like that.

"What I said was thoughtless. I wasn't thinking straight, okay? I know you went out on a limb for us, for me."

"Forget about it." She waved him away dismissively. "You would have done the same for me." She seemed distracted, her eyes unfocused, scratching at the back of her neck.

"Are you okay? You don't look yourself."

"I've had this awful itchy skin all afternoon, makes me very irritable. I feel like the rhino in the *Just So* stories. Probably just need to take a shower."

"You should get yourself checked out. Perhaps you came into contact with something?"

She drained the glass of water in front of her, but struggled to swallow. The drink only seemed to make things worse. She suddenly began to claw at her windpipe, her throat blotchy and red. She was struggling to breathe. She leaned back in her chair, wild-eyed.

Zed panicked, not sure what to do. She was pointing over his shoulder to get help from one of her colleagues. He banged on the glass door to get their attention, feeling helpless. A young Asian woman was the first to react and threw open the door.

"What's going on? Gill?"

"I don't know. She said she was feeling weird. Her skin was itchy. Then she drank some of that water, and this happened."

The Asian woman eyed the glass of water suspiciously. "Gerry!" she shouted over her shoulder. "Get a paramedic in here now!"

\*\*\*\*

While they waited, the Asian woman hastily donned some rubber gloves and a face mask and handed Zed the same. He lifted Gill out of her swivel chair and laid her back on the leather sofa in the corner, placing a cushion under her head and a blanket over her chest. Her eyes were closed, and she was having trouble breathing, her chest rasping and rattling like an old lady.

The paramedic ran in with a green shoulder bag which he dumped next to the sofa, clipping his mask into place. "How long has she been like this?" he said, feeling her forehead and taking her pulse with his other hand.

"I was just talking to her. Less than two minutes."

"If she's ingested something, we need to get it out quickly. I'm going to give her an emetic to make her sick. Grab that bin, will you?"

The paramedic rummaged around in his bag and pulled out a small container labelled Ipecac syrup. Craning her head, he poured some of the liquid into her mouth. The reaction was almost instantaneous.

He inspected the contents of the waste bin but seemed none the wiser. He placed an oxygen mask over her face and looked over his shoulder, calling for assistance.

Two paramedics appeared at the doorway and advanced towards them carrying a stretcher. Gill's condition, far from improving, seemed to be deteriorating rapidly. There was a frothy discharge from her nose and mouth as her chest heaved. One of the paramedics gently pushed Zed out the way, making room for them to lift her on to the gurney and take her to the medical centre.

Zed stood back, his hand to his mouth, watching them leave.

The Asian woman folded her arms. "Who exactly did you say you were?"

"I'm an old friend of Gill's. Zed Samuels. I'm working for the colonel. Look," he said, batting away her questions, "has anyone else been to visit her in the last half an hour?"

"Nope, just you."

He looked around the room, trying to figure out what could have happened, noticing a small ventilation grill directly behind her desk. Was it possible the place had become contaminated? If so, why wasn't he affected? No alarm had sounded, and the lights on the sensor were illuminated and showing green. He looked back at the desk.

"There was a glass right there," he said, pointing.

"What glass?"

There was a water mark but no glass.

# Chapter Thirty-six

By all accounts, the reports from the quarantine camp made for grim reading. The chaplain looked visibly shaken as if the gates of hell itself had opened. He passed the report to David Woods, the politician Riley had met once before. There only appeared to be one printed copy.

Sergeant Jones's advice was troubling her. What had spooked the Americans enough to order an evacuation of all personnel? Perhaps they had seen at first hand the scale of the outbreak.

"How bad is it, padre?" asked Riley, when he had finished reading the report.

"Nineteen dead, hundreds more infected."

"Camp Three was the source of the outbreak," added the politician, removing his cream blazer and straightening his tie.

"How far is that from here?" asked Riley.

"It's a refugee camp for new arrivals just south of Newport. Not far. By the end of the week, we're expecting most of the camp to be infected." David Woods uttered the word "refugee" with particular distaste as if he blamed them for bringing disease to the island. His views on immigration were well known.

"Do we know what we're dealing with?"

"Everything's happening faster this time," said Captain

Armstrong. "Spreading quicker, more deadly. We might be dealing with a new strain."

"Are we sure it's been contained?" asked David Woods, with obvious concern.

Armstrong hesitated as if regretting what he was about to say. "I'm afraid not. Two of the other camps are now reporting similar outbreaks."

"Then we need to get Doctor Hardy and his team back from Porton as soon as possible."

"Do we know their status?"

"They're dealing with a security situation at Porton. Sustained attack by a large heavily armed group. Well-coordinated. Multiple casualties. Suspected gas attack using VX. The colonel has requested immediate evacuation."

"Until they've got control, we can't risk sending our Merlins."

"That's no longer an option, sir. Both Merlins are grounded. One of them got shot up over Southampton yesterday, and the other needs some spare parts from the mainland."

"Peterson, can you spare the Seahawk?"

"We're expecting Sergeant Jones back sometime this afternoon."

"Very well. Let's get a team ready to leave as soon as possible. In the meantime, Camp Three has requested additional resources be deployed. If this is some new strain, then we need to know what we're dealing with."

"Yes, sir."

****

As the meeting broke up, Riley approached Captain Armstrong.

"Captain, I'd like to volunteer to go with the team to Porton. I know the site and, well, Zed and the colonel are there."

"Out of the question. I can't send a civilian into that war zone."

"With all due respect, I'm aware of the risks. I might be able to help. I know my way around Porton."

"The Americans will have operational command. It'll be Sergeant Jones's call, but I'll certainly pass on your offer." He noted her disappointment and suggested an alternative. "Can I ask you something in return? The medical team is short-staffed. Perhaps you would go with the padre to Camp Three? There are going to be a lot of frightened people there. We could do with all the help we can get. Sister Imelda too."

"Whatever I can do to help, captain. Let me have a chat with the sister."

When Riley relayed the captain's request, the padre nodded in resignation, but the sister seemed to draw back, flustered by the suggestion.

"If we're going to be allowed to leave St Mary's, then I'd prefer to return to my own people. They'll need me just as much as anyone at Camp Three."

"But sister, there are no reports of sickness in Ventnor."

"That's not the point. The doctors say that pregnant women and newborn babies will be particularly vulnerable. I need to warn them."

"And risk spreading infection?" challenged the chaplain, before seeming to pull back. "The sister must do what she feels is right," he said, inclining his head, too gracious to challenge what Riley suspected as cowardice. "Perhaps, if you do end up staying, in my absence, you'd be good enough to remain in the chapel where everyone can find you?"

"Of course, father, it would be my honour."

\*\*\*\*

Half an hour later, Riley and the chaplain reported to the car park where a convoy of military vehicles was being readied for departure.

At its head was an armoured personnel carrier followed by two minibuses carrying the doctors and nurses. The windscreens and windows of the buses were reinforced with rusting metal grills, their front bumpers fitted with bullbars and what looked like a snow plough. All personnel had been issued with green hazmat suits with a simple mask that they were instructed to wear at all times when inside the compound.

The crowd at the front gate had swollen further, and hundreds of faces were now pressed against the perimeter fence, watching the convoy load up.

"How are we meant to get out with all these people here?" asked Riley.

"If they don't disperse voluntarily, then they'll use tear gas, same as they did last time," answered the padre.

As if on cue, two guards emerged from their hut with a single-barrelled launcher. They inserted a canister and took aim at the front gate, some thirty metres away. With a soft thump, the canister came skidding to a halt at the feet of the crowd. One of the men stooped to pick it up but was quickly enveloped by a dense cloud of choking smoke.

A second and third canister were fired to left and right of the group, and the tear gas drifted over the crowd. People began clutching clothing to their mouths, coughing. In a few minutes, the protesters staggered away, their eyes streaming. A few remained slumped at the side of the road, heads between their legs, tears streaming down their faces. One man emerged from the gas cloud, pointing and shouting at the soldiers, a gas mask obscuring his features.

A guard unit advanced towards the gate with semi-automatic weapons drawn, cautioning the remaining protesters to disperse immediately. The last stragglers turned and ran.

As soon as the heavy gates were pushed to the side, the lead APC revved its diesel engine and set off down the road, followed closely by the two minibuses.

\*\*\*\*

The senior medical officer briefed them en route. Camp Three housed nearly six hundred refugees in a fenced-off quarantine zone. In any normal cycle, they would be made to wait the required forty-eight hours before being assigned to work parties based on their skills and experience. At the first sign of infection, almost thirty hours ago, the whole camp went into lockdown. Those displaying early symptoms were immediately separated and placed into holding areas.

The officer in charge of Camp Three met them by the front entrance and updated them with the latest information. Over one hundred were already sick or dying, and they expected that number to double over the coming days. A morgue had been set up at the far end of the compound to accommodate the bodies.

"We'll need to take blood samples from all the victims," insisted a grey-haired registrar from the hospital.

"Help yourselves. They're laid out in chronological order. The first fatality is at the far end, working forward through to those that died earlier today nearest the door."

"How many in total?"

"Twenty-three so far. If it goes on like this, we're going to need a bigger morgue. It's not just the refugees either; we've lost two nurses now."

"It's like we're fighting some unseen ghost," admitted his deputy.

The padre's head came up as if stirred by this turn of phrase. "The Spanish Lady," he muttered. "People are superstitious, you see. In Christian iconography, she was a dark exterminating angel, punishing those who had sinned. A *mater dolorosa*, if you like, mother of sorrows, a physical embodiment of God's vengeance, walking among them, spreading disease."

"These people are terrified, padre. They'll latch onto any conspiracy theory. We've already dealt with instances of prejudice, victimisation, racism, anti-Semitism."

"Someone's always to blame. Muslims, Asians, the Jews."

"Yellow, brown or black," cautioned the chaplain, gesturing towards his own skin, "the virus has no regard for the colour of our skin."

"I'm sorry, father. I meant no offence. Everyone's frightened, that's all. They're not thinking rationally."

"None taken. We are all equal in the eyes of the Lord."

"With so many people packed together here from all over the country, it's virtually impossible to control the spread of infection," added a young doctor.

"They said the same thing about the military training camps at the end of the First World War. They were breeding grounds for disease, like the Spanish flu."

The officer in charge led them through to a large marquee being used as a field hospital. The pungent smell of the place caught in Riley's throat. It was almost as if the victims' flesh was rotting on their still live frames.

On every inch of floor space, the sick had been laid out on

plastic sheeting and bedrolls until it became impossible to move between them without treading on someone.

Undeterred, the padre tiptoed from person to person, kneeling beside them on the cold earth, where space allowed, listening carefully to their gasped words of confession. He administered last rites to those with more advanced symptoms. Riley followed closely behind, offering her own words of comfort. One of the Ghanaian victims they attended to looked up at Riley and the padre with terror in his eyes, mouthing something she didn't catch.

"What did he say?" she asked the padre.

"He thinks I'm some sort of witch doctor come to save him."

Several of the bodies were lifeless and could not be shaken awake. He looked back at the officer in charge with a heavy heart, steeling himself for the task at hand.

"Sergeant, can you organise a clear-out? We'll need to make room for new cases."

The usual organised cleanliness that you came to expect of a hospital was strangely absent. In its place was mild panic. They had all experienced this before, the memories still vivid from last time. Most thought they would never have to witness death and destruction on that scale again and yet here they were, not even three years later.

Each curtained-off section they went into was a vision from hell itself. Patients coughing blood, nosebleeds that could not be stopped, young men and women crying for help. The plastic sheeting was sticky with congealed blood. Patients gasped for air like fish out of water.

One of the nurses closest to Riley tried to place an oxygen mask back over a young man's face but in his fever he rolled his head from side to side, fighting for breath. His eyes opened wide for an instant, back arched in agony, staring up lifelessly at his carers. He slumped back spent on the pillow. Riley heard an unmistakable crackling sound from his chest like popping candy.

"What's wrong with his skin?" she whispered to one of the nurses.

"The doctor said it's from lack of oxygen. Their lungs fill with liquid, and they literally turn blue and start to drown. Sometimes, the cyanosis can be so extreme that we can't tell whether the victim is black or white."

Riley felt giddy, and she thought she might faint. She rushed outside, gulping air greedily, trying to steady herself, perspiration beading on her brow and top lip.

In the distance she watched a woman shuffling towards the canteen, dragging her feet along the dusty path. She paused mid-step and seemed to struggle to breathe, sinking to her knees and throwing up the contents of her stomach onto the grass. Riley turned away, taking in the scale of the disaster unfolding before her eyes.

The rest of the medical team joined her by the marquee entrance. She was acutely aware that the camp personnel who brushed past her all wore the simplest of surgical masks that offered minimal protection from the virus.

"And where exactly is the camp doctor?" demanded the senior medical officer from the hospital, emerging from the marquee.

"Doctor Porter is in his office," admitted the camp commander.

"Why the hell isn't he out here helping these people?"

"He's refusing to come out, sir. I think he's had some sort of breakdown."

The medical officer marched over to the Portakabin that

served as the doctor's surgery and waiting room combined. The door was locked, and he hammered several times before his call was answered.

"Have you lost your mind? What the hell are you doing in there?" shouted the medical officer.

The resident doctor clung to the door frame, his knuckles white, squinting at the fading daylight. His eyes were bloodshot, his skin pale and clammy. He had apparently not slept in days.

"There's nothing more I can do for them. They all think I can just give them a flu shot and they'll get better. As soon as I go outside, I get mobbed."

"You'll do your job, man, like everyone else."

"I can't keep lying to them. I'm telling you, nothing is working. They're all going to die," he said, swallowing hard.

"Either you get out there right now, or I'll have you arrested." With that, the barrel-chested medical officer shoved him outside. "Off you go. And hurry up," he said, pushing him towards the marquee before turning to the others. "You see what I'm dealing with?"

A cart passed them in the muddy roadway, pushed by two decrepit-looking women in a semi-catatonic state. The cart was stacked with more than half a dozen bodies, piled haphazardly, one on top of the other. Over the wooden side hung a foot, missing its shoe. A name tag attached to the big toe twirled in the breeze. In red marker pen were the words "Tuesday 19th pm".

Riley half expected one of the women to ring a hand-bell like they had done in medieval times, and call out "Bring out your dead". The scene was surreal and haunting.

"Are you sure this is flu?" asked the padre. "It looks more like cholera to me."

"We can't be sure, but the symptoms of heliotropic cyanosis

and dyspnoea are consistent with extreme cases of Spanish flu. It's worse than anything we've experienced before."

"I've never seen anything like this."

"No one has."

"Sir, sorry to interrupt," said a breathless young guard, "but there's a mob at the front gate demanding to see you."

The commander seemed irritated but curious to know what they wanted. He strode up the roadway towards the motley group shouting about something Riley couldn't make out.

"What's this all about?" he demanded.

"The same thing I was telling this guard. You can't keep us here," warned a thick-set man, red in the face and incandescent with rage.

"It's not right," shouted another woman in a headscarf.

"No one's leaving, not until we get the all-clear. The whole island is on lockdown. We can't risk the infection spreading."

"But if we stay here any longer, we'll get sick, won't we?"

"No, you won't. You've all had your flu jabs. You've nothing to be worried about."

"Then how do you explain all the sick people? We've got rights, you know. You can't keep us here."

"I'm warning you, anyone tries to leave here will be shot."

"We'd rather die trying than wait here."

The base commander turned away, shaking his head. There was no reasoning with these people.

"Corporal, double the guard. Anyone approaches the gate, you have my authorisation to shoot them, am I clear?"

# Chapter Thirty-seven

As night began to fall, the padre tapped Riley on the shoulder and pointed to his watch. "There's nothing more we can do today."

Riley broke off from her vigil, holding the hand of a young Somali girl laid out on a stretcher. She tucked the limp arm under the blanket and joined the padre by the tent door.

"Can we come back here first thing?"

"Of course. The medical team will stay overnight and help."

It had been a long day. They had all witnessed scenes that would never be erased from their memories. The strain on the padre's face was plain to see.

The number of new cases still showed no signs of slowing. In a little under seventy-two hours, the quarantine zone had been transformed from a sanctuary to a scene from hell. Out of some six hundred refugees, there were now only three hundred and forty who remained symptom-free.

"What's going to happen if this new strain can't be contained?" Riley asked when they were outside.

"We just have to pray that doesn't happen."

They wandered back towards the main gate where the medical team from St Mary's had set up a field decontamination unit. One by one they entered a simple tented area where they were sprayed with something that smelled like disinfectant, and their suits scrubbed clean. After washing their hands in a washing-up bowl filled with freezing cold soapy water, they were instructed to remove their hazmat suits and continue on to the waiting transport.

Driving back to St Mary's on the nearly empty minibus, Riley could not hold back the tears, her sobs muffled by the new clean mask she was given.

"Thank you for coming today. I know it wasn't easy," the padre consoled, squeezing Riley's shoulder.

"If that's not hell on earth, then I don't know what is."

"I served in Rwanda and Somalia, and this is the worst I've seen. Suffering beyond imagination."

"I would struggle to believe it was real if I hadn't seen it with my own eyes."

"My grandfather was serving in South Africa after the First World War when the Spanish flu pandemic hit. He used to tell us stories of that time before he died. People dying in their hundreds struck down without warning. The colonials called it *Kaffersiekte* or 'black man's sickness'."

"Why?"

"I suppose they blamed the locals. The truth was the reverse: the new arrivals were the carriers of the virus. The locals thought the Spanish flu was divine punishment for the white man's oppression."

"Sorry, padre, I respect your beliefs, but my family were never very religious." She shrugged half-apologetically. "I suppose I'm a bit of a fatalist about these things. Surviving the first outbreak made me realise that I was being given a second chance, to live my life on my own terms, not someone else's."

"You should consider yourself lucky. We Christians call that beatific vision. So few people experience that. It's a serene and exalted state. The feeling of rapture."

"Epiphany, maybe. I wouldn't call it rapture."

"Trust me, it's God's plan."

"I choose to believe that we have a duty to reject what went before. I don't know, to learn, to choose a different path, not just to survive. That's why life at Hurst was so special. The sense of community, of interdependency, living in harmony with nature and all its cycles. I miss all that."

The padre nodded, staring out the window at the passing fields and woodland to their right. "Once you've stared death right between the eyes, it changes you." His voice was soft and distant. "During the breakdown, I chose to stay with my men at the barracks. Many of them were too ill, too weak to walk."

"Where were you?"

"Barker Barracks, just outside Paderborn in Germany. When people heard about what was going on in the big cities, in Hanover, Frankfurt and Bonn, the local town just emptied of all human life. What they left behind was heartbreaking."

"Go on."

"Scenes so pitiful it almost broke my heart. Dogs left chained in kennels, barking for their owners. Children banging on doors and windows, shouting at passers-by to let them out. Some of those who knew they were infected took their own lives and the lives of their families, rather than wait for the virus to take hold. I saw one man set himself on fire, others too inebriated to care any more."

"Why didn't you leave too, when you had the chance?"

"Where could we go? By then it was too late to leave. We did what we could. We patrolled the city, helped those we could, saw things that no person can forget."

"What did you do?"

"Not much. We used earth-moving equipment to dig trenches and bury the bodies in their hundreds. After a few days, it simply became impractical to move the dead from where they had fallen. That's when the cholera started."

"We've all witnessed terrible things. It was a lottery."

"Perhaps, but our experience was determined by more than simply luck."

"In what way?"

"Never has the gulf between rich and poor seemed so stark. The rich and powerful escaped before things got too bad, to their second homes in the country, or wherever they could find where there was no infection. People came here to the island, thinking they would be safe too."

"We did our best to keep the virus at bay."

"The virus drained all the love and compassion from the world. It made people cold and selfish."

"You don't really believe that, do you? None of us can survive on our own. We need each other now more than ever before."

"Perhaps you're right. Sorry, it's been a long day."

"When did you finally come to your senses and leave the barracks?"

"It was a day I'll never forget. I woke late, to an eerie silence. The normal bustle of the barracks was strangely absent. People in my block had not emerged for the day. The bugle never sounded. I knocked on doors trying to raise people, but most of them had stayed in their beds. Of course, I knew straight away what it was. I suppose it was only a matter of time before it reached us too."

"What did you do?" asked Riley.

"What anyone would have done. We made the sick

comfortable. The men were too afraid to fraternise with each other any more, to eat together, to pray together. We lived in a constant state of fear. I suppose we all retreated into a private world. In the end, we could no longer stay. It was fear that tore our brotherhood apart. We packed our bags and left for the transports waiting to take us home. It was one of the hardest days of my life."

The padre looked at his shoes, trying to hide his tears.

Riley patted his back. No words of comfort would come to her.

****

When they reached the approach road to St Mary's the convoy stopped while they radioed ahead for the main entrance to be cleared of protesters. As the seconds stretched into minutes while they waited for the guards to respond, Riley had a waking vision of the base overrun, imagining they had suffered the same fate as Camp Three.

There was a collective sigh when they all heard the clipped voice of the base commander ordering the convoy to hold in position until the all-clear could be given.

It took around ten minutes to disperse the crowd before the convoy was able to continue up the tarmac. They were greeted by a welcoming hail of bricks and stones thrown by the protesters. Despite the protection of the metal grids on the windows, a large piece of masonry cracked the reinforced glass, sending spiderweb lines snaking in all directions from the point of impact.

Riley found herself breathing shallow, looking around nervously until the heavy gates clanged shut and they were back within the relative safety of the military compound.

Several figures wearing biohazard suits were waiting in the courtyard to debrief them. Riley noticed Captain Armstrong and the sister among them, listening with pained expressions to their first-hand accounts.

"Sergeant!" the captain shouted towards the soldiers standing nearby. "I want you to set up a defensive perimeter around those camps. Anyone who tries to enter that cordon without permission should be shot on sight, do you understand? Relay that command. We must contain the virus, at all costs."

"Yes, sir," said one of the orderlies, hurrying off to make the necessary arrangements.

"Any news from the Americans?" asked Riley.

"They're still upstairs in Operations waiting for Sergeant Jones and the Seahawk. They'll refuel and turn them around. We need Doctor Hardy back here as soon as possible."

"Did you pass on my request to Lieutenant Peterson?"

"I did. We were both agreed. I'm afraid it's much too dangerous for a civilian."

Before she could answer, Captain Armstrong turned his back and began speaking with one of the staff officers.

****

Just after 8pm, the Seahawk helicopter roared over St Mary's, landing lights flashing, announcing its return to base. Riley hurried out to meet Sergeant Jones, but by the time she reached the helipad in the darkness, the Americans were already heading inside for the debrief. She called after him, but her voice was lost in the noise of the rotors as they powered down.

She sat on a plastic bench seat in the corridor that led to the debriefing room, straining to hear their muffled voices. From the heated exchange, she assumed that things had not gone to plan, and she wondered what they had been asked to do.

Sergeant Jones had once used the expression "wet work" to describe an operation. She remembered how hard he had laughed when she asked about diving gear and wetsuits before he went on to explain the reference to covert missions involving extraction or target elimination. She preferred to think of him rescuing people.

After what seemed like hours, the meeting broke up, and the rest of his unit trooped out of the conference suite, laden with equipment, helmets under their arms, weapons hanging from their clips. They had clearly been gone some time.

Sergeant Jones remained inside remonstrating with the lieutenant. Their body language suggested discord. Jones was not in the least bit happy about something. Peterson brushed past him, shaking his head.

"Next time, just follow your orders, or I'll find someone else who will."

Peterson seemed surprised to find Riley outside and delivered a polite but curt "ma'am" before leaving. When he was out of earshot, she heard Jones bang his fist on the table in frustration, sweeping paperwork onto the tiled floor.

Riley gave him a moment to calm down before sticking her head around the corner. He looked up with a forced smile.

"Hey, I thought you'd be gone by now."

"I would, but Adele's only just out of intensive care. She needs some time before she can travel."

He didn't respond and seemed preoccupied.

"I can come back if this is a bad time?" she said apologetically.

"Sorry, it's been a really long day."

"Same here. I've been helping down at Camp Three," she said, still shaken by what she had witnessed.

"Oh, so now you believe me?" he replied tersely.

She studied him carefully, puzzled by his hostility. "Look, if you're angry that I didn't follow your advice…"

"It's not that. You know I can't talk about it."

"I suppose it can't be easy," she said sarcastically, an edge to her voice.

"What's that supposed to mean?"

"Whatever it is you do. Taking lives, eliminating threats."

"You think you're the only one dealing with shit around here?"

"Hey, you started this."

"I'm not in the mood, okay. We've all had a crappy day." Jones hesitated.

He seemed desperate to unburden himself of something, but she knew he would never disclose operational details. Her breath caught in her throat, hands trembling so much she thought something was physically wrong with her. She hadn't realised how fragile she was feeling. The emotion of the last few days had sneaked up on her.

"Look, I said I'm sorry," he relented, seeing the tears in her eyes. "Come here."

He pulled her in tight and wrapped his arms around her.

"The things we saw," she sobbed. "I never thought I'd see people suffer like that again."

"There's so much more you don't know."

She looked up into his eyes, trying to step outside her own private grief. He patted her on the back, rubbing her shoulders. For a few moments, she gave in to her anger and frustration, her inability to help those people.

"I just want the world to stop spinning for a day, so we can all catch our breath."

"I know. That time will come, but not now." He checked his watch and cursed.

"Do you have time for that coffee?" she asked. "I could really do with someone to talk to. If I promise not to ask you any more questions," she added, almost laughing.

"We're heading straight back out again. Sorry."

"Back to Porton?"

"How did you—"

"The captain briefed us earlier. I volunteered to go with your unit, but apparently, it's too dangerous for a *civilian*, let alone a *woman*," she said playfully.

"He's probably right too. Anyway, I wouldn't be able to do my job properly if I was worried about you."

"So what am I meant to do? Just sit here and read a good book?"

"I told you. I don't want you to wait for me. Get out of here while you still can."

"They're saying St Mary's is the safest place on the island."

"They can't protect you here."

"I heard one of the officers talking about Operation Cleansweep."

"Cleansweep is the last throw of the dice. Believe me, you don't want to be anywhere near here when that happens."

"Then where?"

"As far away from here as you can. Just go. Head back to Freshwater. The west of the island is your best bet. Things are only going to get worse. The virus is heading this way, and nothing's going to stop it this time."

# Chapter Thirty-eight

Terra sat in the darkness of a doctor's office on the first floor, staring at the lifeless screen of a television set in the corner, surrounded by dusty medical volumes.

She was so angry with herself for becoming isolated. She had allowed King to come between her and Briggs. With King hospitalised, her path to reconciliation was now clear. Then there was the small matter of Victor's betrayal, and for what? Some small advantage that wasn't worth the price paid.

The door creaked open to reveal the skulking shape of Victor standing rock still, peering into the gloom. She clicked on the portable lantern and motioned towards the visitor's chair, drying her tears.

His ear and neck were strapped up with surgical tape. It was plain to see how much the wound had bled.

"You've got a nerve coming back."

"I'm sorry. Copper told me what happened."

"You sold me out, Victor."

"What King told you, he's lying. He's trying to turn you against me."

"I don't believe you."

"Terra, what possible reason would I have to sell you out?"

"Isn't it obvious? To curry favour with Briggs and King. Suddenly Copper thinks I had something to do with the attempt on King's life."

"I'm telling you this is all King's doing. Anyway, Briggs knows it was a lie."

Terra was so confused she didn't know what to think or who to trust any more. All that mattered now was winning back Briggs. "If King was behind this, then it backfired badly. How is he?"

"Still critical."

"Then who do you think was behind the attack? You really believe those boys had something to do with it?"

"There's no other plausible explanation."

"I know Tommy and Sam from my time at Hurst. They couldn't organise a school trip, let alone an assassination attempt."

"So you're saying they're scapegoats?"

"Maybe. It just sounds a little too convenient. Copper was too quick to blame them."

Victor blew out his cheeks. "If not them, then who?"

"I need to speak to the boys. They must know the truth."

"It's not going to be easy. If Copper catches us…"

"You owe me, Victor."

\*\*\*\*

Victor checked the coast was clear and smuggled Terra along the dark corridor towards another storeroom three doors down. He nodded at the guard and handed him something.

"Five minutes, that's all you're getting."

Inside, Sam and Tommy were dead to the world. They didn't even stir when she shone the lantern in their faces. Terra leaned down and whispered in Sam's ear. There was still no response.

Eventually, she shook him awake, watching him tenderly as his eyes flickered open and consciousness returned. He licked his lips and squinted around the room, unfamiliar with his surroundings. His gaze landed on Terra, and there was a lazy recognition.

"Terra." He smiled. "Is it time to get up?"

"Yes, Sam. I need your help. I don't have much time."

His movements were slurred, and she wondered whether they had been drugged. His hands were still tied behind his back, but she levered him into a sitting position. His eyes were struggling to focus.

"Sam, I need to know what you saw."

He looked puzzled as if the question made no sense.

"Please tell me you didn't shoot those men."

"No, no," he repeated. "We didn't shoot anyone. We were just snooping around, trying to figure out how to get in."

"Doing what? Why are you even here?"

"Will brought us here. He knew his way around. He'd been here before. Look, it's true, we came here looking for King, but we didn't have a proper plan. We got cold feet."

"So you're saying it wasn't you who shot King? Who then? Will?"

"No way," he said, with his eyes closed. He seemed to be struggling to stay awake. "We only had that stupid rifle between us. I kept telling Copper it wasn't us, but he wouldn't listen."

Terra shook her head, not sure what to make of this. "So, where did you get the rifle?"

"Will brought it."

Terra thought back to her brief inspection of the weapon Copper had shown her. There was no physical evidence to suggest the bullets were fired from that rifle. If Copper was trying to frame the two boys, it was amateurish, to say the least. Her instinct was screaming that these two were innocent, but why would Copper lie?

Victor took Terra to one side and whispered, "We're wasting our time, the boys know nothing."

"They're telling the truth."

"Which means Copper is lying."

"It's the only possible explanation."

"Someone wanted King and the professor dead."

Terra was studying Victor carefully. The more she thought about it, the more she was convinced his fingerprints were all over this. It was an odd play for Briggs to have his new partner killed.

Victor read her thoughts. "I know what you're thinking. I swear I had nothing to do with this."

Terra nodded, unsure how much further she could push him without any hard evidence to challenge him with. Besides, he was the only ally she had left. She needed him more than ever.

Terra sat back down next to Sam and put her arm around his shoulders. "I wish you hadn't involved yourself in all this."

"I had to come. For Jack."

"You don't know these people, Sam. They're murderers, all of them."

"If you knew what they did to Jack..." Sam's voice caught in his throat.

She hesitated, unsure whether to admit her part in Jack's death. She still blamed herself for being so naive to trust Briggs. "Sam, I saw what happened. I was there."

"You were there? I don't understand. How?"

"It was me who persuaded Jack to open the gates. Briggs and

King used me. I tried to save him, but no one would help me…" Her voice faltered.

"Why did they hang him?" sobbed Sam. "What had he ever done to them?"

"Revenge. King was angry at being locked up for so long. Jack refused to hand him over to the allies."

"But we treated him well, didn't we?"

"You're not to blame for all this. No one's to blame."

"So King murdered Jack. All this time, I thought it was Briggs."

"No, it was King. He got what he deserved. He's dying, Sam. Justice has been done."

Sam stopped sobbing and wiped the tears from his eyes. "Not until I look into those dying eyes and put a bullet through his skull."

"Let it go before it gets you killed too," cautioned Terra.

There was a knock on the door.

"Time's up. You need to leave now," said the guard.

"We're nearly done," said Victor.

"Listen," said Terra, "I'll try and speak to Briggs. Explain you weren't the ones. Trouble is, I'm not exactly flavour of the month either. In the meantime, just cooperate with Copper, answer his questions. It should keep you alive till I can sort this mess out, okay?"

Sam rested his head on her shoulder. There was a smile on his face, that same sweet smile she was so fond of.

"Somehow I knew you'd come. I never stopped believing you were still alive…" His voice trailed off.

"I wanted to come back, Sam. I wanted to so much, but I couldn't leave. They'd have killed me if I tried."

"Come on," said Victor, getting to his feet. "Time to go."

"Okay, but I need one more favour," said Terra.

\*\*\*\*

They found the professor in a private room on the second floor. At this hour of the night, most of the hospital was deserted. They crept past a guard snoring gently, his rifle leaning against the wall.

The professor was propped up on several pillows with his bandaged leg raised and heavily strapped. His eyes were closed, but he jolted awake, startled at the sound of them entering, sending an open book crashing on to the floor.

"It's me, professor," Terra whispered, holding the lantern high so he could see her face.

"Terra, what on earth are you doing here? Have you brought me flowers?"

"I must have left them in the car." She smiled, squeezing his hand with affection. "I was worried about you. Pleased to see you're still in one piece."

"The doctor said the bullet nicked my femoral artery. I could have bled out if I hadn't have been surrounded by medical professionals. I hear King wasn't so fortunate."

"He's still in theatre," said Victor.

"I don't suppose you know who did this, professor?"

"I heard they'd arrested two boys."

"It wasn't them."

"How can you be sure?"

"Because I know them. They wouldn't hurt a fly."

"I remember three or four shots. Then I must have blacked out."

"Copper says they were from long-range with a high-powered rifle," added Victor.

"It must have been very frightening. Why were you there?" asked Terra.

"Briggs wanted me there to talk about the vaccine. The group from Southampton were going to join us. It was all going so well."

"Professor, there's one more thing I need to ask you about the virus. When Victor and I spoke to the crew from the *Santana*, they called it 'English Flu'. Have you ever heard that name before?"

The professor smiled. "Well, we've had Asian flu, Aussie flu, Spanish flu, so I suppose it's not surprising that the Europeans would blame it on the Brits."

"So you're saying it's just a name?"

"Potentially. There is a precedent though. During the bubonic plague, Europeans called the outbreak *Sudor anglicus* or 'English Sweat'. The word 'influenza' is actually Italian. '*Influenza di freddo*' literally means 'influence of the cold'. But you know Spanish flu wasn't really from Spain?"

"Then why was it Spanish?"

"Because Spain was neutral in the war. Their newspapers weren't restricted by censorship like other countries. They reported it first. I suppose the name just stuck. 'English Flu' is as good a name as any other."

"I'm not so sure. The *Santana* skipper was suggesting that the United Kingdom had been placed under special measures by the United Nations. Exclusion zone, quarantine, etc."

"Well, in that case, there's probably more to it then. They wouldn't invoke special measures unless they had actual proof that the virus originated from these shores. Did they say anything else about a vaccine?"

"I don't think so. They said there were pockets of survivors along coastal regions in northern Spain, Cornwall, Brittany and the Channel Islands."

"Remote areas would have fared much better. Like us, the further away you are from population centres the better chance you have of surviving. Do we know yet whether King's volunteers made it through quarantine on the island?"

"There's no way of knowing," said Victor.

"It's been almost five days since they were infected. Say a forty-eight to seventy-two-hour incubation period. By now, there should be dozens of secondary infections. We can only hope that I was wrong and the allies intercepted them before it was too late."

"What will happen if the outbreak takes hold?"

"I fear it will be similar to the last time the island was devastated by a pandemic."

"The last time?"

"The bubonic plague in the fourteenth century. Entire villages were wiped out. One local priest who survived the initial outbreak wrote in his journal that the plague destroyed the bonds of family and friendship. The very fabric of society was torn apart. Neighbours shunned each other in their time of need. Trust collapsed. People stopped helping each other. Eventually, whole villages were abandoned for decades. It led to wholesale social change, some say for the better."

"Social re-engineering in one fell swoop. That's what Briggs has been talking about for weeks," recalled Terra. "So you really think there's a chance of history repeating itself?"

"King knew full well that natural immunity to this new strain was going to be far lower. It's fairly common with pandemics of this nature. Just when people think they are safe and the immediate danger has passed, a secondary outbreak hits. The same happened with the plague. An airborne, pneumonic strain proved far more deadly."

"We can't just stand by and watch those people die."

"We always knew this was going to happen," challenged Victor. "Whether they die from the virus or some other way."

"We have to warn them. Those are my friends stuck on that island."

"There might be a way," admitted Victor.

# Chapter Thirty-nine

Zed found the colonel in one of the laboratories deep within the Porton Down bunker complex, peering into a large microscope.

"There you are," said the colonel, without looking up.

"Sorry, am I interrupting?"

"Not at all. Just wanted to see for myself what all the excitement was about with this trial vaccine. Want a look?" he said, stepping to one side.

It took a moment for the blue and green cellular structures to come into focus under high magnification.

"These are lung cells taken from one of our volunteers," chirped an enthusiastic lab technician. "Thirty-six hours after contact with the virus and no signs of infection."

"Impressive," said Zed, stepping back, waiting until he had the colonel's full attention.

"Still early days, but Doctor Hardy is already describing it as a 'tipping point'. So what is it I can do for you, Zed?"

"I need to ask you about Gill Stephens."

"Yes, I thought you might. Bad business. Do they know how it happened?"

"If they do, they're not saying."

"The doctor thought it might be a delayed reaction. He

referenced another case in a different department on a different level which may also have come into earlier contact with the VX."

"Possibly. I checked with the maintenance team – the main air filtration system on sub-level two was offline. It was just recycling air within that department."

"So?"

"I'm just saying there's no way the severity of her symptoms was caused by secondary contamination."

"And that's the opinion of the experts, is it?"

"She must have come into direct contact with the nerve agent. That would seem the only logical explanation."

"What about the missing glass you mentioned? Did you ask the paramedics?"

"It's something of a mystery."

"Are you absolutely sure?"

"One hundred per cent."

The colonel leaned forward and whispered into Zed's ear so that no one else would hear. "I hope you're not suggesting a deliberate cover-up? That would be a grave accusation indeed."

"I don't know what to think. But in my experience, once you've eliminated all others, the remaining explanation, however unlikely, is normally correct."

"That Miss Stephens was deliberately poisoned?"

"It's hardly the first time toxic agents have been used in this way. It's textbook counter-espionage. Russian dissidents were routinely poisoned with nerve gas or radiation. The Kremlin admitted training KGB and GRU agents this way. Remember, Kim Jong-Un's brother was killed in Kuala Lumpur airport with a rag laced with VX, and the Skripals with Novichok."

"Really, Zed, you must learn to keep your imagination in

check. This is all beginning to sound like a spy novel. Whatever next? Poisoned umbrellas and fountain pens filled with arsenic? We don't have time for this."

The colonel wandered off, shaking his head in disbelief. Zed watched him leave before banging his head gently on the desk. If he couldn't convince the colonel, what hope did he have with anyone else?

He had witnessed at first hand the doctor's attempts to intimidate Gill. He refused to accept that this was merely an accident. What if someone had tried to silence her? He doubted the doctor would get his hands dirty with something like this, but he could have ordered the attack.

A cough from the open door returned him to the here and now. Ephesus sat in his wheelchair, watching him with some amusement.

"I came to say goodbye. Major Donnelly tells me you're leaving us?"

"We need to get back to St Mary's as soon as possible. There's a helicopter due within the hour," said Zed.

"Before you've solved the mystery?"

"The wall of silence is killing me. Miss Stephens was the only one prepared to go on record, but someone got to her. Thanks to you, I have more pieces of the puzzle to take home with me. I'm afraid the whole picture still eludes me."

"I suspect the truth is somewhat more mundane. Times of war make fertile ground for conspiracies."

"War?"

"What else would you call it?" Ephesus paused, studying Zed as if he was undecided about what he really came to say. "After our last conversation, I took another look through the archive. I couldn't put my finger on it until just this morning. Something's been nagging me. The digital archive has been edited, but I have the original copies in the library."

He handed Zed a single folded sheet of paper and gestured for him to put it somewhere safe. Zed scanned it quickly before sliding it into his notebook. At first glance, it was a photocopied document on headed paper, faded and heavily redacted. Written in bold lettering across the top of the page: "War Office: Directorate of Military Operations and Intelligence".

"You understand, this document never came from me."

He waited for Zed to nod before continuing.

"In May 1943, British Intelligence captured a high-ranking German scientist. Are you familiar with the work of Doctor Vengele?"

Zed shook his head.

"Vengele was Hitler's last great hope. A brilliant man, captured in an elaborate sting. Many of the weapons he was working on at Spandau were rumoured to be expressly designed to spread disease. If deployed against the Allies, they could have altered the course of the war. Weapons that spread cholera, typhus, bubonic plague, anthrax and others were at an advanced stage. Many were tested against the Red Army at Stalingrad. Under interrogation, Vengele described an experimental virus he called *das Lauffeuer*. Translated literally it means 'running fire'."

Zed's eyes went wide. "Or 'Wildfire'?"

"I thought you might be interested."

"But there was no mention of this in the archive."

"Exactly. Officially at least, *Lauffeuer* did not exist, but I assure you Vengele's claims were verified. He was a genius, way ahead of his time."

"But if that's true, then..." Zed's voice trailed off. "The doctor has always maintained that first-generation biological weapons were unstable, difficult to transport, and ultimately did not align well with the Axis goal of developing bacterial weapons that could be used in artillery shells or bombs. He said it was only in the last twenty years that a technological solution became available."

"That's right. Vengele admitted there were issues with stabilisation, accidents were common. We know *Lauffeuer* produced symptoms not dissimilar to Spanish flu, stimulating the body's immune system to start attacking itself."

"Was *Lauffeuer* ever tested in mainland Europe?"

"Not that we know of. Hitler feared retaliation in kind by the Allies. In the end, he chose not to deploy his arsenal of biological and chemical weapons."

"So what happened to him?"

"At the end of the war, he was spirited away, like so many German and Japanese scientists. Granted immunity from prosecution in exchange for continued cooperation. The Allies managed to recover a catalogue of data on human experimentation on a breathtaking scale."

Zed finished scribbling notes in his pocketbook and put the elastic band around it again, patting its cover. There was something about the librarian's candour that made him suspicious. Was this just another false trail to keep him off the path to discovery?

"This is all ancient history, Ephesus. What does it prove?"

"One studies the past to understand the future. Where knowledge is at best fractured and incomplete, we learn to fill in the blanks and understand what motivates. History teaches us about human behaviour. It allows us to extrapolate and interpret actions which otherwise would remain a mystery."

"I suppose it proves that scientists, like Vengele, have been attempting to weaponise viruses for many, many years, long before teams in Iraq or Russia."

"Don't trust anyone who tells you otherwise. The mere fact that documents about *Lauffeuer* were removed from the archive should tell you something. Who knows, perhaps Vengele's programme itself was the original inspiration for Project Wildfire?"

The two men shook hands.

"Thank you. Without your help, I'd still be nowhere. If you think of anything else that might be relevant to my investigation, please let me know as soon as possible."

"Good luck," said Ephesus, his chin raised, straightening his tie. "I hope you find what you're looking for."

\*\*\*\*

At the appointed hour, one of Major Donnelly's orderlies led Zed and the colonel up towards the main bunker entrance, to wait for the armoured convoy. The gigantic reinforced steel and concrete door was ajar, and for the first time in several days, they squinted up towards the night sky from the bottom of the ramp. After two days of hot, sterile recycled air, the cool draught of fresh air from the surface was intoxicating.

They were told to put on their gas masks, checking each other's straps to make sure they were securely fastened. At their feet lay the cutting equipment the engineers must have used. Zed noticed the exploratory hole drilled into the door had barely made an impression, their energies redirected against the locking mechanism. In the end, they had used hydraulic rams to lever them open.

From the far end of the tunnel entrance, Zed could hear the squeak of brakes from approaching vehicles. Two hooded soldiers jogged towards them. Intermittent cracks from distant gunfire suggested they were still involved in skirmishes with the rebels.

"The chopper is ten minutes out. We need to get moving!" shouted one of the guards, urging the team forward.

The colonel paused next to the major to shake hands.

"Good luck. We'll send the helicopter back for the others as soon as we can."

"God's speed."

They hurried up the slight incline to the hanger doors that opened out into a courtyard. The rear doors of the APC were already open, and they were manhandled inside. The cabin was cramped and hot. Zed experienced a moment of déjà vu, remembering the last time he had been in one of these tin cans. The ambush, the explosion, being dragged out by unseen hands, not to mention those hours of torture. He was suddenly nauseous and claustrophobic. The colonel noticed his discomfort, placing a hand on his shoulder.

"It's only for a few minutes. Hold on."

The guards slammed the rear door shut, and the vehicle lurched forward in a haze of diesel smoke. Doctor Hardy sat opposite, clutching to his chest an oversize storage box with a biohazard symbol on the side, like his life depended on it.

Out the front windscreen, they could see the turret of the Scimitar in front begin to swivel to the left. The barrel of the gun recoiled, and a huge boom echoed around the confined space, deafeningly close. The turret rotated again, searching for another target.

Zed covered his ears, ready for the next explosion. The tank fired again. At first, it wasn't clear what they were shooting at. As the roadway veered to the left, the view opened up and they could make out a cluster of trucks in the distance. Thick clouds of smoke and flame were belching from the cab of a flat-bed lorry mounted with a machine gun which had been transformed into a tangled wreck of metal.

"Sixty seconds!" shouted one of the crew from the front compartment.

Zed gripped the seat a little tighter, adrenaline surging through his veins. Ahead of them, he caught his first glimpse of the now familiar grey Seahawk skimming the tree line, keeping low, heading straight for the car park, just inside the fence. The cabin door was open, and their .50-calibre machine gun was firing, raining spent bullet-cases onto the tarmac below.

The convoy screeched to a halt, and the passenger door flew open as the soldier ran to the rear of the APC.

"Keep your heads down!" he shouted, herding the group towards a low wall, near the side of a building.

Zed's heart was beating out of his chest. Above them, the helicopter pirouetted around, kicking up a maelstrom of dust and dirt in its downdraught. As soon as it touched down, the American soldiers took up defensive positions, waving the doctor's team forward.

The colonel half-stumbled on some loose masonry, bumping into Zed. They supported each other the rest of the way. A hand in his back pushed the pair of them into the cabin. Sergeant Jones jumped in behind, and they lifted off, banking right over the buildings, desperate to put as much distance as they could from the small arms fire.

Through the open sliding door, the machine gun spat a ribbon of fire towards the rebel position. Another group emerged from the wood to their right raking the underbelly of the aircraft with gunfire. There was a shout from the cockpit as they banked hard back to the left again.

They stayed low, hugging the lines of warehouses, passing beyond the fence. Trees and buildings flashed past the open door. The pilot pulled hard on the collective, and the Seahawk responded, soaring higher, as Porton Down passed out of sight beneath them.

Sergeant Jones slammed the cabin door shut, moving between them, checking they were uninjured. He signalled for them to remove their masks. The scientists looked terrified, exchanging anxious glances with the crew. One of them retched on the cabin floor.

Zed slumped back in his seat, closing his eyes, trying to regulate his breathing. He promised himself this was the last time he would put his life on the line. He had Heather to think about now. He needed to put his family first. Not this. Who did he think he was? He was an analyst, not a soldier.

When he looked up, Sergeant Jones was staring at him, concerned. Jones shot him a grin and gave him a playful thumbs up.

Zed could just make out an electronic warning from the cockpit repeating every few seconds over the sound of the engine. An amber light above the pilot's head was blinking on and off.

"What's going on?" shouted Zed, struggling to be heard.

"I'll go check."

Jones stuck his head between the two pilots and asked them a series of questions Zed couldn't catch over the noise of the engines. Jones turned and leant close to Zed's ear.

"Oil pressure's dropping. Looks like we took a hit."

From their estimated position, it was less than twenty minutes' flight time. With any luck, they could limp back home. Just what they needed, thought Zed, cursing his luck.

The engine note changed and there was a loud mechanical

vibration that shook the whole airframe. Then it was gone again as the pilot compensated. Whatever it was, it didn't sound encouraging.

"Here, put these on!" shouted Jones, handing out life jackets. "Just in case."

They were all told to strap into their harnesses, now fearing the worst. The engine coughed and spluttered before regaining its rhythm. They were steadily losing altitude.

Straining to see out of the window, Zed could see the reflection of a strip of water ahead of them, the outskirts of Southampton and the container port spread out to their left. From memory, it couldn't be that much further. He couldn't see why they weren't making for Southampton Airport as an alternate landing area rather than pushing on to the island.

Their forward momentum slowed as the pilots wrestled with the controls, yawing from side to side. The co-pilot tensed again, pointing in the direction of something in the distance, but Zed couldn't hear what he was saying. He seemed to be repeating something over and over.

The rattle from the rotor returned, and the airframe began shaking. The pilot fought hard to correct their course and keep them in a straight line, but they dropped again, violently this time.

The helicopter passed low over houses and then a shingle beach, a few hundred feet in the air. There were people on the beach, a fire, and tents and caravans littered the shoreline. Dozens of people emerged below them to point and stare.

"We can't land here. It's not safe," explained Jones. "The *Chester* is standing by."

The expanse of water ahead of them stretched out towards the island, the sea calm and softly undulating in the darkness.

Everyone was straining to see out the window. They were much too low. Surely they wouldn't risk ditching in the sea?

Another set of warning lights came on, and the pilot seemed to react immediately, banking to their right. They weren't going to make it to the island, that seemed certain now. Zed could see the dark outline of the *Chester*, perhaps still two miles away to their left.

An enormous container ship loomed large ahead. Anchored back in the main channel, near the Brambles Bank, the *Maersk Charlotte* had been half-unloaded but still held a patchwork of several hundred shipping containers stacked high on her decks. The co-pilot pointed towards the ship, and they corrected their course.

They lurched lower. The enormous red hull of the *Charlotte* seemed to fill the entire cockpit window. Their engine spluttered as if they were almost out of fuel. For a moment, Zed thought they would crash straight into the side of the ship, but at the last minute the pilot yanked back on the collective and, with a last gasp of power, the nose came up, and they just cleared the container stack.

In a scrape of metal and tyre smoke, they careered across the improvised landing area, bouncing laterally until the helicopter's landing gear caught on a metal ridge, and they veered around to face the ship's bridge, sliding closer to the edge. Zed closed his eyes, bracing himself against the inevitable drop into the ocean below.

# Chapter Forty

The helicopter came to an abrupt stop a few feet from a vertiginous drop into the breaking waves nearly one hundred feet below. For a moment, Zed feared they might still topple over at the slightest gust of wind as it rocked back into equilibrium.

Looking around the Seahawk's cabin, two of the scientists were severely shaken; a box had come loose on impact and landed on them. There was a collective sigh of relief as they picked themselves up.

Sergeant Jones slid back the cabin door and stepped out onto the metal roof of a container, spitting blood from a cut lip. He helped the others out, peering over the edge down into the murky waters of the Solent, taking in how close they had come to disaster.

As the rotors slowed to a halt, they all turned towards the sound of a familiar voice behind them.

"I was not expecting visitors so late," said an out-of-breath Captain Anders Bjørklund, climbing hand over hand up the ladder to the very top of the container stack.

"I'm afraid it was either that or splashdown," Sergeant Jones said apologetically. "Some friendly locals decided to use our helicopter for target practice."

Anders' laugh seemed a little forced. "I think the military is not so popular these days." He glared accusingly at the colonel. "So I should add this to your bill?" he harrumphed, thrusting his hands deep in his pockets.

"Please let's not go through all this again. We won't inconvenience you any longer than we have to."

"The *Chester* will need to send a maintenance crew to look at the damage," added Sergeant Jones, inspecting the underside of the helicopter. "Hopefully it's not too serious."

"Very well, then. Tonight, you are my guests. We should let bygones be bygones, yes? There is much to discuss." With that, Anders gestured for them all to follow him back down the steep ladder to the deck below.

\*\*\*\*

In the cramped crew quarters, the whole place stank of boiled vegetables and unwashed bodies. The ship's cook had prepared a bubbling stew that filled the air of the canteen and steamed up all the port-holes. Stepping over the watertight doorway, a dozen or more men looked up from their dinner to stare at the unfamiliar faces.

"Gentlemen, sorry to interrupt your dinner," said the colonel.

"It smells delicious. What is it, Anders?" drooled Zed, suddenly aware of how hungry he was.

"At home, we call it *Lapskaus*. Norwegian stew. Meat and potatoes. Very good on a cold winter's evening. There is plenty for everyone. Please, come, sit."

Anders' crew made room on the bench seats for the new arrivals. He whispered something to one of the men who reappeared a few minutes later with two bottles of vodka. To a resounding cheer, he handed round a stack of plastic glasses, splashing a few inches of colourless liquid in each.

When everyone had a glass in their hand, Anders made a toast. "To our surprise dinner guests: welcome!"

Jones raised his glass and drained it in one, baring his teeth at the bitter aftertaste.

"It's good, yes?" Anders nodded, enjoying everyone's reaction. "We make our own."

"It takes some getting used to," conceded one of the others with a laugh.

"You can say that again." Zed coughed, to the general amusement of the crew.

Before they could protest, one of Anders' men hastily refilled their glasses. Jones declined the second round and motioned for the other Americans to follow suit.

"Not when we're on duty."

"I think custom dictates you drink as Norwegians do. When in Norway…as they say." Anders chuckled.

"I thought Maersk Line was Danish?"

"To us, the *Charlotte* is a little slice of home." He cheered, dispensing with the glass and raising the half-empty bottle to his lips. "I insist you stay the night. We have plenty of beds for everyone."

"The RIB from the *Chester* won't be here until midnight. If you don't mind, I'm going to get my head down for a bit."

"Be my guest. And you, doctor? You will stay a while longer?"

"Thank you, but no. It's been a long day for all of us."

"What's in the box?" asked Anders, noticing the storage box Doctor Hardy had by his side.

"My team's work. It's a portable refrigeration unit."

Anders nodded slowly, his thoughts elsewhere. For a brief moment, Zed thought he saw a mischievous smile appear on

Captain Bjørklund's lips. Then the micro-expression was gone, like a cloud passing in front of the sun.

\*\*\*\*

After the third bottle, Zed found himself very much the worse for wear, slurring his words, his thoughts muddled. The home-made vodka seemed to have no effect on Anders. Zed wondered whether they were drinking from the same bottle.

The others had made their excuses, thanking the captain for his hospitality before retiring to their bunks. Zed and Anders were the last men standing.

Anders leaned forward, pulling Zed close, his breath hot and stale. He straightened Zed's collar absent-mindedly. "I was very sorry to hear what happened with Jack."

"You two were good friends?"

"He was like a brother to me. We spent many evenings together, like this, drinking or playing cards."

"He was a good man. The best," said Zed, raising his glass.

"People like him, they are not well-suited to this new world."

"What makes you say that?"

"He was old-fashioned, very set in his ways. Inflexible, you might say. Too many principles. Someone you could trust. I enjoyed his friendship. He was someone I could do business with. He would always get me to pay too much for his produce." He laughed. "It was a game I didn't mind losing."

"Trust has been in short supply lately."

"A man's word is not what it used to be."

"What was that with the colonel earlier?"

"Captain Armstrong cannot be trusted. He made promises but left me with virtually nothing. Most of my cargo was claimed by the British Crown."

"Why?"

"They took all the things they needed for Camp Wight, but they paid pennies on the dollar. I am ruined."

"What will you do?"

"Me? I don't know. Maybe go back to Norway. Find out what remains of my country. Find another ship, bring it back here. Or perhaps I will settle down and start a new life."

"You? I can't imagine you settling down. You're like me, too restless by half."

"Perhaps you're right. There's a good chance more Scandinavians survived the outbreak. The doctors tell me a colder climate, fewer people, healthier lifestyle might boost survival rates. And you? What will you do now?"

"I suppose I'm a bit of a nomad too. They relocated us to a hotel in Freshwater. It's all right, but it's not a patch on the castle. I've been at St Mary's ever since."

"So we both have reason to feel hard done by."

Zed shrugged. He hadn't thought of it like that.

"And this colonel you work for? What does he want?"

"He's trying to figure out where the virus came from and how we can eradicate it." He tapped the side of his nose.

"I don't trust that Doctor Hardy. Shifty eyes. I've never trusted doctors."

"He's not that kind of doctor. He's a biochemist. No one knows more about viruses and vaccines than him. He won't talk to me."

"When I want someone to talk, I get them drunk. You should try it."

Zed smiled, feeling his eyelids growing heavy. There was a dull thud beating out a rhythm in his head. "Right, I should turn in."

"So early?"

"While I can still stagger, yes. I haven't had a proper drink in a long time."

"Wait, there is one more thing I wanted to ask you. You remember Victor, my first officer?"

"Of course. How could I forget him? He was one of the men who tortured me," sneered Zed, holding up the stump of his arm.

"I am sorry for what he did. He wasn't always like this, you know. He was like a son to me. Now I think I understand why he takes such an interest in Porton."

"Why did you put up with him for so long?"

"I knew his mother many years ago. She was English. She made me promise to look out for him. I got him the job with Maersk, but he was always ambitious. In this line of work, you meet many people in different ports, all around the world. There are many opportunities to smuggle drugs, exchange counterfeit goods, traffic immigrants. I have seen it many times. Greed corrupts people. I don't blame Victor. He's an opportunist with a thirst for power, as weak as the next man. He would do whatever it takes to get what he wants."

"He's graduated to become Briggs's right-hand man."

"I know. He has become a man without honour, without loyalty. A samurai without a master, like in that De Niro movie."

"His mother was English?"

"Yes, an English teacher. His father was a sailor too. The family lived on the coast near Ventspils in Latvia. Victor pretends he can't speak English very well, but believe you me, he understands everything. All this..." He waved his hands above his head. "The Allies, the Americans, Camp Wight, this is all Victor's doing."

"How do you mean?"

"Victor is the real organ grinder, Briggs is just his monkey. It was Victor who suggested we steer a course for Southampton. He told Lieutenant Peterson about this place too."

"When?"

"When we were all at Port Tawfiq, waiting our turn to get through the Suez Canal. None of us knew where to go. The whole world was falling apart. Looking for a safe port in a storm. Victor told us about the island."

"What's so special about the Isle of Wight? Why not Majorca, Corsica, the Azores, Malta?"

"I'm not sure. I think he came here as a child."

"Why would the Americans trust Victor?"

"You don't know him like I do. He can be very convincing. He's been playing all sides. Like pieces on a chess board."

"Briggs is not a forgiving man. The truth will catch up with him eventually." Zed yawned loudly, struggling to keep his eyes open. "I really should turn in."

"Now I think you can see why I love this ship. Nothing can touch us out here."

"Sleep well, my friend."

"Good night. We can finish talking in the morning."

# Chapter Forty-one

"With all due respect," said the embattled base commander in the operations centre at St Mary's, deploying not inconsiderable diplomacy, "where would you go?"

"That's not the point," said Sister Imelda dismissively, puffing out her chest. "You can't keep us here against our will. It's not right."

"Sister, the whole island is on lockdown. All the roads are blocked."

"Then I'd go cross-country the same way I got here: on horseback."

"You're missing the point. Limiting the movement of people is the best way we have of containing the spread of disease."

"By force?"

"If necessary, yes. You could unknowingly infect the whole of the south of the island. It would be extremely reckless to leave right now. Until we get the all-clear, everyone is stuck here."

"And how long's that likely to be?"

"Could be a few days yet before we know for certain. If you're not happy, I suggest you take this up with the captain."

"That's the first sensible thing you've said all day."

Riley watched her leave, exchanging a knowing look with the

padre. "She's right, you know. They can't keep us here against our will."

"It's for our own protection."

"What about the others? I couldn't forgive myself if something happened at Freshwater while I was stuck here. No, the sooner I get out of here, the better."

"We won't take that personally," said the padre, trying to lighten the mood.

"Sorry, I didn't mean it like that, but I can't rest until I know that the others are safe. I have Heather and Adele to think about. The sooner I get them back to the hotel the better."

"There have been no reports of infection anywhere else. They're saying the outbreak is contained."

"And you really believe them? They can't know that for sure. It's only a matter of time before it spreads."

"I appreciate this is inconvenient for everyone, but it's for the best."

"My mind's made up, we're leaving. I just need to figure out how. You know this place better than I do."

"I can't help you, Riley," he protested impotently. Riley could tell he was conflicted by her request.

"There must be another way out of this compound. Please."

"But if you breathe a word, they'd have me court-martialled."

"My lips are sealed, father."

"The river Medina runs right past the hospital. If you can get to the river, then you can find a boat. Check the map."

"It's a long way round, but I suppose with any luck, we could bypass all the checkpoints and roadblocks in one fell swoop."

"They're watching every waterway and crossing point day and night. It won't be that easy."

"But that's just it. We're not going to the mainland. We could hug the shoreline. With any luck no one will see us. If we left after dark, we could make it round to Freshwater before daylight."

"Can any of you actually sail a boat? It would be foolish to put the lives of those children at risk."

"We don't have a choice. Either we leave now, or we risk being stuck here for weeks. My friends in Freshwater might not have that long."

The padre nodded, smiling weakly. "I fear it will take more than luck."

\*\*\*\*

Riley found Heather playing cards with Adele in the waiting room. The little girl was wearing her Parker jacket with a fur hood, her overnight bag packed next to her. Her cheeks had recovered some of their usual colour.

Riley leaned in close and whispered excitedly. "Grab your stuff, girls. We're leaving."

"Leaving?" started Heather before Riley silenced her.

"I'll explain everything, but not here. Come on."

\*\*\*\*

At 9pm sharp, the three of them met at the edge of the compound. Beyond the fence and the half-finished accommodation block lay farmland that stretched for several miles north towards Cowes. To the north-east lay the outdoor activity centre Sergeant Jones had mentioned.

"Did you get all the stuff?"

The two girls nodded, twisting around to reveal backpacks bulging with warm clothing, food and water for the night's journey.

"Are you sure about this, Riley?"

"As certain as I'll ever be."

"How are we meant to sail halfway around the island in the dark?" asked Adele. "We won't be able to see anything."

"That's the whole point," said Heather bluntly, with barely disguised condescension. "If we can't see them, they can't see us."

"Fine, but who's going to get us there?"

"I can sail a dinghy," said Heather, with typical teenage overconfidence. "Just find me something remotely seaworthy."

Riley cast her eyes around the overcast night sky. The winds were light and somewhere hidden behind a thick layer of grey cloud was a half-moon. They just had to trust to luck that the tide would be in their favour.

"Come on, Adele, where's your sense of adventure?" said Riley, in a cheery voice.

They walked along the fence until they found the area Riley had spotted on the sitemap. The soldiers had cleared one of the warehouses to make way for further accommodation. With the natural barrier of the river on the other side, the fence in this section was rarely patrolled.

By the corner of a building, they waited behind a bush, scanning the darkness for any movement. Other than the two guards they had passed on the way, there wasn't a soul about.

Once they had satisfied themselves that no one was watching, they tiptoed forward. The mesh fence was at least twelve feet high, topped with razor wire. There were no overhanging trees or street furniture to climb on.

Riley considered the building site and weighed up the possibility of dragging back materials to build an improvised tower, but decided it would take too long and risk making too much noise. Their best chance was cutting through the fence, but that would require tools they didn't have.

It was Adele who spotted it first. A fox or some other animal had dug out the earth beside one of the fence posts. With a little further excavation, it might be just large enough to wriggle under.

The girls went first and emerged on the far side, dusting off dirt from their jeans. Riley pushed through their rucksacks and her own. She sat down and slipped her legs underneath, copying what the girls had done. She struggled to contort her shoulders and hips to fit underneath. After several unsuccessful attempts, she retreated and sat back on her haunches, regretting her lack of pilates since the injury.

With her bare hands, she raked at the loose earth, kicking out a few larger stones and widening the gap. She tried again, wiggling left and right until the girls took one boot each and hauled her through. Her sleeve snagged on the metal edge, ripping a hole in her Puffa jacket.

Beyond the fence, they followed the run of a hedge that bordered open fields, making towards the sounds from the riverbank. They stopped next to a single-track lane lined with trees and shrubs. Beyond the lane were the silent shapes of industrial buildings.

The sound of voices to their rear made them quicken their pace. Riley glanced behind, checking for headlights or torches in the darkness, but they were alone on the roadway. They could already smell the sea.

Low voices ahead of them made them stop and listen, crouching low to stay out of sight. Through the fence, they could just make out dozens of tents pitched in a field. Riley checked her watch. It was nearly half past ten. They decided to wait for a few minutes until the noises died away before creeping forward again, stopping every few hundred metres to listen.

At the end of the road, marked with a "No entry" sign, they could hear the unmistakable sound of sail canvas flapping in the wind. Halyards tapped rhythmically against the masts of larger vessels moored in the main channel.

They found the small boatyard and activity centre Sergeant Jones had told Riley about. The soldiers based at St Mary's had converted the site into a base for physical training for the new recruits, complete with single-person canoes, or kayaks as he called them. Jones said he had overflown it several times in the past few weeks.

There were several dozen sailing dinghies on trailers to choose from. Moving them to the water's edge was the challenge. The larger ones were too heavy to move. They found two sturdy day boats already on the water, tied up at the jetty with all of their sails and ropes attached.

Riley couldn't risk turning on her head torch for a fuller inspection, but let Heather climb aboard to inspect the boom and tiller, hauling up the main halyard and making sure there was a working centreboard. With a thumbs up, she confirmed everything was in good order. In the port locker under the seat, they found two paddles and adult life jackets which she handed around. Adele's was several sizes too big, riding up under her chin when she sat down.

Riley took one last look around, checking for any sounds or sign of movement. She could hear the tide flowing beneath the pontoon, but it was hard to tell whether it was coming in or going out. She could see and smell the mudflats, but the floating jetty was far enough out into the tidal channel to be accessible at most points of the tide. They would need to stick to the main channel to avoid getting stuck in the shallower waters.

Riley untied the mooring lines fore and aft and handed them to Adele, before jumping aboard. She grabbed an oar, pushing them out into the tide and paddling downstream. Judging by their rapid progress, the tide was still flowing in their favour.

Heather took the tiller and manoeuvred the dinghy through the lines of motorboats and yachts, growing ever more impressive as they progressed towards the mouth of the river and Cowes Harbour. Ocean-going race boats, luxury yachts and gin palaces. Some looked inhabited, others abandoned. Several marinas they swept past remained a forest of masts, their rigging tapping out a metallic concerto in the light breeze.

As they reached the dim street lights in town, they ducked down, staying hidden as they passed the chain-link ferry and Red Funnel terminal. To a casual observer, it might have seemed that the dinghy had merely broken free of its moorings, drifting lazily out to sea. Heather kept her eyes fixed forward as she carefully steered them between mooring buoys and other obstacles.

A headwind funnelled down the channel, slowing their progress. Riley gave the nod, and they raised the mainsail, tacking back and forth until they were clear of the harbour wall and jetty of what remained of the Royal Yacht Squadron. They hugged the shoreline, wind on their beam, swell building once they were in open water.

It was a straight run of some ten miles down to Yarmouth and the Needles Channel beyond. From there they would head round the Needles rocks and back up the far side of the island to Freshwater in time for breakfast. Riley had estimated it would take them five or six hours at most, depending on the tide, and hoped they would arrive before dawn. It was imperative they passed Yarmouth and the Needles Battery in the darkness. They didn't want to risk being spotted and intercepted.

"I feel sick," said Adele, resting her face on the rail.

"Keep your eyes on the land. That should help."

It was beautiful out here on the water. There was just enough moonlight to see by. The sound of the wind and the waves breaking gently against the beach a few hundred metres away was making Riley feel drowsy.

Heather's seamanship had so far proven impressive. Providing they stayed close into the shoreline, Riley was confident they would make it in no time. She wondered whether they were small enough to avoid the *Chester's* radar systems.

Ahead of them, they could see the dark outline of a massive container ship that could only be the *Maersk Charlotte*. Several port-holes in the crew quarters at the back of the vessel were lit up, casting a ghostly glow on the water below.

Just visible in the distance, she could make out the lights of what she assumed was Yarmouth. She couldn't remember much else on the coast between Cowes and Yarmouth, other than Newtown Creek. The beam of a searchlight or lighthouse swept periodically between Yarmouth and Lymington, several miles ahead of them. One or two of the channel markers remained lit, clanging away in the darkness.

Their progress seemed to slow. At a speed of no more than three or four knots, and running against the tide, they were actually in danger of going backwards. After two hours of sailing, they changed course for shallower water, hoping to lose more of the current.

The tides were notoriously unpredictable round here, back currents and eddies that caught out the unwary. She was unaware of any rocks or sandbanks on their path, but stayed vigilant at the bow, scanning the water for any breaking waves, fighting to keep her eyes open. Adele was soundly asleep, her head lolling against the foam head support of the life jacket.

Riley pointed towards a narrow tidal passage which she guessed was the entrance to Newtown Creek. She vaguely remembered sailing here from her childhood. They dropped their sails and tied up to a buoy in the channel, waiting for the tide to slacken. It was already nearly one in the morning. Once the tide changed, their progress should be quicker than the last hour or so.

"Have a rest, Heather. I'll wake you when it's time to get going."

Riley watched enviously as Heather wriggled lower to shelter from the cold wind, pulling her hood over her head and zipping up the jacket tight under her chin.

\*\*\*\*

Riley waited for as long as she dared for the eastward-flowing tide to slacken. Without waking the girls, she untied the mooring line and pulled up the mainsail, unfurling the jib as it flapped, head to wind. She hauled in the sheet and steered back towards the river entrance and out into the channel. It was hard to tell at first, but she quickly convinced herself it must be nearly slack tide. In a little while, it should turn in their favour and speed them on their way.

Heather rubbed her eyes, yawned and took Riley's place at the tiller, coaxing every scintilla of speed from the boat as it surged through the waves. Nearing Yarmouth, they could see the lights of the Wightlink car ferry moored in the terminal. The low rumble from its noisy diesel engines carried across the water. They were close enough to see the outline of figures on top of Yarmouth Castle and hoped they were too busy to notice their passing.

Beyond Fort Victoria, they turned south-west, watching Hurst Castle slide past them to their right. As hard as she stared into the darkness, she could not make out any signs of activity. No bonfires in the courtyard, no lights in the windows. Its high walls remained as silent as the grave.

With every few minutes, they inched closer to Freshwater and home. The multicoloured cliffs of Alum Bay to their left loomed large in the darkness, and the chalk towers of the Needles rocks now lay directly ahead.

"Do we need to go round the rocks, or can we go between them?" asked Heather.

"There's a deeper channel between the first and second rock. Stay in the middle, and we should be fine."

As Riley stared up at the Needles Headland, she kept an eye out for movement, mindful of Corporal Carter's men. It was still dark enough that they would be near impossible to spot, even with the high vantage point afforded from the cliffs. She hoped their dark grey sails would be invisible against the inky blackness of the ocean.

To her surprise, she noticed a flurry of activity on the clifftop. A lone figure was running as fast as he could towards the gun emplacement. A searchlight powered up and quickly found them in the darkness. Riley stared back, shielding her eyes from the dazzling light.

"Wave, girls. Show them we mean no harm."

In response, tracer bullets angled towards them, ripping up the water ahead of their nodding bow.

"Should I come about?" shouted Heather, a note of panic in her voice.

"No, hold your course. Keep waving."

With a jolt, Riley remembered the radio Carter had given her, and she quickly rummaged around for it in the rucksack. She might only have a few seconds before they opened fire again. As soon as she found the small walkie-talkie, she turned on the power and rotated the dial to channel sixteen.

"Needles Battery. Cease fire, cease fire. We have children aboard. Repeat: cease fire."

"Be advised, you are entering a restricted area. Turn around, or you will be fired upon," came a cold, unfamiliar voice.

"Negative. We have authorisation. We are travelling to Freshwater Bay from St Mary's. Repeat: we have not come from the mainland. Tell Corporal Carter that it's Riley from the hotel, returning with two passengers. We are not infected. Repeat: we are not infected."

"Stand by."

There was an awkward silence as she imagined someone running to wake Corporal Carter to find out whether he had ever heard of a Riley and what exactly he wanted to do about it. Carter's voice came over the radio.

"It's four thirty in the morning, Riley. Bit late for a sail, isn't it?"

Riley smiled her broadest smile and punched the air. "Sorry to disturb your beauty sleep, corporal. We were just trying to make it home for breakfast."

"It may have escaped your attention, but the whole island is on lockdown. You're lucky my boys didn't sink you. You know I should turn you round, send you back where you came from."

"Please. We're just trying to get home."

There was a heavy pause as Carter no doubt played out various scenarios in his head.

"I'll send a team to meet you in Freshwater. Don't make me regret this, Riley. Needles Battery, out."

# Chapter Forty-two

The next morning, the fast RIB from the *Chester* returned for the remainder of the colonel's party, shuttling them the rest of the way to Cowes and from there by road to St Mary's.

Zed woke to find the Americans had already left during the night, leaving behind a pair of mechanics working in the pre-dawn gloom under portable lights. Anders said they were replacing the fuel line and the other damaged helicopter components. The doctor too was nowhere to be seen. He must have left with the soldiers to deliver urgent vaccine samples to the hospital. Despite a thumping hangover, Captain Bjørklund had seen them off with a cheerful farewell.

Clambering down the ladder, Zed stepped uncertainly onto the rigid rubber seat of the RIB. The roll of the waves half-propelled him into the arms of a waiting seaman. He could just hear Anders' laughter from above, mocking his unsteadiness.

Bouncing across the placid waves towards the island, Zed fought to keep down the contents of his stomach. He wasn't sure if it was the Norwegian stew, the home-made vodka, the motion sickness or a combination of all three. The colonel was po-faced, unamused by Zed's condition.

Arriving at the hospital, the atmosphere seemed altered.

Gone was the quiet confidence and efficiency of a military-led relief effort. In its place, Zed could detect a palpable tension. This had become a fortress under siege from an unknown threat that might attack at a moment's notice.

An orderly handed them each a face mask and instructed them to wear them at all times. Arriving without them had prompted mild horror as if their negligence was wholly irresponsible.

The orderly led them through the operations centre up the stairs to a large conference room, whose walls were covered with lists, maps and plans. Lieutenant Peterson, Captain Armstrong, the politician, the padre and Doctor Hardy were already waiting for them.

"Welcome back, colonel," saluted Captain Armstrong.

"What have I missed?"

"It's been a busy few days."

"For all of us, captain."

"The allied pockets around Southampton docks and Portsmouth Harbour have come under sustained attack. They were reinforced by the two new companies deployed from Camp Wight."

"How many more men?"

"All told, about three hundred."

"And we're sure they were ready?"

"As ready as they'll ever be. We have a further two hundred in training, ready for deployment later this month. On the advice of the medical team, we've separated out those units to reduce the chance of infection."

Zed looked across at Doctor Hardy whose face was lit up by the dull glow from his laptop. He had barely looked up and seemed engrossed in running calculations on a spreadsheet, shaking his head from time to time as if unimpressed by the results.

"And, doctor, where are we at with the vaccine?" asked Captain Armstrong, hands on hips.

"Right now, none of us have any idea how our prototype will perform against the new strain."

"But the early indications were good?"

"Captain, I'm well aware of the critical situation we face, but my team cannot be hurried into making mistakes. It's a painstaking but necessary process. We can only learn through trial and error."

"With all due respect, doctor, your team has been given everything they've asked for, at considerable sacrifice to other units, I might add. My men have scoured the local hospitals and pharmaceutical manufacturing centres. We need results, and we need them fast."

"Look, you all need to understand, we're looking at the greatest medical holocaust in history. The Millennial Virus is now on an altogether different scale from previous pandemics."

"Then there must be more we can do."

"If it keeps mutating, the best advice would be to avoid all contact with the virus. We could be looking at a final death toll in the billions."

"Our quarantine measures were sub-standard," said Lieutenant Peterson.

"What about all those people already infected? We can't just abandon them," challenged the padre. "We promised them a fresh start. A chance to rebuild their shattered lives."

"The padre and lieutenant are both right," said Zed. "This is our failure. The quarantine camps were set up to protect the island from infection. We can't leave those people to their fate."

"They came here seeking sanctuary and all they've found is fresh suffering," admitted the padre. "That does not sit well with me."

"There's nothing more we can do for them." The doctor shrugged. "The camps are part of the problem. They've become incubators for disease."

"But, doctor, we have a duty of care."

Doctor Hardy shook his head, avoiding their eyes, and continued tapping away on his laptop.

"The medical teams from the hospital are doing everything within their power to treat those affected," said the captain. "But without a vaccine, we're simply treating the symptoms rather than addressing the cause."

"We always knew this would happen. This is all part of a natural process," protested the doctor. "In every pandemic, there are always successive waves of infection as the virus mutates and new strains emerge. We saw the same cycle with Asian flu, bubonic plague and the Spanish flu. We all want solutions, but you've got to give me more time to study this new strain."

"Time is the one commodity we have in short supply," admitted the captain. "Meanwhile hundreds of refugees are dying by the day."

"As inconvenient as it sounds, there is always a price to pay for scientific progress."

"Doctor, I refuse to accept that," challenged the colonel. "Either we make a stand right here, right now, or this is going to turn into a massacre."

"What would you suggest? Go back to the mainland? It was only a few weeks ago we were saying the island was our best hope."

"Aren't we forgetting the threat posed by the rebels? We're losing the war on the mainland," admitted the captain.

"The virus is much more of a threat than any rebellion."

"I agree with the doctor," said the colonel. "If we don't take a stand, there'll be nothing left. We fight or we die."

"Colonel, look around you," interrupted the politician. "Since you've been gone, people are deserting in their droves. Morale is crashing. They all remember what happened last time. People are losing hope."

"We simply can't allow that. Anyway, that's your and the padre's responsibility. Perhaps if the carrot is no longer working, then it's time for the stick," suggested the captain. "We need to make an example of any deserters and punish dissent. They'll soon get the message."

"If people have stopped caring, threatening them with punishment is not going to help. Without hope, what do we have left?" challenged David Woods.

"I simply refuse to believe the spirit of the people can be vanquished that easily," said the padre. "The will to carry on in the face of adversity. I choose to believe in man's indefatigability. The promise of a future vaccine would give them that hope."

"I want to believe that too, padre, but look around you," cautioned the politician.

"The human spirit shines brightest in the face of adversity. Pestilence never created anything but grief. It's only when our backs are against the wall and our lives in the balance that we discover what we are capable of."

"I hope you're right."

"I saw the same thing at Paderborn," said the padre. "I assure you, our finest hours lie ahead of us."

"We need to give these people hope, set our collective sights on a brighter future."

"We've allowed ourselves to live in the shadow of grief and the threat of further destruction for too long. I don't know about you, but over the past few weeks, I've witnessed so many small acts of heroism and self-sacrifice. Each time it reaffirms my faith in humanity."

"Padre, please. We should put our faith in science," said the doctor.

"You all had your chance. Science has been humbled by the scale of destruction unleashed by this virus."

"I'm surrounded by luddites and religious fanatics," the doctor muttered under his breath.

"For all your empty claims about scientific progress and genetic engineering, none of you could stop the death of millions, could you?" spat Zed, coming to the padre's aid. "Your so-called experts know just as little about the Millennial Virus as the quacks knew about the bubonic plague six hundred years ago."

"That's rich coming from someone atoning for past failures," scoffed the doctor. "You're the one with blood on your hands, not me. You're still crippled by the guilt of taking this country to war under false pretences. The consequences of your incompetence have been devastating. September 11, 7/7, not to mention terrorist attacks in Paris, Brussels, Nice, Madrid and dozens of other major cities. That's what's really eating you, isn't it?"

Zed shook his head but remained silent. The doctor had touched a raw nerve, an unacceptable truth he would never escape from, however hard he tried.

"This is getting us nowhere," warned the colonel, losing patience. "Unless you two set aside your differences and start working together, none of us are going to have a future. We need both of you to focus on the present and making a difference to our predicament."

"Gentlemen, we can't afford to get distracted," implored the captain. "The fate of everyone on this island rests in our hands. Doctor, if we're going to mount a viable relief effort, then we need immunity from infection."

"Like I say, I can't give you that. The best I can suggest is the provision of masks and hazmat suits."

"We still don't have enough for everyone," continued the captain. "Meanwhile, that virus is knocking our people down like bowling pins."

"Then until you can protect everyone, I suggest we pull them out and buy our scientists more time."

"We should start by issuing health warnings," suggested the politician. "The sooner we tell people about the outbreak, the more support we can expect."

"That's out of the question," dismissed the captain. We can't risk fomenting civil disobedience. We have to keep a lid on this."

"And ignore the lessons from the past?" said the doctor. "With MERS and SARS we learned that changes in public behaviour can make the biggest difference."

"Democracy had its day," continued the captain. "Politics was always a sideshow. A performance but never the solution."

"Nevertheless, planning and communication are going to be the key to our survival," insisted the politician, pointing to the boards and maps that surrounded them. "Re-establishing rule of law, bring these outlaws to justice."

Zed pushed back his chair and walked to the window, looking back towards the main gate where the protesters were waving placards, pressed up against each other. He sighed and turned towards the nearest notice board, half-covered by a grey blanket. He could just make out a series of mugshots, most likely taken from Home Office records: police, passport, driver's licences, or similar.

He lifted up the corner of the blanket and studied the faces. Some like Briggs and Copper he recognised, but others had no photo available, just nicknames written underneath such as "Cutter" or "The Blacksmith". Several of the faces had been crossed out with black marker pen. With a small shudder of delight, he recognised Damian King.

"King's dead? When did that happen?"

"Yesterday," said Lieutenant Peterson flatly, looking over his shoulder. "Sergeant Jones's team have confirmed kills against seven high-priority targets. They're going back out later today to hunt down more of the ringleaders," he added, before readjusting the blanket to cover the remaining faces. "That's strictly between us though," he whispered.

"Understood." Zed nodded.

"Any update on the transmitter?" asked the colonel from behind them.

"We're still having issues throughout the area. Been that way for several weeks now."

"Do we know what's causing all this interference?"

"Best guess is that the main transformer burned out when we turned the power back on. We've had spikes across the network. Equipment failing in all sectors."

"But has anyone actually been up there to check?"

"We don't have the manpower. Cabling's a mess. We're having to run replacements throughout the island and reset the equipment until we find the fault. In the meantime, we keep getting white noise and static."

"If I didn't know better I'd say our communications were being jammed somehow," suggested the captain.

"You think the rebels had something to do with this?"

"I suppose it's possible, but to pull that off you would need some fairly heavy-duty equipment. In the circumstances that doesn't seem likely."

"All the same, sergeant, can you get your team up to Rowridge and take a look as soon as possible?"

"Yes, sir."

\*\*\*\*

As the meeting broke up, the padre stood patiently behind Zed while he finished writing up his notes.

"We haven't met properly. I wanted to introduce myself."

"Of course. I've heard a lot about you. I'm told your spiritual council is helping keep everyone sane around here. After the sisters stirred things up, you're a breath of fresh air."

"Oh, they're not so bad." He laughed. "I got to spend some time with Sister Imelda and the others." He paused as if realising his stupidity. "Sorry, I'm being a bit slow on the uptake this morning. I had the pleasure of meeting your lovely daughter, Heather, and your good friend, Riley."

"How are they?" said Zed, struggling to hide his guilt.

"With any luck, they'll be back in Freshwater by now."

"As far away from here as possible, I hope."

"Quite. So how long have you been a man of the cloth?" asked Zed, changing the subject.

"Twelve years. My father was an officer in the army. I supposed I wanted to be like him. The adventure, the glamorous overseas postings, but I never liked the guns. Most of what I do is pastoral care."

"What does that involve?"

"We're embedded with the ground troops, so we deal with everything you can imagine. People are happy to talk to me because I'm not their commanding officer, but I can still help and advise them.

"I've never met a real-life army chaplain before, let alone a…" He hesitated, trying to think of the politically correct term.

"Man of colour? We're somewhat of a rare breed. Before all this, there was a big push to recruit more ethnic minorities into the armed forces and those from different faiths. I don't suppose there are many like me left now."

"Well, then, it's good to have God on our side," he ventured awkwardly.

They both laughed, but in truth, the mention of Riley and Heather had thrown Zed off-kilter. His last conversation with Gill had made him realise how much his family meant to him. He had secretly hoped he might find them all here at St Mary's on his return.

He had already made up his mind to quit at the next available opportunity. Latterly, he had come to realise that his work for the colonel was a fool's errand. There could be no knowing what caused the outbreak. He was merely going through the motions, locked in a loop from his past. He yearned to break free and start afresh with the remaining people that still mattered to him.

"If you'll excuse me, padre, I have something I need to do."

# Chapter Forty-three

There was an urgent knock at the door to Zed's cramped office, and Doctor Hardy's sheepish face appeared at the crack.

"I've brought you a peace offering."

In one hand he gripped two mugs of tea. Tucked under his arm was a packet of chocolate digestives. Zed remained seated, and pointed towards the visitor chair. Was this a trick or a genuine olive branch?

"I suspect you're wondering why I'm here."

"You could say that."

"Look, I know we haven't always seen eye to eye, but in the circumstances, perhaps we could set aside our differences? Or at least try." He grimaced.

"Look, we all want the same thing."

"It's nothing personal, I assure you. I know you have many questions for me, but there are some things I am simply unable to discuss. I'm happy to cooperate with your investigation, where I can."

"Very well, then. I'll keep my questions general. How much do you know about Spanish flu?" said Zed, gesturing towards the three piles of reports and printed documents on his desk.

"It was the focus of my PhD years ago. What do you need to know?"

"I've read all the various studies contained within the archive. To a layman like myself, the similarities with the current outbreak seem striking. But then, as you keep telling me, I'm not a real scientist."

"Sorry, I didn't mean that. Heat of the moment."

"Absolutely. Water under the bridge."

"Well, as you will have read, Spanish flu is clinically quite different from seasonal influenza. Symptoms typically start within thirty-six to forty-eight hours. Delirium, intense headaches, very high temperature, profuse bleeding from the nose and mouth. In extreme cases it would feel like the lining of your throat and lungs were being ripped out. Black and purple swellings under the armpits like the bubonic plague. Really nasty."

He frowned, dipping a chocolate digestive biscuit into his tea and snapping it between his teeth.

"After the Great War, it became a widely held belief that Spanish flu was an indirect result of the poisoned gas attacks, of rotting corpses left decomposing in No Man's Land, of cholera outbreaks. In reality, scientists spent years analysing the causes of that pandemic. There still remains considerable disagreement as to the aetiology of the virus."

"Aetiology?"

"Sorry, where the virus came from. And you're right, there are some remarkable similarities between Spanish flu and what we're seeing now. Both viruses cause an extreme auto-immune response. In many cases, the healthier the victim, the more extreme the reaction. Organ failure and inflammation of the lungs is typical. We always hoped that the circumstances that produced the 1918 pandemic were unique, unlikely ever to be reproduced."

"By which you presumably mean the thousands of young people from different backgrounds and geographies thrown together into training camps, in close proximity with livestock and fowl, exposed to death and disease on an unimaginable scale? Not to mention the gas attacks, poor hygiene and the filth of No Man's Land?"

"Precisely. Are you familiar with the work of Professor John Oxford? He was one of my former colleagues at the Royal London Hospital Medical School. I knew one of his daughters when I was up at Trinity. Brilliant man. He spent years researching the causes of the 1918-1919 pandemic. He hoped we could all learn the lessons of the past and avoid such an outbreak happening again."

"How?" asked Zed, leaning forward in his chair.

"Well, the professor believed that Spanish flu victims buried in the permafrost of the Arctic Circle might provide scientists with sufficiently preserved internal organs for viable tissue samples. They exhumed countless bodies, hoping that the genetic sequence of the virus could be decoded. When the tissue samples were analysed, what they discovered was that a single strain of bird flu had successfully adapted to infect humans."

"A single strain? But you said flu viruses were always mutating?"

"That's right. We call it antigenic shift. Viruses are always evolving, exchanging genetic material with other viruses. The trick is to find the specific moment when that leap occurred. We're forever playing catch-up with Mother Nature's ingenuity. In some ways, it's like following a river back to its source."

"Then what turns a common or garden seasonal flu virus from a nuisance into a global killer?"

The doctor studied Zed carefully before answering. "The

honest answer is that we simply don't know. That's not the answer you want, but that's the truth."

"So you're telling me that after a hundred years of scientific analysis, with all your resources and technical know-how, we're still essentially fumbling around in the dark?"

"I wouldn't put it quite like that. The progress we've made in the past twenty years has been breathtaking. Genetic engineering has ushered in a new dawn."

"What about this so-called 'gain of function' research?"

"It's a very exciting area. Closely guarded. Porton Down is one of only a handful of facilities worldwide qualified to undertake that research."

"And off the record, was your team engaged in any offensive bioweapons studies before the outbreak?"

The doctor smiled. "You know I can't answer that. I can show you the door, but you need to walk through it yourself."

"The door to where?"

"You asked me before about these so-called chimaera viruses Russia and North Korea were supposed to be working on, and whether two viruses could be spliced together in a lab to create a hybrid. Let's say, for the sake of argument, a virus with the infectiousness of seasonal flu but with the mortality rate of Ebola."

"You mean like the Millennial Virus?"

"Look, let's be candid. We were aware of several clandestine programmes that tried and failed to develop weapons that could strike against the West. Various terrorist groups were known to be experimenting with anthrax and other home-made bacterial weapons. The trouble is, it's much harder than it sounds. Amateur biochemists with a grudge against the world normally kill themselves long before they pose a risk to the general public."

"But if it's only a matter of trial and error, they'll keep trying until one of them pulls it off. The intelligence services can't keep track of them all."

"Look, I know Ephesus has been helping you."

Zed's face remained a mask, giving nothing away.

"That old fool," the doctor laughed. "Filling your head with stories of Nazi super weapons. The sooner you accept that this was a terrible accident of Nature, the sooner we can all move on and deal with the consequences."

Zed thought about defending Ephesus but didn't want to distract the doctor. He seemed to be building up a head of confessional steam.

"Let's, for a moment, assume you're right," encouraged Zed. "Is it possible that the current outbreak on the island is just a seasonal spike linked to the onset of winter?"

"The team are looking at that possibility. Seasonal spikes are closely linked to reduced levels of vitamin D. During the summer months when we spend more hours outdoors in the sunshine, our natural levels of vitamin D rise. Unfortunately, it looks like we're dealing with a new, more potent strain."

"That's emerged as part of this antigenic shift," confirmed Zed, checking his notes. "Is it possible the rebels could have given Mother Nature a helping hand? We heard rumours that the group at Lymington Hospital was running experiments with different strains."

"Manipulating a virus in this way takes highly specialist equipment, far beyond the capabilities of a local hospital. This is cutting-edge science, Mr Samuels."

"But through trial and error might they be able to find and incubate a more potent strain?"

"With enough time and resources, I suppose it's possible. You would still need to somehow bypass the allies' quarantine protocols, not to mention maritime and land-based defences."

"Humour me for a second. How would you go about infecting people on a secure island? Presumably, you can't just do what the Americans did with *Bacillus globigii* and release a cloud of virus to drift over the water."

"Air release is only effective for chemical or bacterial agents." He sighed. "The influenza virus is airborne but extremely vulnerable to sunlight, wind, or even temperature change. Viruses generally cannot live long outside of a host. Your best chance would be to use a human vector. Infect some unsuspecting person and hope that their symptoms don't materialise before they clear quarantine."

"And from there?"

"Nature would run its course. The virus would jump from person to person, camp to camp, town to town until the whole island became infected. Without a viable vaccine, it would be unstoppable."

There was a knock on the door, and the colonel and his aide entered the room. He seemed pleasantly surprised to find Zed and the doctor together.

"If I'm interrupting, I can come back…"

"You're not. We're just exploring some ideas."

"Good. I'm afraid we need you back in Operations. The Americans are getting very hot under the collar."

"About what?"

"They're trying to throw our epidemiologists under the bus, blaming them for inadequate controls. Perhaps you can come and explain?"

****

The doctor leaned back in his chair and threw his head back in annoyance, staring down Lieutenant Peterson.

"Look, the quarantine protocols were drawn up by the very best. Porton Down's own senior epidemiologist, Gill Stephens, was heavily involved."

"Then perhaps we can get her in here and explain why two of my men are in the morgue," said Lieutenant Peterson.

"Unfortunately, she can't be here. She was injured in the attack." The doctor glanced at Zed. For a moment, Zed thought he saw a hint of a triumphant smile on his lips.

"She was poisoned," corrected Zed, staring back defiantly.

"We don't know that for sure."

"Gentlemen," interrupted David Woods, the politician. "I totally refute the allegation that we were not well prepared. The UK Government developed its quarantine protocols based on WHO guidelines. For years now we've been conducting contingency exercises involving the police, military, fire brigade and the NHS. We did everything we could. We stockpiled antivirals, designated schools and leisure facilities as treatment centres and morgues. The island was our best chance."

"Then how do you explain that those measures so spectacularly failed?" asked Peterson. "If your boys had done their jobs, Mr Woods, none of this would have happened."

"Please," interrupted the colonel. "Blaming each other is not going to get us anywhere. Doctor?"

"I worked closely with Miss Stephens. The contingency plans were robust and well designed. Mother Nature simply found a way. The virus adapted."

"And your report states that this latest outbreak could be far deadlier?"

"If I'm right, the first pandemic was just the dress rehearsal for the 'real thing'."

"Meaning?"

"Look, we're still playing catch-up. We need to think differently if we're to get ahead of this."

"We knew we were sitting on a ticking bomb," claimed the American. "Experts have been warning us for years. All that planning and preparation counted for nothing."

"If our models are right," continued the doctor, "without a viable vaccine, we could be looking at a species-defining extinction event. The end of human life as we know it."

Peterson laughed, shaking his head. "You Brits. All you seem to do round here is drink tea and talk about the end of the world," he mocked. "This situation requires definitive action. Operation Cleansweep was designed for exactly this scenario."

"We're not at that stage yet, lieutenant," cautioned Captain Armstrong.

"It's the only way we're going to get ahead of this. Look, if you all lack the backbone—"

"Lieutenant," interrupted the colonel. "Whether you like it or not, we're in this together."

"Perhaps you are not aware," shot back Doctor Hardy, "but your country is just as much to blame for our present circumstances."

"You're not suggesting we had something to do with the outbreak…"

"You keep implying Porton Down was somehow responsible. Let's be honest, the WHO's Sentinel programme absorbed huge budgets and resources, but delivered very little of real value," snarled the doctor. "Mr Samuels here has investigated enough illegal weapons programmes to recognise the hallmarks of a biological agent. He maintains that there are sufficient grounds for us to be suspicious about the origin of the Millennial Virus."

"An agent bioengineered for a specific purpose," Zed said,

taking over from the doctor. "As a collective, we'd be foolish to dismiss these lines of investigation. And while everyone's been pointing the finger at Iraq, North Korea and Russia, there's emerging evidence that America was conducting the bulk of the research in this area."

"That's ridiculous! What would the US have to gain from developing biological weapons like these?"

"Isn't it obvious? A new world order. The annihilation of all human threats in one fell swoop. Leaving all the civilian infrastructure intact and operational for an invading force."

"Have you lost your mind? We were the first line of defence, for God's sake. The protector of the free world. No country did more to enforce the Biological Weapons Convention, to roll back the years on the proliferation of WMDs."

"What a government says and does can be quite different. I'm here to tell you that the Americans were one of the worst offenders," claimed Doctor Hardy, rising from his chair and leaning across the table to lend authority to his words. "The USA applied all its industrial might to research and production. At the end of the Second World War America possessed more than one hundred thousand tonnes of poisoned gas, more than every other nation on earth put together."

"But that's ancient history."

"I wouldn't be so sure. At the end of the Cold War and the fall of the USSR, we all knew what really happened to those Russian specialists. They were recruited by the Americans."

"That is just conjecture."

"No, lieutenant. I saw at first hand the continuing scale of those programmes. I toured Camp Derrick in Maryland, Horn Island in Mississippi, Granite Peak in Utah. There was an exchange programme between our two countries. The American teams were pioneering working with highly infectious organisms, including the influenza virus."

"Yes, but as part of a robust defence strategy, doctor. You can't seriously be suggesting that the UK's oldest ally was using these technologies to develop first-strike weapons?"

"No one is suggesting that yet, but it's well known that Porton Down restricted our research to biological weapons where there was a known cure, whereas places like Camp Derrick took a very different approach. In many cases, they concentrated their efforts where there was no cure. It became a race against time to stay one step ahead. Our primary defence was intelligence, learning about the current focus of numerous research programmes, including yours, and preparing the West in case of biological attack."

"With a virus like this, it would only take one mistake. We know that industrial accidents occur—" Zed began to say.

"None of us know what really happened," countered Peterson. "We've been marooned on this God-forsaken island for so long, who knows what's going on in the rest of the world?"

"That's right," continued the doctor. "Since we lost all communications we only have your word for what happened."

"We've told you already!" shouted Peterson in disbelief. "The virus was everywhere. We saw at first hand in Pakistan, India, Oman, the UAE, Saudi Arabia, Egypt that the world was a total goddam mess. They were all battling infection."

"We have no reason to doubt you," admitted the captain, "but you see, you are the first and only visitors to these shores since the outbreak. We have no way of corroborating what actually happened."

"So, what, you think those TV and radio reports before the blackout were all faked?"

"Please, let's all take a step back," pleaded the colonel, trying to calm things down. "No one's seriously accusing anyone of deliberately starting the outbreak."

"Aren't they? It sounds to me like the doctor was suggesting the *Chester* was going around infecting the world!"

Doctor Hardy smiled back. He seemed to be enjoying the lieutenant's temporary loss of control.

"Well, I for one don't feel like we've ever had an adequate explanation for why the Americans came here in the first place," challenged David Woods. "Why choose the Isle of Wight when you could head home or anywhere else, for that matter?"

"I've told you before. We triangulated your radio traffic, we knew there were survivors here. With the geographical advantages of a large island with natural resources, I admit, the Isle of Wight was on our shortlist. It had everything our planners needed to kick-start a relief operation. We came here to help you, for Christ's sake."

"You showing up out of the blue was a bit of a surprise to all of us. A welcome one, I might add," admitted the colonel.

"This whole region was a hot mess when we arrived. You could barely organise yourselves, let alone a relief operation. Give us a little credit. We were the catalyst that got this all started."

"No one's denying the role you played."

"Well, it doesn't sound that way to me, sir. Look, if we're not welcome any more, you be sure to let us know, and we'll find someplace else."

"My apologies, lieutenant. We didn't mean to hurt your feelings. Your timing was fortuitous, that's all."

"Look, I get it, everyone's strung out. It's been a difficult few days, but let's not get distracted."

"The lieutenant is right," said the colonel. "The search for a cure is what matters. We simply have to find an answer."

"One of the other main reasons we came here was because of the proximity to Porton Down," admitted Peterson. "We are all hoping the doctor's team could figure out the answer before it's too late."

"I appreciate your vote of confidence, but we still have nothing. A promising prototype with limited effectiveness against some strains of the virus."

"Doctor, without a vaccine, we're looking at the final rout of our civilisation."

"We're all aware of the urgency of our situation. Whatever it takes. How can we help you?"

"We'll need a reliable source of test subjects. Children preferably, with immature immune systems."

"Go on."

"Look, I'm not indifferent to the question of medical ethics, but the discovery of a viable vaccine will vindicate every sacrifice that has been made in its creation."

"So, spell it out. What are you really asking for?"

He hesitated as if what he really needed was too bold to give voice to. "Infants, unborn foetuses if possible."

There was a silence round the table as they each came to terms with the real meaning of sacrifice.

"I can raise this with the sisters, but the likelihood of them actively supporting what amounts to human experimentation on aborted foetuses is, I'm afraid, zero."

"Then someone needs to explain that this is the price we need to pay. For scientific progress."

"One way or another, it must be done. We have to find a way, whatever it takes. It's our biological imperative to survive."

"If we are to get through the next few months, then we must

set aside this squeamishness," suggested the doctor.

"Pointing fingers at each other and indulging in conspiracy theories will get us nowhere," agreed the American.

"Between the virus and the rebellion," began the colonel, "a state of emergency exists that permits us, the acting government, to ask everyone to make sacrifices for the greater good. Our obligations to medical ethics and the rule of law must become secondary to our primary need for survival."

"We fight together or we die together," confirmed Peterson with an air of finality.

"Then if we are all agreed. May I suggest—"

From outside came a sound that Zed initially struggled to identify. A low whine that built up into the full wail of a hand-turned air raid siren. It evoked black-and-white war movies from Zed's youth, of Spitfires and Messerschmitts criss-crossing the skies.

Everyone turned as one towards Captain Armstrong. He seemed momentarily lost for words. The door was thrown open and an aide ushered them all outside.

"Follow me, please. We'll take you to a safe location."

# Chapter Forty-four

Downstairs in the central atrium of the hospital building, there was an air of panic as people raced to their appointed stations, elbowing others out of the way. The base commander stood rock-like in the middle, directing groups as they flowed around him.

The colonel, padre and Zed fought their way towards him.

"Commander!" the colonel shouted several times before making himself heard. "What's going on?"

"There was an attempted perimeter breach behind the Albany Prison compound. We're getting initial reports of disturbances throughout the island."

"Where?" asked Zed, thinking about the others at Freshwater.

"Ryde, Cowes and Newport, so far."

"And we think the attacks are coordinated?" asked the colonel.

"We don't know that yet, sir. We're interrogating two of the intruders, but they're not talking. There was a breakout from Camp Three earlier this morning."

"How did they get out?"

"Apparently, they rushed the gate, overpowered the guard unit and took their weapons. We've sent an armoured convoy to intercept, but they've disappeared. Probably gone cross-country."

"Or they've headed west instead, away from here?"

It made perfect sense to Zed. Why would civilians risk going head to head with a heavily armed group? More likely they would make for less populated areas in the south and west of the island.

"St Mary's is on high alert, just in case they come here to link up with the protesters."

"Have we tried to speak with the ringleaders? Perhaps we could send our resident MP, David Woods. They might listen to him," suggested the padre.

"We've tried. They blame the allies for not doing more to protect them. They're threatening a mass uprising. They intend to take back the whole island for themselves. Now, gentlemen, if you'll excuse me, shall I find someone to take you all to the command bunker?"

"That won't be necessary, thank you. We know where we're going."

They pushed through the crowd. With all the talk of island-wide disturbances, Zed was worried about Riley and Heather, and the new dangers heading their way.

Outside, it was just beginning to rain, a thin drizzle. Dark clouds were blowing in from the north, threatening a heavier downpour.

As they rounded the building, chants from the protesters at the front gate grew louder. Zed was surprised to see people ten-deep, pressed up against the fence as far as the eye could see.

"It might be safer to take the long way round."

"Wait. I should try talking to these people. Maybe they'll listen to me."

"Not now, padre. They're about to use tear gas again. I don't think we should stick around," urged the colonel, retracing his steps away from the commotion.

Soldiers were already setting up barricades and taking up secondary defensive positions as if they expected the fence to give way at any moment. The guards nearest them were unpacking what looked like smoke grenades and a launcher.

The padre lingered, and Zed found himself frozen to the spot, caught between them, unsure what to do. He reached out to lead the padre away, but he shrugged him off.

"We can't let this escalate. Someone has to try," he said purposefully, advancing from cover.

"Wait, don't..." started Zed, but it was too late. The padre set off towards the fence.

For a moment, Zed stood and admired the chaplain's courage, his refusal to accept that this confrontation was beyond resolution.

The chaplain was no more than ten metres from the fence now, close enough for the ire of the crowd to become more focused. Then something unexpected happened. A pocket of silence seemed to radiate out as a sea of grubby faces stared back at him, puzzled by his boldness.

"Don't be fooled by the uniform. I'm not a soldier; I'm the chaplain here." His voice carried a calm assurance, sustaining an eerie quiet as those further back strained to hear. He pointed to the small cross embroidered on his uniform.

"I need you all to listen. We need everyone to return to their homes. There's been a new outbreak, just south of here. You're all in danger if you stay here. Help us deal with this."

He paused while his message rippled out to the others behind.

"There's no need to be alarmed. We've beaten this before, and we'll beat it again."

"That's easy for you to say. You're on the other side of the fence," pointed out a mean-faced woman with grey hair.

"This is our island, not yours!" shouted another, to the jeers and boos of those around her.

"Please," he said, appealing for calm.

"Your sort don't belong here."

The chaplain bristled at the implied racial slur but carried on. "If you don't disperse and return to your homes, the soldiers behind me are under orders to disperse the crowd, whatever it takes," he said, pointing at the men behind him readying their weapons.

The padre's voice was lost in a chorus of dissent, as more people shouted abuse at him. He seemed to hesitate in the face of such ferocity, glancing over his shoulder, appealing to Zed for moral support. The crowd latched onto the hesitation as a sign of weakness. He was isolated and exposed.

Zed felt duty-bound to stand shoulder to shoulder with the chaplain but noticed soldiers to his right moving forward, taking up firing positions behind a low wall as if anticipating trouble.

"Father!" shouted Zed, realising the danger he was in. Somehow he had to get him back to safety. He looked around for anything he could use.

A single shot silenced the crowd as everyone turned towards its source. Along the fence, near some bushes, a hooded youth stood trembling, barely able to hold the smoking handgun steady in his shaking hands.

The padre staggered for a moment, a look of disappointment settled on his features. He collapsed on the grass, clutching his side.

Those around the youth stood motionless. The weapon was quickly torn from his hands. The crowd closed around him, smuggling him away.

Without a thought for his own safety, Zed ran towards the body prone on the grass, throwing himself on the ground to shield him from further harm.

The padre's jaw was clenched as he gritted his teeth against the surging pain. His eyes flickered open long enough to recognise Zed.

"I had to try."

Zed checked him over quickly. His right side was already soaked in blood.

"I'm sorry."

"Can you stand?"

"Just save yourself."

Behind them, a guard unit hurried forward, firing over the heads of the group beyond the fence. One of the soldiers broke off and ran towards Zed.

Between them, they levered the injured man upright. He could barely stand, groaning, his body bent double in agony. The guard noticed Zed's prosthetic arm.

"Help me lift him," implored Zed.

The guard helped hoist the chaplain's trembling frame over Zed's shoulder, crying out with the effort. They staggered back towards the building as another shot kicked up a sod of grass by his feet.

Zed felt the impact of the next bullet as much as heard it. A dull thud as the padre was hit again in the lower back. His whole body went limp.

Zed reached the brick wall and rounded the corner, shielding them from further fire. The colonel helped lower the padre down, cradling his head against the crumbling masonry.

"Medic!" cried the colonel above the distant shouting and intermittent rifle shots. Two paramedics from the hospital were already running towards them. One carried a green medical bag. They barged their way through the small crowd and knelt beside the padre's body, checking for vital signs.

"He's still breathing."

Zed sat back on his haunches, pointing towards the chaplain's right side.

"Two shots. One in the stomach and one in the back."

"Okay, let's get a drip set up. Stand back, please. Let me work."

Zed flinched as a machine gun started firing behind them. Screams from the crowd shook him to the core.

They cut open the padre's camouflaged jacket, exposing his chest and silver cross hanging from a chain. On his right side, just below the ribcage was a neat entry wound that pulsed with a steady flow of blood that trickled down his side. The paramedic half rolled him to the right.

"Single entry point to the lower abdomen. No exit wound. Second entry wound lower back. Again, no exit."

Zed's hand covered his mouth, watching the paramedic work. The man pushed his glasses back up his nose with gloved fingers, considering what he could do to keep him alive. He rummaged in his bag and ripped open a packet containing sterilised gauze. He tore strips off and stuffed the fabric directly into the bullet holes to staunch the bleeding. At the other end, his partner began giving chest compressions.

"Can you get a trolley up here? Quickly, please!" he shouted towards a passing group of nurses hurrying towards their station.

"Blood pressure is still falling," said the other paramedic. "He's losing too much blood."

The padre's face was expressionless, almost beyond pain. They worked relentlessly, waiting for the trolley to arrive, but their exchange of looks betrayed what they already knew. The colonel put a hand on Zed's shoulder and led him away.

"He thought he could make them see sense," half-whispered Zed, shaking his head.

"Who shoots a man of the cloth, for God's sake?" said the paramedic, noticing the cross on his uniform for the first time.

"How were they to know?" mourned Zed.

After several minutes the other paramedic ceased chest compressions. "I'm sorry."

"You did your best," said the colonel. "You couldn't have done more."

"He didn't deserve this. Not after everything he's done," lamented Zed, as the colonel escorted him away.

"Come on, we still have work to do."

****

They followed the colonel's aide down a metal staircase towards the basement complex of the largest hospital building. This underground rabbit warren of interconnected storerooms had been designated as a backup operations centre in case of attack. A number of workstations were already set up to accommodate the various personnel relocated here.

Zed's hands were still shaking. After what had happened to Gill and now the padre, he felt numb. He was drowning in a rising tide of futility. What did any of this matter? Sooner or later they were all going to die. He cursed the nonsensical nature of a world turned on its head.

At the doorway, the enormous frame of a professional soldier stood guard in his immaculate uniform, polished boots, and brass buttons. There was a holster on his hip. It took Zed a moment to recognise the man.

"Flynn? Why, you…" Something in Zed snapped. He barged the larger man back against the wall, catching him cold. Flynn's head smashed against the rough concrete as he wrestled with Zed.

Flynn grabbed hold of Zed's collar, forcing him back against the opposite wall. Zed's blood was up, spoiling for a fight. He'd made a promise to himself that if he ever saw Flynn again, he'd make him pay for what happened back at Hurst.

"Have you both lost your minds?" shouted the colonel as he tried to separate them.

"Get him off me!" cried Flynn in the scuffle.

They were finally prised apart. Zed fought to free his arms, straining to have another swing at the soldier. Flynn straightened his jacket and stooped to pick up the beret from the floor.

"What's this all about?"

"He attacked me, sir."

"You know why—"

"That's enough. Get a grip, Samuels."

"You should be locked up. You're unstable!" shouted Flynn.

"You didn't lift a finger to help him, did you?"

"What are you talking about?" asked the colonel, looking from one man to the other, waiting for an answer. "Explain yourselves."

"Jack got himself killed. He was his own worst enemy. He wouldn't listen to any of us," said Flynn.

"Bullshit! Your men did nothing to stop it."

"How could we? There were too many of them. They overran the castle."

"You're a coward, Flynn." Zed surged against those restraining him, almost breaking free again.

Flynn stood up taller, towering over Zed. "I'm not scared of you."

"Did no one tell you who I am?"

"You're nothing, a pencil-pusher," he sneered.

"No, Flynn. I'm your worst nightmare. You really think I'll have any trouble bringing someone like you to justice?"

"My men will back me up. You've got nothing on me. You're pathetic," he spat, looking Zed up and down, sneering at his prosthetic arm.

"Corporal Flynn!" interrupted the colonel. "Either you show Mr Samuels the appropriate respect, or you'll be back on the frontline before you know it. Do I make myself clear?"

"Yes, sir." He snapped to attention, staring at the wall beyond the colonel, his top lip trembling with indignation. He dipped his head in acquiescence, whispering under his breath. "You haven't heard the last of this, Samuels."

"That's enough, sergeant!" commanded the captain, arriving behind them. "You're relieved. Get a grip of yourself."

Flynn brushed past Zed and headed outside. The colonel waited until the others had gone and leaned in close to Zed's ear.

"I will not tolerate another outburst like that. Do we understand each other? I expect you to conduct yourself like an officer, or not at all. Clear?"

"Crystal."

"This ends here."

"Yes, sir. Perhaps you'd be good enough to tell me why the corporal is here in the first place."

"Hurst Castle was abandoned weeks ago. Didn't you hear?"

"Since when?"

"We couldn't spare the men. They were needed elsewhere. Now go and make yourself useful. Find Doctor Hardy. He'll be in the lab."

Zed retraced his steps back up to ground level, punching the plaster wall in frustration. He stared at his skinned knuckles, shaking with anger.

The main concourse and thoroughfare were deserted. Aside from the last stragglers hurrying to where they should have been half an hour ago, he had the road to himself and time to think.

From the direction of the main gate, he could see smoke now billowing above the two-story outbuildings. The mob had been driven back, but he was sure they would come again.

Zed approached the checkpoint in front of the new science block. The guard looked him up and down, stiffening as he approached. Zed flashed his pass, and the guard waved him through.

One of the orderlies at the main desk directed him towards the secure laboratories where they worked with more hazardous substances.

He passed room after room filled with empty cages and intermittent animal noises of birds, cats, dogs, or chimpanzees. It was hard to tell from the cacophony. At the end was a prep room where lab workers were scrubbing down, sealing each other into pressure suits.

Through a large perspex panel, he could see Doctor Hardy already inside the lab, wearing an oversized headpiece that exaggerated his features. He was unpacking the blue storage box he had brought from Porton. He looked up as Zed entered and held his arm up in welcome.

"They've just gone in," said a junior lab assistant, standing next to Zed. "You're welcome to wait, if you like. There's coffee next door. Help yourself."

Within the sealed room, the doctor was checking inside the storage container again as if hunting for something. He placed the vials of liquid on the countertop and counted them again.

Several of the slots appeared to be empty.

The doctor approached the glass viewing panel and pushed the intercom button. "You're sure no one has tampered with this?"

The lab assistant nodded, confused by the question.

"Then I don't understand," continued the doctor. "This box has been in my possession since leaving Porton Down."

"What's he looking for?" asked Zed, puzzled by their exchange. "The vaccine samples?"

The lab assistant hesitated. "I guess so. Or the other items they brought back."

Zed struggled to hide his disappointment. He had naively assumed that the portable refrigeration unit contained a treasured source of hope and salvation, but now it appeared the unit might also hold the seeds of their destruction.

# Chapter Forty-five

Victor led Terra back to the doctor's office within Lymington New Forest Hospital, locking her in to avoid arousing further suspicion. He promised to return as soon as he had spoken to Briggs.

All the clocks in this part of the management suite had stopped and, without a watch, the minutes felt like hours. Trapped in her makeshift cell, she wondered what lies Copper was telling Briggs and whether Victor could ever really be trusted again. She was caught between a rock and a hard place. Without his help as her advocate, she didn't have many options left. How on earth could she get a message to the allies now?

Copper's henchmen returned at first light. She had named them Little and Large. She regretted her earlier choice of words. It was not advisable to bite the hand that fed you.

The two men delivered Terra to Copper's care in the central atrium. From the waiting room next door, she heard Briggs's voice and strained to see around the doorway. He emerged a few minutes later, staring straight ahead as if in a trance. Was he still angry with her or was there something else troubling him?

Sat on the sofas in reception were two people she didn't recognise. One was a stout fellow with a heavy beard and close-set eyes, in his early thirties. There was a self-satisfied air about him that Terra took an instant dislike to. The other was older, with a soft round face, used to taking orders.

"King's dead," said Briggs flatly. "They couldn't save him. Copper, I want you to take over responsibility for the hospital. He would have wanted that."

"Yes, boss."

Copper seemed downcast, but the others shrugged at the news. Perhaps they had already expected the worst.

"Then long live the new king," said the bearded man with an Irish accent, trying to be clever, but trying too hard. Briggs's eyes narrowed, unamused.

"Seamus and Henry, your Highcliffe unit will come under Copper's command." Briggs nodded towards the new arrivals. "Victor, you want to explain what we just discussed with the others?"

"Sure," he said with undeniable relish, clearly enjoying being back in Briggs's favour. "Between the virus and the disturbances we've set in motion, the allies' focus will be on the island. That leaves Lymington wide open."

"Our scouts say there's a token force there," said Briggs. "With more units being redeployed to Fawley Refinery, Southampton docks, and Portsmouth Harbour, their line is stretched very thin. Now's our chance."

"We'll teach those boys a lesson," boasted Seamus.

"The cars are waiting. Good luck," said Briggs, shaking hands with each of them.

"What about that little job we discussed for Terra?" asked Victor.

Briggs glanced at her, his expression loaded with begrudging remorse.

"Copper owes you an apology."

Briggs' demand was met with a dismissive shrug from Copper as if it was the last thing on his mind.

"He'd got it into his thick skull that you were behind the attack on King. That you were conspiring against us, but I set him straight. I mean, why would you want me and the others dead?" He smiled with heavy irony. "I told him, you're headstrong, yes, and you don't know when to put a lid on it, but you're not a murderer."

There was a knock on the door, and a young boy was led in. He made a beeline for Briggs.

"There you are. Come over here, son."

Terra studied the boy, curious to know more. He looked about ten or eleven with brown hair and freckled good looks. There was a sadness about him like the last few years had hollowed him out and left nothing but emptiness.

"You know who this lady is?" Briggs asked the boy.

The boy shook his head, holding on to the armrest of Briggs's chair.

"She's going to be looking after you from now on. Name's Terra."

The boy blinked up at her, his expression blank.

"What's your name, darling?" she said, going down on one knee.

"Connor."

"Connery is one of my favourite names. It was my dad's name."

"Just Connor," he corrected.

"Victor tells me you used to have a kid, Terra. I thought you might like someone to look after. Go on, Connor, tell the lady who your father is."

"I don't have a father."

"Now, now, don't be like that. That's no way to speak about family."

"His name was Zed, Zed Samuels."

Terra could barely contain her astonishment. "My God. Where on earth did you find him?" she said, cupping the boy's chin. "Where have you been all this time, darling?"

"Living in a caravan park in Hayling Island."

"All on your own?"

"I was with a group. I got separated when we moved to the island with the other refugees."

"Separated from whom? Your mum?"

"No, my big sister."

"Is she here too?" she asked, barely believing her ears, glancing at Briggs.

Connor just shrugged like he didn't care.

"He doesn't know. One of my men found him at a school near Newport where they put all the kids with no family. Apparently, he refused to give them his last name," whispered Briggs. "When he did, one of Victor's informants recognised the name right away, put two and two together, brought him here."

"Where have you been all this time?" she asked again.

"They locked me up with all these sick people, said I was infected too. I was there for weeks. Left us there to die. You have no idea what they did to us…" he said, tears welling in his eyes.

Terra tried to put her arms around him, but he pushed her away.

"Of course not. I can't imagine. So, what happened to your sister?"

"She never came to collect me," he said through clenched teeth.

"You poor thing."

Briggs motioned behind Connor's back that he might have some unresolved mental issues. "You were a bit messed when we found you, weren't you, lad? Had a rough time of it. Saw things no kid your age should see. But," acknowledged Briggs, "it's made a man of you. You survived. That's what counts."

"I don't want to be treated like a child any more."

"Of course you don't. You've got a new family now. We're your family, isn't that right?" said Briggs, encouraging Terra to take him under her wing.

"Come on, Connor. I'll take you to your new home. Can someone give me a lift to Walhampton?" She smiled confidently, wondering whether she was now free to leave the hospital. Briggs's eyes narrowed for a moment, considering her request, then nodded his consent.

Terra guided Connor towards the door. Briggs got to his feet and followed them out. The hairs on the back of her neck prickled in anticipation. He caught up with the pair of them, falling into step.

"Listen, Terra, I know things were said, things we both regret. There was stuff going on, stuff I couldn't talk about."

"I know," she said with a smile. "I'm sorry I doubted you."

"It took me a while to realise something."

Terra stopped mid-stride, unsure where he was going with this. He seized on her puzzled expression.

"You still can't see it, can you? You and I, we've always wanted the same thing. I kept telling you, but you wouldn't listen."

"I was worried King was manipulating you. I realise now I was wrong. It was the other way round all the time," said Terra, knowing she was reaching for something she only half-suspected was true.

"King was just a jumped-up northerner, blinded by greed. All he cared about was power. Still, he served his purpose, got us this far. I'll give him that but, like anyone else, he failed to see he was dispensable."

His words hung in the air like a veiled threat.

"Then tell me what I'm missing."

"It's been staring you in the face all this time, but you can't see it. Did you never wonder why I chose you?"

She shook her head, stroking Connor's hair absent-mindedly. From a distance, she imagined they might look like a family.

"When I first heard about you, I knew straight away."

"Knew what?"

"Most people around here saw the breakdown as an opportunity. People like King or Seamus were driven by rage, to get one over, to take something that didn't belong to them. They were so blinded they forgot who they really were, what they stood for, but you didn't, did you?"

"I suppose we all did what we thought was right."

"Exactly. You see, you and I still yearn for a time when honour and respect actually meant something. We share the same values."

Something clicked for Terra. She had always been puzzled why she was attracted to men like Jack and Briggs. Perhaps they had something in common after all.

"Sometimes, it takes something terrible to make something good happen," he continued. "This country used to be the best place in the world. I'm not talking about the Swinging Sixties or Cool Britannia. I'm talking about years before, after the war, when people made do with nothing. The stories I grew up with of families pulling together, of community. When all that other stuff is stripped away, people are forced to understand what really matters."

"Then tell me what you really want."

"A fresh start for you and me and the others. I want my island back. I couldn't care less about power. That's what drove King. Not me. I'll give it back to the people it belongs to. Not these cuckoos."

"But how? You're not the only one who wants that place."

"There's going to be a purge. Things are going to be different now King's not around. It'll be just like old times, but better."

There was a renewed confidence about Briggs. Terra got the impression that, far from being a setback, this was what he had wanted all along.

"People keep underestimating you, don't they?" she said, reaching out a trembling hand to stroke his face.

"They always have."

"Just give me another chance," she pleaded. "I can change too. I can be what you want me to be, you'll see."

"You still don't get it, do you? I want you to stop pretending and be who you really are."

"I don't know what you mean," she lied.

"I've been surrounded by liars and cheats all my life. Don't you think I see through all that?"

He pulled her in close, gripping her arm so tightly it began to pinch. He pretended to kiss her cheek but whispered in her ear, "I told you, you'd learn to appreciate me," taking her earlobe between his teeth. "Now take the boy back to the school before I change my mind."

"What do you want me to do with him?"

"I haven't decided yet. I figured he might come in handy when the time comes."

He released his grip and smacked her on the bottom. Connor watched them with dead eyes.

Outside, there was a car parked by the entrance with its engine running but no one inside. She looked around but there was no sign of the driver.

Behind her, she heard Victor's voice, laughing with someone, patting him on the back like an old friend.

"Wait in the car, Connor. I'll be with you in two minutes," said Terra, craving closure with Victor before she went. Terra and Victor waited until the others were inside the vehicle so they would not be overheard.

"I've taken care of everything," claimed Victor. "I'll get Sam and Tommy out tonight."

"I don't know what to say. How?"

"The guard will leave their window unlocked. They can get out the same way they got in."

"Thank you." She sighed with relief. "Can I speak to them before I leave?"

"They're waiting for you. They know nothing. If you go now, there should be no one around. The guard will be expecting you. You owe me. Now go, quickly."

Terra wasted no time, staying in the shadows, making sure no one could see her from the balcony above. The guard stood up as she approached, and unlocked the door.

Sam and Tommy seemed much better than the last time she had visited. She hugged them both and stepped back.

"There's no time to explain. I'm getting you out."

Sam blinked back at her, barely able to take it in, waiting for her to continue. She explained Victor's plan, making sure they understood what needed to happen.

"Turn yourselves into the first allied patrol you find. It's vital you deliver a message to Captain Armstrong. Can you do that?"

"Of course."

"Tell him this new strain of the virus came from Lymington Hospital. It was King's doing. The professor says it has a longer incubation period and a higher mortality rate. Got that?"

"Longer incubation, higher mortality. Why is the professor helping them?"

"He doesn't have a choice. They made him do it. There's one other thing. When you see Zed, tell him Briggs has his son. Can you do that?"

"Sure. Come with us, Terra. Tell him yourself."

"Not until I've finished what I started."

"Why? You don't need to stay."

"It would take too long to explain. There's a car waiting. Look, I'm doing this for you, Sam. For Hurst." She kissed him, tears in her eyes. "I'll never forget you, Sam."

"Just make sure you come back."

"When this is all over. Wish me luck, I'm going to need it."

With that, she turned and left, striding past the guard and down the corridor with renewed purpose. As she took the steps two at a time, she heard the heavy metal door behind her slam shut. She took a deep breath, eyes closed, steeling herself for the final part of her plan.

# Chapter Forty-six

It was still dark when the dinghy carrying Riley, Heather and Adele rounded the Needles rocks and beat back into the wind and waves, spray lashing the open boat.

The high cliffs of the Needles Headland and Tennyson Down sheltered them from the worst of the strengthening north-easterly wind. Every now and again the wind would flip around in the opposite direction as it raced between gullies above their heads. Heather remained alert to the danger. The waves too were confused as wind and tide collided. Sweeping in from the channel, they could hear rollers surging up the beach in front of the old Lifeboat station to crash among the pebbles and rocks.

Riley was anxiously looking ahead, trying to figure out the safest way of getting ashore. They could take their chances and risk wrecking the boat on the beach or tie off against one of the buoys at the western end of the bay nearest the waterfront hotel. It would mean one or more of them would have to swim the remaining twenty metres to shore.

Riley volunteered to drop the girls in the surf and paddle back out to the buoy. She figured they might need the dinghy again. Between them, they stowed the sails as best they could. For now, they hoped the dinghy would survive till dawn on the mooring.

With any luck, they could persuade Sam to swim out later and sail her back around to Yarmouth Harbour.

Riley went as close as she dared, struggling to control their approach in the surf. A larger wave caught them unawares and almost tipped the boat. It grounded for a second on the shelving beach as she grabbed the paddle and pushed off before the next roller swept towards them.

The girls jumped one after the other into the freezing cold water, gasping and shouting as their heads popped up again. As they found their footing, they pushed the bow round, back the way they had come. Riley threw the rucksacks one by one, hoping they could reach them in the surf.

She fought hard to keep the bow head onto the breaking waves, paddling as hard as she could. The cockpit was already ankle-deep in water, making her feet slip and slide, struggling for purchase.

She could see the buoy directly ahead of her now. She was soaking wet, spray in her eyes, salt water in her mouth, gritting her teeth at the supreme effort to escape the last few yards beyond the breakwater.

The buoy reared up beside her, and she lunged for it, nearly losing the paddle over the side. Gripping the buoy tightly with one hand, she reached for the painter, looping the line through the eye and tied it off on the cleat at the bow. Once all the other gear was safely stowed, she checked her life jacket was securely tightened and stepped over the side.

The cold water took her breath away. She surfaced and wiped water from eyes, struggling to get her bearings as a wave broke over her head. She sighted Adele and Heather waving on the shingle and set off towards them. Her clothing and shoes acted like a sea anchor making it difficult to swim, but she persisted.

She could sense a strong current sweeping her along the beach towards the prominent rocks at the far side of the bay.

Before she knew it, Riley could feel the steeply-shelving shingle shifting under her feet. Standing up she stumbled the rest of the way, exhausted by the effort. Heather and Adele came rushing down to meet her, helping her upright and supporting her to the concrete hard.

She recognised an army truck from the Needles Battery already there to meet them. Two dark shapes walked towards them, carrying armfuls of blankets.

"Courtesy of Corporal Carter," said the taller of the two, handing them one each. They kept their distance as if they didn't dare come any closer. "You need to come with us. Our orders are to take you back to the Battery."

"But we only live up there," said Riley, shaking uncontrollably with cold, pointing to the Freshwater Bay Hotel. "I told the corporal earlier, we've only come from St Mary's. We're not infected."

"You're still subject to quarantine."

Behind the soldiers, she noticed a small crowd of people making their way towards the beach, carrying torches and lanterns to light their way. She held up her hand to shield the light in her eyes, struggling to make out their faces.

"Now what's all this about? Making such a racket in the middle of the night," said a voice she recognised instantly as Liz. "Riley? Is that you? You lot look like drowned rats. Who are you two?" she said, shining the torch in the soldiers' faces.

"They're Carter's men. They're trying to take us back to the Battery."

"Is that so? Can't you see they're freezing to death? I suggest you get Carter on the radio."

"We've got our orders. We're not leaving without them."

"Then you best come inside too. There's a hot brew back at the hotel.

"Listen, you've got your orders, I've got mine," Riley bluffed, holding up the radio as if it were proof. "Unless you want me to wake up Captain Armstrong?"

Being this close to home, she was in no mood to argue. The two soldiers glanced at each other, wrong-footed by Riley's lie.

"Captain Armstrong? Perhaps there's been some misunderstanding then," one of them mumbled, unsure what to do.

Liz glared at the two boys in uniform. "I suggest you get that corporal of yours to come back in the morning. He knows where to find us."

"Come on, Ben, we're wasting our time." The larger of the two shrugged, noticing Will eye-balling him. "We'll come back at first light."

"You do that. We'll be waiting," said Riley, shivering so much she could barely speak.

****

Back at the hotel, news had spread fast. Everyone was already up, and an early breakfast had been laid out for the new arrivals.

Riley spotted Scottie brooding by the front entrance. She nudged Liz who led the girls inside to find them a change of clothes. Scottie casually handed her his cup of coffee, but in place of his usual smile was a furrowed concern.

"We thought you weren't coming back," he said, shaking his head. "You've been gone for days. Where have you been?"

Riley took a deep breath and explained what had happened with Adele's extended stay in hospital, collecting Heather from Ventnor, not to mention the attack at St Mary's and the outbreak at the quarantine camp.

"If we hadn't left when we did, I'm not sure we would have got back here at all."

"There's been some trouble with the locals. The soldiers refused to do anything."

"I know, Scottie. I'm sorry I wasn't here. I made a promise to Zed. I had no choice, okay?"

"We always have a choice."

"Look, can we talk about this another time? We've got bigger issues to discuss. I've asked Liz to gather everyone together in the hall in twenty minutes. We don't have long."

****

The dining room fell silent as Riley climbed onto a table to address the room. After speaking with Scottie and Will, she had quickly changed into dry clothes and towel-dried her hair. She was still shaking from the adrenaline and the cold, she couldn't tell which, massaging her arms and hands to get blood circulating back to her extremities.

Scottie and Will took up positions below her, arms crossed, body language muted as if they hadn't yet made their minds up about what she had proposed.

Riley looked around the room at the expectant faces, searching for Sam and Tommy but not finding them. While they were waiting for the last few to arrive, she bent lower as Scottie explained what had happened.

"I told them not to go." Scottie shrugged. "But Sam wouldn't listen. Ask Will, he was the one who went with them."

"Why, Will?" she berated, turning her attention to the South African. "Why go back? Have you forgotten what happened last time we went there looking for you? It didn't turn out so well—"

"When we found out what the hospital group had done to

Jack, we couldn't let it go. We had to do something. Sam wanted to go on his own, but we wouldn't let him. I agreed to take them."

"So where are they now?"

"Briggs knew we were coming. There were too many of them. I'm sorry. I was the only one who got away."

"We'll talk about this later. Not now."

She shook her head, too tired to be angry. If King and Briggs had captured them, then they were probably already dead. There was no helping them now. She had the safety of the remaining group to worry about.

"Is everyone else unaccounted for?"

"Everyone's here if you don't count Zed."

"Did you track him down?" asked Will.

"We kept missing each other. He went back to Porton in search of answers, but other than that, I don't know."

"Who's the new girl?"

"You didn't hear? That's Zed's daughter."

"You're kidding!" Will laughed incredulously, the pitch of his voice higher than usual, looking Heather up and down.

"It's not something I'd lie about." Heather smiled, to the amusement of those around her. "If you'd met my dad, you'd understand."

"Met him? I've had to live with the bugger these last few years. Most of us owe him our lives, in one way or another."

Heather seemed dubious but took the statement at face value.

"That's the last of them!" shouted Liz, escorting the last of their group into the dining hall. "We're all here."

Scottie put his fingers to his lips and wolf-whistled for quiet.

"Now, listen up!" shouted Riley, struggling to make herself heard. "Thanks for coming at this early hour. As you know, we've just returned from St Mary's. I wanted you all to hear what's really happening east of here. The soldiers aren't telling the whole truth. There's been a fresh outbreak. There could be thousands of people heading our way."

Scottie had to silence the room again.

"We all know from previous experience what happens. We can't let that happen again here."

"They told us the island was safe."

"I know, but we can't stay here. Whatever we do to secure this site, we can't stop the virus."

"We've only just got here. Where would we go? The soldiers won't let us leave Freshwater. The whole island is on lockdown."

"Back to Hurst. We know we can defend ourselves there."

The room fell silent as they digested Riley's proposal.

"Flynn's hardly going to welcome us back."

"His men are gone. We just sailed past the castle. There was no one there."

"What if you're wrong? That's a big risk," shouted a voice from the back.

"Anyway, they say soldiers are shooting people just for trying to leave," said another.

"We're all worked our butts off to get this place ready and now you want to give all that up? No, this is crazy," challenged Liz.

"Listen, the allies are dealing with much bigger problems right now," said Riley.

"What about Carter?"

"Look, I'll talk to him," she said, checking her watch. "He should be here any time. He'll listen to me."

"How are we going to get there? We can't all fit in your wee dinghy." Scottie laughed at the thought.

"What about the *Nipper*?" suggested Will. "Sam left her on a river mooring in Yarmouth. With any luck, she should still be there."

"You really think we can just waltz back to Hurst and pick up where we left off?" said Nathan, shaking his head.

There was a knock at the door, and Corporal Carter appeared, flanked by the two soldiers from earlier.

"Can I speak to you in private a minute?" he said tersely, holding the door open.

Riley nodded and followed them into the reception area.

"May I remind you that the quarantine measures exist for our protection? They're not just petty rules that anyone can choose to ignore. You could have infected every person here, without your knowledge. You do realise that?"

At the sound of raised voices, Will and Scottie came out to join them.

"Everything all right, Riley?"

The soldiers squared off silently against the new arrivals, gripping their weapons a little tighter.

"How on earth did you convince these two muppets to disobey a direct order? They were meant to bring you back."

"Sorry, Carter, I didn't have much choice. I told them I was working for Captain Armstrong."

"And they believed you? I'm disappointed, Private Field," spat Carter, dressing down the more experienced of the two men.

Turning back to Riley, Carter's stance seemed to soften a little. "Is it as bad as they say?"

"Worse."

"But we're in no immediate danger out here?" he said, intending it as a statement rather than a question.

"With respect, no one can protect us from what's heading this way."

"Then why come back here? Why not stay in St Mary's?"

"I'm not staying. We're sitting ducks here. We plan to head back to Hurst. We'll have a better chance there. We know we can defend the castle."

"And you expect me to just turn a blind eye? Ignore my orders?" Carter blew out his cheeks and ran a hand through his hair. "The way things are going, I don't know how much longer we'll be here either. They're pulling back to secure the strong points at Southampton and Portsmouth. Flynn's team pulled out weeks ago from the castle. The allies are in full retreat on the mainland. You'd be on your own. Hurst will be exposed. No one will be there to protect you."

"I know, but we've done it before. We know what we're asking."

"Look, until someone tells me otherwise, my orders are to protect the western approaches to the Solent. Having your lot at Hurst Castle might actually be a good thing. Another set of eyes and ears. Since Flynn left, the Battery has picked up double the work."

"We'd help in any way we can. Before Flynn arrived, we kept watch, mounted patrols. We could bring you food and supplies, if you like."

"Look, I'm not going to try and stop you, if that's what you're really asking, but I do have some conditions."

"Sure. Anything, within reason." She smiled.

"There's another group I know would kill for this site. It's one of the best on the island. If your team does a proper handover and you leave everything in good working order, beds, furniture, tools, everything, then…" His voice trailed off. "I'd need a few of your people to stay behind for a couple of days till it's all sorted."

"That's fine. We're planning to send an advanced party over to the castle as soon as we can, find out the lay of the land and what needs doing. Do you know if anyone is still living there?"

"I doubt it, but it wouldn't take long for word to get around, especially if the soldiers left anything behind."

"There's one more thing," she ventured, pushing her luck. I don't suppose you could spare us a couple of shotguns? Just in case."

# Chapter Forty-seven

Zed had made up his mind: he couldn't stay at St Mary's while the people he cared most about were in danger.

He barged into the colonel's office without knocking, interrupting a conversation with a military aide.

"Why don't we finish this later?" suggested the colonel, noticing Zed's impatience. He waited for the staff officer to collect his papers and leave the room.

"If you've come to apologise about earlier—"

"I'm leaving," snapped Zed. "I have to get back to Freshwater. The virus could be there any day now."

"Of course. I understand your concern. If my family were still alive, I'd want to be with them too." He nodded thoughtfully. "But let's say I did allow you to go back there, what would you actually do?"

Zed hesitated, unsure how to answer the question.

"If you really want to help them, you'll stay here and finish what you've started."

"But I keep telling you, I'm getting nowhere. I'm slowing Doctor Hardy's team down. They'll close ranks at the first suggestion of blame."

"What did you expect? Your line of questioning puts them

on the defensive. You've repeatedly suggested Porton shoulders some of the blame."

"It's going to take more than a bunch of second-hand rumours and conspiracy theories to convince them to play ball. You know full well that the evidence I've gathered so far is at best circumstantial."

"Don't be so hard on yourself. You've got this far, haven't you? In time, more pieces of the puzzle will fall into place. You'll find them, I know you will."

"Doctor Hardy is still the block. No one can force him to talk."

"You said yourself, the longer he spends away from Major Donnelly, the more co-operative he'll become. Even in the last few days, he's softened his stance. In a few more weeks, who knows what he'll volunteer? Trust me, I've been involved in enough interrogations of foreign agents and terrorist suspects to know that a little kindness goes a long way."

"Perhaps."

"You have to admit, you two would make a formidable team. His scientific knowledge and your investigative skills. In my experience, there's nothing like creative conflict."

Zed looked at his shoes, reluctant to admit that the colonel was right. What difference could he make if he was at Freshwater with Riley? His best chance of saving them was right here. It was a stark choice, but in the end, logic would win the day.

"If I agree to stay, I need your assurances that the soldiers will protect Freshwater Hotel, whatever comes their way."

"I'll make the necessary arrangements. You have my word."

"Four more weeks, then I'm out of here, whatever happens."

"If you can get the doctor to talk, who knows, you could be home in two. Now, if we're done," he said, rising from his chair.

"The captain wants us all back in the command centre for three o'clock."

Zed followed the colonel through the dimly lit corridors that ran beneath the hospital. The largest storeroom had been cleared of boxes and redundant machinery to make room for a large boardroom table and chairs. Temporary lighting had been rigged up, casting long shadows across the highly polished surface, half-illuminating the faces of Captain Armstrong, the doctor, Lieutenant Peterson and the other senior members of the allied team.

In the centre of the table, a military radio transmitter had been set up, its digital fascia lit with a series of numbers and settings.

"What's going on?" whispered Zed in the colonel's ear.

"Remember the engineers we sent to the transmitter at Rowbridge? They think they've got everything working again."

There was a crackle of static.

"Try that," said a voice. "Any better? Do you read us, over?"

"Loud and clear, sergeant," answered the captain, leaning closer to the set. "So, what seemed to be the problem?"

There was a short delay as the sergeant could be heard discussing with another senior engineer their collective response.

"There's no question, captain. This was sabotage."

"How can you be sure? Last time we spoke, you thought it was just a transformer burn-out."

"Process of elimination, sir. When you've replaced everything you can think of, you start investigating the less likely causes. It took us a while, but eventually, we found it."

"Found what?"

"Broadcast equipment that shouldn't be here, sir."

There were some puzzled expressions around the table.

"Broadcast what exactly? We're not following you."

"A signal powerful enough to drown out everything else for miles. Static, interference, white noise, whatever you want to call it."

"Then how were we able to make and receive radio comms before now?"

"Nothing long-range has been working for months. Except for very local transmissions. Line of sight, point to point. It's like a blanket smothering the whole region's communications. Power outages probably didn't help either."

"And you say the transmitter is working now?" asked the captain.

"It appears to be, yes. We're scanning all frequencies but not picking up any transmissions."

"Understood. Stand by, sergeant."

The captain muted the channel so no one outside the room could hear, and looked around the room. Everyone seemed as dumbstruck as Zed felt. So many questions crowded out his thoughts. Who could have done this and why?

"Do we have any idea why it has taken us this long to find out what was going on?" demanded the colonel. "I thought we looked into this ages ago."

"This has the hallmarks of a sophisticated attack. Flynn reported something similar at Hurst. The rebels used police jamming equipment to disrupt communications and isolate the team there," said the captain.

"This attack is on an altogether different scale."

"My men checked the transmitter a few weeks ago when we restored power. We found nothing." The captain shrugged.

The American remained silent, listening to their exchange.

"What's the range of this thing?" asked the colonel.

"It covers the south coast of England, potentially hundreds of miles."

"So we can use it to contact other groups?"

"The world is listening."

"If people tried to contact us before, they would assume our silence meant everyone was dead."

"Ever since we got here," volunteered Peterson, "the *Chester*'s communication systems have been playing up."

"What are your orders, sir? We're standing by," came the sergeant's voice on the radio.

"Sir, we should put out a test message. See who else is out there."

"Then we're all agreed?" said the captain, his eyebrows raised, waiting for each of them to nod in turn. "Sergeant, I want you to open the line. Turn up the signal as much as possible."

"Just give me a minute to make the connections."

The captain dipped his head in deference towards the colonel. "Sir, as the ranking officer, it should be you who does this."

The colonel nodded in agreement, thinking through what he wanted to say. "Of course. It would be my honour, gentlemen." He raised his eyebrows at the heavy burden conveyed on him. It seemed beyond hope that the rest of the world was merely waiting passively for them to make contact.

Zed found his breaths becoming shorter. In his head, he imagined pockets of survivors just like theirs spread throughout Europe and beyond. Perhaps, like them, they were waiting, focused on their own survival.

"We're all set here. Open channel in three, two, one..." The man's voice trailed off, followed by a baseline static that filled the room.

The colonel leaned forward and cleared his throat, coughing

into his sleeve, taking a deep breath. "This is Allied Commander Colonel Abrahams speaking to you from St Mary's on the Isle of Wight in the United Kingdom. Calling all survivors of the Millennial Virus, do you read me, over?"

There was silence, bar the static.

"Keep trying. We have no idea if this message is getting through or not," encouraged the captain in a low voice. "Someone out there has to be listening."

"To all survivors of the Millennial Virus, this is Camp Wight—" He was suddenly cut off by a loud digital burst, like a set of beeps and then dashes, almost like Morse code. Then silence.

"Hello, your message was garbled. Repeat, please."

A faint male English voice said: "Hello, hello. Can you hear me? We can hear you, colonel."

The captain leaned in and increased the volume, adjusting another dial to boost the signal from his end.

"Yes, go ahead. Repeat, this is Colonel Abrahams at Camp Wight, on the Isle of Wight. We hear you."

"It's very good to hear your voice on this sunny day in Jersey," said the voice brightly with a local burr.

"New Jersey?" whispered the lieutenant.

"No, I suspect he means the Channel Islands," mocked the captain.

"And yours too. How many in your group?" asked the colonel.

"Here? Oh, just me and the wife."

There was a collective outlet of breath as if they all realised this was too good to be true.

"Just the two of you then?"

"And the dog…" The voice trailed off, perhaps sensing their

disappointment. "But there are other groups. Quite a few of them, actually. Here on the island and Guernsey. There are others we trade with on the Cherbourg Peninsula and down into Brittany."

"Thank God. We were beginning to think we were the only ones," admitted the colonel. "What's your name?"

"Cyril. The wife's Deidre. We've not heard from the UK mainland for months since…" His voice fell away and all they heard was the word quarantine.

"Sorry, Cyril, you cut out. Can you repeat?"

"I said that we haven't been able to reach anyone back in the UK since the quarantine came into effect."

"What quarantine?"

"Where have you been? There's been a ten-mile exclusion zone around the British coast for two years."

"By order of whom?"

"The United Nations."

The colonel looked around the table, but they were all as puzzled as the next person.

"Sorry, Cyril, you're saying the whole country was quarantined?"

"Or at least that's what I heard."

"Then why has no one come here in all that time?"

"I expect they'll get to you in due course. They've probably just got their hands full right now. You're not the only ones, you know."

"What about a vaccine? Does the UN have a vaccine?" asked the doctor, hopeful.

"I can ask Deidre, if you like. She might know. A vaccine, you say?"

The doctor leaned in towards Zed and whispered, "Of all the

people who could have answered our call, we're stuck with this moron with a CB radio."

"Cyril, perhaps you can pass on a message to the other groups you're in contact with and advise them that there's a military-led relief operation based at St Mary's hospital, in Newport, on the Isle of Wight. We urgently need to speak with anyone in authority. The police, the military, civic leaders."

"I'll see what I can do, but it might not be for a few days. It's a bit of a trek into town from here. I'll see if I can pop down later, mind."

"We'd appreciate that, Cyril. We'll be waiting. Camp Wight out."

"Corporal, disable the channel, will you?" ordered the captain.

"Confirmed, transmission ended. Just us now."

"I want you to keep trying, on all frequencies. Make contact with whoever you can. If there's one group in Jersey, there might be other groups within range of the transmitter. Report in as soon as you know more. St Mary's, out."

The captain sat back in his chair, exhausted. "So it would appear we are not alone. If there are survivors in the Channel Islands, then there must be survivor groups throughout the region."

"It stands to reason," confirmed the doctor. "Our pandemic modelling indicated that coastal and rural areas had the best chance of survival."

"We suspected this would be the case, but we didn't dare hope," admitted Captain Armstrong.

"Now we know, the question is, what do we do about it?" asked the colonel.

"We're in no position to expand our range of operations."

"But we are in a position to ask for help."

"Aren't you forgetting that until the country is free of infection, we're still subject to international quarantine? We cannot allow this new strain to spread further. You know how this works."

"I'm aware of that, captain, but if we're going to survive, we need their help now, before it's too late."

"Then we don't tell them about the new outbreak until we've secured their support," suggested the politician.

"That would be grossly irresponsible."

"I agree, but it might also save lives and get help here quicker."

"And risk a second global pandemic? Have you lost your mind?"

"I'm just saying it's an option that would get us the resources we need earlier."

"No, we come clean and explain what's happened. That's the only responsible path. We take our chances and hope the United Nations is in a position to send help."

"Very well, then. Let us hope this is the turning point."

Zed sat back in his seat, trying to take it all in. He had been studying Lieutenant Peterson during these final exchanges. While everyone else around the table had reacted with myriad emotions, his face had remained a mask. He kept looking at his watch, perhaps distracted by another agenda that superseded their own. It was almost as if this was all part of a larger plan that Zed could only guess at.

He thought back to the printed report on his desk. On a whim, he had pulled some data on communication systems, curious to know more about the Roweridge transmitter. He had stumbled across a paragraph about ELF, the system American submarines used to communicate over long distances, virtually anywhere on the planet. If he could prove that the *Chester* had ELF, then their claims about communication blackouts must be incorrect. The Americans might be the only ones who really knew what was going on in the outside world. It was another intriguing puzzle that had jumped to the top of his list.

Right now, the only person he could really trust was Colonel Abrahams. This fresh outbreak gave him a renewed urgency. If he was going to get closure before his self-imposed four-week deadline expired he would need to eliminate all distractions, redouble his efforts, work every hour until he found the answer. It might be the only way to save his daughter and Riley, assuming it wasn't already too late.

# Chapter Forty-eight

No one knew quite what to expect back at Hurst. Corporal Carter had already confirmed what Riley guessed: the castle was abandoned.

When the fighting moved east towards Southampton and Portsmouth, Hurst had become an unjustifiable outpost in the allies' sphere of influence. With resources stretched to breaking point, Captain Armstrong could ill afford three squads of men twiddling their thumbs while the danger moved closer to their centre of operations.

That said, Riley knew only too well that no major site would be left empty for long. As soon as the soldiers pulled out, the castle would have been taken back by groups travelling east from Bournemouth or Christchurch.

Carter's truck from Needles Battery dropped the first group from Freshwater Hotel later that morning in Yarmouth. They waited by the quayside near the ferry port for Scottie to bring the *Nipper* round from its river mooring.

With some amusement Riley watched the locals going about their business. It reminded her of a scene from the Blitz. Children in school uniform, blazers and ties, wearing surgical masks, heading to the park. The youngest of them held hands in pairs, gawping at the group from Freshwater like aliens from another world. The teacher at the rear hurried them along, glancing at Riley with suspicion.

Two soldiers from Yarmouth Castle strode over to check their paperwork before one of Carter's men interceded.

The journey across to Hurst Castle was short and uneventful. Aside from a light swell from Christchurch Bay, it was a dry, grey, overcast day. It felt good to be back out on the water; the sea air, the open space, the peace and quiet.

It was clear from a distance that the castle had seen various alterations over the past few weeks. The soldiers had wasted no time in bolstering the castle's defences. Rolls of barbed wire lined the seaward-facing walls, repainted in camouflaged stripes that seemed to serve no purpose other than decorative. Perhaps Flynn's men simply wanted to leave their mark on the place.

As they approached the end of the Hurst Spit, they could see the eastward-facing dock had been further upgraded to allow stores to be uploaded from larger vessels. In all likelihood, following the latest set of powerful storms, deliveries to the castle could only now be made by sea. The roadway that ran along the top of the shingle bank back to Milford had been repaired many times during their tenure.

It was approaching high tide, so Scottie ignored the East dock and continued round to the small harbour nearest the castle gate where the ferry used to deposit day-trippers.

Parked near the main castle entrance was an army truck with a flat tyre. The castle drawbridge was down and the gates left open. The group waited onboard the *Nipper*, scanning the ramparts for movement.

There was further evidence of the soldiers' upgrades to the fortifications. Surrounding the main gate were rolls of barbed wire and the scars of previous battles, bullet holes and scorch marks in the stone. The drawbridge had been reinforced with inch-thick armour plates.

There were other small differences, too numerous to take in and yet, despite the meticulous attention of the military, slowly but surely, Mother Nature was beginning to reassert herself here on the spit. The grass grew long, and every crevice in the walls was colonised by weeds. Brambles and wildflowers swayed in the breeze, indifferent to their return. The signs above the entrances had been smartly repainted in red and black.

When they were satisfied there was no one there, Riley waved them forward, a pair of shotguns at their head. A dog barking made them stop and listen, checking around them.

"Be careful," she whispered.

Will and Joe went first, disappearing around the corner towards the Tudor gate, making no sound. They were gone for several minutes, just long enough for Riley to start to worry. She heard the dog again, joined by another, alarmed by the men's approach, growling and snarling. Two shots fired, and then silence.

Will and Joe jogged back into view, signalling it was safe to approach.

"It doesn't look like anyone's here." Will shrugged.

Riley split them up into pairs to search the rest of the large site, room by room. Liz went with Riley to check out the old kitchen canteen. They found the store cupboard bare, aside from a few tins of vegetables.

"Why do they always leave the green beans and horse chestnuts?" Liz wondered out loud.

In the cold cupboard were some fresh items gathering mould, a jug of curdled milk, the white bone from a leg of lamb that had been picked clean. Judging by the state of it, Liz said it would have been boiled several times. Liz had her hands on her hips, lamenting the time it had taken to fill the storeroom. It would take weeks of scavenging to return the kitchen to its former glory, with enough stock to sustain the group over another harsh winter on the spit.

A gust of wind made the door creak on its hinges, groaning in protest. There was dried blood on the ground by the door. Riley stooped to touch it, but it was weeks old, possibly from the last attack on the castle.

They met the others back inside the Tudor gate in the courtyard at the heart of the castle complex.

"Storeroom's bare," announced Riley. "Someone's eaten us out of house and home. How did the rest of you get on?"

"The soldiers must have left in a hurry." Will said. "Anything they couldn't carry got left behind. There's a 50mm GPMGs up top plus boxes of ammunition."

"There's what's left of an armoury in the cellar. Three semi-automatic rifles, ammunition, two pistols, a few grenades, tactical vests, helmets, the lot."

"Excellent. How did you get on, Nathan?" asked Riley.

"The soldiers have been busy. They must have been worried about getting attacked again. There are lots of upgrades. Repairs, barbed wire everywhere, concrete posts to stop people driving up the spit, new defensive positions with sandbags covering the East dock area."

"What else?"

"All the water butts are full. The main storage tank too."

"There's tonnes of army-issue clothing, spare bedding and mattresses in the storehouse," said another, already wearing a new blue sweater with a Royal Marines insignia on the chest.

"Someone's been repairing all my guttering and pipework," said Will, following the line of the roof with his eyes.

"I'll be sure to thank Flynn next time we see him," suggested Riley with heavy sarcasm. "What's the bad news?"

"All the animals are gone."

"I expect they were slaughtered weeks ago."

"Or maybe the soldiers moved them back to the farm at Keyhaven," suggested Greta hopefully. She was fond of riding the horses along the beach in the surf. Riley said she only did it because Scottie found it titillating.

"No, there were a few butchered animal carcasses by the lighthouse."

"Not the horses?" pleaded Greta.

"I think so."

"There appears to be a family living over there. I don't think they're very pleased we shot their dogs."

"Should have kept them locked up then. You did the right thing. They could have been rabid."

"Did the family say anything else?"

"Yeah, friendly bunch once they'd calmed down. Apparently, most of the soldiers left weeks ago."

"I know no one else gives a hoot, but half the stuff in my museum has been nicked," cursed Scottie.

"Our museum, don't you mean?" corrected Will. "We all helped you lug that junk back here. The paintings, the heavy sculptures, books, records, film props. For posterity, you said."

"Because it's important. Well, some genius sprayed graffiti on some of my paintings and used the sculptures for target practice. My Picasso's ruined."

"Philistines."

"And loads of books are missing from the library. Some of

those were first editions. They've burned all the furniture."

"Shame. Still, maybe Picasso would have approved of someone reusing his canvas."

"Very funny. Well, I don't."

"None of those things matter," challenged Liz. "Getting the castle back is what counts. Having a roof over our heads for winter."

"Vandalising a Picasso doesn't matter? Is that what you're saying? Art doesn't matter? What about Dickens, Shakespeare, Larkin, or Keats? I suppose none of them matter either?"

"Get over yourself, man. It's just stuff," dismissed Will. "You can't take those books with you, can you? You live your life, then you're dead. Make the most of it."

"Typical bloody South African. If it's not a stuffed animal or lion's head as a trophy on your wall, it's nothing."

"Don't stereotype me, Braveheart," he shot back testily.

"The true mark of a man is what he leaves behind." Scottie nodded. "His legacy, whether it's something tangible, like a book or a painting, or something intangible like the Nobel Peace Prize. That, my friend, is how we transcend our time on Earth."

"No way!" Will scoffed. "It's what we do that makes us who we are. Actions are what define us, not just pretty pictures or words on a page. Making a difference to our fellow man. Freedom, equality, liberty."

"You can start by making yourselves useful," interrupted Riley. "Like cleaning up this place?"

"At least now we know that, whatever we do, wherever we go, we'll never be safe," cautioned Will. "All these guns and high walls may not be enough, you realise that?"

"Until someone finds a cure, we'll always live in the shadow of the virus."

"Let someone else worry about that." Scottie shrugged. "Jack would have wanted us to carry on. To do what's right. Our first duty has always been to survive."

"We don't need a bunch of fancy scientists for that. At least here we can hide from the virus like we did before. Jack's quarantine measures kept us safe for two years. We can do the same again."

"I'd rather live out our remaining days and die here together." Greta smiled, stroking Scottie's back.

"Greta's right. If this is going to be our end, then to hell with it!" shouted Scottie with renewed vigour. "We die with our heads raised high, not running in fear into an uncertain future."

"Then this is where we make our final stand, at Hurst Castle," proclaimed Riley with growing authority.

"We'll shrug our shoulders and carry on."

"In honour of Jack and the 'spirit of the blitz' he always talked about."

In a moment of solidarity, they embraced each other in turn. Riley pulled Scottie in close and whispered something in his ear. He nodded with a smile and hurried off towards the stores.

"Go on, the rest of you. Let's put this place back the way it was."

Riley watched everyone go back to their former dormitories and workstations to make repairs and prepare for the arrival of the others on the next ferry trip from Yarmouth.

She wandered back through the castle gates, heading west along the roadway alongside the towering stone walls facing back towards Keyhaven and the salt marshes, eager once again to enjoy the solitude of the spit and the uninterrupted views back towards the Needles.

To her right, she passed the firepit where they had burned the dead. The stench still took some getting used to. Will was not far behind her, wheeling the carcasses of the dogs they had shot.

The barrow's rusted wheel squeaked on its half-inflated tyre. Riley helped sling the limp bodies of a Golden Retriever and a Labrador over the raised edge into the pit below.

As she turned to leave, something near the rim caught her eye. If she wasn't mistaken, there was a body with a thick mooring rope tied around its neck, trailing up the slope. Its features were barely recognisable, charred and disfigured, half-covered with lime. Riley shuddered and turned away, realising that this must be Jack. She closed her eyes and hurried past, not daring to look again.

Stepping on to the rocks and the spit stretching back towards Milford, she bathed her face in the afternoon sun, staring back towards the island. There was a light sea swell. Shadows from passing clouds hurried across the waves.

From here, the island looked so tranquil, like a haven from the chaos of the last few years. She now knew the true horror. The island was as damned as anywhere else. One way or another, without a vaccine, those who remained would fall victim to the virus. Those who fled faced an uncertain future on the mainland.

Looking back towards the castle keep, she saw Scottie had kept his promise. Fluttering above the Gun Tower was the Union Jack in all its glory. It was a fitting tribute to their former leader and all he had achieved here. He would not be forgotten.

Riley looked around the lichen-covered castle walls, feeling nostalgic, remembering the good times they had enjoyed here and acknowledging the bad. She closed her eyes, inhaling the sea air. It felt good to be back.

She made a solemn promise to herself. They would keep the home fires burning until Zed and the others made it back here alive. It was up to her now. They would survive or die fighting for what they believed in. There could be no other way.

Made in the USA
Monee, IL
18 March 2020

23331515R00252